OCEAN SPACES ISLAND WORLDS

CHRISTOPHER FARLEY

OCEAN SPACES ISLAND WORLDS

AN EXTRAORDINARY ADVENTURE OF DISCOVERY AND TRANSFORMATION

You must understand that the pages
inside this book grant access to ancient
wisdom kept purposefully hidden
from outsiders for centuries.

As you venture into the rich mythology
of pre-contact Hawai'i, know that this
unique culture was nearly destroyed
by early Christian missionaries.
Despite threats of persecution, many
Hawaiians secretly preserved their
customs, beliefs, and rituals within
the privacy of their own homes.

In recent years, as descendants
of these wisdom keepers neared the
end of their mortal journeys, many
agreed it was time for the tabu
to be lifted so that everything once
forbidden may now be shared.

Before it's lost forever.

I'm grateful for my apprenticeship with
some of those wise elders, and having
written this novel for future generations
in their honor, I've done so with the
utmost respect and responsibility
of preserving ancient wisdom they
so generously shared with me.

ISBN: 979-8-218-20784-7

Developmental Editor: Kimberley Lim

Editor: Becky Sweeney

Proofreader: Constance Renfrow

Design and Typesetting: André Manoel

To my father, John, whose lessons in nature's wonders
and the pursuit of worthy goals have charted my course.

To my mother, Mary Anne, whose teachings of creativity,
familial bonds, and honored traditions have shaped my heart.

To Adam and Larissa, my cherished children, this book
is crafted for you—a compass for life's magnificent voyage,
a *Beginner's Manual for the Living*, as it were, distilled
from the wisdom I've gained throughout my own journey.
May it illuminate your path to true happiness
and purposeful living.

And to the lineage from which I stem, to those who came
before, to those who walk beside, to those yet to be
—a timeless thread that weaves
our stories as one.

✦TABLE OF CONTENTS✦

✦ *FOREWORD* ✦

The emerald isle of Kaua'i is a place of astonishing beauty, but for me, it's much more than that. It's a place of profound and mystical connection, a place that awakened a hunger within me to explore the ancient wisdom of the Hawaiian people. This journey began decades ago when a young man from Michigan, fresh out of college and seeking adventure, set foot on the island for the first time.

I remember it like yesterday. As I stepped off the airplane and breathed in the fragrant air, a jolt of recognition surged through me—a feeling that I was being reacquainted with something long forgotten yet deeply significant. It was a sensation that would haunt me even as I boarded the plane to return home, where I felt the invisible roots that connected me to the island being torn away, leaving me yearning to return.

And return I did, year after year. With nothing more than a plane ticket and a backpack, I journeyed across, around, and between the Hawaiian Islands, hitchhiking, camping, and sailing. In libraries and bookstores, at garage sales and flea markets, and in remote corners of the land itself, I sought to uncover the secrets of ancient Hawaiian life.

It was a quest that led me to many gifted healers who practiced their ways in secret, steadfastly guarding their knowledge from those who would condemn it. As I listened to their teachings, a common sentiment emerged: the time had come for the knowledge to be shared, for the tabu of secrecy to be lifted.

So here I stand, humbly offering you my first novel: Ocean Spaces, Island Worlds. It is the culmination of a journey that spans more than thirty years—a journey of discovery, wonder, and reverence for the people of Hawai'i, whose wisdom holds the power to heal not only our planet but every living being upon it.

As you turn the pages, may you too feel the roots of connection, and may the ancient wisdom of the Pacific guide you on your own journey.

My intention has flown; it is free to manifest.

Me ke aloha pumehana,
With all the love of my heart

Christopher Farley
May 2023

ʻA ʻohe hana nui ke alu ʻia.
No task is too big when done together by all.

Ancient Hawaiian proverb

✦ PROLOGUE ✦

In a time before time, far across the vast, fathomless sea, Earth Mother Papahānaumoku and Sky Father Wākea gave birth to the Hawaiian Islands, igniting the genesis of time and existence.

While there is plenty of thoughtful speculation and theory about the first intrepid explorers who discovered the particular archipelago that many have come to know as Hawai'i, exactly where those brave souls might have originated remains a mystery to this day.

What we do know is that the exploits and contributions of many important historical figures from this region were passed down from generation to generation through oral chants, hula, myths, and legends, elevating these figures to the status of gods and goddesses.

As such, being taught from birth that they were the descendants of these celebrated ancestors and siblings of the islands on which they lived, a unique culture of language, customs, craftsmanship, artistry, navigation, and empowerment developed that was wholly unique to those who would eventually become the Hawaiian people.

Here is a very special outrigger built by a master canoe builder under strict ceremony with the intention of carrying us back in time to Havai'i Nei, where we will experience ancient life among an intuitive people who understood the importance of using prayer to maintain a poetic and harmonious relationship with nature, and of passing down legends and myths as a means of understanding the world around them.

There, our sail is full...

OCEAN SPACES

THE FIRST JOURNEY

❖ CHAPTER 1 ❖

O Taua'i, the eldest sibling of Havai'i Nei, is a land of beauty and mythic splendor, born from fiery ocean depths. Both wild and inviting, its varied landscape of golden sand beaches, lush rain forests, soaring black cliffs, emerald-green mountains, and red-earthed canyons is a masterpiece sculpted by hands skilled in the heavenly manifestations of absolute beauty and paradise. At the near center and highest elevation of the island stands Mount Vaiareare, its sacred plateau cloaked in mystery beneath a perennial shroud of rain-swollen clouds. For this reason, mortal inhabitants believe this earthborn temple to be the very navel of the island.

From realms of the divine, the perpetual wreath of clouds adorning the heights of Vaiareare fosters countless waterfalls with sacred, life-giving waters. Among these is Vairuanuiho'āno Falls, two gushing white cascades forging twin rivers through the uplands of Puna and down across the floor of Vaiareare Valley before finally merging with the sea along the eastern shores of Taua'i. It is here we find the coastal village of Vairuanuiho'āno, *Great Sacred Vairua of Ho'āno*, a region extending from the high mountain ridges of Tarepa and Nounou to the eastern shores of Vairua Bay. At the center of this immense royal compound is the grass palace of Ruling Chief Vahanui himself. Son of Ho'ano, the late, beloved leader after whom this Tauaian kingdom was named, his genealogical oration extends back to a time when gods walked the earth.

Ruling Chief Vahanui achieved his envied status through a carefully maintained bloodline that could be traced back hundreds of years to the birth of the gods. Although the blood of many great ancestors courses through his veins, he must nevertheless earn the respect of those he governs.

Since birth, Vahanui has undergone ancient and sacred training, preparing him for absolute control over the lives, lands, and properties of his subjects. He alone is responsible for using the powerful spiritual power entrusted to him by his ancestral gods to maintain military forces, impose taxes, and preside over all religious rites that affect the health and well-being of the island.

Currently, Ruling Chief Vahanui oversees all of Taua'i, which includes the six districts of Puna, East Tona, West Tona, Nā Pari, Harere'a, To'orau, and the detached seventh district of Ni'ihau, Ta'ura, and Nihoa, a group of small islands southwest of Taua'i across the Tauratahi Channel. While the entirety of Ni'ihau is its own district, each of the Tauaian territories are divided from the center peak of the island down to the sea. This ensures each mainland district has access to all of the island's resources—timber from the upland forests, richly soiled lowlands for farming, and abundant fishing along the coast—and the ability to sustain a prosperous, productive community.

Each of these districts is, in turn, managed by high chiefs of the purest blood—in this case, seven of the ruling chief's younger brothers. Their responsibilities include supervision of the common people, who support the royal compound by harvesting the agricultural fields, maintaining the inland fishponds, and ocean fishing. In most cases, each community is comprised of family groups that barter among themselves and with nearby villages for various goods and services. Elders oversee all matters pertaining to the family, and are accountable to the chief land manager of their district for the weekly collection of taxes, including food and clothing, to support the ruling chief and his court.

While other islands have been conquered and retaken multiple times over the years, Taua'i has an extraordinary reputation for being immune to invasion, separated as it is from the other six eastern islands by nearly a full day's travel by canoe across rough seas. However, they are not immune to internal squabbles. While geographic separation has certain advantages, the isolation makes Tauaians prone to the occasional interisland flare-up.

One notable dispute occurred ten seasons ago, when Manu—high chief of West Tona district—fell in love with Nuna'ea, the wife of Utumehame, high chief of East Tona. Discovery of the affair caused three years of embittered skirmishes between West Tona, who called people in East

Tona 'Wind Eaters,' and the people from East Tona, who called those from West Tona 'Sun Eaters.' This explosive rift threatened to destabilize the kingdom of Taua'i's long-standing prosperity.

Well aware of the drama between these districts, Ruling Chief Vahanui initially decided it was best to let these squabbles work themselves out. But after a long time without resolution, he eventually sought the counsel of his supreme high priest and most trusted advisers to determine what rites might be performed in order to return peace to the island. After several days of deliberation within sacred temple grounds, it was decided Vahanui would summon his brothers to the royal compound in Vairuanuiho'āno to begin mediation. Much to his surprise, both brothers agreed. Upon arrival, each brother was accompanied by hundreds of their own counselors and family members. Needless to say, tensions quickly ran high, and discussions grew heated. By midday, an argument of minor significance erupted into a fistfight. The conflict quickly escalated as the people of East and West Tona, loyal to their respective leaders, took the altercation to the sands of Vairuanuiho'āno Beach. There, many lives were tragically lost in what became known as the *Battle of Beating Heart*.

That was almost seven lunar years ago and, aside from the occasional use of foot messengers, the three brothers haven't spoken or seen one another since. To this day, violent memories of that battle weigh heavily in the hearts of all Tauaians.

This particular day, however, brings a glimmer of hope.

The star cluster *Eight Little Eyes* appeared ten moon phases ago and villagers have been closely watching the evening sky. Tonight, when the rising constellation in the east falls in sync with the setting sun in the west, the new crescent moon's position will mark both the change of season from summer to winter and, more importantly, the official start of the Matari'i-hiti season, the widely anticipated celebration of the new year. During this time, priests temporarily retire the idol of Tū, god of war, and erect the idol of Ro'o, the patron god of fertility, agriculture, and peace.

As legend has it, the ancestral deity Ro'o fell in love with a beautiful chiefess named Taitirani. The two lived in bliss until a mortal chief from a neighboring land became smitten with Taitirani and began courting her in secret. On nights when her husband was away, the chief serenaded Taitirani with songs and chants until, one evening, Ro'o returned home unannounced.

Assuming he'd caught his wife being unfaithful, Ro'o killed the mortal and then turned his fury on his wife, savagely beating her. As she lay dying in her husband's arms, Taitirani plead her innocence and, with her final breath, whispered her eternal love for Ro'o. Distraught by his irreversible acts of violence, Ro'o traveled from island to island challenging any man he met to a playful boxing or wrestling match in the hope his grief would leave him. Unfortunately, it never did.

Originally a time of games honoring Ro'o's deceased wife, Matari'i-hiti has since evolved into an important season of peace and rejuvenation for both the land and its people. It is also a much-needed opportunity for hard-working villagers to rest, reconnect with family and friends, engage in sports, and celebrate with lots of feasting and dancing. For the next four lunar months, labor will be prohibited, island laws will be lifted, and most importantly, violence of any kind will be forbidden. The latter was both an important lesson carried over from the cautionary tale of Ro'o and his wife, and a symbol of hope to the many villagers praying that this would be the year brothers Vahanui, Manu, and Utumehame finally reconcile and put an end to unrest on the island.

But there was one person who couldn't have been more indifferent to all this. While most commoners were soon to be freed from labor, farmers were among the very few who still had much work to do during this time when the earth was most fertile. And Matani, just days away from his seventeenth rotation of life, happened to be a third-generation taro farmer.

As remembered through family chants, four generations after the first Tahitian settlers migrated to Havai'i, Matani's grandfather, Namotaha'i, sailed from Tahiti as an apprentice to a well-respected farmer named Retuatua. Early on in the long ocean voyage, Retuatua unexpectedly died in his sleep. The highest ranking chief aboard the double-hulled canoe made Namotaha'i responsible for all twenty varieties of taro his mentor had carefully packed in watertight baskets. This was no small request; taro was considered to be a gift from the gods. Cooked and pounded into a pasty food staple called *poi*, the cultivation of taro is not only an important source of sustenance and spiritual nourishment, it also symbolizes prosperity and abundance. Namotaha'i was told in no uncertain terms that if a single leaf of taro so much as wilted, he would be put to death and fed to the sea. As merciful gods would have it, by the time their leaking hulls scraped ashore the long sands of Vairua, every last taro plant had not only survived, but had thrived under extremely difficult conditions, thanks to Namotaha'i's cultivation skills.

Regrettably, despite his family's serendipitous beginnings on Taua'i, Matani's inconsistent genealogy afforded him little respect according to social norms, thus placing him among the lower class of people. And, as was common amongst commoners, he was underfed and overworked, of medium height for his age, and with dark-brown skin from daily exposure to the elements, unlike the lighter skin of the nobility, who had the luxury of avoiding the sun—aside from their rejuvenating baths in the saltwater sea using a variety of scented, skin-softening coconut oils.

Burdened by the daily tasks of his so-called genealogical superiors, Matani's dark-brown eyes peered angrily through thick strands of black, sweat-soaked hair as he made his way from the inland taro gardens and out to the village border for the tenth time that day.

Useless, self-serving worms!

The society Matani had been so reluctantly born into was comprised of four different levels of social class. The first were ruling chiefs, high chiefs, and lesser chiefs that ruled the territories and were considered to be descendants of the gods.

Priests carried out sacred religious ceremonies at the temples, while master craftsmen with expertise in medicine, religion, and natural resource management ranked near the top of the social scale.

Commoners—the largest group of people on the islands, by far—carried out all menial and productive labor as builders, fishermen, and farmers, providing royalty with a life of leisure.

Then there were the 'untouchables,' social outcasts who were either lawbreakers or war captives, and typically attached to a master in a life of servitude.

Although Matani had no master and wasn't forbidden to interact with others—though he often chose not to—he most certainly considered himself a slave to the rules of a miserable society he'd had no say in creating.

Why can't I wear feather cloaks or hair necklaces with whale tooth pendants? Why can't I have luxurious scented mats? Or eat the humuhumunukunukuapua'a fish? Or live in a cavernous house filled with far too many wooden platters and decorative bowls to use for eating food I made no efforts to catch, kill, or grow?

As was his wont, Matani interrogated himself ruthlessly.

Perhaps there is a good reason?

What reason? To make me wish I was dead?

Regardless of the burning jealously of his desire for the material possessions reserved for highborns, Matani kept his focus on the work that needed to be done. Tradition dictated Ruling Chief Vahanui must receive full payment of taxes from all districts in his domain before Matariʻi-hiti could begin. This was more important than the weekly offerings that afforded commoners the right to live on the land. If Roʻo was displeased, he wouldn't bring the much-needed winter rains to soften the land for another fertile year of farming. And, as every ruling chief knew, healthy agriculture meant survival and success for himself and his people.

As the big night approached, all people of the land were occupied in preparing offerings to appease Roʻo. Under the guidance of their mothers, young girls gathered to beat tapa and weave leaf baskets and mats. Tahunas of various skills would craft all manner of things, from bowls and platters, to elite weapons made from wood of the esteemed koa tree. Fisherman fashioned lines and nets using cordage made from plant fibers, while bird catchers, having spent all season in the mountains, returned with plumes of yellow, black, and red feathers. Farmers harvested sweet potatoes, yams, bananas, coconuts, breadfruit and, the most important crop of all, taro.

Lots and lots of taro.

Sadly, even without the additional labor required after the start of Matariʻi-hiti, Matani would have been unhappy anyway. His mother had died when he was very young, leaving him to be raised by a father with whom he'd always had a difficult relationship. Sure, Matani had relatives like everyone else, and fond memories of spending time with them when he'd been much younger... but for reasons he didn't quite fully understand, at some point they had disappeared from his life, suddenly and without explanation.

"Family," Matani scoffed, swiping away the sweat pouring down his face. "And why is it so stuffy in these trees?"

Not a moment later, a refreshing breeze rattled the leaves, cooling his skin. But Matani barely noticed, focused as he was on the annoying echo of wooden mallets pounding bark into cloth. On most days, he hated this sound as one might hate the point of a dagger shoved into their ear.

But why do I hate it so much?
The relentless monotony reminds you of your own life.
So, what's the point of being alive?
None, obviously.

This was how it always was, the voice of negativity pushing Matani to admit his hidden doubts and insecurities. Before he could contemplate the origins of these biting thoughts, a grumbling stomach reminded him he hadn't had time to eat a single bite today. And that wasn't likely to change anytime soon. At sunrise tomorrow, the parade of royal priests reenacting Ro'o's ancient tour around the island would arrive, expecting to receive the finest goods from each district. Failure to provide an abundance of taro—the most important crop of his people—would be to affront Ro'o and risk bringing a year of bad luck upon the island.

A sudden echo of laughter filled Matani with seething resentment. He followed the sound to a cluster of thatched-roof homes along the valley floor, where many of the villagers had gathered to prepare additional gifts for the great god of agriculture.

What are you all laughing about? You might not have to work after tomorrow, but for me, its work, work, work! Yeah, that's all I ever do! Gotta keep those lazy highborns fed and fat!

Adjusting the carrying pole, Matani descended toward the edge of Puna. Each district had a boundary intersecting a network of paths that encircled the entire island. At each of these boundaries was a sacred altar of stones topped with the wooden image of a pig's head stained with red dirt, representing one of the many forms Ro'o could take during his earthly visit. It was at the base of this ancient idol where the bountiful offerings of land and sea were laid.

Lost in thought, a peculiar sensation lured Matani's gaze to a colorful rainbow far out to sea. He'd seen many rainbows during his lifetime, but there was something odd about this particular one.

It seemed to be looking back at him.

Remembering how his mother had often told him that rainbows were a bridge used by deceased ancestors to visit their living descendants, Matani grew even more annoyed. Virtually everyone he knew had grown up being taught the traditional ways of religion, believing that spirits could be found in non-human beings and objects. But for many years now, Matani had struggled with this unsubstantiated concept. Sure, he'd heard stories from other people who claimed to have had miraculous experiences with ancestral spirits, demigods, and gods, but nothing even mildly out of the ordinary had ever happened to him.

That's me. Just some boring, common, ordinary farmer.

I've told you how to fix that.

Yes, I know.

Well, make up your mind.

Lost in his usual barrage of troubled thoughts, Matani stumbled over a twisted root and plummeted headlong down a hill. The carrying pole snapped, and both calabashes of taro hit the ground and began to roll. Unable to control his somersaulting, Matani slammed stomach-first into the stone base of the sacred pig altar. As he lay there, the wind knocked out of him, Matani gazed up at the ancient wooden head teetering precariously above, feeling the weight of its legacy pressing down upon him. The idol, known as *Tamapua'a*, was much more than a mere wooden carving; it was a symbol of connection to the land and the gods, a manifestation of divine power that sustained and protected the island and its people.

"Please don't fall, please don't fall, please don't fall," Matani repeated in a frantic chant. But despite his desperate words, the pig idol continued swaying unpredictably as he stood at the ready to catch it. Just when it seemed that the wooden head was about to topple off the stone pedestal, it gave one final shudder before coming to a stop.

Collapsing with relief, Matani looked up to see a chunky warrior dressed in a shoulder-length cape of red and yellow feathers standing over him.

"The priests just finished cleaning this, you witless slug!"

It was Uanini, second son to Ruling Chief Vahanui. This particular chief wasn't as tall as the others, but he had a bigger belly than most, and the craftiest, cruelest eyes Matani had ever known. The truth of it was, not many commoners liked Uanini or his blatantly awful people skills, but society dictated that everyone must respect the chain of command—at penalty of death.

Everyone except Matani, that is.

While most disrespectful commoners could be expelled from a district, or even put to death, Ruling Chief Vahanui had acquired the taste for a most delectable taro that only Matani could grow from an ancient cultivating method passed down from his grandfather. While Matani would often say that taro tastes like taro, no matter who grows it, the ruling chief's very different belief afforded Matani the opportunity to get away with far more than most commoners would ever dare.

To the great displeasure of Uanini.

"Clumsy fool!" the chief yelled, shaking his head at the mess of vegetables strewn across the ground. "I won't present Ro'o any taro contaminated by your commoner filth! Gather up this slop and feed it to the pigs!"

Instead of pointing out that taro didn't magically grow from the earth, untouched by his lowly commoner hands, Matani settled for another response. "Sure," he said, holding up a smashed corm of taro. "Shall I start with you?"

Uanini's face darkened. "More and more, the son becomes his father."

By now, everyone on Taua'i—and beyond—had heard the many tragic stories from the Battle of Beating Heart. The story that had given the battle its grim name actually involved Matani's father, Tumatua. As told by those who had been on the beach that day, after the skirmish between the ruling chief's brothers, Manu and Utumehame, escalated into a raging battle, the Puna chiefs brought in commoners and slaves to help end the confrontation. Among those recruited was Tumatua, who had a staunch reputation for being short-tempered. As rival Sun Eaters and Wind Eaters merged in a clattering storm of bodies and weapons, Tumatua boiled with anger as he watched friends and family wounded and killed in a battle instigated by the elite ruling class.

Fueled by resentment, Tumatua marched right up to where Chief Manu stood on the beach that day and screamed, "Why must we fight your battles? Especially one over a woman!'"

As Chief Manu stood flummoxed by a commoner daring to scold him, in the midst of battle no less, his enraged brother Utumehame saw the distraction as an opportunity.

"Move!" Chief Manu warned Tumatua.

But Matani's father stood firm in his anger. "Why should I listen to you? What makes you think your blood is better than mine?"

It wasn't until a chilling expression colored Manu's face that Tumatua fell silent, barely a moment before Utumehame's spear exploded from his chest. Tumatua dropped to his knees, staring in shock and horror at his own severed, glistening heart hanging from the spear's tip before him. It was still beating. He collapsed lifeless upon a hunk of lava embedded in the sand beneath Manu's feet, which many later realized was in the shape of a tear.

Tumatua's Tear, as it would be called forever after.

Matani had been ten, and the horrific image from that story haunted his thoughts and dreams ever since.

The battle abruptly ended after the gruesome incident, with both sides returning to their respective districts under a cloud of shame and regret. And while the number of skirmishes had lessened over the years, the feud between Manu and Utumehame was still very much alive to this day.

"Your father's anger lives in your blood," Uanini snarled. "It will destroy you one day, just as it did him."

Matani clenched his teeth in fury. "At least he wasn't a lobster!"

Although rarely spoken of publicly, nearly everyone knew that Uanini wasn't very useful in combat. After only a few training battles as an apprentice, he'd quickly earned the nickname 'lobster.' Much like the spiny crustacean, he'd developed a reputation for propelling himself in the opposite direction of danger. Many assumed that this was why Ruling Chief Vahanui had relieved Uanini of warrior status and given him the role of district manager of Puna. As such, in addition to collecting tributes, his primary responsibilities included the enforcement of island laws and overseeing the coordination of property, including water and fishing rights, land distribution, agricultural use, and general maintenance.

"Call me a lobster again," Uanini dared, pressing his bloodstained stone club against the farmer's forehead. "And I'll reunite you with both of your parents."

"Go ahead," Matani said, his eyes devoid of emotion.

Glancing down, Uanini gave a crooked smirk. "Take this with you," he said, plucking a white hibiscus from a small bush beside them. "Your mother's favorite, wasn't it?"

Matani averted his eyes from the flower, as if from a blinding flash of lightning.

Those who'd known Mahina, Matani's mother, described her as caring, kind, and generous. While the details of her face had faded for Matani over the years, one thing he'd never forgotten—could never forget—were her eyes, unusual by Havaiian or even Tahitian standards, for they were a bright, cool blue that shimmered with white webs, giving them the hypnotic appearance of two small galaxies. It was the memory of unconditional love in those compassionate blue eyes that had often kept Matani from disappearing under the unbearable weight of grief after her death.

Unfortunately, not long after Matani first learned to walk, his mother fell and broke her hip. A village doctor diagnosed her with "brittle bone disease" and prescribed an intense combination of psychic, spiritual, and natural treatments. But by the time the weather changed from cool to warm, Mahina—who had once stood strong and straight—had become bent over like a dying tree. Eventually, she lost her appetite and rarely left the family's sleeping house. One afternoon, young Matani sat beside her as she lay on a stack of floor mats, helping her drink cool water from a coconut shell. Seeing freshly cut flowers around the base of the family altar, one in particular made him smile.

A white hibiscus. Her favorite.

Matani brought the flower over, hoping it might offer a moment of peace. Despite barely being able to force a smile past the lines of pain drawn across her face, Mahina's love for her thoughtful baby boy could not be dimmed, shining ever so brightly from those adoring, blue-galaxy eyes.

Breathing in the flower's beloved scent, she sneezed and died.

The expression of surprise and pain on his mother's face was something Matani would never forget, nor the final, awful moments watching the light of consciousness fade from her eyes.

The bone doctor explained that the force of Mahina's sneeze had caused her spine to collapse, killing her instantly. Matani's father was furious. Until the day of his own death, he never forgave Matani for giving his beloved wife that stupid flower.

And neither had Matani been able to forgive himself, or the unsympathetic gods who'd ignored the prayers of a young boy asking them to spare his mother's life. After all, he'd been taught since birth that almighty beings could heal the sick or keep loved ones from death through ritual, prayer, and offerings. After witnessing his mother die in spite of his pleading for help over and over again, Matani eventually realized that neither gods nor ancestral spirits could ever be trusted again.

"What do you know of death?" Matani said in a mocking tone, slapping the offensive flower from Uanini's hand.

"That I can grant it to whomever I please," Uanini sneered, somehow growing larger and taller as he stepped forward, wrapping his chubby fingers around Matani's throat. "Your disrespect for the royal bloodline is tiresome, and I would be within my rights to kill you."

"Then do it," Matani calmly replied, relaxing into his fate. "Saves me the trouble of doing it myself."

"No," Uanini said, shaking his head with repulsed bewilderment. "You're a stone. And wallowing in misery, year after year, is a far worse punishment than my club could ever bring upon you." With a final glare, the embittered chief released and walked off, leaving Matani crumpled on the ground.

Gasping for air, Matani's gaze moved up the pedestal of fitted stones to the wooden pig idol looming over him, its long snout pointed to the cloudless sky. "Why am I here?" he mumbled.

"Looks like someone's day is off to a great start!" came a whisper so loud, the female voice that spoke it might have well just used their regular voice.

"Better than most," Matani replied sarcastically. He got to his feet, seeing Heiana—a rosy-cheeked girl his age—step out from behind a nearby tree. She was carrying several neatly folded reams of freshly made bark cloth, an offering to Ro'o from the female members of her family. When she turned toward Matani, he saw a purple-black bruise under her left eye, probably from the most recent weapon she'd gotten her hands on.

"Still trying to be a warrior?" he asked with a disapproving smirk.

"I'm already a warrior," she replied with her typical confidence.

When the two were younger, Matani hadn't cared much about what Heiana said or did, but eventually, he'd come to appreciate how often she spoke her mind. And while this was unusual behavior for a female in the community, Heiana was so determined to do the opposite of what was expected of her that no one ever had the guts to tell her otherwise. For example, instead of keeping her hair short with turned-up edges above the forehead and a wash of white clay at the temples like most women in the village, Heiana's hair was long and natural. And instead of spending her entire day learning to pound bark into cloth or making clothes and blankets like her mother, aunties, and younger sisters, Heiana would often slip away to practice her battle skills in secret, aspiring to become the greatest warrior the islands had ever known.

But in the end, Matani supposed that the most trying thing about Heiana was that she'd always known who she was and what she wanted from life.

And he did not.

Nonetheless, Matani constantly found himself intrigued by their differences and was unable to decide whether he liked her or not. While her strange ways confused him, Matani couldn't deny how many times he'd stolen glimpses of her large, expressive, hazel-colored eyes (that could magically change from brown to gold depending on the light), making his heart both ache and flutter at the same time. Like his mother, Heiana's eyes possessed the ability to soothe his internal frustrations with the world. Unless she got mad, of course. Then, those calming eyes could shift into something as cold and dangerous as a winter storm.

"Let me guess," said Heiana, placing her offering among several other items surrounding the pig idol. "You're upset that the royals have the best houses, finest mats, largest canoes, tastiest foods, and are the only ones allowed to wear feather cloaks and helmets, right?"

"Don't forget how the world hates me!" Matani reminded her, slamming one piece of 'defiled' taro after another into a carrying gourd.

"Or how meaningless your life is," she added.

Matani tossed her an annoyed smirk, unable to deny that she knew him all too well. "Yours isn't?"

"Not at all," she said, picking up three taro behind him. "I find meaning in sharing life with family and friends."

"And then after life, what?" Matani shrugged. "We die and that's it? No more family? No more friends?"

"Grandfather says life is like a flower," she replied. "It sprouts, lives, dies, then sprouts again."

"Sprouts where, exactly?" Matani asked with genuine interest. "And when?"

Heiana could only shrug. "I guess we'll have to wait and find out."

Matani spat air. "Yeah, well, I hate flowers," he said, wanting to be mad at Heiana but always finding it difficult somehow. "Anyway, don't you need to go pound more bark somewhere?"

"After I pound you!" Heiana laughed, dropping to the ground. In one swift move, she spun on her hands while sweeping her legs in a low arc, knocking Matani's feet out from under him. "I got that one from watching the warrior apprentices train the other day."

"Don't practice your dumb fighting moves on me!" Matani scrambled to get back up. "My feet hurt enough as it is."

Heiana paused, thoughtful. "Grandfather says aching feet are a sign you're going on a journey soon."

"The only journey I'm going on is back to those muddy taro patches," Matani snorted. "I still have to make enough hard poi to last the season for us all so the highborns have enough fresh taro to stuff their fat faces."

"Okay, okay," Heiana said soothingly. "Let's finish cleaning up."

Wondering why he still put up with her, Matani always ended up answering his own question with the same old story. After losing his father at just ten seasons old, none of Matani's blood relatives had come forward to raise him. It was only due to Heiana's relentless urging that her own parents eventually took him in. Even as a child, she always stood up for others, refused to do anything she didn't want to do, and typically made her own rules. Yes, she was a pretty remarkable person, and Matani knew full well that if it weren't for her selfless compassion, he probably would've disappeared into emotional oblivion long ago. And so, for a time, Heiana, her parents, grandparents, and cousins were the closest thing to a family Matani had.

As they quietly collected the remainder of the spilled taro, Heiana repeatedly glanced over at Matani.

Rolling his eyes, he finally gave in. "Okay, what is it?"

She giggled awkwardly. "Vatua, that new warrior apprentice, wants me to meet with him after the water splashing ceremony tonight."

The ceremony was an important celebration during Matari'i-hiti when the community bid a symbolic farewell to the old year and welcomed the new. Come nightfall, great bonfires would be lit all along the beach to offset the chilly weather and everyone, both commoner and highborn, would wade out and submerge themselves in the ocean, symbolizing re-entrance into the mother's womb. Emerging from the salt water reborn, all past mistakes would be forgiven. After drying themselves by the fires, old clothes of the previous year would be burned, replaced by fresh new loincloths or decorated skirts. The ceremony would end at sunrise with the birth of a new day, a new year, and the chance to reset one's path in life.

A path, it seemed, that Heiana and her new little highborn friend (probably muscular and handsome . . . and conceited, too) might soon be walking together.

Tell her how you feel!

No way! She'll just laugh at me!

He's right. She will. Just like last time.

"Never heard of him," was all Matani said, but that wasn't entirely true. Just days earlier, he'd overheard a few other farmers talking about a particular young chief by the name of Vatua, who had apparently caught Heiana sneaking around the warriors' compound, trying to watch some of the older apprentices train. Rumor had it that they had met in secrecy later that night.

"He's a warrior apprentice from Ni'ihau," she said with an air of haughtiness. "Son of High Chief Opoa."

"Yeah, and you're a commoner," Matani said. "Don't you understand the danger you're putting yourself in?"

While Heiana enjoyed defying social norms, hierarchy was a serious matter. For a commoner to have any kind of relationship with a highborn, whether it be romantic or simply friendship, was considered extremely dangerous. Any perceived threat to their status could be met with punishment, including death.

"We've only met a few times," she replied. "And it's always after dark."

"If anyone finds out, *you'll* be the one sacrificed," Matani said with genuine concern. "Not him."

Heiana's eyes narrowed, her fiery spirit refusing to be tamed by such warnings. "I won't let fear dictate my life. No one controls my heart or happiness."

What about my heart?

You had your chance. You blew it.

Three summers ago, shortly after Heiana's thirteenth lunar year, something changed in their relationship. While the two were picking limpets from rocks along the beach, an unexpectedly bright and colorful sunset exploded in the clouds above them. Matani experienced a sudden rush of feelings and tried to kiss her. Surprised, she dodged his clumsy attempt, then jumped up and ran off giggling. Neither of them had spoken of the incident since.

Shortly after that horrible embarrassment, Matani moved into the abandoned house of an elder fisherman who'd disappeared at sea a year earlier. While he and Heiana remained close at first, over time the two grew more and more independent of each other. While she continued pushing the boundaries of expectation by teaching herself the ways of a warrior, Matani found that being around other people was much too uncomfortable and chose to spend more and more time alone.

And while most people let him be, Heiana would not. This confused Matani, because if she didn't want to kiss him, why wouldn't she just leave him alone like everyone else?

Because Heiana does what she wants.

With this thought, Matani gave a defeated shrug. "Well, then go to the ceremony with Vatua. Just be careful."

Shaking her head in frustration, Heiana threw down all the taro she'd picked up. "Fine, I will! Since no one else is going to ask me!"

Hold on. Does she want me to . . .?

Of course not! It's a trick!

Heiana grunted at Matani's silence. "You need help, you know that?"

Matani threw his hands in the air. "What did I do now?"

"What you *always* do," she yelled, on the verge of tears. "Nothing!"

Confused as always when it came to Heiana, Matani could only watch her turn and walk off.

Should I go after her?

Why? So she can reject you again?

Heiana stopped suddenly, then turned and walked back to Matani, wiping tears from her eyes. "I know I can never fully understand the pain you carry from losing your parents, but I really try. Maybe it's time you find out why your family left?"

Matani winced slightly at her words. All of his mother's relatives lived on Maui, and due to the complications of long-distance travel for commoners—especially farmers—he'd never met any of them. And though he recalled many fond memories with the aunties, uncles, and cousins on his father's side, they had all abruptly picked up and moved to the To'orau district when he was six seasons old. When Matani asked what had happened, his father refused to talk about it, saying only that he and his brother had a disagreement. When his father died, the mystery of what happened died with him, haunting the shadows of Matani's mind ever since.

"It's been too long," he said quietly. "Besides, I've gotten along just fine without them."

"Oh, obviously," Heiana said, unconvinced. "I know you hate when I say this, but maybe you should try praying again?"

Matani chuckled bitterly. "Here we go."

"Well, maybe you're doing it wrong!" she replied. "Words are spells, and only with words of substance will we receive substance in return."

Groaning, Matani returned to gathering up the last of the spilled taro. "I have work to do."

Heiana knew when to stop wasting words on Matani, but she stayed to help finish picking up the taro anyway. As the two worked in silence, Matani felt his guilt creeping up on him. He knew all too well that she was the only person who was always honest with him, even when it was something he didn't want to hear. About to apologize for hurting her feelings, Matani happened to look over just as she bent to pick up a corm of taro. Her hair dropped down, offering a glimpse of her left breast.

Looks larger than I remember.

The surprising thought embarrassed Matani so much, he forgot to look away.

"What are you gawking at?" Heiana snapped.

Matani blinked, startled. "What? Nothing!" he blurted. "My eyes just happened to be aimed that way when you—"

She suddenly turned to face him, pushing her long black hair behind her shoulders, giving Matani the full view of both her breasts.

Matani was careful to keep his eyes on her face. "W-what are you doing?"

"Do you want to touch them?" she purred.

To Matani, this was highly unusual behavior. Especially considering that they hadn't spent much time together in quite a while. Still, he couldn't stop himself from imagining his finger tracing her soft, feminine curves.

She's just teasing you because she's mad!

But she's flirting with me, isn't she?

Why would she flirt with you? What can you possibly offer her?

You're right. She deserves better.

The moment quickly turned awkward, broken only by Heiana whisking her hair back over her breasts in a huff. "Forget it!"

Matani wrinkled his brow, both confused and insulted. "Well, I wouldn't want to upset your new boyfriend."

"He's not my boyfriend," Heiana replied, pausing for dramatic effect. "Yet!"

"Oh, good, then there's still time for him to come to his senses," Matani shot back.

Heiana's mouth fell open in an offended gasp just before she, rather impressively, lifted one of the half-full calabashes of taro above her head and heaved it at Matani with everything she had.

Barely dodging it, Matani could only watch in horror as the calabash flew past, slamming into the ancient altar behind him. Both Heiana and Matani stood rooted in shock as the sacred wooden head of the pig teetered one way, back the other, then toppled to the ground.

"Oh gods!" Heiana gasped. "What have I done?!"

Out of the corner of his eye, Matani saw Uanini doubling back on his rounds. His next thought was immediate and, surprisingly, without any internal discussion.

Protect Heiana!

"Hide!" he whispered, careful not to move his lips or even so much as glance in her direction. Heiana immediately dove into a thicket of ferns as Matani hurried over and tried to lift the pig's head back up onto the stone pedestal before the bloodthirsty chief arrived. But it was too heavy and too late.

"Sacrilege!" Uanini shouted, spotting the defiled idol in Matani's arms.

"It wasn't me!" Matani pleaded. "An evil spirit knocked it over!"

Uanini's enraged expression mutated into a repulsive grin. "By authority of the gods given to me by blood," he shouted, unhitching his stone club, "I sentence you to death!"

Stunned, Matani glanced over at Heiana hidden in the ferns and saw her lips form a single, urgent word.

Run.

✦ CHAPTER 2 ✦

Havaiians had always centered their lives around *Mana*, the incorporeal force originating from the ancestral gods that flows out into the world, giving life to all things. Mana is born of the nonmaterial world but felt in the material one, and in humans, manifests itself as an intellectual skill or physical talent—such as land management, leadership, martial arts, canoe carving, fishing, or house building—which is passionately maintained through consistent offering and prayer. Commoners possess little mana, because their bloodline is impure and genealogies incomplete, while royalty can trace their impeccable heritage directly to the gods, thus assuming the role of gods themselves.

Of the five classes of Havaiian chiefs, the highest ranking are those with the most pristine genealogies. If these bloodlines are not kept pure, a ruling chief's efficacy as a leader is greatly diminished, risking famine, disease, or destruction of the lands under their control. To avoid calling down such terrifying wrath from the gods, the priests and highborns created a system of island laws in order to protect their mana from mingling with that of lesser beings. Because it is believed that commoners possess little mana (with outcasts and slaves having absolutely none), they are forbidden to touch the clothing, hair, or even so much as a fingernail clipping of royalty. Since it is prohibited to enter the homes or living spaces of chiefs, eat from their bowls, or touch, look at, or even cross shadows with them, it is incumbent upon lower members of society to stop whatever they are doing and bow or prostrate themselves in the presence of all high-ranking individuals. However, these more stringent rules don't apply to lesser chiefs, who themselves possess less demanding tabu rights, thus allowing them to more effectively manage commoners within their district.

To ensure fealty to this most rigid tabu system, nearly all offenses are punishable by death. The most common penalties involve strangulation, clubbing, stoning, burning, drowning, or—if the crime is truly heinous—being offered to the gods as a human sacrifice.

Ultimately, this all centers around the most sacred hosts from which all mana originates: the ancestral gods.

And this was why, in Matani's case, the mishandling of a sacred altar to a primary god—on the eve of his seasonal arrival, no less—needed to be dealt with swiftly and severely. In fact, his death was vital to preventing the island from imminent disharmony and potential collapse. No matter how much Ruling Chief Vahanui enjoyed his taro.

Why do I have to follow ancient customs I had no say in creating?

Because you're a commoner.

That's just a label someone came up with. What if I believe I'm something more?

Believe you can fly, if it makes you feel better, but the reality of jumping off a cliff will ultimately disappoint you.

I hate being so powerless.

Then stop running and let Uanini kill you, so it can finally be over.

Racing through strobing columns of dusty light—dead brown mulch below, sunlit leaves above—Matani could hear the snap and crack of chasing footsteps catching up to him. Glancing back, he saw Uanini leap over a downed tree trunk, his eyes focused but wild, his thin lips curled into a crazed grin. For some reason, this made Matani chuckle as he wove through a blur of tropical plants and palm trees. The chuckle turned to maniacal laughter as Matani found dark irony in the absurdity of his predicament. Moments like this had given him a lifetime of training, constantly forced to outrun far too many disciplinary smacks and head clubbings. By the time he'd lived to see seven harvests, no one on the island could catch him. Not even his father.

In full flight, eyes wide and terrified, Matani ran headlong through the community working plaza where he spotted old man Poutoru sitting on a worn stump teaching his grandson the art of chipping rocks into various handheld tools. Hearing the pounding of footsteps, both looked up. Accustomed to seeing Matani being chased by one angry person or another, Poutoru just sighed and shook his head.

"What did you do now, boy?" asked the old stonecutter.

"He thinks I knocked over Tamapua'a!" Matani yelled in passing.

Poutoru's expression shifted from weariness to concern. "Better get yourself to the temple of refuge," he warned.

While Matani had angered Uanini more times than he could remember, this was the first time he'd ever angered him enough to actually need physical protection. Short of suicide, which some lawbreakers preferred, there was but one single opportunity to evade punishment: if a tabu breaker could reach a temple of refuge before getting caught, the resident priest could offer sanctuary to the fugitive and perform sacred rituals to absolve them of their misdeeds, allowing them to return home with full immunity.

This was without dispute. No pursuer—including a high chief or even the ruling chief himself—could follow any guilty party into a temple of refuge without risking death at the hands of the resident priest or even his underpriests and attendants. A necessary fail-safe for those who had absolute power over the life and death of their subjects.

The closest temple sanctuary Matani knew of was Hauora, located at the mouth of Vairuanuiho'āno River within the Hitinaatarā City of Refuge, which wasn't all that far. But in order to get there, he'd have to make it past the royal compound and across the bay without getting caught. Or drowning.

"The only temple you're going to is Pori'ahu!" Uanini shouted from behind, knowing full well where his fugitive was headed.

Matani laughed, but it was forced. Pori'ahu was a temple named for the snow goddess—a sister of Pere, the volcano goddess—infamously known for its ritualistic use of human sacrifices.

Bounding across the valley floor, Matani made a winding course between several commoner dwellings, some small, simple constructions that were low to the ground without walls, while the larger walled residences with straight or curved rafters were built on stone platforms. Curiosity finally got the better of him and he looked back, capturing another image of Uanini—this time with teeth gnashed in a hateful grimace. At first impressed by how committed he was for someone so clearly out of shape, Matani quickly became worried.

He might actually catch me.

Good.

Exploding from the tree line into the wide-open panorama of Vairu-anuihoʻāno River, Matani found himself barreling straight toward a gathering of women washing clothes along the water's edge. Launching himself over their unsuspecting heads, the bottom of his foot grazed a few strands of someone's hair before he splashed down into the milky-brown river water on the other side.

Not a moment later, Uanini burst from the trees, his blazing eyes morphing into comical surprise when he realized he was on a collision course toward the same group of women Matani had just barely cleared. Locking his feet, the stout chief quickly lost control as he skidded down the embankment and crashed through wooden racks hung with freshly laundered clothes.

Treading water, Matani locked eyes with Uanini and burst out laughing.

Uanini's face grew hot with rage. "I'll knock that laugh out along with your teeth when I catch you!" he vowed, struggling to untangle himself from the wet clothes.

Matani spun and swam down the northern fork of the twin rivers, looking for a place where he could make his way over to the southern one. Something whistled past his ear, splashing the water in front of him. Matani looked over and saw Uanini running alongside him, carrying a handful of rocks.

"Chiefs of Vairuanuihoʻāno!" Uanini shouted, launching another barrage. "A tabu breaker is fleeing in the river! Help me catch him before he reaches Hauora!"

A sharp lava stone grazed Matani's cheek, but it quickly became the least of his concerns when he saw three chiefs emerge from the trees just ahead. Each carrying a long spear.

Think you can outswim their weapons?

Hearing the crescendo of something whizzing through the air, Matani made a blind move to get out of the way just before a rock struck him in the shoulder. He dove under, screaming bubbles of pain as more projectiles streaked down through the water all around him.

The river was thick and powerful with mountain runoff from a recent winter storm, making visibility extremely poor. Quickly losing his sense of direction, Matani instinctively concentrated on the flow of the water and the angle of shadows on his hands. Determining where he was in relation to the northern and southern banks, he decided to swim for the shadier side of the former. Lungs about to burst, he was relieved when his fingertips touched the rocky shallows of the riverbed. Lifting his head for a hasty gulp of air, Matani moved quietly through a tunnel of long grass curled over the riverbank and held himself as still as possible, feeling his heart banging hard in his chest.

"I lost him!" Uanini shouted.

Matani jumped. The voice was right above him.

"He's probably underwater! Don't let him get past you!"

Shivering in the cold mountain water, Matani waited for Uanini to move on. After what seemed like an eternity, he was about to climb from the river when soft, raspy breathing stopped him cold.

Uanini's still there.

Reaching into the slimy mud beneath his legs, Matani felt around with both hands until he found a small rock, then got on his haunches and flung it as far upstream as he could. It hissed through the leaves before hitting a distant tree with a loud knock. Above, Uanini grunted, followed by the sound of feet stomping off across dead leaves. Relieved, Matani turned onto his stomach and crawled down through the grassy tunnel, glimpsing several more warriors and royal guards.

As staying put was far too risky, Matani reluctantly climbed up the opposite bank of the opposite river fork he needed to be on. Crawling through thick ferns, he suddenly found himself staring at two crisscrossed sticks with white balls of cloth on top: a grave warning for commoners not to trespass. With little choice, he ignored the ancient symbol that meant 'obey or die' and entered the grounds anyway.

Moving stealthily through the hot, dusty shadows of several thatch structures, he stepped on something that made him scream out in pain and surprise. Clamping both hands over his mouth, Matani saw the fragment of a shark's tooth protruding from his heel, having likely broken off any number of weapons used by the chiefs who resided here.

It's an omen. You shouldn't have ignored the tabu cross.

"I see tracks over here!" a voice shouted. "Looks like he crawled this way!"

No turning back now.

Matani dashed for the shadows of another thatch house. Looking back, he was horrified to realize he'd left blood-spotted footprints in the sand. He yanked up a handful of nearby ferns and hurriedly swept away as much of the evidence as he could.

Betrayed by my own blood once again.

Hopping on his good foot through a huddle of free-roaming chickens, dogs, and pigs devouring fruit and vegetable peels on the ground, Matani made his way into the shadow of another, much larger thatch structure. Hearing two young toddlers coming around the corner, he dove through its low doorway. Assuming an elder was more than likely not far behind, Matani froze until he heard the sound of heavier footsteps shuffling past. Relieved to find the structure was empty, Matani determined from the long wooden tables on the ground that it was the chiefs eating house.

Now where do I go?

This was a question Matani had asked of himself many times. As always, it unleashed waves of depression that encouraged him to simply lie down and give up.

They're going to find you eventually, anyway. Just make it easy on yourself and stay put.

Trapped and terrified to the point of tears, Matani closed his eyes. "Mother . . . Father, please help me."

The faint scent of ripe banana caught his attention. He opened his eyes and saw the source of the smell, a rotting banana under one corner of the larger eating table. He snatched it up and immediately began peeling the brown, overripe skin, but stopped when he noticed an altar against the far wall. It was an upright lava stone placed on top of a circular fan of ti leaves. Conditioned by years of upbringing, Matani averted his gaze from its supposed sacredness. While he himself had lost faith in such things, most others believed that when gods or familial ancestors were invoked through certain rituals, their spirit could occupy a particular object and be consulted or supplicated in times of need.

Matani regarded the spirit stone for a moment, struggling with all the things he no longer believed. "It's just a rock," he muttered.

But then something Heiana had told him came to mind: *Words are spells, and only with words of substance will you receive substance in return.*

So, here I am once again, faced with little choice but to ask for help from imaginary forces.

Even if he could find the correct words or intention, the blunt truth of it all was that Matani had been without both parents for much of his life. And the impact of their loss had proved nothing short of debilitating. At least when they were alive, he'd still believed there was a chance help would come from above. But experiencing such traumatic losses had directly informed his utter lack of belief in anything even remotely supernatural.

So why would I believe now?

Because you're stupid.

An image of Heiana interrupted his cruel thoughts. Her warm hazel eyes, that beautiful smile that he had come to miss seeing every day, but mostly all the things that remained unspoken between them. Important things.

And now I may never get the chance to tell her.

This sobering thought brought Matani before the altar, staring at it for a good long moment. "I'm in trouble," he finally began, "and ask with a humble heart if you would consider passing along a message to my ancestors."

Waiting for a sign, Matani was relieved when he heard the light, cheery whistle of a bird on the roof right above him.

Definitely a good omen.

"For your hunger, for mine," he recited, then rested the banana he'd found before the spirit stone. "Even though my hunger is probably stronger than yours right now," he added, before reconsidering. "Okay, forget that last part."

Dipping his hands into a gourd of salt water on the ground beside the altar, Matani froze, startled by an angry face glowering back up at him.

"Who are you?" he whispered. "Where did you come from? Where are you going?"

While the reflection gave no answers, what unnerved Matani the most was how much he looked like his father now—the furrowed brow hanging like storm clouds over unhappy eyes dimmed by years of hurt and pain. The image disturbed him more than he dared admit.

A tear slid down Matani's cheek and into the water, erasing the unsettling image in a blur of circular ripples. He dipped his fingers into the calabash, sprinkled the stone with salt water, then took a piece of bark from a small pile and placed it on top. Taking a deeper breath this time, he stepped back, got down on his knees—first the right, then the left—and touched his head to the ground.

"For anyone listening," he whispered, then assumed a cross-legged position. Eyes wide and head held high, he repeated an opening prayer used often by his mother at their home altar.

> "Lift up, the purified prayer for life.
> Lift up, to the shining heavens, lift!
> Lift it to the gods of places on high!
> Sacred spirits of the mountains,
> wise companions of the sea,
> seek and find, find my fault that I may atone.
> Go prayer, but return to me with reinforcements.
> Here is a prayer from Matani,
> here are my troubles:
> Gods, you brought me into this life as a commoner, separated
> me from my relatives, and took my parents. Now, it seems, you
> want to take me, too. Why? Whatever I've done to offend you,
> I am sorry. But are my wrongdoings so horrible that you can't find
> the compassion to forgive me? If not, then I offer this banana
> along with myself as sacrifice, because I can't take much more.
> There. The prayer has flown; it is free to manifest."

As was customary, Matani waited for the essence of the banana to be consumed by the spirits before eating the physical aspect of the offering himself. If his words had the meaning and substance he hoped they did, the answer to his prayer would come to him in a dream within the next few days.

If you live long enough to receive it, that is.

As he peeled the banana with hungry anticipation, an energy thick with mystery descended upon the interior of the eating house, followed by a swirling breeze that was strong enough to shiver the thatched roof and all four walls.

It carried intermingling scents of the sea—brine, fish, salt water—mixed with the unmistakable perfumes of earth: plants, flowers, and pine.

His prayer had been received.

The hairs on the back of Matani's neck stood on end as sounds of clattering and grunting filled the air. Racing over to the opposite end of the eating house, he peered through perforations in the thatch. In an open courtyard across the way, two young chiefs were sparring with blunt spears. Beside them, two more of similar age bounced on their toes, practicing kicks and punches.

Warrior apprentices.

Matani couldn't help but notice that they weren't that much older than himself—though certainly far more muscular, as Heiana often enjoyed reminding him. In fact, to anyone that had never visited the islands before, highborn and commoner could very well appear as two completely different races.

Just then, a smaller figure entered the courtyard, carrying a precarious stack of calabashes and breaking the concentration of one particularly mean-looking trainee, who was practicing a series of spin kicks on some hanging bags of sand.

"You made me miss the last one, Vatua!", shouted the young chief with a fiercely chiseled jaw.

"Maybe you need more practice," the smaller apprentice replied.

Matani snickered quietly. But then he recognized the name. Vatua was the apprentice from Niʻihau that Heiana had mentioned earlier.

The one she's going to get naked with at the water splashing ceremony tonight!

Rock Jaw—as Matani dubbed him—walked over, a smug expression on his broad face, and brazenly knocked the stack of calabashes from Vatua's arms, drawing the attention of the other three trainees.

"Aren't you gonna say something?" a trainee with a large head brayed, running over to them.

Vatua answered with a sarcastic smile. Rock Jaw's fist slammed into his mouth. Shaking it off, Vatua touched his lip and saw blood on his fingers.

The other three trainees cackled loudly as they formed a tight circle around Vatua. But even still, despite his size, the young apprentice didn't seem intimidated in the least.

"He's got guts, I'll give him that," Matani whispered.

As if somehow sensing this admiration, Vatua seemed to casually glance across the compound, straight into Matani's eyes.

"Eee!" Matani inhaled, backing away from the peephole.

Before he could determine if he'd been spotted, Matani heard footsteps staggering past the eating house, accompanied by the fatigued voice of Uanini. "You four," he stopped, out of breath and huffing, "Come with me!"

Through the peephole, Matani saw Uanini doubled over in front of the warrior trainees, trying desperately to catch his breath. "A tabu breaker (*huff, puff*) is on the loose!"

"Who?" asked a trainee with a rather thick neck.

"A puny farm boy," Uanini snapped. "He desecrated the border idol and is trying to reach Hauora to escape punishment. Whoever helps me catch him can share in the glory of spilling his blood!"

The trainees howled with gleeful anticipation as they raced to the weapon rack, fighting one another to grab from the display of beautifully made spears, strangling cords, rock slings, wooden clubs, and daggers.

Uanini turned to Vatua, as if noticing him for the first time. "You're the apprentice from Ni'ihau, yeah? Opoa's son?"

Vatua nodded. "Yes, Chief."

"You see a commoner run through here?"

Here we go. The spoiled little highborn gets to have Heiana all to himself now.

"Now that you mention it," Vatua replied, "I did see someone that seemed out of place running that way not too long ago."

Prepared to make a break for it, Matani was surprised when he saw Vatua point in a completely different direction from the eating house.

Maybe he didn't see me after all.

Uanini grunted, surveying any number of possible escape routes. "Could be heading back upriver to throw us off so he can find a different way to reach the temple."

"We'll get him!" assured Rock Jaw.

"Good," Uanini said, then clapped Vatua on the shoulder. "Go spread word of the unlawful farmer. Warn everyone that offering him any assistance is punishable by death!"

"Right away," Vatua promised.

Matani stood motionless, not taking his eyes off Uanini and his trainees until they were very far away and then some. When he looked back at the compound, his throat hitched to see Vatua walking straight toward the men's eating house. Before Matani could find another way out, Vatua ducked through the entrance.

"I'm not here to turn you in," he said quickly, both hands raised in a nonthreatening manner.

Matani was skeptical. "W-why did you lie? If Uanini finds out you helped me, he'll kill you."

"You're Matani, right?"

"How do you know my name?"

"Heiana speaks of you often," Vatua said, rather candidly. "Mostly to say how alike we look."

"Oh," Matani said, suddenly feeling competitive. "She's never mentioned you before."

Vatua nodded with a smirk that seemed tinged with a hint of jealousy. "Well, she'd never forgive me if I played any part in your death."

"Me neither," Matani quipped, moving slowly for the doorway. "So, you'll let me go?"

Vatua nodded. "Of course."

"Okay, well, whatever happens, can you tell Heiana I said we're even now?"

Vatua replied with a puzzled look.

"Long story," was all Matani would afford him as he turned to leave.

"Wait," Vatua whispered, grabbing Matani's arm. "Across the river, there's a small canoe landing that only the ruling chief and high priest use. It has a path that leads straight to Hauora."

"Are you crazy? What if I get caught?"

"Says the person who's already in a place he shouldn't be."

"Good point," Matani agreed. "Where exactly is this canoe landing?"

"Once you get across to the southern river, look for a bamboo grove on the other side. The path starts there, between two temple guardian idols."

Matani's first reaction was that Vatua was trying to trick him somehow, but something in the young chief's light-brown eyes convinced him that this was a genuine person of good character.

With so much at stake, are you sure you can trust your instincts?

"Better hurry," Vatua said. "There's a big ceremony taking place on the beach right now with warriors from all over the island, but it will be ending soon."

Nodding farewell, they crawled through the doorway of the eating house, Vatua first, followed by Matani, both running in different directions without a second glance.

Matani crept through a thick patch of ferns back down to the river's edge. Spotting the bamboo grove on the southern river's bank, he decided the best route would be to swim straight across, then make his way down under the cover of trees.

I'll have to stay underwater until I reach the other side to avoid being seen. Impossible! You can't hold your breath that long!

Breathing in and out a few times to prime his lungs, Matani took one last fateful inhale, then sank quietly into the water. Careful to keep the current pushing against his right side, it wasn't long before he felt his body involuntarily rising to the surface. Diving back down as far as he could go, he searched the bottom of the river until he found a good-sized stone to weigh him down. Clutching it to his chest, he rotated his body until the current pushed against his right side again, then started kicking his way forward through the water.

Matani had no idea how far across the river he was until warm, silky water started pulling on his legs.

Salt water.

Dropping the rock, he quickly rose to the surface, surprised to find that the freshwater current had carried him all the way down to the mouth of the river, about to be pulled into the sea. Spotting the temple of refuge across the bay, Matani had barely reoriented himself when he heard someone shouting.

"I see the farmer!" It was Thick Neck. "He's caught in the rip current!"

"Well get him!" Uanini ordered.

"Rip current?" Matani repeated, confused, as a powerful undercurrent yanked him underwater, slamming him to the ocean floor. Pulled into the depths of the sea, his lungs convulsed, inhaling water.

This might actually be the end of me.

Feeling himself losing consciousness, Matani fought his way out of the deadly current into tamer shallows. Stumbling ashore, he collapsed face down on the wet, hot sand, vomiting salt water. As he forced himself onto his feet, Matani smelled cooked pork in the air that made his stomach tighten with hunger. Blinking the saltwater fog from his eyes, he could see he was standing on the immense, curving golden sands of Vairuanuihoʻāno Beach.

Seeing the temple of refuge even further away now, Matani groaned. Glancing behind him in search of other options, his jaw dropped at a gathering of canoes lined up across the beach—at least three hundred magnificently crafted single- and double-hulled vessels. Their sails were brailed up to their respective masts, and each of their bird-shaped bows aimed valiantly seaward, anxious to fly across the waves. Almost every canoe was covered with fragrant garlands of vine, orange flowers, and sacred ti leaves, indicating that whatever expedition they were about to embark upon was an important one.

Matani was momentarily lost in the skills a master builder must have in order to construct such beautiful contraptions able to withstand the wild waves and weather of the sea. The upper third of each hull was natural wood, polished with coconut oil. The bottom sections were stained black with a mixture of charcoal and plant sap used for their water sealant qualities. Matani noticed that several of the hulls bore blemishes of stone and spear divots, souvenirs of countless battles and untold adventures.

I should take one of these and leave the island!

And do what?

Start over! Find a new island and be whoever I want to be!

Oh, please. You don't know how to work a canoe.

How hard can it be?

Well, whatever you're going to do, do it fast.

Why?

Look behind you.

Matani turned to find Uanini and his four trainees stomping around the southern end of the beach. Without thinking, he spun back and ran straight between the canoes—where his shifting perspective revealed an army of no less than four thousand warriors sitting in complete silence on the beach before him.

Frozen in place, Matani recalled Vatua mentioning something about warriors and a ceremony happening somewhere, but only in that moment did he realize the gravity of his mistake in dismissing the warning. Staring into a terrifying abyss of privileged highborns who held all the power, should a single pair of eyes among the thousands spot Matani, his lowly status as a commoner witnessing such a sacred event would be a swift and immediate death sentence. Praying for invisibility, Matani's heart began pounding so hard against his ribcage, he felt like his entire body was about to explode.

♦ CHAPTER 3 ♦

Just beyond the beach, under the late-afternoon shade of gently swaying palm trees, was Ruling Chief Vahanui himself, dressed in a magnificent cloak of bright, yellow feathers. Like all royalty who devote themselves to the development of bodily and mental superiority, Vahanui was a tall, muscular figure of a man with kind brown eyes. Though youthful in appearance, the gray infiltrating his thick black hair reveals the stresses of leadership. As with all highborn, his daunting physique was attributed to the excellent care given all children of nobility, with better life conditions, food, and a regimen of healthy sports and exercise.

Seated cross-legged on plush, handwoven mats before his audience of warriors, he wore a feather helmet to match his cloak featuring a thick, high crest arching from the back of his neck to his forehead. On his right, the short-caped royal signet bearer stood holding a staff made from the long bones of an old rival topped with hawk feathers—a prestigious symbol of any ruling chief's power and divinity. And to his left were three male personal attendants wearing yellow feather loincloths, each ready to fulfill their ruler's every wish and whim.

Matani had only seen the ruling chief and his entourage in person four times throughout his entire life. The first few times, he was at a considerable distance. The third and fourth, he was able to hide behind a tree or boulder. Now, here, under the ill-fated circumstances of his fifth encounter, he was much closer, and way more exposed than he could have ever imagined. Still, Matani had wits enough to notice that not one warrior among the thousands moved a single muscle—knowing full well that the slightest disturbance was punishable by death, even for high-ranking chiefs such as these.

Of course, Matani wasn't being still and silent out of respect. He was a powerless victim of oppression paralyzed by absolute fear.

Thankfully, all eyes were currently closed in reverence for the sacred chant being performed by Supreme High Priest Hunumaniani, the preeminent leader for all seven sacred temples of Vairuanuihoʻāno. As with all religious ceremonies, it fell upon the exalted priest to make sure the performance was flawless in order to please the gods. Considered one of the most powerful priests in all the islands, Hunumaniani had a long white beard and a matching head of hair. His intimidatingly tall, white-robed frame was draped in a cloak of red feathers that contrasted with a black feather helmet with white plumes. Though wrinkled and withered by weather and time, the priest moved with a subtle grace as he raised aloft the sacred sennit cord, a symbol of the ruling chief's genealogical relationship with the gods.

"Repair and renew Vahanui's pristine bloodline, braided like this cord in my hand, connecting the strength of all ancestors before," the high priest chanted with perfectly cadenced phrasing. "We call upon your wisdom and compassion to return peace and unity to Tauaʻi!"

Everyone on the island had heard the many dark and chilling tales of Hunumaniani's sorcery. His eyes—the left a vibrant brown, and the right a lifeless, milky white—allowed him to see into both worlds of the living and the dead. As a Knower of the Unknown, it was said that all time belonged to Hunumaniani—the then, the now, and the afterward. He walked with the gods in his dreams, accessing powers of the infinite that enabled him to gaze into the future. And, perhaps most chilling of all, it was also said that he could return life to the dead with the utterance of a single word . . . or pray it away.

Seeing Hunumaniani turn in his direction, Matani forced his wobbly legs to propel him backward, only to trip over an outrigger boom attachment and fall into the bottom of a canoe hull. Terrified, Matani froze until he heard the priest's chant proceed unbroken. Staring up at tangles of rigging strumming in the ocean breeze, he was reminded of how his mother would entertain him with string animals when he was child.

Imagining her smiling, blue-galaxy eyes looking into his was enough to help him breathe again.

"We call upon your infinite mana to be used in defense of darkness, to fend off death," the supreme high priest chanted evenly. "Shelter these warriors on their seaward journey across the mysterious depths, from unforeseen dangers in the east and west, to the north and south; from zenith to horizon, of the upper and lower strata."

Matani gathered the courage to peer over the canoe's rim, searching out every possible place to run but unable to commit to any of them.

You can't possibly think you're going to get out of this one, do you?

While Matani had grown numb to the blunt and unsupportive nature of his own thoughts, he couldn't deny that this particular one might actually be right.

There was no going farther up the beach, that much was obvious. He couldn't go south; a search party was likely scouring every possible path to the temple at this very moment. And while risking a swim across deadly rip currents swirling in the bay could be a last resort, he actually had one other, less risky option. The north end of the beach was wide open with a row of canoes, and plenty of hiding places between them, spanning nearly the entire distance.

Infused with a sliver of hope, Matani hatched a new plan that was actually inspired by what Uanini had said earlier. He would make his way across the beach, careful to stay hidden behind the canoe fleet, then go inland under the cover of trees, way, way, way past the royal compound, then go east beyond both rivers and back down the other side to reach the temple of refuge before nightfall.

After climbing out into the open, about to execute his new plan, Matani looked down the beach and groaned.

Huddled together just a few canoes down were Uanini, Rock Jaw, Back Scar, Big Head, and Thick Neck. And judging by their expressions, they were just as impressed by the unexpected gathering of warriors and voyaging canoes as he had been.

"Is this a launching ceremony?" Thick Neck blurted out. "Where are they going?"

"I've heard talk of a gathering on O'ahu for Matari'i-hiti," said Big Head. "Or whatever they call it there."

Thick Neck looked confused. "So why isn't Uanini going with them?"

"Only high chiefs are invited," Back Scar told him.

"Lower your voice, you dumb logs!" Uanini snapped as he approached them from behind, then looked over at Hunumaniani as fearfully as prey watches a predator.

"Are you sure the farmer came this way?" Big Head whispered. "The temple is on the other side of the bay!"

"Yes, I know the temple is on the other side of the bay," Uanini replied mockingly. "But he was taken by the rip current, which pulls this way."

Back Scar shrugged. "Okay, so where is he?"

Uanini grinned slyly, then pointed at several evenly spaced divots in the wet sand.

Matani gasped. Although considerably melted by the incoming tide, his own tracks could be seen in the wet sand, leading to more solid footprints in the dry sand, leading straight toward him. He immediately scurried on elbows and knees past several canoes, dangerously exposing himself to the supreme high priest and his ministers, who were now walking through the crowd of prostrated warriors, purifying them with sprinklings of seawater in the closing practice of the ceremony.

Forging ahead, he counted the canoes as he passed them. At around fourteen, Matani glanced back to see where Uanini and the others were, then looked forward again, nearly ramming his face into a large, wooden steering paddle. Fearing that going around it might leave him exposed, he dove underneath the raised platform of the double-hulled canoe it was attached to instead.

Surprised at how deceptively spacious the crawl space beneath the deck was, Matani felt like he was inside a miniature house. The massive hulls on either side of him were the length of nine men and easily as thick as he was tall—each carved from a single, centuries-old koa tree and connected by nine crossbeams about twelve forearm lengths across, with a tenth curved crossboom in the center that gave the deck a slight arch.

Pivoting, Matani looked anxiously around the back of the righthand hull and saw his bloodthirsty pursuers ransacking the canoe he'd just been hiding in. Fortunately, their progress was slow, as they, too, were wary of drawing attention from the high priest.

Finding more fresh foot divots in the sand, Uanini pointed frantically, whispering something that sent Big Head and Thick Neck in a crouching run along the ocean side of the canoes toward the beach's north end.

Of course they are.

Well, there goes your brilliant plan. What now?

Why don't you come up with something?

Sure, I've got an idea. Give up!

Matani shook his head and raced to the fore end of the twin-hulled canoe, where the rectangular opening framed bright layers of sand, ocean, and sky. To the left, he could see Big Head and Thick Neck working their way back down the row, searching every canoe from front to back. To his right, Uanini and Back Scar were doing the same, quickly working their way right up to where he was.

"Powerless," Matani whispered despondently.

Out of options, he balled himself up, closed his eyes, and began to pray for the second time that day. Not so much with thoughts or words this time, but through his emotions of desperation and loneliness.

As he did, the sound of footsteps grew louder and louder, until, almost mercifully, the anticipation ended with shadows of doom slithering across the lumpy sand just outside the perimeter of the two-hulled canoe.

Time's up.

Ready to accept his fate, Matani crawled from his hiding place to turn himself in.

Wait. Look up.

I wouldn't, if I were you.

Through a tight space between the deck and hull above him, Matani saw a burnished brown lizard with light stripes on its back and a sky-blue tail looking back down.

"What are you doing here?" he hissed. "Come to see me get killed?"

The little brown creature twitched its bright-blue tail, then licked the transparent membrane shielding its right eye before skittering off at someone approaching. Matani tried pulling himself up to where the lizard had been, but the combination of his sweaty feet and a recently oiled hull made it difficult to gain purchase.

It's over. You're not strong enough.

Yes you are! Pull yourself up! Now!

Gathering every bit of strength left in his already burning biceps, he pulled himself up onto the dark-gray deck, just before Big Head and Thick Neck crawled under the canoe right beneath him.

Matani rolled onto his back and remained absolutely still.

"This is the last canoe," Big Head said nervously. "Should we search it?"

"Only if you've got a death wish," Thick Neck snorted. "Let Uanini do it if he wants."

Not fully processing their exchange, Matani rolled over onto his stomach and spotted a small thatch shelter lashed to the deck between the canoe's twin masts. It looked large enough to fit five or six men, open at both ends, with a ribbed framework of curved bamboo and sennit that was tightly plaited with dried leaves.

Hide in that canoe house. You'll be safe there.

With no time to question his thought, Matani quickly pulled himself along the heavily worn wooden deck, his nostrils filling with the pungent scent of sun-heated ash used to stain it, and climbed over a low hanging cord mesh into the canoe house. Typically used for sleeping and shelter from the elements on long voyages, the interior of the thatched shelter was packed with gourd containers, baskets, calabashes, and piles of coconuts. Though he rarely appreciated his slight frame, he knew he wouldn't have been able to squeeze his way into the tiny space behind all the cargo without it.

Okay, what now?

Don't move or make a sound.

Hearing footsteps circling the canoe, Matani went rigid when he saw the heads of Uanini and the others appear through the half-moon-shaped opening of the shelter that faced the sea. For the first time, he noticed the front endpieces of the canoe had been carved to look like enormous shark heads, decorated with lava rocks for eyes and real shark teeth.

That was when it finally hit him.

Of all the canoes he could have picked, Matani felt immediately betrayed by his thoughts for telling him to hide on the most infamous war canoe in all the islands.

"*Mano'nahu*," he whispered in horror, which meant *shark bite*.

"It's my brother's canoe," Uanini's voice seethed indignantly. "Why would I be afraid to search it?"

Hunumaniani's chant abruptly stopped, blanketing the entire beach in silence. Uanini and the others dropped to the ground and skittered under the canoe.

Matani carefully climbed over several loose coconuts to look through the cord mesh at the other end of the canoe house, facing the beach. It appeared that the sudden silence was just part of the ceremony. Unfortunately, it was also in that moment that the wind shifted, bringing a delicious whiff of freshly cooked pork to Matani's nose from distant earth ovens, prompting a growl in the empty pit of his stomach.

"You hear that?" a voice whispered below.

Feeling his tightening stomach about to grumble once more, Matani noticed all the different containers surrounding him. Quietly lifting the lid from a gourd directly beside him, he found some handmade cordage, fishing lures made of animal bones, and wooden plates. The next few containers held red and yellow bird feathers. A few smaller ones were packed with sea salt and ginger. Valuable items, to be sure, but little help in quelling his severe hunger pangs. Searching through the surrounding stacks of gourds and calabashes, he found several filled with fresh water. After drinking his fill from one, he peeked under the lid of the next gourd, both surprised and pleased to see it was stuffed to the brim with perfectly ripe, golden bananas.

You better not!

My stomach is going to give me away. I have to!

Matani grabbed the biggest banana he could find and held it above his head. "For your hunger, for mine," he quickly recited. Peeling its unblemished skin and devouring the tasty fruit inside, he was about to replace the cover when his thoughts intervened.

I don't think my stomach's quite ready to be quiet yet. Maybe I should eat another.

Sure, why not? Consider it your last meal.

Matani pulled out another fine-looking banana, noticing three more under it that looked too scrumptious to ignore. He grabbed those as well. But beneath those three were a few more on the verge of becoming overripe, so he thought he'd spare the intended recipient any offense by graciously adding them to his growing stockpile of food.

Outside, Hunumaniani's chant resumed. "O Ta'aroa, god of the sea, a payment, a gift, an offering, a sacrifice to you."

Clutching bananas in each hand, Matani moved to the back of the canoe house and placed an eye to a small hole in the thatch just in time to see the supreme high priest holding up a basket of food.

"To gods above and gods below, of wind, of sky, and waves, guide and keep safe this fleet, until the island of destiny is reached!"

Hunumaniani handed the basket over to two underpriests, who carried it to the shore and set it afloat as the first offering of the coming feast. "The sacredness has been profound," Hunumaniani exultantly shouted to the heavens. "The prayer is freed!"

"FREED OF TABU THAT I MAY STAND, THAT I MAY WALK!" came the thunderous reply from the mouth of every single warrior on the beach. "FREED BY THE DECREE OF GODS!"

"Now, the prayer is free! Now, the prayer has flown!" Hunumaniani exclaimed, then turned to face his ruling chief. "And how was the ceremony you and I have performed?"

As a direct descendant of the gods, serving as the intermediary between the immortal and the devout, Vahanui sat a moment in silent consideration. "I heard no barking dogs or crying babies. Not one omen of dissatisfaction." He shifted his serious gaze from the priest to his warriors before a smile stretched across his face. "The gods are favorably impressed. The ceremony was perfect!"

"THE CEREMONY IS SUCCESSFUL!" the warriors answered, rattling every last container surrounding Matani in the canoe house.

The sound of conch shells signaled the official end of the ceremony, releasing the tabu of movement placed upon the congregation of warriors. They leaped to their feet, unleashing a cacophony of rowdy cheers, chatter, and laughter. The sea of muscular, suntanned bodies flowed up the beach and converged around the earth ovens, where priests served them coconut water and leaf platters laden with succulent pork and sweet bananas.

Matani turned back from the peephole, staring apprehensively at the heavy breakers framed within the front opening of the canoe house. It wouldn't be long before all those warriors would finish eating and come down to board their vessels. The time had come to initiate his last—and potentially fatal—resort.

Well, if I'm going to risk it, now's the time.

As Matani navigated carefully past the teetering stacks of calabashes to escape, the entire canoe lurched to one side. Just inside the dim shelter, he saw a figure clambering onto the deck, their sunlit form matrixed by natural perforations in the tubular shell of layered grass. He scurried back into his hiding place just as a pair of stocky legs appeared in the opening of the canoe house, a familiar stone club hitched at the figure's waist.

"Be ready if he makes a run for it!" Uanini shouted above the din of the celebrations, then bent down to peer inside. "You in here, Stone Boy?"

Matani shrank behind a stack of gourds, the discomfort of hunger churning in his stomach once more.

Oh gods, please don't growl!

Uanini pushed the mesh gate down and started climbing in.

"What are you doing up there?" shouted a gruff voice.

Matani couldn't see the voice's owner, but whoever it was sure startled Uanini.

"Oh, I'm, uh . . . I'm hunting a tabu breaker!"

"You lost another one?" Another voice cackled with a sound like a pig being strangled.

"I haven't lost anything," Uanini mumbled. "Can I just look inside—"

"Get off!" the first voice ordered. "We're leaving soon!"

Uanini banged his fist against the canoe house, stealing one last dissatisfied look inside before jumping down with a sandy thump. Matani poked a peephole in the thatch just in time to see him wither before the owners of the two voices, both dressed in shoulder-length capes and helmets made of sharkskin. They wore matching hair necklaces with shark-tooth pendants the size of a man's hand.

"Shark Warriors," Matani whispered with a mixture of fear and awe.

In general, Toa warriors served to protect the lands, natural resources, and status of most ruling chiefs. But then there were the Shark Warriors, a special operations force comprised of the five most-feared men in all Havai'i, whose reputation preceded them on every island. Known as Ruling Chief Vahanui's elite team of commandos, each was skilled in the ancient martial art of Raputu'iarua (also known as *rua*)—a mysterious and powerful technique of self-defense known only to a select and worthy few. An important component of the Tauaian defense in times of conflict, this small unit of men had conducted many perilous missions that involved anything from capturing or eliminating high-level targets, to gathering intelligence behind enemy lines.

Rumor had it that the Shark Warriors trained under the cover of night, in far-off hidden temples, to prevent enemies from learning their secrets of joint locks, strikes, throws, pressure point manipulations, weapon techniques, and battlefield strategies. Countless tales of thrilling exploits—like how these highly skilled combatants could break every single bone in a man's body with a single punch—had given them celebrity status throughout the islands. Everyone knew each warrior by name, including Matani, who quickly identified the two standing before Uanini. The first was *Pui the Crazy*, with his trademark cackle, frizzled hair, and wide, bulging eyes full of mischief. The other—a mountain of a man with short, coarse brown hair and a matching beard—was *Imo the Giant*. He was as tall as he was wide, made entirely of muscle.

"Hey, give that back!" Uanini shouted, as Imo snatched his stone club and kept it out of reach, before finally throwing it to a handsome warrior garbed in the same shark uniform.

"Aw, what a cute baby's toy!"

The warrior's wavy black hair falling around his perfectly angular features, imperious nose, chiseled jaw, and excellent arrangement of pearly white teeth told Matani he had to be *Tari'i the Handsome*, swooned over by women across the archipelago. He was tall, with a dark, reddish-brown complexion that suggested he spent more time in the sun than his counterparts.

If nothing else, Uanini was persistent. Already winded, he refused to give up on getting his club back and stumbled for Tari'i even as it flew over his head and into the hands of a fourth Shark Warrior, Timoa the Monster, named after his half-melted face that had been disfigured—as the story went—during vicious combat in a burning cave several years earlier. A scar ran from his hairline through his right eye—which was disfigured into a squint—to the corner of his mouth. One cheek was smooth and pretty, while the other was bunched up like a dried jellyfish. He had an intimidating presence, with the typical large shoulders and forearms of a frequent paddler.

"Very funny," Uanini said. "Can I have it back now?"

Timoa just stared dispassionately at him while spinning the club around both shoulders with impressive fluidity. There was something about this particular warrior's cold stare that sent a chill up Matani's spine. Not a drop of joy or playfulness there, they reflected back to the world a twisted, painful darkness.

By now, a crowd had gathered. Every toss and catch of Uanini's stone club by the Shark Warriors was rewarded with boisterous cheers, while every missed interception by Uanini was met with obnoxious jeers. Seeing the shame and embarrassment on Uanini's face almost made Matani feel sorry for the old lobster. Almost.

Under their stares, Uanini turned and saw the apprentice warriors watching from the crowd, each trying their best to keep a straight face. "What are you fools looking at?" he shouted bitterly. "Find the farmer or I'll sacrifice one of you in his place!"

The trainees nodded and disappeared into the crowd, leaving Uanini to wallow once more in embarrassment.

"A farmer got the best of you now?" Timoa smirked, dangling the stone club in front of Uanini. "Wasn't that last lawbreaker you couldn't catch a fisherman?"

"This one isn't getting away," Uanini wheezed, swiping lamely at the air as his stone club flew over his head and then back again. "He knocked over the border idol."

I did not!

"Ready for launch!" bellowed a heavy, commanding voice. All eyes turned to a sharkskin helmet bouncing through the crowd, setting off a chain reaction of excited greetings from every chief and warrior it passed.

When the sea of bodies parted, Matani's jaw dropped at the arrival of *Hano the Bone Breaker*, esteemed leader of the Shark Warriors. Not only did he radiate an aura of prestige and respect from being the first son of Ruling Chief Vahanui, Hano was also his father's trusted prime minister and chief advisor on military strategies.

Easily the tallest of them all, Hano was a wild and impressive man with dark, compelling brown eyes brimming with strength and vigor, and a strong jaw of good proportions. "The sea is calm now," he warned, "but like any powerful woman, she'll eat us alive if we forget our place!"

Every warrior roared with laughter.

Hano's own stolid face even cracked a grin, but it was short-lived. "Pui, tighten that cordage!" he ordered. "Get her ready for launch!"

"No troubles!" Pui answered, scrambling up onto the deck.

About to point out his tormenters to Hano, Uanini's club thumped against his back and landed at his feet. Hearing the sound, Hano turned with a start.

"Little brother, what are you doing here?"

Uanini just shook his head. "Why does everyone keep asking me that?"

Hano gave a hearty laugh. "Maybe you belong somewhere else!"

"As the son of Ruling Chief Vahanui, I should be welcomed anywhere my brother is," Uanini replied, reeking of self-pity.

"Oh, if you've been to one of Po'omanu's celebrations, you've been to them all."

"Well, I've never *been* to one before," Uanini replied glumly.

"Inferiors, prostrate yourselves!" shouted four retainers carrying special staffs that warned of an advancing tabu. "The great ruling chief comes this way!"

An even cadence of drums and a sudden crescendo of voices drew Matani over to a poke a new peephole at the back of the canoe house.

Six court attendants moved through the crowd, holding long poles topped with the royal insignia of brightly colored feathers. Right behind them was Vahanui, inside a perimeter of guards, followed by a troupe of eight drummers. Lower-ranking chiefs stopped whatever they were doing and promptly sat on the sand as a sign of respect, while high chiefs remained standing but kept a customary distance as the esteemed ruler passed.

"'Ano'ai," Hano said with a welcoming smile, giving the common verbal greeting among people, which meant *not one greater than another*.

Both men touched noses, inhaling each other's mana. Of course, notoriously protective over his pristine mana, the ruling chief would never engage in this age-old nonverbal greeting with just anyone, which involved touching noses and inhaling each other's mana as a way of welcoming a person into their space and sharing the breath of life.

"'Ano'ai, my son," Ruling Chief Vahanui replied.

"Congratulations." Hano smiled proudly. "The ceremony was perfect."

Vahanui nodded graciously. "Though it will surely pale in comparison to the grand departure of you and your fleet."

Pondering the similarities between Hano and his father, Matani noticed Uanini slinking up behind them clearly intent on eavesdropping. Vahanui unexpectedly turned, nearly colliding with him.

"What are you doing here?" Vahanui blurted.

Uanini rolled his eyes, ignoring the question that seemed to plague him. "Is there something going on, Father? Are we attacking Oʻahu?"

Vahanui placed a firm hand on Uaniniʻs shoulder. "No, we are not attacking Oʻahu," he said definitively.

Uanini glanced between Hano and his father, not fully convinced. "Well, if it's just a celebration, why aren't you going with them?"

"The same reason you aren't," Vahanui answered in a slow, deliberate tone that one might use with a child. "There is much work to be done before Father Roʻo's arrival."

"Can't someone else drag that old hunk of wood around the island this year?" Uanini shouted, immediately regretting his complaint.

"Of course," Vahanui answered sharply, "but then who will escort the Short God?"

Uanini clenched his jaw.

Father Roʻo was the name given to the material form that represented the esteemed god of winter: a straight wooden post with the image of a bird at the top, and a slightly longer crosspiece that was decorated with feather wreaths, taupō bird skins, and long streamers of white tapa cloth. Also called *Long God*, this grand idol would tour the island on a twenty-three-day journey in a clockwise procession to each village along the coast. At the same time, a smaller, less cumbersome version called *Short God* would tour in the opposite direction throughout the more remote homesteads in the upland canyons and mountains. This was a difficult and far less prestigious task that few chiefs and priests enjoyed doing.

Uanini didn't want to push his luck. "I've already picked someone for the honorable task," he mumbled, then stomped off, trying not to look like he was stomping off.

Hano and his father shared a subtle smile before the ruling chief's expression changed to one of concern.

"He certainly has his mother's intensity," Vahanui said.

Hano shook his head. "If only he had his father's good sense."

Vahanui found Uanini looking lonely among the crowd, and his eyes filled with compassion. "Not all flowers bloom at the same time, Hano. Give him a chance."

"Of course," Hano replied, nodding respectfully.

Vahanui faced Hano again, his expression now more serious. "I do hope you're able to get to the bottom of these war rumors. If Po'omanu has been planning an attack on Taua'i, you know as well as I we're in no position to defend ourselves."

Recent months had brought gossip from other islands that O'ahu was not faring so well. There had also been rumors that Ruling Chief Po'omanu had learned of the discord on Taua'i and was considering an attack to plunder the island's resources. Knowing this, Ruling Chief Vahanui and his advisers had decided to have the Shark Warriors attend the celebration on O'ahu under the guise of bringing Po'omanu a veritable bounty of provisions.

"We'll know the answer soon enough," Hano said matter-of-factly. "I'm certain that gifting such a large portion of this island's offerings will get me an audience with him—at the very least."

"And if he is not amenable to a peaceful solution?" Vahanui asked pointedly.

"You still have five other districts," Hano reminded him. "And they will not fail you."

"I pray you're right," replied Vahanui. "But the two Tona districts make up nearly half my army, and my brothers and I haven't spoken for more than seven years. I'm grateful the gods have kept outside conflict from our shores all this time, but if that should change, my brothers may not contribute their forces so willingly."

High Priest Hunumaniani, who had been idling nearby, came forward with steepled fingers. He placed a supportive hand on the ruling chief's shoulder. "As we approach a celebration of new beginnings, perhaps the time has come for the three of you to make amends?"

Vahanui turned to Hunumaniani with a heavy sigh. "If only actions were as easy to accomplish as uttering the words that describe them."

"Miracles have been known to unravel the impossible," Hunumaniani said with a mysterious air.

"He's right," Hano agreed, his eyes shining with confident optimism. "Besides, we have four months before any potential war is a concern. Should it come to that, I can't believe my uncles would ignore their brother's call to defend this island."

"I'm not so sure," Vahanui sighed.

Despite Vahanui's fears, there was some solace in the fact that strict religious customs dictated war was absolutely forbidden by Ro'o during the four months of Matari'i-hiti season. As the reigning god of peace, this meant no surprise attacks or underhandedness of any kind were allowed during his visit on earth. But should conflict be unavoidable after Ro'o's departure, any battle or war—and their assigned day and location—would be agreed upon between opposing parties well in advance.

Vahanui inhaled deeply as he pulled himself from his thoughts, then snapped his fingers, materializing a servant holding a neatly folded cloak of red feathers. "I want you to bring this gift for Po'omanu."

Hano admired the finely crafted featherwork and piping of human teeth sewn into the bottom of the cape. "If your generous offering of food and supplies doesn't get me in front of him, this most certainly will."

"Still, I can't help but be wary of the timing behind Po'omanu's celebration," said Vahanui. "Why would he invite chiefs from every island when he has nothing to celebrate?"

"Po'omanu's gatherings are legendary," said Hano lightly. "I'm sure he knows that all his guests will bring him portions of their riches as a show of respect and gratitude. Just as we're doing."

"Yes. Perhaps if he receives enough contributions, any thought of war could be swayed," Vahanui said with a degree of hope. "Do you think I should send more?"

Hano laughed. "I think three hundred canoes packed with the finest goods this island can produce is plenty."

"Yes, perhaps I'm being a bit excessive," Vahanui said with an embarrassed grin.

"The time has arrived," interrupted Supreme High Priest Hunumaniani, motioning for Vahanui's attendants to come forward. "Escort his greatness into position for the launching ceremony."

The attendants immediately prepared a new path to the center of the beach. Before leaving, Vahanui grabbed Hano and hugged him tightly.

"May good fortune prevail on your ocean voyage, my son."

Sensing the weight of his concerns, Hano whispered affectionately into his father's ear, "Remember what you always say when something causes me worry?"

Vahanui stood back, his face flooded with nostalgia. "No cliff is so tall it cannot be climbed."

"Good words," Hano said with a smile, then winked. "Now please try not to make any bad decisions while I'm gone."

"I will miss your wise counsel until your return," Vahanui said, forcing a smile that failed to reach his eyes as he turned and walked to the center of the beach.

Before Hano could leave, Hunumaniani gently held his arm. "A moment?" It was a polite request, but he was already leading Hano to a more private area behind *Manoʻnahu*.

Matani maneuvered past a stack of gourds to the opposite wall of the canoe house, poking a new hole through the thatch. Just below him, Hano and Hunumaniani stood talking in the vessel's long shadow.

"These past months, I have had recurring visions of an evil lurking on Oʻahu that threatens to spread darkness across Havaiʻi like a storm."

"What form does this evil take?" Hano asked, both concerned and intrigued.

"Unfortunately, my visions are impeded by a dark and powerful force such as I have never encountered before," said the priest. "But I have seen crops withering, animals dying, people gone mad with hate and hunger. And fragments of ponds and rivers sinking into the earth under rains of blood."

Hano absorbed the priest's mysterious warning, then nodded confidently. "If there's evil on Oʻahu, my men and I will find it."

"Oh, it will find you," Hunumaniani said chillingly. "I have seen in the clouds that you each have an important role in combating this evil, but you're going to need help."

"Help? Us?" Hano blinked. "What kind of help?"

"The supernatural kind," the priest replied. He leaned in closer, speaking too softly for Matani to hear. But whatever the high priest said, it tinged Hano's face with a mixture of consternation and doubt.

With a solemn expression, Hunumaniani rubbed noses with the warrior, sharing the breath of life. "Your journey will be a difficult one," he said, his voice carrying a weight of foreboding, then placed a gentle hand on Hano's chest. "Keep your heart intact and trust in the path set before you."

As if in response to the priest's cryptic words, frothing waves surged up the shore like the tides of fate, splashing against the bow of every canoe. Distracted by the strange happening for barely a moment, when Matani looked back, Hano was standing alone.

Hunumaniani had vanished, leaving no trace behind.

Where did he go?

Hano chuckled to himself in a way that seemed to convey that this was a common occurrence with the priest, then turned to look up at his magnificent vessel. In a fleeting moment, Matani caught the wide-eyed excitement of a child steal across the warrior's life-hardened gaze.

"Warriors!" Hano called excitedly, leaping up onto the deck in a single bound. "The sea is eager to carry our fleet to O'ahu. Let's not keep her waiting!"

Matani nearly jumped out of his skin when the feather cloak gift for Ruling Chief Po'omanu flew into the canoe house, landing before him in such a way that its ornamentation of human teeth formed a twisted grin.

Better get off the canoe or you're as good as dead!

A conch shell cut through the murmuring crowd of seabound warriors, followed by three of the most terrifying words Matani had heard all day.

"Prepare to launch!"

◆ CHAPTER 4 ◆

More seashell horns trumpeted long, throaty tones across the beach as Matani bounced nervously from one peephole to the other inside the thatch confines of the canoe house, watching in absolute horror as thousands of warriors filtered through the long row of canoes waiting to embark on their ocean journey.

I'm surrounded!

Yes, you are.

Maybe that riptide doesn't sound so bad now. Should I make a run for it?

If you think you can get past all these highly trained warriors, sure.

Two assistant priests approached Pui and handed him a ceremonial basket of food tied up with a cord, then scurried off.

"Let's push this island out from under us!" Hano shouted. Then, in an impressive display of strength, he began shoving the massive vessel across the sand all by himself.

"Show-off!" Pui quipped, throwing the basket up onto the deck before he and the other Shark Warriors each grabbed pieces of *Mano'nahu's* twin hulls to help push her into the water.

"Haul on!" Hano strained, kicking off a time-honored chant that all the other warriors joined in on.

"Haul, haul!
Push on, push on!
Cast off, cast off!
Keep the sails wrapped!
Keep the rigging tight!"

The deep bellow made Matani's spine straighten.

What should I do?

Give up!

The deck vibrated beneath him as its twin hulls scraped the sand, followed by a silent sensation of weightlessness. Matani looked through the back of the canoe house and saw Supreme High Priest Hunumaniani standing at the shoreline beside Ruling Chief Vahanui and his entourage, palms aimed at the sky.

"Uplifter of the heavens, uplifter of the earth!
Uplifter of the mountains, uplifter of the ocean!
Who delegates the night?
Delegates the day?
The parental gods above!"

Hunumaniani lowered both hands and turned to Vahanui. "Ruling Chief of Taua'i, how is the launch? Is it good?"

"Yes," Vahanui answered. "The launch is very good!"

Having received approval of the highest order, every warrior—now turned navigator, steersman, and oarsman—erupted with whoops, hollers, and rowdy thumping of oars.

All at once, the Shark Warriors climbed aboard *Mano'nahu*, bouncing the canoe house so violently, Matani had to contort every available part of his body to keep the stacks of gourds and calabashes from toppling over and drawing attention.

"Look ahead!" Hano cautioned, and not a single pair of eyes among the thousands dared transgress, knowing full well that even glancing towards shore during a launch would curse the voyage.

"Oars ready!" he continued.

Pui jumped down into the forward left hull, in front of Timoa, both setting their paddles at the ready. Tari'i had already posted himself in the front right hull, with Imo squeezing into the seat at the opposite end behind him. Finally, Hano claimed his territory at the rear deck, helming the enormous steering oar—which was nearly half as long as the entire canoe.

With barely a word, all five warriors worked their paddles to guide the war canoe from the bay. It was astounding to see how each of the other

canoes—of smaller or equal size—had anywhere from six to twelve paddlers, while the Shark Warriors did the same job with only five.

Imo cleared his throat extra loud before leading the oaring chant,
striking the hull on the paddle's return stroke with each verse.

"That large (thump) canoe!
That long (thump) canoe!
That broad (thump) canoe!"

"Pui, feed Ta'aroa his offering!" Hano prompted, using the steering sweep
to aim *Mano'nahu* toward the ocean, as his fellow warriors helped maneuver
her past the incoming waves.

"No troubles!" answered Pui, scrambling from hull to deck.

He picked up the huge basket of food the priests had given him, quietly recited a few ceremonial words, then heaved the offering overboard.
It landed with a deep, thunking splash, bobbing on the surface for a moment
before being consumed by the sea.

Content with the successful execution of this most important ritual—which ensured a safe and successful journey across Ta'aroa's watery
realms—Hano cupped both hands around his mouth, reciting the closing
words of the launching ceremony.

"The final offering is given! The tabu is lifted!"

It was now safe for all crew to look back at the beach without fear,
which many did, already pining for loved ones left behind. Barely a short
distance across the water, an offshore breeze sprang up in the bay and
pulled several folds loose from the bundled sail, making it whip and pop
impatiently. Matani startled when Tari'i jumped onto the deck just outside
the canoe house.

"I think she's hungry for this wind!" Tari'i shouted, unfurling *Mano'nahu's* front sail with a forceful, windy crack.

Pui landed with a hard thud behind the canoe house and loosened the
hoisting lines to open the rear sail. "Then let her feast!"

Matani poked his finger through the thatch ceiling to get a better look.
Both sails were constructed of overlapping strips of fine matting connected
to horizontal booms and vertical spars topped with red feather streamers
swimming in the open wind.

In nearly perfect synchronization, Tariʻi and Pui grabbed lines of cordage that ran up and over U-shaped horns at the top of each mast, lifting both spars and booms to open the sails. Harnessing the wind, both booms bent to a curve and created deep wind-pockets in the sails that gave the distinct appearance of two giant crab claws. The entire deck lurched heavily and bucked before the canoe settled into a smooth, loping glide across the waves. Matani watched Hano wave once more to his father at the shoreline before turning his focus back to leading the Tauaian fleet around the southern headland of the bay.

Through the rear of the canoe house, Matani spotted Hauora, the temple of refuge, and it gave him pause. Considering a last-ditch effort to bolt across the deck and jump into the ocean, he stopped when he saw a row of four wooden images that stood near the river mouth, watching over all of Hitinaatalā. Not a moment later, he spotted the small but recognizable figures of Uanini and his apprentice minions approaching the temple grounds. They ran past the wooden guardians just before the entire temple disappeared from view behind a barren outcropping of the adjacent coastline.

Even if I'd made it, they would've killed me anyway. Sacrilege or not.

Entering deeper waters, *Manoʻnahu* broke free from the lee of the island, twin sails catching the mighty force of the whipping winds and surging the canoe forward. Matani watched how both shark-head pieces worked to keep the twin bows from driving straight into the back of increasingly larger swells, splitting the face of any following waves that might otherwise swamp the canoe from behind.

Once far from shore, the Shark Warriors removed their sharkskin capes, helmets, and necklaces and tossed them into the canoe house. Intrigued by the matching tribal tattoos on the left sides of their bodies, abstract depictions of past adventures they had shared, Matani nervously reached out to touch the iconic wardrobe of the legendary Shark Warriors; rough and gritty under his fingertips.

If they find you in here, they'll kill you.

As if I needed the reminder.

Hey, it's what I'm here for.

For many, many years now, each day had been virtually the same for Matani: wake up, work, be miserable and unfulfilled, make someone frustrated or angry, fake an apology, work some more, go to sleep, then do it all over again. But now, Matani had no idea what was going to happen next. Or how he might feel about it. And while he couldn't deny that he had every right to be anxious about being discovered, the uncertainty was actually exciting.

I haven't felt anything like this for a long time.

As many similar thoughts coursed through his head, Matani was struck by how his view of the entire district of Vairuanuiho'āno fit rather unremarkably in the tiny half-moon opening of the canoe house.

There it was, the tiny stage for every single experience he'd ever had and every person he'd ever encountered. And, rather surprisingly, there was only one person he had any sense of longing for.

Heiana.

Thinking of her somehow distanced Matani from any immediate fears, allowing him to settle back on a stack of mats, watching the lush green island of Taua'i grow smaller and smaller on the wide blue horizon. And as though distance was equivalent to time, the farther away he traveled from the only home he'd ever known, the deeper he sank into old memories. Starting with the most recent and dramatic events of the day, he relived countless experiences in reverse chronology, taking him further and further back to his earliest years as a child.

Eventually, the images became more and more nebulous until Matani was left with the sum total of a brief and unremarkable life stained with regret.

Out of all those years, why didn't I use one stupid moment to tell Heiana how I feel about her?

Because, as I've told you many, many times, she would have rejected you.

I'm not so sure.

Entranced by the gentle motions of the canoe, Matani gradually nodded off.

Each time he opened his sleepy eyes, Taua'i looked a little bit smaller. At first an island . . .

. . . a green mountain . . .

. . . a faded blue hill on the horizon . . .

. . . then gone.

And just like that, everything Matani had ever known vanished, leaving him in the middle of nowhere with five fearsome warriors who would almost certainly kill him should they find him hiding on their canoe.

When they find you.

Ugh. Couldn't you have stayed behind on Taua'i?

That's not how it works.

Deciding it better to remain conscious and aware, Matani focused on the Shark Warriors as they settled into their respective routines, quickly developing his own initial impressions of each warrior.

Timoa the Monster clearly had the most abrasive personality, constantly ordering the others around. Curiously, everyone ignored him, making Matani wonder if the cantankerous warrior had done something in the past to lose their respect, despite his constant demand for it. And while the others regularly conversed with one another, Timoa spent most of the time by himself in his left rear portion of the hull, chewing loudly on dried fish as he carved away at a small log with a stone adze. Based on a few sarcastic comments from the others, Matani gathered that this was a new hobby.

Then there was Tari'i the Handsome, who, aside from constantly preening his hair and scrubbing his super-white teeth with his finger, was the most devout of the group. He spent much of his time reciting prayers on a narrow plank that ran from the front deck to a crossboom that connected the twin prows.

Imo the Giant seemed to be the most liked by all the Shark Warriors. He spoke very little but, when he did, it was usually to diffuse an argument with humor or to sing in a surprisingly beautiful voice that didn't quite fit his imposing exterior. But while his eyes radiated kindness and affection, there was an underlying intensity that the others seemed wary of triggering. Matani also gathered that he was the official cook aboard *Mano'nahu*, spending much of his time at the cooking box behind the canoe house, where he was even now baking sliced bananas and yams.

Pui the Crazy was the team's comic relief, whether or not he intended to be. He appeared to also be a very hard worker, often mumbling or chuckling to himself with every chore. Positive to the point of annoyance, his response to any complaint or concern was his trademark, "No troubles!" And out of them all, he was the one who tended to Hano's needs the most, constantly bringing him food and water.

And speaking of Hano the Bone Breaker, who had not left the canoe's massive steering handle even once, Matani's first impressions were that he was intense and quiet, but also the clear leader of the elite squad, which he managed with as much precision and control as he did *Mano'nahu* herself. Beyond that, Matani couldn't quite get a good read on him, but his eyes—mild and generous—suggested he was a man of good character. Curiously, he also wore a subtle but constant smile, as if he knew things no one else did.

"Pui, clear the way!" Hano shouted across the deck.

"No troubles!" answered Pui, tightening the lines that connected the front of each hull to the top of both masts. "How's that?"

"Better," Hano said, then tilted his head with closed eyes, feeling the angle of the breeze on his face. "Yes, the wind is coming nicely over the right hull now. We should have a smooth ride until we hit deeper waters."

And just as he predicted, the fleet sailed without incident for a long while, passing through a large gathering of black-footed albatross harvesting the deeper pelagic waters for fish eggs, squid, and floating debris. Circling with intense curiosity, it wasn't long before several of the braver birds landed on the canoes, scavenging for food. One wily little bird made its way into *Mano'nahu*'s canoe house, looking straight into Matani's eyes. Matani tossed it a piece of banana, which it grabbed in its long, dark beak before turning and flying off. Another bird with a lame leg had the nerve to swoop down beside Timoa, who was intently focused on carving, and brazenly snatched a piece of dried fish right out of the warrior's mouth.

Timoa swung his oar at the confounded bird until it flew beyond reach.

"Careful," Tari'i warned, rushing to gather feathers fallen from their wings. "Any one of these birds could be Ro'o!"

"These are pests, not gods!" Timoa shouted, swatting his oar at the winged annoyances and nearly hitting Pui and Tari'i in the process.

Stopping to catch his breath, Timoa noticed Imo laughing at something beside him. He turned to find the lame bird perched on the canoe house next to his head, the dried fish it had stolen still in its beak. Timoa brought his oar down on the cylindrical roof of the shelter, punching a small hole right above Matani, sending him scrambling for a new corner to hide in. Ultimately, Timoa's attempts were futile, as the precocious bird continued to outmaneuver him before flying off unharmed, leaving the warrior muttering many colorful unpleasantries.

Through the rear of the canoe house, Matani saw gourds, coconuts, and several pieces of taro floating in *Mano'nahu*'s wake, failed projectiles that frustrated passengers on other canoes in the fleet had thrown at the bothersome birds.

A loud gurgle from his own stomach startled him.

Oh, come on! After all that food you just ate?

But eating another banana only seemed to exacerbate the sensation, making his stomach lurch and churn as if possessed by some malicious force. He swallowed, but the sour taste in his mouth only taunted his stomach to expel its contents. Then it finally dawned on Matani that he was stricken with the ancient malady known as *hautae*, a curse brought on by the never-ending motion of the sea.

In other words: he was seasick.

Up and down, side to side, round and round went Matani's entire world. His hands shook uncontrollably as the canoe house closed in on him, smaller and smaller, sucking every last breath of air from his lungs. Shutting his eyes did little to suppress the vicious ailment, serving only to amplify every sound on the canoe, from every little stretch and contraction of the rigging to the hollow sounds of water splashing against the hulls. Up jumped the horizon and down dropped the canoe as Matani's fragile world sat precariously at the back of his throat. His skin turned cold, then hot, then clammy, then all three at once as his quivering insides further destabilized.

I have to get out of here!

If you go out there, you're as good as dead!

I don't care anymore. I'll die if I stay in here!

Desperately massaging his queasy stomach, Matani glanced around at all the containers surrounding him; each filled with an array of treasured items fit for a god.

"And I'm taking some of these things with me," he whispered, grabbing a beautifully decorated bowl of carved koa wood to collect as many valuables as he could. Handfuls of red and yellow feathers, a mother of pearl shell necklace with matching bracelets, a few handfuls of sea salt, several strips of dried 'o'opu nani fish, and three large breadfruit were quickly added to his collection. Greedily clutching his treasure trove of all things forbidden to commoners, Matani quickly realized that having them in his possession changed nothing—certainly not his unhappy state of mind, nor his debilitating motion sickness.

After burping up liquid convulsions, Matani's saliva turned sour, sending him past the point of no return.

"Oh no," he groaned.

Tossing aside his bowl of valuables, he dove across calabashes, gourds, and anything else that stood between him and the fresh, open air, launching from the forward opening of the canoe house for the big finale—projectile vomiting the entire contents of his stomach onto the deck of the double-hulled canoe that belonged to the five most feared warriors in all Havaiʻi.

"Where'd he come from?" Imo shouted in surprise, shooting a confused glance up at the sky.

Despite his miserably spinning head and stomach, Matani chuckled. As footsteps rushed across the deck, Matani instinctively noted the position of the sun and managed his shadow, careful not to let it fall upon so much as a toe of any of the Shark Warriors.

Timoa grunted with revulsion, taking several steps back from the splash of puke oozing between the slats of the deck. "Disgusting."

"Now you know what we feel like looking at your face," Imo said dryly.

"Shut up!" Timoa barked.

"Must've been hiding since launch," Pui said, sticking his head inside the canoe house.

Hano craned his neck to see what was happening. "Anyone else hiding in there?"

"No," Pui confirmed, then raised a finger. "Wait, didn't Uanini say he was looking for someone?"

"Yeah, some farmer broke a tabu," said Timoa, using the cracked, yellow nail of his big toe to lift Matani's chin. "Is that you?"

"It washhnnt me," Matani slurred, his words thick and sludgy with seasickness.

"Then who *are* you?" asked Pui.

Matani was at a complete loss on how to answer this question, on many levels, but desperate times called for desperate measures. In the few seconds he had to come up with something plausible, an idea popped into his head. It seemed like a good one in the moment.

"Answer," Timoa said with a chilling calmness. "Or I'll empty the rest of what's inside you onto this deck."

"My name is Vatua," Matani finally blurted. "I'm an apprentice at the warrior compound."

"Why do I know that name?" Hano asked. "And what are you doing on my canoe?"

"Well, I-I w-was," Matani sputtered, searching for a good explanation. "I was loading supplies, and then, well, the launching ceremony started, and I got stuck in here, you know? Because I, uh, didn't want to risk upsetting the high priest!"

"So, why didn't you get off when the ceremony was over?" asked Hano.

"It was a very long ceremony," said Matani. "I must've fallen asleep."

"That makes two of us," Imo cracked.

An expression of great concern crossed Timoa's face. "We have to kill him before the gods curse this voyage."

Hano waved a disinterested hand. "All right, all right, Timoa. We're not gonna kill him for falling asleep."

"But the runt ate our food, too!" Timoa reminded them.

His merciless comment echoed the kind of sentiment Uanini might express, triggering a knee-jerk response that Matani immediately regretted. "Help yourself," he said, gesturing weakly to the acidic mush in front of him.

Imo's entire body shook with laughter. "Ooh, I like him!"

Hano reprimanded Matani with a glance. "I'd watch my words if I were you."

Matani immediately shrank and nodded.

"Look at him!" said Timoa. "He's way too scrawny to be a chief!"

"I haven't started my physical training yet," Matani lamely interjected.

"Okay," said Timoa. "If you are who you say you are, recite your genealogy."

Now this was a problem. Every child was taught to memorize their genealogies as oral evidence of their family lineage and personal status. As genealogies were used to measure the passage of time, the degree of mana inherited from one's history was what made a chief a chief and a commoner a commoner, thus preserving the rigid social order.

Sadly, having become disconnected from his own family over the years, Matani had long since forgotten many of the names in his own genealogy—not that remembering them now would have helped him very much.

"I w-would," Matani stammered. "But my father warned me not to expose the bones of our ancestors to strangers."

"Strangers!" Timoa shouted, nearly choking on the word. "Everyone knows who we are! *You're* the only stranger on this canoe!"

Hano squinted at Matani from where he still sat beside the steering oar, trying to bring the stowaway's features into focus. "I visited Uncle Opoa three or four summers ago, and he did have a son named Vatua."

"Which makes him your cousin!" Timoa pointed out incredulously, before dragging Matani by his neck across the deck so Hano could get a better look. "Do you recognize him?"

Hano looked Matani up and down. "I don't know. I do remember him being a little scrawny back then, and his black hair and brown eyes look familiar."

"So do my mother's!" Timoa snapped. "Is this your cousin or not?"

"You have a mother?" Imo asked with perfect innocence.

Timoa shot him the blackest stare imaginable. "Let's see how funny you are with a doomed voyage!" he said, then pointed a damning finger at Ruling Chief Vahanui's prized gift crumpled up under Matani, one corner of its meticulous featherwork spattered with vomit.

All eyes turned to Hano, who was unsettlingly calm.

Pui quickly reached down and snatched up the cloak, sending Matani into a half spin across the deck. "No troubles! With a little fresh water and some coconut oil, I can make this as good as new!"

But it was too little, too late. Visibly angry, Hano nodded to Timoa, who grinned. Before Matani even knew what was happening, he found himself tossed unceremoniously overboard into the untamed sea.

"There!" Timoa laughed. "Now you can sleep as long as you like!"

Hitting the water, Matani's seasickness disappeared almost immediately but was just as quickly replaced by a flood of panic when he saw the distance growing far and fast between himself and *Mano'nahu*.

"Leave him where he is!" Timoa called to the rest of the fleet.

Matani had never been this far out to sea in his entire life, and his imagination was rampant with any number of dreadful creatures that might lurk in the unseen depths below his dangling feet. Against his better judgment, he dunked his head underwater, seeing nothing but a bottomless blue void.

Surfacing and seeing *Mano'nahu* carried farther and farther away by an unending march of waves, Matani lost patience with every single person in his life who had made it their personal mission to determine his fate. A rage erupted inside him so fierce that he had no room for any other emotions, including fear of death. His eyes darkened and lost focus, becoming portals to a dimension even more limitless than the sea around him.

He had one last thought before blacking out.

Take the wind from them.

While Matani had long struggled with believing in anything supernatural, there was one lingering sliver of dispute inside him, fueled by an unusual story that surrounded the night of his birth.

As his mother had explained to him, shortly after she had gone into labor, a terrible hurricane hammered the island, forcing Matani's parents to seek cover in a cave. Through a long night of painful labor and screams that rivaled the roaring winds, Mahina gave birth to her first and only child. Looking into her newborn's tiny brown eyes, she said she saw a bighearted soul that was both wise and intelligent, like a gentle breeze, but also as stubborn and turbulent as a hurricane, and so she decided to name him *Matani*, meaning *Wind*.

As he grew older, Matani complained about not having a brother or sister, and his mother always reminded him that he had many brothers and sisters in nature. Because of this, and a few other odd experiences with winds and breezes, he'd often wondered if he could influence the weather. Or at least impact it in some meaningful way. But whenever he asked, his father would tell him to stop talking nonsense, and his mother would just say, rather mysteriously, that he was capable of a great many things. And despite a few purposeful attempts to control the weather—which usually resulted in a gap in his memory that lasted a couple of minutes to a few hours—he had dropped the silly notion altogether some time ago.

But here and now, hanging in the depthless eternity of boundless horizons, it was happening again.

Had Matani not fallen into a catatonic state, he would have felt the wind completely disappear, flattening the sea around him, leaving every canoe in the fleet spinning helplessly. Even mighty *Mano'nahu* hung in the water, both sails flip-flopping listlessly. He would have also heard Hano tell the other Shark Warriors that having the wind disappear this far out into the wilder seas of the channel was nothing short of impossible. And he would have heard an argument among them that Pui started, over whether or not the stowaway had something to do with it. He would have seen the sails of *Manoʻnahu*—and only those of *Manoʻnahu*—catching wind from the wrong direction, spinning her completely around before pushing the dual-hulled canoe straight back toward him.

"Over there!" Tariʻi shouted, pointing at a large bank of clouds appearing on the northeastern horizon.

By the time Matani came to his senses, a wall of wind was already coming at them filled with ethereal voices that seemed to emanate from everywhere and nowhere all at once. Still in and out of consciousness, he was vaguely aware of being back aboard *Manoʻnahu* and of a blasting gust of wind so fierce it stirred up white-tipped waves, straightening the feather streamers on every canoe in the fleet.

"Looks like we got our wind back!" Hano shouted, eyeing the gargantuan clouds that seemed to move and shift with curious intelligence. "Trim that sail!"

Tariʻi and Pui quickly yanked rigging attached to the front and back sails, harnessing the massive forces of the wind. The left hull dipped underwater, dropping the deck so dramatically even seasoned sea legs lost their balance.

Imo grabbed Matani around the waist before he could topple back overboard. "Oh no you don't!"

Continuing across the channel between Tauaʻi and Oʻahu, the mysterious return of the winds brought heavy swells that even the twin bows of *Manoʻnahu* could not entirely stave off, spraying Matani where he stood. Blinking twice, bringing consciousness back to his eyes, he was surprised to see the intrigued faces of Imo, Pui, and Timoa circled around him.

"H-how did I get back on the canoe?" Matani asked, visibly confused.

"I told you he was in some kind of trance!" said Pui.

"Back to work," was all Hano said.

All four warriors quickly dispersed, leaving Matani alone for an awkward moment before a gourd thumped him in the chest hard enough to make his teeth clatter.

"My right hull is pulling!" Hano shouted, pointing. "Start bailing!"

Recognizing that his life had just been spared for reasons he didn't understand—but wasn't about to question—Matani simply nodded and picked up the gourd, happily accepting his new responsibility. "No troubles!"

Hano and Pui traded expressions of bemusement while Matani jumped down into the hull and began scooping out the seawater that had collected there.

Feeling someone watching him, Matani looked over and saw Timoa glaring suspiciously at him across the deck.

"Something's not right about you," Timoa whispered in a low, terrible voice. "And I'm gonna find out what it is."

✦ CHAPTER 5 ✦

Compared with the endless expanse of the surrounding sea, it wasn't difficult to comprehend that even gods passing overhead might barely notice a fleet of insignificant vessels below. With no more than a few yards between them, *Mano'nahu* confidently guided the entire armada on a seemingly pathless journey across the wide channel between Taua'i and O'ahu, lifted to windward by taut, bulging sails. Heavy swells continuously broke across her sharkhead hulls in sheets of spray, keeping Matani very busy with his new bailing duties.

Other than some heated whispers between Timoa and Hano, which Hano quickly put to an end with a terse grunt and stern wave of his hand, nobody spoke a word about the mysterious incident of the disappearing and reappearing wind. Matani, having no clear recollection of the incident himself, was only mildly aware of the warriors casting puzzled looks at him every now and again.

"Vatua! Water!" Hano demanded.

Matani dropped the bailing gourd instantly, dashed over to retrieve a calabash of fresh water from the canoe house, then raced back across the deck with it. As he stood waiting patiently for Hano to drink his fill, Matani was struck by the navigator's perspective of nothing but a constantly changing tableau of sea and sky, wondering how anyone could possibly know where they were going without any concrete landmarks to guide them. Especially since Hano hadn't left his position once since their departure.

It must have something to do with that steering oar.

Barely aware that his left hand was gravitating toward the long handle of the oar, Matani jumped back at the slap of Hano's hand.

"Need more work?" the warrior barked. "Pui! Get Vatua going on coconuts!"

"No troubles!" Pui answered, waving Matani over to meet him at the canoe house. "First rule on this canoe: no one touches Hano's steering oar but Hano."

"Why?" Matani asked, tossing the emptied calabash into the shelter. "What's so special about it?"

"Hano and *Mano'nahu* are strongly connected," Pui said, his tone almost reverent. "Always talking to each other."

Matani looked at him. "About what?"

"The great world around them," Pui said, sweeping out his hand. "But you and I? We're gonna talk about coconuts!"

Although Matani already knew how to prepare a coconut, he listened patiently as Pui explained how to crack them open, collect the water inside, then scoop out the oily white meat onto shells so they could be passed out for the rest of the crew to snack on.

"And save the husks," Pui said, as he left to perform other duties. "Imo cooks with them."

Matani nodded and went straight to work, husking coconuts long enough for a wide, sparkling trail of late afternoon sunlight to stretch behind them all the way to the horizon.

"Vatua, come clean this mess!" Timoa bellowed from the other side of the canoe.

Expecting to hear another voice reply, Matani momentarily forgot about his new identity. "Coming!"

Timoa gave Matani a hard stare as he jumped into the hull to gather up the wood shavings that had collected at his feet. Staying longer than he should to sneak a glimpse at Timoa's carving, Matani flinched when Timoa turned with an angry grunt to shield his secret whittling project. "Okay, go!"

Matani leaped from the hull, suddenly plagued by a new wave of seasickness. He grabbed hold of some rigging to steady himself, but it did little to help his spinning head.

From his cooking box behind the canoe house, Imo held up a stub of sugarcane. "Vatua, try chewing on this."

"Blessings," Matani said appreciatively, taking it from him.

Imo flashed a friendly grin, laying several coconut husks on the bed of sand inside his cooking box. "Don't take it personally, the way Timoa treats you," he added. "He got a hole in his head that makes him grumpy."

Matani looked up in surprise. "A hole?"

"Long time ago, a spear caught him right here," Pui said, peeking over the canoe house, pointing at his own head just above the left ear. "The doctor fitted him with a piece of coconut shell and covered it with pig skin."

"Yep," Imo nodded, rubbing two sticks together until a small ember appeared. He fed it with coconut husk fibers. "Ever since then, he gets a lotta angry-making headaches."

The entire deck abruptly heaved to one side. Clamping the sugarcane tightly in his teeth, Matani used both hands to balance himself, stubbing his toe for the umpteenth time on a long tree branch lying beside the deckhouse.

"What is this stupid thing?" Matani yowled, straining to lift the object that was about the size and thickness of a man's leg. "Can I throw it overboard?"

"No!" returned a chorus of voices.

Matani immediately dropped it with a thud.

This time, Tari'i popped his head above the canoe house. "Imo doesn't fight with finely crafted weapons like the rest of us. He prefers that clunky old thing."

"He uses a tree branch in battle?" Matani asked, somewhat baffled.

"Not just any tree branch," Imo said, laying tuna loins onto the bed of smoldering coconut husks. "A while back, I was in a forest on the big island of Havai'i being chased by this crazy chief who accused me of sleeping with his wife."

"Chief Nāhi'ena'ena," Pui threw in.

Imo nodded. "He was coming fast, about to run me through with his dagger when this branch fell—pow!—right in front of me. I picked it up, surprised by how heavy but well balanced it was, like it was custom-made for my hand, you know? I barely swung the thing, and it knocked Nāhi'ena'ena right out of his sandals."

Matani burst into laughter. "Really?"

"Yeah," Imo continued with his broad-faced, bearded grin. "Poor guy just sat in the dirt with this stunned look on his face, pointing and shouting,

Leg from Heaven! Leg from Heaven! before running off. Never bothered me again, I can tell you that!"

"You forgot to tell him the most important part," Pui prompted.

Imo's face went blank. "What's that?"

Pui smirked at Matani while pointing his thumb at Imo. "He *did* sleep with that chief's wife!"

"Oh yeah." Imo shrugged, chuckling deviously.

As Pui squeezed past to make an adjustment on the rear sail's rigging, Matani noticed a double-pronged dagger shoved into the waist of his loincloth. "Is that your weapon of choice, Pui?"

"My talking dagger is much more than a weapon," he replied with a hint of mischievousness, then held it up to his ear, listening. "Mm, that's right. We do."

Matani's wide eyes conveyed his curiosity. "It speaks to you?"

"The spirit inside does, yes," Pui said with a sage grin.

Matani nodded mechanically, finding the whole thing a little far-fetched, but unsure whether Pui was just teasing him.

Pui listened to his dagger again, then raised an eyebrow at Matani. "No, I don't think he believes us, either!"

"Oh, be quiet, Pui," Timoa mumbled, irritated. "Your brain is broken."

"So is your penis!" Pui shot back loudly, and everyone around the canoe burst out laughing.

Matani felt Timoa's judgmental gaze on him again and, feeling bold, turned to face him. "What weapon do you use, Timoa?"

"I *am* my weapon," Timoa answered darkly.

"Ah," Matani said, bobbing his head while trying to appear passively impressed. But a nervous gulp gave him away.

"Timoa's hands bite like sharks," Imo said, making a claw with one hand. "I've seen him dig his fingers into a man's thigh and rip the skin clean off."

"Pui! Tari'i!" Hano shouted from behind. "She's turning!"

"No troubles!" Pui hollered, racing over to the back mast as Tari'i made his way to the front. They exchanged a quick nod before simultaneously letting out both sails.

"Much better!" Hano shouted, focused on the sea ahead. "Now, let her loose a little more, then pull her back!"

Matani watched the rigging slide one way through the horns, then back again to tighten up the curve of the sails. "Is turning bad?"

"The entire canoe gets off-balance if either hull turns into the wind," Pui explained. "The trick is to keep both sails slacked a bit without letting *Manoʻnahu* get too close or too far off the wind so she doesn't swallow too much."

Matani glanced up at the twin crab-claw sails with fresh worry. "What happens if she swallows too much?"

Pui held out his hand palm up and flipped it over, cackling. "We capsize!"

"Don't worry," Tariʻi said reassuringly. "The ingenuity of our ancestors, and Hanoʻs skills, will always keep us on the right side of the deck."

"I never realized how complicated sailing was," Matani admitted.

"Why does my left hull feel heavy now?" Hano shouted, this time at Matani.

"No troubles!" Matani replied, tossing Pui an appreciative grin before running off to resume bailing.

It wasn't long before the fleet hit their stride and found themselves on an even southeastern course to Oʻahu. By then, *Manoʻnahu* was so well balanced thanks to her experienced crew, Hano was able to lash his steering oar to the deck and let the vessel sail herself windward for a long while, allowing him to rest. When he wasn't bailing, Matani rearranged cargo under the direction of Pui to weigh down the back of the canoe to offset its balance against the wind. Meanwhile, Imo patrolled the canoe, singing pleasantly as he inspected her masts, sails, and rigging for any signs of fatigue, and Timoa crouched in the left rear hull, heavily immersed in his carving and whittling.

After disappearing into the canoe house, Pui brought out his fishing gear and dropped a trolling line off the back deck, where he sat with his legs dangling over the water. "Oh, great roving fish, swim this way," he chanted to the sea.

"Come to Pui who calls you,
  bring fish in large numbers,
  enough for a god,
  enough for our navigator,
  enough for our crew!"

Meanwhile, Tari'i perched on his narrow plank with a calabash, praying as he sprinkled water onto the waves that rushed between the hulls. Matani walked over to him, curious. "What's that you're doing?"

His eyes still on the sea, a peaceful smile grew on Tari'i's face. "It's important to give offerings to Ro'o in return for good weather."

Again, Matani tried to hide his cynicism. "Do you really believe the gods hear our prayers?"

Tari'i nodded emphatically. "I do."

Matani just looked at him, recalling once more how Heiana had told him that words are like spells. "Will they not answer if a prayer doesn't have the right words?"

"Words aren't as important as one's intention," said Tari'i. "Intentions come from the heart, not from the mouth or mind. A prayer without intention is like sailing a canoe without a destination."

The answer stung Matani with both its insight and ambiguity.

An understanding smile grew on Tari'i's face, as if he could read Matani's thoughts. "There was a time I wondered why my prayers weren't being answered, but I eventually came to realize they were, just not in ways I expected."

"Fish on the line!" Pui yelled, reeling in his catch hand over hand.

"Oooh!" Imo crooned, lumbering across the deck. "Big one, too!"

Tari'i grinned at Matani. "Sounds like two prayers just got answered, yeah?"

Matani smiled back, then rushed to see Pui drag a dorado the size and weight of a young child onto the deck. Flopping wildly, its brightly colored scales flashed green, yellow, and silver in the setting sun. Pui held the fish down while Imo struggled to remove the hook from its gasping mouth, only to get whacked squarely in the face by its dripping wet tail. Wiping slimy fish mucus off his face, the dorado wriggled from Pui's grasp and flopped right past Imo and Matani's comically grabbing hands before finally making its escape off the deck and over the side.

Thoroughly entertained by the entire scene, Pui cackled uncontrollably as the fish disappeared beneath Mano'nahu's wake. He then turned to see Imo's bitter expression and reassured him, "No troubles, Imo. There's more fish out there."

"Well, hurry up and catch'em," Imo said with a frown. "I'm hungry."

It wasn't long before things settled down again, and Matani realized he was the only one actually working. And while it didn't bother him so much— it was much more fun to work a canoe than to labor in the taro fields—he did find himself facing a burgeoning problem. Seeing how the crew ate with their hands and bathed in salt water scooped from the sea, it was apparent just how primitive life could be aboard a voyaging canoe. While he had already learned a few ways of adapting to ocean life—like leaning his body this way or that to adjust for the constant tilt and sway of the deck, or how to anticipate the shifting sails and spars so they wouldn't knock him overboard—for the life of him, Matani could not figure out when or where it was appropriate to pee.

"Water!" Timoa called out with ironic timing, not even bothering to use a name this time.

"Coming!" Matani answered, diving into the canoe house to fetch another calabash of fresh water. The sloshing sounds it made didn't help his dilemma at all. "Okay, I give up," he said, approaching Pui. "How do you go to the bathroom out here?"

"Seriously?" Pui cackled in a poor attempt to speak lightly.

"Very," Matani said, his tone much more serious.

"Just hang off the side and release your problems into the sea!"

Thank the gods!

Matani immediately raced around the deck until he found a blind spot from the rest of the crew. Setting down the calabash, he leaned over the hull and pulled back his loincloth. About to relieve himself, a dark shadow moved through the water right below him, disappearing under the canoe.

Matani leaped back in terror. "Something just went under us!"

"I'll put *you* under us if you don't bring me water!" Timoa demanded, just as a gray blur flew up and over the bow, raining down seawater.

"Off our right!" Tari'i declared. "Dolphins!"

Matani peered nervously over the hull and saw the miraculous sight of several hundred dolphins coming right up beside *Mano'nahu*, swerving back and forth between her twin bows. He marveled at the way their gray backs glistened with sparkles of sunlight as they flew effortlessly through the waves.

"See, Timoa?" Pui said. "Would Ta'aroa have sent us escorts if he didn't approve of our journey?"

Judging by the hard line of his mouth, Timoa clearly wasn't convinced.

His biological needs on hold, Matani was fully enraptured by the spectacle unfolding all around him. From one moment to the next, the watery spaces among the fleet were infiltrated by hundreds upon hundreds of glorious, frolicking creatures of the sea.

Everywhere I look, dolphins!

"Over here!" Tari'i alerted the others.

Nearly slipping several times as he raced to the front deck, Matani jumped onto the plank next to Tari'i, who directed his attention to six dolphins riding in their wake.

"What are they doing?" Matani asked, his face stretched wide with a grin.

"What we're all supposed to be doing," said Tari'i. "Having fun! Enjoying life!"

Matani stretched out on his stomach, chin in his hands, watching refracted images of dolphins plow through the clear blue water below him like spears of light. Every so often, one of the sea mammals would break the surface long enough for him to hear their small, mouthlike blowholes clicking and chirping. "I wonder what it feels like to fly through the water like that."

And then, as if by some silent command, the entire pod of dolphins disappeared.

Matani circled the deck, looking everywhere. "Where'd they go?"

"Something must've spooked them," said Imo.

Matani moved around the canoe, anxiously searching for the beautiful creatures, finding only long bubble trails popping on the surface. Leaning precariously over the right hull, he spotted something in the water right below the canoe.

A rather large and dark something.

"Careful over there!" Hano warned not a moment before a monstrous beast launched itself from the water, its head rising up in front of Matani, high enough to block out the sun, before crashing back down against the left side of the canoe.

Matani dropped flat onto the deck, watching in horror as the gigantic, gray-and-white blur sank under the waves in a shower of seawater.

"Whales!" Pui shouted.

The canoe bounced wildly as Imo raced across the deck, tracking the creature. "He's under us!"

"More whales over there!" Tari'i shouted, pointing out three more massive gray backs arcing through the water, easily three times the size of any canoe in the fleet.

"Are we leaking?" Hano asked, pointing at the port hull.

Imo leaned over and examined the exterior of the hull where the whale had made contact. "A few scrapes, but it looks okay!" Then he bent over and picked up a handful of busted barnacle shells the whale had left behind, holding up two that were dripping with a mixture of salt water and blood. "Looks like he used our canoe to scrape these off his belly!"

Out of nowhere, clouds of seabirds filled the sky, wanting in on whatever food might be stirred up by the whales. Matani counted the shining backs gliding through the water—nineteen, twenty, twenty-one, twenty-two whales just ahead. Having only ever seen a whale once or twice from afar when he was much younger, Matani was utterly dumbfounded at just how enormous they actually were. "How can something so big exist?!"

"The limitless creativity of gods!" Tari'i sang as a trail of five geysers sprayed into the air behind him.

Whoosh! Whoosh! Whoosh! Whoosh! Whoosh!

Why aren't you afraid? They could easily capsize this canoe, you know!

Before the negative thought could contaminate Matani's joyful spirits, one of the whales breached off the right hull, heaving its entire body from the water. Every single person stopped, watching in awe as the amazing creature spun on its tail and fell on its back, sending a tidal wave of white water crashing across *Mano'nahu* and drenching everyone aboard. Matani stood a moment in stunned silence before he burst out laughing, laughing in a way he couldn't remember doing for a very long time.

In mere moments, the entire fleet found itself infiltrated by a mega pod of at least seventy humpback whales. Things quickly turned chaotic as hundreds of canoes went in all different directions, maneuvering to avoid the whales and one another. Forced to make a hard turn, one outrigger lost its wind and stalled right across *Mano'nahu's* bow.

"Paddle on the right side!" Hano alerted, pushing his steering oar to the left. "Drop the sails!"

Mano'nahu veered hard, barely missing the smaller outrigger.

"No troubles!" Pui yelled, racing to the rear mast.

Tari'i got there first and released the front sail, but before Pui could release his he stepped on a jagged barnacle shell that sent him dropping onto the deck with a painful howl. Wind caught the unmanned sail, sending the lower spar swooping wildly across the deck—the entire scene unfolding before Timoa, who wore a devious grin.

"Vatua, watch out!" Tari'i yelled, but it was too late.

The boom slammed into Matani's back, sending him flying overboard.

"Why didn't you say something?" Tari'i shouted.

Timoa just shrugged, flashing a sheepish grin. "Oops?"

Back once again in the wild sea, Matani felt his heart pounding like never before—and not so much from having the wind knocked out of him. He suddenly felt the reality of being barely a mote among a watery land of giants.

Even the smallest of those whales could eat you whole!

Barely able to see above the rise and fall of the waves, Matani feverishly kicked his legs, spinning helplessly.

"No troubles, Vatua!" Pui's voice echoed across the waves. "We're coming back around!"

"Definitely a little worried," Matani muttered to himself, looking for signs of any creatures beneath him.

Treading water, he watched nervously as *Mano'nahu* made a wide arc. Shouts came from several other canoes, but they were too far away for Matani to make out what they were saying. Then, Matani noticed one of the warriors pointing frantically at something—just as he became aware of an ominous presence in the water with him.

"Okay, a lot worried now!" he yelled, followed by the involuntarily evacuation of both his bladder and bowels.

Dropping his head down under the bright-blue water, Matani saw three blurry figures lumbering in his direction through rings of shimmering sunlight. Almost directly beneath him, they rose higher and higher, slowly coming into focus.

This is it! I'm dead!

At first mistaking them for sharks, Matani realized they were actually whales. As they drew closer, he could make out the ventral grooves defining each of their chins, and with both ears submerged, he could hear three distinct vocalizations coming from them.

A deep, purposeful moan.

A lighter, melodic intonation.

And a higher-pitched, almost questioning series of inflections.

Matani's terror quickly diminished as he realized this was a family of whales on a leisurely swim.

The one he guessed to be the mother, nearly as long as *Mano'nahu*, floated just below the rippling waves with her newborn closely hugging her side. And suspended in the water right beneath them was the father, slightly smaller than the female, keeping a protective eye over his small family.

Matani lifted his head above the water to inhale a gulp of air, then dove back under again, compelled—however foolishly—to risk getting closer to these giants.

The mother whale's enormous tail muscles flexed slowly up and down to propel herself through the water as the newborn calf maneuvered slightly above, using its small dorsal fins to support itself atop her wide head. The image reminded Matani of how his own mother had carried him on her shoulders when he was a toddler, bringing a fond smile to his face. Refracted sunlight from above danced and wriggled in nebulous patterns on the sleekly contoured bodies of the whales, accentuating a number of fist-sized bumps covering their heads. And while the skin of the calf looked new and smooth, both parents were aged and pocked with scars, with the father having what looked like bite marks from a good-sized predator or two.

Then, something remarkable happened that Matani knew he would never, ever forget.

The calf pulled away from its mother, giving a few flashing white flicks of its flippers to propel itself up toward him.

Vaguely aware that he could hear and feel his own heartbeat, Matani let himself hang motionless at the surface. Unsure of what might happen next, he felt more excitement than fear.

Can you hear my thoughts?

Where do you come from?

What are you doing here?

Where are you going?

Like a dream, the blurry gray shape of the creature came into focus as it rose closer and closer to the surface. Although small in comparison to its parents, the whale calf was easily bigger than most of the canoes in the fleet. And it made Matani suddenly aware of just how fragile and finite human life really was.

How could I possibly have thought so little of this amazing gift? And all the unexpected experiences like this that come with it?

Matani surfaced first, followed by a misty geyser bursting from the calf's blowhole, sounding eerily similar to a human exhale. Its large, bumpy head lifted above the water, revealing an equally large, brownish-gray eye. And maybe it was his imagination, but the whale seemed to be looking at him with friendly affection.

No, not just looking at him.

This incredible being was actually seeing Matani through the iris of a whole new universe bursting with brand-new possibilities.

Nervously reaching through the water, the moment Matani's fingers touched its smooth, spongy skin, a jolt slammed up his arm and exploded deep inside his chest so mightily, his entire body straightened. There was no pain, no fear, but for a moment he could see and feel everything, as if he were connected to the very universe itself.

Reconnected.

The brief but powerful moment culminated in a silent, radiant light.

And then it was gone, taking with it the blinding darkness that had veiled Matani's spirit for so long.

Blinking slowly, as if he'd just risen from a long, dull sleep, Matani marveled at the colors of the world exploding all around him. The ocean wasn't just a solid blue, but rather comprised of countless subtle hues: azure, aqua, royal, sky, and midnight blue, with shades of turquoise deeper down. He saw every single pore and ridge of the whale's skin, every haunting detail of its eye: the lens, cornea, pupil, and retina. Matani watched this big, beautiful eye scan the length of his body before meeting his gaze again, and then the whale calf sounded a long, soulful note that rose in pitch at the end.

I will.

Having intuitively answered a question he wasn't wholly certain of, Matani knew only that it was important, perhaps the most important question he'd ever been asked in his life. A life for which he had, up until that very moment, held such little regard.

The whale calf's massive body spun in the water, flashing its white belly at the sun before moving closer to Matani, lightly but purposefully nudging him with its nose. Matani burst out laughing when he realized the little whale was playing with him.

Eventually, the machinations of time returned to normal and Matani watched the friendly creature fall away through the water, returning to the loving care of its mother and father below.

"Vatua!" called a distant voice.

Matani looked up and realized the voice wasn't distant at all. *Manoʻnahu* was right alongside him, and Pui tossed down a length of cord attached to a stick. Matani grabbed it, and Pui reeled him up onto the deck.

"My third catch of the day!" Pui joked. "You okay?"

Matani thought for a moment, realizing, "Well, I don't have to go to the bathroom anymore!"

Pui doubled over in laughter. "Maybe we gotta tie you down so you don't fall off again, yeah?"

Matani smiled, then turned his attention back to the whales. They stayed close to the fleet for a while before eventually heading off on a northwestern trajectory, leaving every traveler in an unspoken communion of silence, reflecting upon the day's events in their own personal way.

For Matani, he knew he'd just experienced something incredibly powerful and profound. It was as though the whales had helped him move past himself, the way a boulder might be moved from a stream, allowing the water to flow more freely.

Not an easy task, by any means. But a necessary one.

Rising above all those languishing emotions of sadness and loneliness, Matani rediscovered a tiny flame of optimism that had somehow remained alive somewhere in the suffocating darkness.

No longer a stowaway tossed upon the stormy seas of life, he realized—and truly understood—that he was part of something greater. Something that pulsed with the heartbeat of the universe itself. Gazing dreamily across the dimming infinity of heaving waves before him, Matani could barely make sense of exactly what that something was . . . but he no longer felt so alone in the universe.

He was not alone.

And in that knowing, he found solace.

✦ CHAPTER 6 ✦

With a wavering orange sun just touching the western horizon behind them, *Mano'nahu* guided the Tauaian fleet across the deepest, darkest waters of the voyage. A balmy evening wind vibrated through her rigging as the gentle rise and fall of waves performed gentle creaks on the sturdy wooden instrument of the sea. As always, Hano manned the helm, with Pui right behind him trolling for fish. Imo and Timoa were engaged in minor repairs to the canoe house and sail rigging, while Tari'i sat cross-legged at the foredeck, eyes focused on the deepening blue pastels on the eastern horizon ahead.

With an energized spirit, Matani sang quietly to himself while carrying out his chores. Which was most definitely a first; he'd never sung when doing work of any kind. After organizing the cargo inside the canoe house for the umpteenth time that day, he circled around the outside, by now having memorized exactly where to skip right to avoid stubbing his toe on Imo's *Leg from Heaven* without even looking. And despite a constant stream of abusive grumblings from Timoa, Matani felt content in a much brighter world that somehow seemed easier to breathe in.

"Gotcha!" Pui screeched, his body flailing about as he struggled to reel in the trolling line.

The entire canoe dipped under Imo's weight as he lumbered across the deck to help Pui haul in a hefty, gleaming ahi tuna. "You're not getting away this time!" he shouted, tightly hugging the fish on the quickest path across the deck to his cooking box. "Now, catch another one for the rest of you!"

As if by Imo's divine request, no sooner had Pui thrown the line back into the water than he was hauling a second tuna of nearly equal size onto the deck. "Woo! I should've used this hook earlier!" Pui said, struggling to keep his knee on the fish's wriggling head.

Seeing that Imo had already begun preparing the first tuna, Matani darted over to Pui's side. "How can I help?"

"Get that hook off its mouth for me," Pui grunted, grappling with the tuna's desperate thrashings. "It's special."

It took a few missed grabs before Matani finally secured the bucking head of the tuna firmly enough to unhook the bone fishhook from its gasping mouth. He stood holding the fishing line before him, watching tiny sparkles of salt water slide down the tightly woven coconut fiber onto a magnificent lure of pearl shells and yellow feathers.

"What's so special about it?" Matani asked. "Are there spirits in here, too?"

Pui's mouth quirked into a sentimental smile. "Even better. My father's mana," he said, carefully attaching the fishhook back onto the cord around his neck. "He loved fishing, so I made this from his bones after he died so I could keep catching fish as well as he did."

"Vatua, bring me that other tuna before it escapes!" Imo summoned, restlessly scratching his beard.

Matani struggled to carry the surprisingly heavy tuna over to Imo, who was waiting impatiently with a wooden dagger poised for cutting. "Here, help me cut 'em up."

Taking the dagger, Matani was well aware that ahi tuna was off limits to commoners. Not only that, having subsisted mostly on poi made from taro and goby captured from mountain streams, he certainly didn't have much experience cutting fish of this size. After several nervous attempts, Imo stopped him.

"Haven't you ever cut a fish before?"

Matani shrugged. "Only little ones."

"Okay, I'll teach you," Imo asserted, positioning both tuna side by side on the deck so Matani could mirror him. Using the edge of his hand, Imo outlined the four parts of the fish. "They both got four loins. Two on top, two on the bottom. Start by cutting off the head and tail so the body can lie flat, yeah?"

Matani nodded and placed the point of his dagger on the tuna's head. Imo adjusted the blade slightly, positioning it just below the gill.

"Don't forget to thank Ta'aroa for the catch!" Tari'i reminded them from the foredeck.

Imo shook his head, waving his hand impatiently. "Oh, be quiet and let him cut the fish already. I'm hungry!"

Looking down at the tuna, its lidless, lifeless eyes staring back, Matani slid the dagger beneath its gill, feeling its delicate skin tear. Its dark-pink flesh was slowly revealed, emitting a fragrant, oily smell.

"Not so hard, yeah?" Imo said, arching his eyebrows. "Now, cut from the gills to the tail here, here, and here, but be careful not to push the tip down too deep or you might get some backbone in there."

Matani carefully followed Imo's instructions, peeling off four loins—each as long as his arm. "Now what?"

Imo smirked as if the answer was obvious. "Get some coconut husks so I can start cooking!"

Matani crawled into the canoe house and brought back as many husks as he could carry. Imo immediately started pulling apart the dry fibers, arranging them on the sandy base of his trusty cooking box. Then, as he had before, he took out two sticks. Rubbing the sharpened tip of one stick up and down the long groove carved into the other stick, which he held between his feet, through friction, he manifested a trickle of smoke that was quickly coaxed into a flame.

"Vatua," Hano shouted. "My left hull's heavy again!"

"No troubles!" Matani answered, jumping for his bailing gourd.

Maybe this is my life's purpose? A life at sea!

Until they find out who you really are.

Can't you let me be happy for a moment?

Why? You know as well as I that happiness never lasts very long.

Having just finished a welcoming ceremony to the first few stars arriving in the dimming eastern skies ahead, Tari'i noticed Matani smiling. "Enjoying yourself over there?"

Matani stopped shoveling water from the bulkhead and looked over his shoulder, grinning. "Just happy to be here!"

"You're welcome to bail all the way to O'ahu," Tari'i said with a raised eyebrow. "That's the one job we all hate on this canoe!"

"Oh, this is nothing compared to farm—" Matani quickly cut off the potentially ruinous word and maneuvered his mouth to say another. "—far-uh-fighting! Training! Fight training!"

Matani looked around to see if anyone had noticed his verbal blunder.

He had trouble seeing in the waning daylight, but it seemed the others were all focused on something else, thankfully. He rushed over to the right hull, tripping over something that made him fall and hit his head on the deck hard enough to blur his vision. Blinking both eyes until they refocused, he saw Timoa slowly pulling back the handle of his oar with a sadistic grin.

"You did that on purpose!" Matani shouted.

"Mind your tongue," Timoa snarled. "Or I'll cut it out."

He knows what you almost said. Do something before he ruins your new-found happiness.

Matani's breezy attitude instantly crumbled into the depths of himself, distorting into a rage that he poured right back into Timoa's vicious eyes.

Without warning, a massive lightning bolt crashed down into the water not a stone's throw from Timoa in a blinding burst of intensely heated light. Stunned by the unexpected strike, he looked back and saw Matani's face, twisted into a sneer of triumph.

"Where did that come from?" Imo yelped.

More confused shouts ricocheted across the water from the rest of the fleet as dozens of fingers pointed up at a sky filled only with the merging colors of sunset and dusk.

Curiously, the only visible clouds were on the distant horizon.

"Get ready," Hano said, studying the weather's intent across the shark-head bows.

A trail of foam and spray suddenly bubbled up from the swells, racing toward them like the wake of an invisible god.

Matani noticed his own heart pounding. "Is it Ro'o?!"

"Ta'aroa," Timoa corrected him. "He's come to punish us all because of you."

Cupping both hands around his mouth, Pui called out the phenomenon by name, "Rain Squall!"

Out of nowhere, a rush of cold air slammed into the canoe, punching *Mano'nahu's* sails hard enough to bend her masts, forcing both hulls down into the water.

"It's charging us!" Tari'i yelled, pulling in the forward sail to keep them from leaning to one side.

Hano secured the handle of the steering oar under his powerful bicep.

"Close those sails before we flip!"

With the deck heaving and swaying under his feet, Pui imparted a quick word of advice as he ran past Matani. "Hold on to something!"

Matani could only nod as he watched Pui and Tari'i finally wrangle the rigging lines, securing both sails to their masts.

In the blink of an eye, a heavier darkness smeared across the horizon as white, frothing tips ignited across the waves. The deep-blue sea turned slate gray, reflecting a ceiling of rain-heavy clouds moving in quickly overhead.

A cavernous, spine-chilling moan filled the air as the rain finally broke, driven horizontal by a charging wind that slammed into *Mano'nahu* again, making every inch of her shiver violently. The rough waters nearly ripped the steering oar from Hano's grip a number of times as the back of the canoe launched up into the sky, then plunged back down in one explosion of water after another.

Taking Pui's advice, Matani clung to the canoe house framework. "How can I help?"

"Stay out of our way!" Timoa snapped, digging his paddle into the raging sea to keep *Mano'nahu's* bow aimed into the wind.

The entire canoe quivered, then bucked so violently that Hano lost his grip and rolled backward across the deck. Had he not grabbed hold of the right hull's endpiece, he'd have slid straight off into the sea. Pulling himself back up on deck, he watched helplessly as the unmanned oar began knocking loudly back and forth in the steering column, sending *Mano'nahu* into an uncontrolled spin.

Finally seeing an opportunity to be useful, Matani raced across the tilting deck.

"No, Vatua!" Hano warned, struggling to right himself.

But it was too late. Matani had already grabbed hold of the long wooden handle, completely unprepared when it knocked him off his feet. In a daze, he looked up to see the steering oar coming right at his face. He flattened himself onto the deck, barely escaping what could easily have been a deadly blow. Shoving Matani clear of the danger, Hano reined in the oar and deftly pulled *Mano'nahu* out of her spin.

"Secure that cargo!" Tari'i shouted at Matani, pointing to a cracked calabash rolling across the deck and spilling taro everywhere.

Through the wind and rain, Matani saw that the rope gate on one side of the canoe house had split open, and he nearly swallowed his tongue when he noticed the lavish gift for Ruling Chief Po'omanu inching its way out into the open. He dove with outstretched hands, barely snatching one of the feather cloak's decorative teeth between his thumb and forefinger before stuffing it back under a weighty stack of bark cloth. As he made some minor repairs to the rope gate, water started gushing up through seams in the deck.

"Everyone, grab a paddle!" Hano ordered.

Needled by freezing rain, Pui and Tari'i raced to their hull positions, digging their wooden blades into the turbulent waters.

"Where's Imo?" Hano yelled. "I need his paddle, too!"

Thinking the worst, all eyes searched the deck only to find Imo behind the canoe house hunched over his cooking box. Pui and Tari'i shared a bemused glance as they watched him use his entire body to shield the sizzling tuna loins from the rain and crashing waves.

Feeling eyes on him, Imo looked up. "What?" he shouted, clearly bothered. "Let the kid do it, I'm cooking!"

Hano shook his head impatiently, then threw Matani a confirming nod.

"Me?" Matani gulped.

No! Not you! You're not nearly strong enough to do Imo's job!

"Stop thinking!" Hano yelled. "That's when fear sneaks in!"

Terrified, Matani jumped down in back of the right hull, parallel to Timoa, and clamped his hands in a death grip around the worn handle of Imo's paddle, offering a quick mental prayer. The atmosphere had darkened even further under heavy sheets of rain, but he could still see dim shapes of the fleet all around them. In every direction, hundreds of voices shouted themselves hoarse, trying to survive the powerful storm. Off to his left, Matani saw two canoes collide, erupting in a spray of splinters and water. To his right, an outrigger rammed straight under the deck of another double-hulled canoe, sending both of its immense hulls in different directions.

We're all going to die.

Matani looked around at the Shark Warriors, expecting to see them sharing his fear.

But what he saw surprised him. None of them looked the least bit afraid;

in fact, they actually seemed to be enjoying the terrifying ordeal. It was the first time Matani had considered the possibility that not everyone had the same emotional response in a shared situation.

And this realization made him wonder.

Is fear a choice?

"No burials!" Hano shouted through the rain.

"No funerals!" the Shark Warriors answered back in unison

Matani looked over at Pui, who answered before he could ask, "It means no one dies today."

Inhaling sharply, Matani jammed the blade of his paddle into the blustering sea, emulating the other warriors' movements as best he could.

No burials, no funerals.

His stomach dropped as *Mano'nahu* lifted up on the back of a mountainous wave, giving him a spine-tingling bird's-eye view of the entire convoy below, appearing as nothing more than flimsy wooden toys in the middle of watery chaos. But the view barely lasted a moment before Matani's entire world dropped back down the height of a mountain, exploding onto a thunderous splash of white water.

People don't belong out here!

Out of nowhere, he pictured Heiana back home, without a care in the world, completely oblivious to what he was going through right now.

She's probably getting ready to go with Vatua to the water splashing ceremony.
Probably.
Does she even care if I'm alive?
Probably not.
This is so unfair. She's the one who knocked over that pig idol in the first place!
Yeah, but you were the one stupid enough to take the blame for it!

But as always, Matani couldn't find it in him to stay mad at Heiana for long. The truth of it was that he knew he could have managed their relationship better, but all he felt now was guilt, knowing that certain actions could not be undone, or certain words unsaid. With a startled blink, he returned to the storm in time to see a section of rigging on the horizontal spar snap apart.

Before he could warn anyone, *Mano'nahu's* foresail unexpectedly burst open with a deafening crack, and the entire canoe lurched, pushing both hulls down into the water again.

Hano's gaze bounced between each of his crewmen as they fought against the wild sea, making a dozen complex calculations in an instant before his gaze settled on Matani.

"Vatua, drop that sail before it capsizes us!"

This decision made sense, of course. Hano needed stronger arms on the paddles. Without hesitation, Matani leaped from the hull and made his way across the slippery, teetering deck. Searching the base of the mast through the biting rain, he found some tangled cord. His oar-blistered fingers were difficult to manage in the cold, but he finally loosened several knots, untangling the securing lines, and was able to close the sail.

Mano'nahu slammed back down onto the water.

Wondering what horror they would encounter next, Matani could barely believe it when the sky suddenly lifted.

Within moments, the squall moved off, dragging a thick curtain of rain behind it.

Hoots and hollers of joy and relief mixed with adrenaline erupted as the winds quickly abated and the unruly sea calmed to a light chop. Matani had no idea how long the entire ordeal had lasted, but all that remained of the day was an afterglow of sunlight on the western horizon.

Rattled and disoriented, the exhausted fleet circled around *Mano'nahu*, seeking Hano's leadership. There was a brief exchange between Tari'i and some shaken warriors in one of the other canoes.

"A few injuries, but nothing fatal," Tari'i reported. "We lost four outriggers and a double, along with their supplies."

"Yeah, the slightest weather can eat these newer canoes alive," Hano said, shaking his head. "What about their crews?"

"All survivors were taken aboard other canoes," Tari'i assured him.

Concerned voices continued calling out to Hano, asking where the storm had taken them. For a tense moment, he just stared out at the sea and the sky, saying nothing.

Matani watched Hano very closely, wondering what he was looking for. At one point, the warrior pressed his hand against the sky. "Before, there weren't any clouds. Now, there's too many," he mumbled.

As the fleet drifted along on bare poles, nothing seemed to please Hano for a very long while—until a dozen black noddies appeared from the west, flying directly over the fleet.

"Our winged escorts have arrived!" Hano declared, pointing at the birds. "Raise the sails!"

"How far off are we from Oʻahu?" Tariʻi asked, making his way to the forward hull.

"The storm carried us pretty far southeast," answered Hano, pushing the steering oar to redirect *Manoʻnahu's* bow in the direction of the noddies. "Pui, Tariʻi, get our sails open. We should be able to raise the island by sunrise."

"The birds told him all that?" Matani whispered to Pui.

"Not exactly," Pui said, giving Tariʻi a quick nod so both could open the front and back sails together. "Certain birds fly to their feeding grounds in the morning, then back home at night with food they've collected for their families. So, if they're heading back now, it means we should see the island in that same direction after a little while."

Returning to his bailing duties to rid both hulls of seawater, Matani had only just begun to understand the many hidden signs available to a navigator at sea.

"Let's eat!" Imo's voice rang cheerfully from behind the tuna-flavored steam that rose from behind the canoe house. "Vatua, come help me hand out this food."

Imo gathered up the bones of the fish he'd prepared and wrapped them in ti leaves as an offering to Taʻaroa. With a prayer of personal thanks to his grandmother, who had taught him how to prepare this particular meal, he threw the offering into the sea.

Handed four bowls of baked fish, Matani carried them across the deck to where Tariʻi, Pui, and Timoa had already gathered around Hano in the dark, talking like old friends. Famished hands saved him the trouble of handing out the food.

"Should I light some torches?" Matani asked, wanting to be helpful.

"No," Hano replied, offering no further explanation.

Pui raised a patient hand. "He sees the stars better without them."

This remark puzzled Matani even further.

Why does he need to see the stars and not the ocean? Do they use some unspoken language only highborns can hear?

"This smells amazing!" Tariʻi declared, closely studying the tuna preparation in his bowl. "What's this on top, Imo?"

Imo plopped down among the circle of men with a heavy thud, palming a coconut shell of piping hot tuna in each hand. "A light crust of crushed tutu'i nuts and a pinch of sea salt."

Pui squinted enviously at Imo. "Hey, how come you get two bowls?"

Imo threw him an indignant look, then handed the second bowl to Matani, who was standing obediently outside the circle. "It's for Vatua."

Inhaling the good smell of fish, Matani stepped forward and took it, then stepped back.

"What are you doing?" Imo laughed, forcing Timoa aside with the thrust of his rump to make space between them. "Come sit and eat with us!"

Doing his best to ignore Timoa's irritated glare, Matani joined the circle. Ever since his embarrassing introduction earlier that day, combined with the effects of intermittent seasickness, he'd thought he'd never want to eat again, but the heavenly aroma of Imo's steaming, savory creation far outweighed the risks. Not only that, the thought of defying one of many unjust laws made the forbidden dish all the more enticing.

As Matani reached into his bowl for a pinch of tuna, Imo gently touched his arm in a wordless request to wait.

He wasn't sure why until Tari'i spoke.

"To those not with us," Tari'i began, placing one hand over his heart. "To those who helped our canoe across the sea, and to those who never came home but are still always a part of our journey."

Still confused, Matani then saw everyone hold up their bowls, reciting in one voice, "For Mau! Until we meet again!"

After the warriors emerged from their individual moments of silence, Matani asked, "Who's Mau?"

"He was the best of us," Pui said with a hint of mournful affection.

Hano swallowed a large chunk of tuna, nodding wistfully. "On our way to Havai'i one summer, we ran into a bad storm."

"Way worse than today," Pui added.

"What happened?" Matani asked, momentarily forgetting about his own bowl of food.

A painful look filled Hano's eyes. "A rogue wave knocked him overboard."

"We searched for as long as we could," Tari'i said quietly, "but the sea refused to give him back."

After a prayer to the gods and to their individual ancestral spirits, the warriors ate and exchanged memories of Mau that included weapons, battles, and the mysteries of women. Matani hung on to every word, which reminded him of something Imo had mentioned earlier. Waiting until Timoa was focused on eating, Matani glanced over to see if he could spot the piece of coconut in his skull.

Timoa turned sharply, with eyes so fierce they pierced the darkness. "What are you looking at?"

"N-nothing!" Matani stuttered, stuffing a chunk of tuna into his mouth. Then his eyes exploded with surprise. "Wow, this is the most amazing thing I've ever eaten!"

"Food always tastes better after a near-death experience," Pui laughed.

A raucous sound of excited whistles and voices suddenly rose across the fleet, directing all eyes to the eastern horizon.

"Lunar Light of Life!" Tari'i exclaimed, jumping to his feet. He raced over to the canoe house and brought out a conch shell. Facing west, he blew into it with the full force of his lungs. "O Hina!" he called out. "Matriarch of our people, mother of those born and yet to be born! Your arrival today reminds us of the eternal continuum of life, death, and rebirth!"

Each moon phase was a nightly reminder of humankind's origins as spiritual beings, determining things both to be done and avoided on certain days. Its appearance this evening not only symbolized that first shard of heavenly light to penetrate the realm of night, but also the birth of a new day, month, and year.

At this very moment, having faithfully observed the nocturnal heavens day after day, studying the recurring phases of the moon, the galaxies of stars and the revolving planets, the holy staff of every temple across the island chain was carrying out ancient and sacred ceremonies to temporarily retire Tane, Tū, and Ta'aroa of their heavenly positions.

During the next four months of the lunar harvest festival, Ro'o—god of peace and agriculture—would rule the mortal realms of land, sea, and sky.

Tari'i returned to the circle of men carrying a bottle gourd tooled with ornate etchings. "This 'ava is from the root of our homeland," he said, removing the wooden stopper with a quiet pop, releasing a strong, pungent smell into the salty air. "It's the drink of gods that reminds us of where we came from. For the gods above us, all around, and in front of us, we offer our gratitude."

As was customary, Tari'i first handed the ceremonial drink to Hano, who ranked highest among them. "The honor is yours, navigator and chief."

Hano nodded graciously, raising the bottle. "To new beginnings," he said, taking a swig.

"New beginnings," his fellow warriors celebrated, followed by several hearty grunts of approval.

Receiving the bottle from Hano, Pui took the next swig, then handed it to Imo. Before he was finished, Timoa reached for it.

"Vatua's next!" Imo grunted, jamming his elbow into Timoa's side.

"What for?" Timoa asked, clearly disgruntled. "I'm a higher-ranking chief than he is!"

"No ranks," Imo persisted. "After Hano, we go in order of the circle."

Timoa reluctantly handed the bottle to Matani with mock politeness.

Don't drink it!

Yeah, believe me! I know!

While fisherman and farmers often drank 'ava to soothe sore muscles after a hard day's work, Matani purposefully avoided the concoction because of how it impaired his father, often exacerbating his already potent anger. Nervous about the effects it might have on him, he also knew that not drinking it might arouse suspicion. Hoping it was too dark for them to see, he faked a sip, then quickly passed the bottle to Timoa.

"No, no, no!" Pui said, snatching the bottle from Timoa's pursed lips. "A warrior doesn't sip 'ava like a baby! He gulps it like a god!"

Under the pressure of everyone's gaze, Matani smiled nervously, then took the bottle and tilted his head back, filling his mouth. The moment he swallowed, a terrible burning sensation raced down his throat and into his chest, sending him into a coughing fit.

This must be how I die.

Pui slapped his knee and cackled. "Now you feel it, yeah?"

"I can't feel anything," Matani said, touching his lips. "My mouth is numb!"

"Here," Imo said, breaking off a small piece of his sugarcane.

Still coughing, Matani took the cane and sucked on it until the sweet flavor cooled his throat. "Does sugarcane cure everything?"

"It does for me!" Imo laughed.

By the time the bottle gourd of 'ava had made two more rounds, Imo and Pui were starting to sway back and forth in a lighthearted way, which quickly turned into a shoving match. Things escalated, and they were suddenly on their feet and circling in a ceremonial warrior dance. They bent their knees, widened the whites of their eyes, and stuck out their tongues in an attempt to intimidate one another.

But what caught Matani's attention the most was how they moved their hands, like they were pulling something from the air into their bodies.

"What are they doing?" he asked of no one in particular.

"Gathering mana," Hano answered.

Matani wrinkled his brow. "I thought mana was in the blood?"

"Mana is everywhere," Hano said, almost mystically, circling his hands in the open space before him. "With proper intention, we pull it from the earth, the sea, the heavens, and into our flesh and blood, giving us strength, confidence, and focus."

This was a stunning revelation for Matani. He'd been raised by society to believe that mana could only be inherited—raising all sorts of new questions. "Is mana what makes you great fighters?"

Imo was the first to answer. "It's not always about fighting."

"Yeah, it's also about understanding energy and how to use it," Tari'i said. "Sure, we can break bones, but we also know how to unbreak them."

Matani's jaw dropped. "How do you unbreak a bone?"

"A properly trained warrior can transfer their mana to a person who is sick, wounded, or dying, and help them recover," Hano replied.

Bored by the conversation, Timoa turned his attention to heckling Pui and Imo. "You two danglers gonna flap your tongues all night or what?"

"Patience," Imo said, just before throwing a blinding-fast punch that Pui caught under his armpit.

"And skill," Pui added—then, in one impressively fluid move, spun Imo around and bent him over until he was flat on his back.

Imo gave Pui an eager grin as he brushed himself off and got back on his feet. "I give you that one 'cause we brothers!"

Circling each other once more, Pui threw the first punch this time, but Imo dodged it and grabbed Pui's entire face with his enormous hand, slamming him onto the deck with such force, the entire canoe bounced.

Matani's jaw hung open. "How many people have you killed?"

"Not as many as we've saved," Hano answered sharply. "Resolving conflict is not about winning; it's about wisdom."

"What kind of wisdom?" Matani asked, genuinely curious.

"Just because you can take a life, that doesn't mean you should," Hano replied.

"Speak for yourself," Timoa said with a pernicious grin.

"We aren't murderers," Tari'i countered, shooting a disapproving glare at Timoa. "The art of battle is about being *pono*," he said, meaning *in proper balance with all things*. "There's a time to be hard, like a man, and a time to be soft, like a woman."

"Like a woman?" Matani asked, surprised by this concept.

"No matter how we refer to ourselves, we each have the energy of both men and women inside us," Tari'i explained. "Masculine energy is always pursuing, planning, and focusing, while feminine energy wants to create, dream, and unfold. Getting these two energies inside us to marry peacefully creates healthy emotional balance in our hearts."

This confused Matani even more. "If I have female energy in me, why don't I understand them better?"

"Ha! What you wanna know about Timoa?" Pui cracked.

"Shut your maggot mouth," Timoa murmured.

Tari'i reached out and tapped Matani's knee. "Women need to be both seen and heard."

"That's it?" Matani asked, unimpressed.

"Well, there's more to it than that," Imo said. "You gotta actually listen when she talks, because it's how she heals."

"Talk little," Hano seconded with a nod. "Listen a lot."

Imo nudged Matani with a friendly wink. "Why you wanna know all this? You got a girl back home or something?"

"No," Matani said, but somehow that single word gave him away.

"Come on now!" Imo pressed.

"Okay, yeah," Matani finally admitted. "There is this one girl."

Pui laughed. "Isn't there always?!"

"Well, she's not my girlfriend," Matani tried to explain. "But I've known her since we were little."

"You ever kiss her?" Imo asked.

Matani hesitated. "Well, I tried once, but she laughed and ran off."

"Ooh, that hurts," Tari'i sympathized.

"Ever try again?" asked Pui.

"No way!" Matani countered. "She made me feel like a fool!"

"Listen to me," Pui said in a more serious tone. "I'm no expert, but since you guys met so young, you're probably both still trying to figure out what you really want."

"Or, if she does know," Tari'i said, "she might just be testing you to see if you can protect her."

"Protect? Her?" Matani said, incredulously. "She's a *waaaay* better fighter than I am!"

"I don't mean physically," Tari'i clarified, gesturing to the others. "Men are physical."

"He's right," Imo said, giving Timoa a playful shove. "You see how we always knock each other around and give each other a hard time, yeah?"

Tari'i nodded. "Well, women are emotional beings. More than her physical body, this girl you like needs to know you're going to protect her heart and her feelings."

"Trust," Pui said, boiling it all down.

"Trust?" Matani repeated.

"Yes," Hano said. "And for anyone, trust in a man is only as good as his word."

Matani pushed frustrated fingers through his hair. "Girls are complicated."

"Oh yeah," Imo said, followed by grunts from the other Shark Warriors, each nodding in commiseration.

Imo chuckled to himself before sharing a thought. "My tūtū always told me and my brothers that men are just the seeds of existence. Women are the gateway all human life passes through. Make 'em angry, they'll stuff us back between their legs and send us back where we came from!"

As everyone shared a good laugh at that—even Timoa—Matani looked around at each of the warriors, realizing the importance of encountering such interesting male mentors at this time in his life. Feeling both buzzed and relaxed from the effects of 'ava, his heart swelled with a grateful, albeit unfiltered, appreciation.

"I love you guys!" he bellowed in a drunken slur, then pounded an earnest fist against his chest. "Well, maybe not you, Timoa, but definitely the rest of you!"

To which Timoa raised an eyebrow in mock offense. The other warriors traded looks of silent bewilderment just as something flew from the dark ocean atmosphere, tracing a starlit arc through the air before delivering an unceremonious slap across Matani's face.

As he toppled to the deck, the culprit revealed itself—a fish, of all things, with wings that flapped in protest beside him. "Are you from sea or sky?" Matani asked in awed wonder.

Waiting for the strange sea creature's reply, his vision blurred, and reality seemed to withdraw into the tranquil arms of oblivion with whimsical reverie, where neither laughing warriors nor flopping bird-fish could intrude.

⁘ CHAPTER 7 ⁘

Sallow, formless clouds whirled like unwieldy spirits, making it difficult to see anything, but the unmistakable sensation of sand indicated a beach underfoot.

Not being able to see anything was terrifying enough, but then came the wicked, disembodied whispers.

Pathetic.

Helpless.

Confused.

Useless.

Hopeless.

Trapped.

Afraid.

Alone.

Lost.

Powerless.

Racing through a prison of blinding fog to escape them, Matani finally, mercifully breached its nebulous boundaries to find himself at the base of an emerald-green mountain so enormous, to even guess its height was impossible. Its conical peak was faded by the upper atmosphere and further obscured by a cloak of feathery clouds where unfamiliar, winged creatures dared to orbit.

Deciding that any attempt to ascend a mountain of such mythical proportions was beyond the realms of rationality, Matani stepped back just as a peculiar, vibrating energy grabbed hold of him, wresting him forward against his will. Though he tried to resist, the overwhelming sensation became jarringly uncomfortable. Trying to understand what this all meant, he saw something that twisted his heart with unspeakable terror.

The mountain was breathing.

With a meek grunt, Matani awoke, vaguely aware that someone had covered him with a scratchy bark cloth blanket that smelled lightly of mildew. Unused to waking up to the gentle rise and fall of a canoe at sea, he found the lack of forest sounds unsettling.

No crickets or birds, no breeze-fluttered leaves. Just the creaking of a wooden vessel, the light flapping of a sail in the breeze, and the gentle wash of water on hollowed-out hulls.

Matani peered through a small, misshapen hole in the blanket at the dark water swishing past. Poking his head out like a turtle from its shell, he glanced up—struck breathless by an explosion of bright, blazing stars across his entire field of vision.

"Oh!" he blurted, covering his mouth in surprise.

Matani had seen stars before, of course, but large portions of the sky had always been obscured by the sharp black outlines of mountains or trees. Out here, among these wide-open ocean spaces, it felt like he could see the entire universe—radiant freckles of light spattered clearly across the dome of heaven from one luminescent horizon to the other, shimmering wondrously on the undulating surface of the waves.

"Beautiful, yeah?"

Startled, Matani followed the voice to the back of the canoe, where he found the featureless outline of Hano against a sparkling trail of crescent moonlight, still seated diligently beside his steering oar.

"Never seen anything like it," Matani whispered.

"These are the same stars our elders sailed under," Hano said. "Think about that."

The concept didn't have the same meaning for Matani as they did Hano, but he smiled politely anyway. Assuming that was the end of their interaction, he was surprised when the warrior's silhouette waved him over.

Uh-oh.

Wrapping the blanket tightly around himself, Matani stood and made his way nervously across the cool, damp deck. Sliding one hand along the salt-crusted rigging, he saw the rest of the fleet sailing quietly behind, a collective menagerie of lightly bouncing sails reflecting the twinkling lights above. Timoa's foot suddenly stuck up from the port hull, twitching under the spell of a dream. Tari'i was splayed on his stomach across the plank between the front endpieces, his fingertips dragging in the water rushing between the hulls. Pui was propped up against the canoe house, leaning on Imo's bulky form, his breath whistling out in faint, nasal snores.

"Cute couple, eh?" Hano chuckled, then held up a strip of dried fish.

Matani devoured it ravenously, taking in the harmonious sounds of wind and sea all around them.

After a long while, Hano cracked his neck, grunting with relief. "This your first deep-sea voyage?"

"Yes," Matani confessed, sinking to the deck in a seated position before Hano.

"You did good in the storm today. Once you started doing what I told you."

"I was pretty scared."

"Well, like Tari'i said, it's all about being pono," Hano reminded him. "You gotta find that spot between courage and fear."

Once again, Matani found himself intrigued. "You really believe balance is always an option?"

"As above, so below," Hano answered with a confident nod. Then his eyes focused with a potent intensity. "When we find balance between what appears to be two things, only then do we understand they aren't separate at all."

Matani took the words in but was ultimately unable to decipher them. "How do you mean?"

"Look at Mano'nahu's sails," Hano began, pushing the steering oar and redirecting the canoe until both sails collapsed. "I go too far left, they lose the wind. Same as if I go too far right." He then moved the steering oar in the opposite direction, again leaving the two sails deflated, dangling lifelessly. "Although I can choose between two directions, there's really only one wind, so when I find that sweet spot in between—" he explained, adjusting the steering oar to aim the canoe until the sails filled with wind again, "—everything's pono."

Matani smiled. "Okay, yeah. I get it."

"Just like in life," Hano continued, suddenly seeing something through the darkness that made him push on the steering sweep to reorient the canoe. "Sometimes we make good choices, other times bad. This doesn't necessarily define us as a good or bad person, but it does show the importance of balancing our choices."

Following the warrior's gaze across the bow, Matani tried to discern what had caused his adjustment on a seemingly pathless path. Of course, all he saw was more endless, ambiguous darkness. "But what if things come up in life where balance isn't a choice?"

Hano eyed him thoughtfully. "Like what?"

Go on. You can trust him.

Are you crazy? No, you can't!

"Like being lost." It was difficult for Matani to actually say the words out loud, but he knew he needed to tell someone . . . before it was too late.

"Ah," Hano replied, seeming to understand the weight of Matani's statement. "Well, I'd tell them what my father always told me: you just haven't come to that part of your path yet, where you can see what's ahead."

Matani leaned back in contemplation but was ultimately unsatisfied by the answer. "Okay, but where's the position of balance between being lost and found?"

A broad smile grew on Hano's face. "Patience."

With a self-aware smirk, Matani nodded. "Yeah, I seem to have a problem with that."

"Most of us do," Hano said, jerking his chin at the other sleeping warriors. "When we were younger, all we did was train. Day and night. When we got a little older, it wasn't enough, so we started fighting each other. And I mean really fighting. I remember our teacher telling us if we didn't do something about it, we were gonna kill each other."

"What did you do?"

"Well, we had to figure out other ways to release that adolescent energy inside us," Hano explained. "Even now, Pui fishes, Imo cooks, and Tari'i prays." Then, as an afterthought, he added, "And he has adventures with many women." He laughed at that, then made an airy sound with his mouth. "But Timoa, well . . . he still hasn't found anything he likes better than fighting, but we'll see how wood carving works out for him."

"What did Mau do?" Matani asked.

Hano smiled fondly. "Ol' Mau, he liked pounding bark cloth with his mother and sisters, actually."

"Really?"

Wait until Heiana hears this! A warrior who liked pounding bark cloth!

If you ever see her again.

Hearing Hano speak more than he had the entire trip, Matani wondered if the sea had something to do with it. Or maybe the canoe. Or maybe, just maybe . . . it was that *something* else. "Are you religious, Hano?"

"Nah, Tari'i's religious. I'm more . . . spiritual."

"What's the difference?"

Again, realizing what a big question this was, Hano took a moment to gather his thoughts. "To me, religion is man-made, like a house or canoe. Don't get me wrong, we need these things. But spirituality is more natural, centering around a personal connection with the world. Both are meant to work together, I think."

"Well, I definitely felt something when I touched that whale today."

"Whales are profoundly sacred beings," Hano said with a reverent tone. "The *Creation Chant* tells us they were born during the time of darkness and helped usher humanity into the time of light. Maybe that little one brought you out of the darkness, too?"

"I did see a bright light," Matani said, recalling the powerful moment almost as if it were happening to him all over again. "It was like being woken up from a long sleep."

"Or maybe something awakened inside you," Hano suggested. Then he looked Matani square in the eye. "So, tell me. Did you mess with the weather today?"

Matani knew he couldn't play dumb, but the direct question took him by surprise. "Me? Why would you ask that?"

"Has it ever happened before?" Hano pressed. "Can you do it on purpose?"

Remaining cautiously quiet a moment, Matani decided to be truthful. "Every so often, I experience things I can't explain," he said. "But honestly, I don't really remember much. It's like I black out when they happen."

"Your mind was definitely somewhere else when the wind disappeared," Hano said, humming thoughtfully. "Though you seemed pretty awake during the squall."

"Yeah, that's never happened before."

"Until the whales, yeah?"

This revelation gave Matani pause. "Yeah, I hadn't thought of that."

"Do you have a teacher or someone helping you with this?"

"No," Matani said. "I've never actually told anyone about it before."

Hano blinked in disbelief. "What about your parents?"

"Well, they knew, but they just kind of ignored it," was all Matani said.

Sensing Matani's discomfort, Hano didn't press the matter. "Do you remember how you felt just before that lightning hit the water?"

"Angry," Matani replied without needing much thought. "Right after Timoa tripped me. Why? Do you think it means something?"

"I think it means you don't like Timoa," Hano said, making Matani laugh. "You probably won't want to hear this, but you two are a lot alike. He struggles with his emotions, too. When we train, that's the main thing we work on with Timoa. Self-control."

Matani couldn't deny the accuracy of Hano's assessment or the comparison. Both he and Timoa seemed to be bitter, angry, and resentful people. While not necessarily a good thing, at least now Matani finally understood how others must see him.

"What do you tell Timoa when he loses control of his emotions?" Matani asked.

"We can tell him lots of things, but it doesn't do much good," Hano replied. "Training the head is way harder than training the body."

"How do you get through to him, then?"

"I always remind him that it's better to learn strengths and weaknesses from friends than enemies. On a battlefield, there are some mistakes you won't walk away from."

"Why is Timoa so angry?"

"Oh, he's angry about lots of things," Hano replied with a chuckle, but there was compassion in his words. "His heart carries a lot of rage, but it's also very loyal. I would never go into battle without him at my side."

Matani made a derisive noise. "If you say so."

"Listen, whatever's at the root of your anger, you better figure out a way to resolve it before it consumes you the way it has Timoa."

"I think I'm just angry at the world."

"Why?"

"Because it offers me nothing."

"Well, that's your problem," Hano said. "The question you should be asking is: What do you have to offer the world? More importantly, the people you share your life with? Your community?"

"I'm still trying to figure that out," Matani replied with an irritable glare, but he knew it wasn't being a farmer.

Once again, Hano looked up at the sky behind him, then back across the bow, pivoting the steering oar to the right for a bit, then a little to the left again, before settling back in satisfaction.

Matani's head spun in all directions.

Okay, what did he just see?

Standing abruptly, Matani stomped across the deck to the bow of the canoe, not caring in the least this time if he disturbed the others. As expected, he saw only indistinguishable waves stretching through endless darkness to a dim glow on the horizon. Visibly irritated, he strode back to Hano.

"Okay, how do you know where you're going without any landmarks? Without the sun? What are you seeing that I'm not?"

Hano snorted. "Signs."

Matani hesitated, thinking Hano was being sarcastic, until he realized that the warrior's expression had remained genuine. "What signs? Are they hidden?"

"Sometimes," Hano said with a knowing grin. "All my senses are attuned to the dance between sea and vessel. During the day, I follow the sun, wind, clouds, and ocean swells, but right now, I'm following the stars."

"Oh, come on," Matani said, churlishly. "How can stars possibly tell you where you're going? There are way too many!"

Hano stretched out his arm and rotated his shoulder from one horizon to the other. "They rise in the east, arc overhead, and set in the west, defining points on the horizon that can be used as guides."

Raised a farmer, Matani obviously understood how the moon helped with knowing when to plant certain crops and not others, but he'd never considered stars to be very useful. "Do they always move the same way?"

"Yes, but not all the lights up there are stars," Hano said. "There are five small moons that have colors and paths all their own."

"Five moons?" Matani asked in disbelief. "Who told you that?"

"Hunumaniani," Hano said. "He taught me everything I know about the night sky, including the path of several important stars on any given night."

Matani looked up, intimidated by the numberless points of light. "How long did that take?"

"Oh, a thousand years or more."

Matani stared at Hano, perplexed. "A thousand years? How old are you?"

"It's not me that's old," Hano chuckled. "It's the knowledge of my ancestors, going back to that first navigator who unlocked the secrets of celestial navigation."

The only knowledge I ever acquired from my ancestors is how to slave in mud under a hot sun.

The scornful thought made Matani laugh, but there was an edge to it.

Hano raised both eyebrows. "What? You don't believe you're the culmination of your ancestors' wisdom?"

Matani shrugged. "Oh, I believe it all right. I just don't think that what they passed on to me is very wise."

"It's not about you," Hano said, unmoved and unimpressed. "Have you heard the old saying, *The branches grow because of the trunk?*"

"Yes, my father used to say it all the time," Matani said, rolling his eyes. "It means without our ancestors we wouldn't be here."

"That's right. Our ancestors are the doorway to our past and hold the truth to who we are." Hano paused, thoughtful at first, then annoyed. "You know, not one person has been back to Tahiti since before I was born."

Nonplussed by the information, Matani played along just to be polite. "Why not?"

"It's a very long voyage," Hano replied. "At least twenty moons there, twenty moons back. The last one to go was a ruling chief on Maui. By the time he returned, his entire island and all six of his wives had been taken over by his two stepbrothers."

"Well, you're not a ruling chief with any land to lose yet," Matani said. "Why don't you go?"

"Believe me, I dream about going to our homeland every day," Hano said. "But these new double hulls, with their single sails and narrow decks, rely more on paddling than wind power. They're only good for short trips and warfare."

Matani looked out across the fleet, noticing for the first time that every other canoe in the fleet had only one sail and their shallower hulls rode much closer to the water. "What about *Mano'nahu?*"

"Oh, she's a voyaging canoe," Hano said. "The last of her kind. On Taua'i, anyway. But a little old to withstand a lengthy pounding from the sea."

"How old is *Mano'nahu?*" Matani asked.

"She was built back on Tahiti when my father was a child," Hano replied.

"The main reason I keep using her is so the younger generation don't forget where we came from."

"What if I'm not interested in living the same life as my ancestors?" Matani asked, his words carefully chosen.

"What life do you want to live?" Hano asked with a discerning look.

Matani opened his mouth but could only muster a deflated expression. "I have no idea."

"Well, that's just it. When we lose connection with those who lived before us, we not only forget the skills and knowledge they worked so hard to master, we risk losing our own identity."

Hano fixed a concentrated stare on Matani. "It's like navigation. I determine my course by knowing where I started and the distance and direction to my destination."

"Meaning what, exactly?" Matani asked.

"Knowing where you came from is as important as knowing where you're going."

Matani glanced over at the empty horizon behind them, remembering he could no longer see Taua'i. Almost immediately, a rather unexpected sense of terror crashed down on him.

"Don't be afraid," Hano continued, pointing up at the sky. "See those three stars clumped together up there?"

Matani followed the navigator's finger above the twin masts, searching the tapestry of light. "That big star with the two little ones behind it?"

Hano nodded. "Every island has its own zenith star, which helps a navigator find it, no matter where he is on the sea. That big one, called Humu, is Taua'i's."

"Is Humu a god?"

"No, he was a famous navigator from long ago. He sailed on the first fleet from O'ahu to Taua'i. As the legend goes, Humu's two sons—both named Humu-mua—were on the lead canoe. Familiar with celestial lore, they were constantly arguing with the elder steersman about which star to follow. Having a big ego, the steersman got so fed up with the brothers telling him what to do that he threw them both overboard. Humu, who was in the last canoe with the ruling chief of O'ahu, left the rest of the fleet to rescue his sons. Following the stars that they believed in, Humu and his sons eventually reached Taua'i, while the rest of the fleet ended up lost at sea. So now, when you see those stars, you'll always remember that Humu is the brightest one and the two swimming behind him are his sons on their way to Taua'i."

Matani studied the three stars intently, committing them to memory. "But how do you use Humu and his sons to find your way to Taua'i?"

"Envision their path across the sky, from where they rise in the east to where they set in the west." Hano outstretched his slightly tilted hand to the sky, keeping his four fingers vertical while sticking his thumb out horizontally. "You aim your top fingers at the star you're following while touching the horizon with your thumb. Where the path of the star touches the ocean is where you'll find Taua'i."

Focused on the Humu cluster, Matani estimated where they may have risen in the east, then made his best guess envisioning their path across the sky, all the way down to the western horizon. "There?" He pointed dubiously.

"That's it," Hano confirmed with a quick nod.

Matani let out a long sigh of relief. "It's strange, even though I can't actually see the island anymore, it feels better at least knowing what direction home is."

"Home is the anchor of our hearts," Hano agreed. "For me, there's always comfort in knowing that when I return from a long journey, my family and friends will be there waiting for me."

These words stung Matani deeply. The only person who might be waiting for him was Heiana.

Does she even wonder what happened to me?

Doubtful.

I bet she'll like Vatua even more when he tells her that he helped me!

Probably.

Watching Matani struggle with his thoughts, Hano gestured behind him. "Do you know what that small flat piece is on the back of my right hull?"

Matani got up and quickly spotted a thin ledge sticking out slightly just beneath the right rear hull covering. But it wasn't on the other hull. "A mistake?"

Hano laughed. "Looks like it, but no. It's called *momoa*, and there's an oral tradition behind it that goes back many years. Piri-ta'aiea, a chief from Raiatea Island with a pristine genealogy, was chosen by a great priest and master navigator named Pa'ao to rule Havai'i. As they departed the homeland, Maumatuataumana, a priest who was expecting to accompany them, cried out from a cliff that he'd been left behind."

Matani tilted his head. "What did the priest do?"

"Pa'ao told him the canoe was full, so the priest said he'd find a place for himself. After leaping from the cliff and changing from a man into a spirit, he chose a small projection at the back of the hull. Ever since then, the momoa has been considered a seat for the 'aumakua."

"Your 'aumakua is a shark, right?" Matani surmised.

"A giant tiger shark named Niho'ino," Hano replied. "The form my great-great grandfather takes when he visits this world."

From a very early age, Matani had been taught that when a family member died, they resided in *Pō*, the underworld. But from time to time, they could return to the living in specific animal forms to offer guidance and protection. *Makua* meant 'parent,' and *'au* meant 'time,' making the two words together 'parent in time.' The 'aumakua played an important role in a family's identity as a messenger between the worlds of spirit and flesh. In the flesh, the 'aumakua visited through physical forms of many things—sharks, owls, birds, trees, rocks, thunder, and many other aspects of nature. Most families prayed to their ancestral 'aumakua at the dawn of each day, but this was a habit Matani had lost interest in after his parents passed.

"When I was little," Hano continued, "I got the dumb idea to swim really far from shore until I found myself surrounded by ten hungry white-tip sharks. Out of nowhere, Niho'ino came and helped me fight them off. By the time we were done, I was so tired from swimming that he let me take hold of his dorsal fin and brought me to shore. Since then, Niho'ino has become our family's 'aumakua. To this day, my elders feed him and ensure his body remains free of barnacles."

"I wish I had a shark 'aumakua from my ancestors," Matani admitted with a hint of jealousy

Hano listened attentively. "What form do they take when visiting?"

"Well, this striped lizard with a blue tail's been following me around a lot."

"Interesting," Hano replied with a knowing glance. "Most legends describe lizards as female shape-shifters, capable of appearing as slim, beautiful beach maidens, or gigantic, cave-dwelling dragons." He then paused, looking Matani in the eyes. "They're also believed to have knowledge of forgotten magic that can control the weather."

Matani remained silent, wondering if Hano was starting to realize that he wasn't who he'd said he was.

If he does, he'll probably kill you when you least expect it.

Sensing his discomfort, Hano pointed out a wide swath of glowing stars, gas, and dust that stretched from one edge of the sky to the other. "See that long, celestial rope of light above us?"

"Taupe'a," Matani said easily, having learned about this particular asterism from his mother many years ago, *Lizard's Backbone*.

"A powerful symbol of genealogy that connects us all," Hano added. "Each vertebra is an ancestor that links the patriarch of a family's lineage across time, carrying the chant of history."

"The lizard's head looks into the future," Matani said, continuing the story. "Its front feet are the children, exploring all they come across, and its firm hind legs are the parents."

"And behind them, its spine—the interlocking bones of elders," Hano finished, flashing a grin.

For some reason, Matani suddenly felt compelled to confess who he really was, but quickly changed his mind for fear of ruining what had become an unexpectedly meaningful conversation.

"Here, take her on for a while," Hano said, stepping aside as he gestured to the handle of the steering oar.

Matani was dumbfounded, nervous, terrified all at once. "Why me?"

Hano glanced over at the momoa, then back again. "Because Niho'ino wants you to."

And Matani could tell he was dead serious.

Are you sure?

I . . .

It's a trick!

But . . .

Trust me, you'll just end up being disappointed again!

"Still got those bugs buzzing around up there, yeah?" Hano asked, tapping his head.

"Oh yeah." Matani nodded heavily. "They never shut up."

"In the final moments before my great grandfather died, do you know what he regretted most?"

Matani could only think of his own regrets with Heiana. "Not being able to tell someone how he felt about them until it was too late?"

"Well, that's a pretty specific answer," Hano laughed. "But yeah, he regretted many things he hadn't done."

Matani took this concept deeply into his heart, thinking of all the things he'd never done or accomplished—but wanted to. Or at least thought about doing. "I never realized until today how many new things there are out in the world to experience."

"In the same way you can't learn about the ocean without sailing on it," Hano began insightfully. "You can't possibly learn about life without living in it."

He's right.

No, he's not.

I've been hiding.

You've been protecting yourself.

It hasn't helped very much.

Don't be ridiculous.

Frustrated by the negative thoughts still holding claim somewhere inside his head or consciousness or wherever they existed, Matani realized something a bit daunting.

The whales may have shone a light upon the darkness within me, showing me what's possible. But talking with Hano, I clearly have a lot more work to do before I'm free of it entirely.

Are you ready to do the work?

Nah. He's too weak and stupid.

What work?

See?

Matani punched his right fist into the palm of his left hand, determined to ignore his fears and clashing thoughts.

You're wrong. I am ready. Whatever it takes.

Then he stood and, albeit nervously, took hold of the steering oar.

The instant Hano stepped away, Matani felt the immense weight of *Mano'nahu* in his hands, and the great responsibility for its passengers and all the souls following behind them. "Okay," he said apprehensively. "Which way do I go?"

Hano reached out and gently squeezed the crown of Matani's head, instantly calming the distracting thoughts bouncing around inside his mind. "The questions we ask ourselves are more important than we realize. Always be specific, especially when setting a course for your destination."

Words are spells.

"How do I find my way to O'ahu?"

Satisfied, Hano nodded and pointed at the sky. "The course is south of east on the path of that bluish-white star up there called Hiti'aumoana."

Matani held his hand to the sky, well aware it was shaking with eagerness. And perhaps a little fear, too. Aiming his fingers to Hiti'aumoana, he visualized its path down to where his thumb touched the southeastern horizon. "Is it there?"

"Only one way to find out," Hano said. "Like my tūtū says, the gods put our greatest lessons behind fear."

At the same time, both Hano and Matani heard someone stirring in the darkness.

It was Pui, blinking in disbelief at seeing Matani manning the steering sweep. "Is that—?"

"You're dreaming," Hano interrupted. "Go back to sleep."

Pui nodded obediently and closed his eyes, returning his smiling face to Imo's shoulder.

Matani shared a quiet grin with Hano, immediately replaced by a look of concern "Wait, will you tell me if I'm going in the wrong direction?"

"Maybe." Hano shrugged. "Just pay attention to the signs. If they get confusing, don't give up. Dig down deep and find the confidence in yourself to stay the course."

Is he telling me I'm going the wrong way already?!

Of course he is! If you follow the wrong star, you'll end up lost at sea like in that story about Humu and his sons!

"Conquer those negative thoughts," Hano said with conviction. "Don't let them conquer you."

Matani froze, staring fearfully across the intimidating expanse of the sea. Quickly losing confidence, he searched the sky for Hiti'aumoana again, found it, then traced its arc several times over to make sure *Mano'nahu*'s twin bows were aimed for the correct spot on the horizon.

That was when he noticed something.

Wait, what is that?

Nothing. Just a bunch of clouds.

There were clouds, yes. But something inside Matani told him they weren't just *a bunch of clouds*. That there was, in fact, a subtle difference about them.

"Do you see that?" he asked tentatively.

"Seeing what I see is easy," Hano told him. "It's feeling what I feel that's hard."

The words only made Matani even less confident. "Well, I feel like those clouds on the horizon—" Matani stopped, thinking that maybe his eyes were playing tricks on him.

That's right. Keep your mouth shut. You don't know what you're talking about.

"Stop trying so hard," Hano said in a gentle whisper "When you're on the hunt for the island, trust in your instincts . . . and allow for a little bit of magic."

My instincts are horrible, and I don't believe in magic.

Are you sure?

Of course he's sure!

It's okay, Matani. Tell him what you see.

No! I'm warning you, Stone Boy! Don't tell him anything!

"Those clouds," Matani whispered. "They aren't moving like the others. It's like they're stuck."

"Go on," was all Hano said.

Squinting through the inky darkness, Matani finally saw the distant peak of a mountain sticking up from the lighter coloring of clouds.

"Is that . . .? I mean, can you . . .? It seems impossible, but I think I see it!" he exclaimed, pointing vigorously.

"You think? Or you know?"

"I see it! I definitely see land!"

"Congratulations, you've found O'ahu," Hano said with little fanfare. "Now take us there."

Finally sure he was going the right way, Matani pushed the steering oar with confidence, experiencing *Mano'nahu*'s true power as it rotated the entire sea and sky at his command. He struggled with the interplay of her twin sails with the wind and waves for a bit, but eventually, he framed the stuck clouds between the two shark heads.

Matani looked at Hano, exhaling with immense relief.

Hano chuckled. "You okay?"

"Everything's pono," Matani said, smiling. "But now I actually feel a little sad because finding the island means the voyage is coming to an end."

"There will always be new islands to pull from the sea," Hano said reassuringly. "What's important is knowing that if you're no different at the end of your journey than you were at the beginning, then it wasn't a very good journey."

"You have no idea—" Matani began, only to be interrupted by Hano raising his hand.

"Get some sleep, Vatua. The new sun will bring a busy day."

Knowing better than to question Hano, Matani returned the steering oar of *Mano'nahu* to its rightful owner and walked quietly back to where he'd awoken.

Awoken. Yes.

Wrapping himself back up tightly in his smelly old blanket, Matani sat and watched O'ahu slowly enlarge on the horizon as he sifted through his thoughts. Entranced by the quiet, vast, and twinkling stars above, he wondered where following any one of them might lead.

So many choices.

Too many.

Limitless, really.

Yes, but now I know that where a star sets on the horizon is as important as where it rises.

Floating between infinite realms of sea and stars—and several moons, too—Matani felt content and at one with the universe. If he paid attention to the signs, listened to his gut, didn't give up, and allowed for a little bit of magic, he'd eventually find his destination out there. Somewhere.

Breathing slow and deep, Matani nodded with cautious optimism, smiling a navigator's smile.

✦ CHAPTER 8 ✦

Matani awoke to find that the rich, dark, twinkling ceiling of lights he'd fallen asleep under had been replaced by the soft, incandescent blue of predawn. Still wrapped in his musty blanket, its smell of old earth and dampness now oddly comforting, he watched silently as the brightening atmosphere extinguished the last few remaining stars, one by one.

Here and here.

A few more there.

Then gone.

Sitting up as four white birds flew overhead, Matani now understood that the birds were going out to their morning feeding grounds. Much like the guiding rotation of stars across the sky last night, he traced their flight path from the direction they'd come, where he easily found a grainy, faded-blue haze of land outlined by luminous gradients of orange and red on the horizon.

Watching the far-off island slowly rise from the swells, more and more details appeared with every passing moment until the briny, salty air he'd grown accustomed to was suddenly permeated by wisps of earth, pine, and flowers.

He inhaled the fragrant air deeply, then exhaled the island's name. "O'ahu."

As the first glowing sliver of sunlight breached the dark-blue line that connected sea and sky, it wasn't long before an entirely new and unfamiliar island landscape loomed off *Mano'nahu's* bow.

I wonder what new experiences I'll have there.

Have you forgotten the evil Hunumaniani warned Hano about?

Several caged roosters sounded off abrasive greetings to the breaking shadows of a new day, the ill-timed omen sending a cold shudder down Matani's spine. Aware of movement to his right, he looked over and saw Tari'i awake and seated on his plank with a calabash in his lap, sprinkling water from it onto the waves rushing underneath.

"Another prayer?" Matani whispered.

"An offering." Tari'i smiled, his face aimed at the rising sun. "A gift of fresh water blessed by Supreme High Priest Hunumaniani for Ta'aroa, showing him gratitude for our fleet's safe arrival."

Thinking of his conversation with Hano, Matani was interested in Tari'i's perspective on the differences between spirituality and religion. "Do you believe gods watch over us?"

"Yes, but they only hear us if we acknowledge them with spiritual offerings," Tari'i said with sincere devotion, replacing the lid on his calabash.

"But I've given offerings before and bad things still happened."

"I think, maybe, these are opportunities meant to test our character and faith."

Matani nodded out of respect, but his expression was reserved. "I guess I've just never had a defining experience that makes me believe supernatural things exist."

Tari'i's gaze wandered in thought for a moment. "It's not so much about believing in supernatural things as it is understanding them. In my experience, people fear things they don't understand."

Matani's brow wrinkled. "Fear of what, though?"

"The truth," Tari'i said with an eerie tone. "We are physical beings living in a spiritual universe governed by spiritual laws. And for me, once I opened that sacred door, everything I thought I believed or didn't believe got turned upside down."

"Why?" Matani asked. "What happened after you opened it?"

"I knew I could never go back to my old way of thinking."

Matani couldn't deny the subtle sparks of curiosity detonating somewhere deep inside him. "So, which way are we supposed to understand? Religion or spirituality?"

"That's just it. Religion and spirituality aren't separate at all," Tari'i replied. "And neither are the natural and supernatural worlds. Everything is happening at the same time. Gods, spirits, nature, and humans—when all are conscious, connected, and pono, good mana flows."

Pui popped his head up over the canoe house, having apparently been listening. "You know, I only found out recently that these so-called gods are actually real people from a long time ago."

"Well, of course they are," said Tari'i. "Remembering our ancestors is how we show respect for what their deeds teach us."

"But if that's true, then who really created all this?" Pui asked, opening his arms to the world of sea and sky around them.

"I believe it was our esteemed ancestors, Tane, Tū, Ta'aroa, and Ro'o," Tari'i replied. "But in their ascended spirit forms."

Pui grunted loudly, stretching his waking body. "Well, when I'm out in the middle of the ocean like this, my gut tells me there's something else out there. Something so big and powerful, it's beyond comprehension." Bending to one side, several bones finally popped in his lower back. "People see what they want, or what they can make sense of, but in the end, I think we're all tapping into the same source. Everyone just calls it by different names."

Tari'i beamed with delight. "Pui, I didn't know you had such deep thoughts!"

"Because I spend too much time around you and Hano!" Pui snorted, moving to the back of the canoe. "Always making me think!"

"Glad you're all enjoying yourselves while my canoe is dragging!" Hano interrupted from the navigator's seat.

"No troubles!" Matani shouted back, immediately jumping into action. He gathered up his bailing gourd and, with his newly experienced eye, quickly spotted the heavier hull and jumped in to scoop out water that had collected there during the night.

Bringing a calabash of fresh water to Hano, Pui suddenly stopped with confused recollection. "Hey, I think I had a dream you let someone else steer *Mano'nahu*. Funny, yeah?"

"Not one bit," Hano said flatly, then shot Matani a savvy wink.

By midmorning, the rest of the fleet had tightened their formation around *Mano'nahu* as they made their way on a northern course parallel to O'ahu's eastern coastline. Imo was the last to wake, and his first task was to heat up coconut husks in the cooking box and prepare thick slices of dried banana, sweet potato, and seabird eggs.

"Finished!" Timoa shouted from his usual spot in the rear left hull.

Everyone looked over to see the typically stoic warrior with a grin on his face, proudly holding up the long-awaited result of his secret carving project.

"What is it?" Pui asked bluntly, trying to squint the object into focus.

"It's a shark!" Timoa answered indignantly.

Pui voiced a wild laugh. "Looks more like a dog's penis!"

Timoa studied his woodworking endeavor with a discerning eye, rotating it this way and that, then he looked up and saw his fellow warriors choking on their stifled amusement.

"Bah!" he spat angrily, flinging his sculpture into the waves.

"Well, so much for that hobby!" Pui remarked, setting off a barrage of cackles at Timoa's expense.

Seeing Matani trying to wrangle his own smile, Timoa banged the hull with his fist.

"Wipe that grin off your face before I do it for you!"

Matani returned to bailing, mumbling under his breath, "Only if you wipe the ugly off your face first."

"What did you say to me, you little rat?" Timoa shouted.

"Nothing," Matani said, hiding his smile.

It wasn't long before the island of Oʻahu loomed overhead, capturing the entire fleet in its wind shadow. The going was hot and slow for a while as *Manoʻnahu* led the fleet up and around the northwestern tip of the island, coming up on a dramatic peninsula covered with lava rocks and boulders.

"Kaʻena Point," Hano announced, his pronunciation odd-sounding to Matani.

Manoʻnahu's position at sea offered a simultaneous view of the northern and southern coastlines of Oʻahu, with a breathtaking spectacle of waves coming in from two different directions on either side of the rocky point.

A mysterious shiver raced up and down Matani's spine. "What is this place?"

"The westernmost tip of Oʻahu," Tariʻi answered, pointing. "Locals call it the *Leaping Place of Souls*."

"Why?" Matani asked.

"Because they believe this is where the dead jump into the spirit world to meet their ancestors," Tariʻi said. "Every island has a place like this. Tauaiʻi's is the *Falls of Rīhuʻe*."

Matani swallowed nervously as he searched the desolate landscape for any sign of ghosts or spirits. Seeing none, he didn't know whether to be relieved or disappointed.

More stories.

Soon, the fleet hit the trades in full force, riding winter waves the size of great blue mountains. A powerful wind drove the canoes past a long stretch of rocky terrain that appeared to shiver and glow in the morning heat. One of the fleet's twin-hulled vessels powered by only one sail was coming up fast on the windward side of *Mano'nahu*. With a crew of five strong-backed paddlers in each hull furiously pumping their oars in the water, its navigator stood up on the vessel's narrow deck, waving to get Hano's attention.

"You sea turtles wanna race?!"

"Paddles versus sails!" Hano shouted back.

The race was on.

Clipping along at a good speed, the hulls of both canoes bounced and crashed on the waves, sending great, sparkling arcs of water across their bows.

Seeing his challenger's canoe coming up fast alongside them, Hano tightened his grip on the steering oar. "Get ready to pull those sails in when I tell you!"

"I'll do one!" Matani shouted back, dropping his bailing gourd as he eagerly leaped from the hull, beating Pui to the rear mast.

"Oh, someone's getting cocky!" Pui laughed.

"Let him!" Hano ordered.

Pui threw up both hands and stepped back with a smile. "She's all yours!"

Tari'i locked eyes with Matani. "Ready?"

"Ready!" Matani shouted back, coiling the sail's rigging in one hand.

Hano waited patiently until the rival paddlers made their move to pass. "Now!"

Off Tari'i's cue, Matani pulled in his line at the exact same time he did, allowing both sails to grab hold of the veering wind. *Mano'nahu* sprinted forward, its left hull flying high on the water as she kept the lead and stretched it further along an inshore route.

"Look who's the turtle now!" Hano jibed, easily gliding ahead of their opponents. "So much for you knobs and your paddles!"

The crew returned their own gestures, stroking imaginary penises.

"What you give us, we return to you!" Hano laughed as Pui and Imo joined him in making their own offensive enactments.

Passing a large manmade fishpond, the rocky coastline turned to undulating sand dunes, populated with flocks of albatross, many nesting out in the open on freshly laid eggs. Several could be seen among them performing fidgety dances, attempting to attract mates.

"Timoa!" Pui yelled, dropping down into the opposite hull. "You dance like those birds, maybe you get a girl, too, yeah?"

"Maybe shut your mouth!" Timoa barked.

Matani watched rolling dunes end against a black lava cliff that shot straight up into the sky, unfazed by waves exploding in white sheets against it. On the other side of the cliff, three tide pools came into view, with dozens of people bathing in them. Noticing the enormous fleet, several began waving excitedly, offering shouts of welcome.

"Here we go," Hano mumbled to himself. "Vatua, get our capes and helmets!"

Matani raced over to the canoe house and rummaged about inside before returning with separate stacks of apparel. Watching them don their shark-tooth necklaces and sharkskin outfits, transforming into the Shark Warriors, Matani noticed a subtle change in each of their demeanors. For the first time, he couldn't help but notice how obvious it was that they were putting on costumes, as if getting ready for a performance.

Is life really just a big story? If so, who came up with the narrative? Who created all the characters and decided their roles? And what if I want to write a different one?

"Warriors, I have something important to tell you," Hano said with a quiet forcefulness, letting everyone know he meant business. Once everyone had gathered around with their full attention, he made a point to look each of them straight in the eyes. "Before we left home, Supreme High Priest Hunumaniani warned me of an evil somewhere on this island. He didn't know what form it would take or exactly where it would be, but it seems we're destined to cross paths with it."

"So, we bring our weapons, yeah?" Imo asked, unfazed.

"Rope belts only," Hano said. "We must be careful not to disrespect Ro'o during this time of peace if we want him on our side."

The warriors returned a sober nod and dispersed, knowing not to question him further.

Suddenly full of apprehension about their arrival, Matani lowered his voice to a whisper. "Hano, do you think I have something to do with—?"

"Yes," Hano said, cutting him off with a sharp nod. "I just don't know how, yet."

Pui handed out several lengths of rope, which the Shark Warriors tied around the waists of their loincloths before dropping into their hull positions.

"Get ready," Imo said as they approached a notch in the coastline.

Leaving the open and wild sea behind, Hano and the other warriors angled *Mano'nahu* across rolling breakers into calmer gradient shades of blue until she was gliding across crystal-clear turquoise waters. Rounding groves of palm trees, a gorgeous bay seemed to magically appear before them, teeming with thousands of people spread across a lush, deep valley cutting inland from the sea.

"There are more people than trees!" Matani shouted, staring incredulously at the multitudes of bodies swarming the bay. "How does the island not tilt under the weight of them all?"

"Welcome to Waimea!" Pui sang, followed by many voices across the fleet behind them calling out preparations for landfall, then turned to Matani. "It means *reddish waters*."

Scanning the beach, Matani spotted a rusty-red river making its way from a lush green valley down to the ocean. "How many times have you been here?"

"It's been a while, but we used to come several times a year for one celebration or another," Imo told him.

Every crew in the fleet reveled in the singing and laughter that danced lightly on the air as they passed a monstrous lava rock formation lodged in the bay. To Matani, it resembled a gigantic petrified whale that might've fallen from the heavens. Hundreds of people were cliff-diving off the very top, exploding in great white splashes of water below.

"I think they should call that rock the Leaping Place of Souls," Matani joked, but he was also kind of serious. "How is no one getting hurt doing that?"

"Oh, many do," Imo said humorlessly.

Sounds of celebration and smells of roasted delicacies filled the tropical air. Matani saw even more people scattered throughout the surrounding hills and rocks beyond the bay. Others were perched on rooftops, hanging off tree limbs, or cramming the bay beyond capacity with their bodies. And thousands of canoes—in which they'd all come from across the entire island chain—covered the entire beach.

"Doesn't look to me like there's anything evil going on here," said Pui.

"And one isn't stung by a camouflaged scorpionfish until they step on it," Hano said, maneuvering *Mano'nahu* past crowds of people standing knee-deep in the surf, smiling and waving. Amid the sustained roar of humanity, a chorus of voices could be heard chanting, "*Mano'nahu, Mano'nahu!*" as children climbed onto parents' shoulders to get a better look at the famed Shark Warriors.

"Coming through!" Tari'i warned, as they glided past clumps of bodies surrounding the Tauaian fleet on all sides.

"*Lonoimakahiki!*" cheered two brave men climbing aboard Mano'nahu, a celebratory word meaning *Lono in the time of Makahiki.*

Without breaking a sweat, Imo grabbed each of them by their hair and shoved them overboard. "Lonoimakahiki!" he replied, waving to them.

Matani looked down and saw the two men congratulating each other, not offended in the least; they would likely brag about their brief interaction with Imo the Giant for years to come.

Another older man tried to climb aboard to do the same, but Timoa popped him in the face with the blade of his paddle, knocking him backward into the water. He came up with a bloody nose and broken tooth, laughing hysterically.

Timoa looked down at him with a viciously pleased grin. "Lonoimakahiki!"

After joining Pui to close the sails, Tari'i brought out his conch shell and blew it three times, officially announcing the arrival of the Tauaian fleet. "Blessings to gods and ancestors for bringing us safely to O'ahu!"

Hano waved at Matani to get his attention. "Vatua, get my father's gift for Po'omanu." Then he leaped off the canoe. "The rest of you get down here and help me push her ashore!"

Not wanting to be alone anywhere on this strange island for even a single moment, Matani raced over to the canoe house, quickly gathered up the feather cloak, then made a running jump off the canoe. A blinding pain exploded up both shins the moment he hit steady ground, causing him to drop the feather cloak.

With *Manoʻnahu* successfully beached, Pui looked over and saw Matani writhing in agony. "Don't tell me you're landsick now?"

"Better not puke on that cloak again," Hano warned, helping Matani onto his feet with one hand while picking up the feather cloak in the other. "Listen, I know we talked about a lot of stuff last night." He paused, handing Matani the cloak, then curled one edge of his mouth into a smirk. "But the truth is, nobody really knows anything. Everyone is just guessing their way through life. Including me."

Stunned by this revelation, Matani stood speechless as Hano ruffled his hair, smiled, then turned to address the rest of the fleet.

"Tauaian warriors! Let's get these offerings unloaded and over to the border idol!"

Barely turning to walk up the beach, Hano was approached by two midlevel chiefs, clearly eager to speak with him.

The first one, with heavy brows, appeared desperate and nervous. "Hano, blessed be the gods you're here. I am Kaleo, and this is my cousin, Hakau," he said, gesturing to the slightly older man beside him. "We are chiefs from Maui, of the ancestral line of Olowalu."

"Anoʻai," Hano greeted them, his expression more curious than annoyed. "Is there a problem?"

"See for yourself," Kaleo said, motioning to the crowded beach. "Notice anything strange?"

Hano studied the scene until something registered. "Only highborns," he said, disquieted. "Where are all the commoners?"

"We've heard that droves of them went insane with thirst and hunger from a recent drought on this island," said Hakau. "Others are said to have poisoned themselves."

"And since the rise of the winter moon, hundreds more have been sacrificed by Poʻomanu," Kaleo added somberly.

"Hundreds?!" Matani blurted in disbelief.

Hakau nodded, his eyes darting suspiciously to anyone who walked past them. "Ruling Chief Poʻomanu blames them for the poor harvest this year and has been trying to appease the gods with an unreasonable number of human sacrifices."

"As if there's a reasonable number," Matani muttered to himself.

"Yet he continues to indulge in feasts and debauchery," Kaleo added in a voice only a step above a whisper.

Hakau looked nervously around. "Have you heard how his cousins who controlled Ko'olaupoko, Kona, and 'Ewa, mysteriously died in the past year?"

"All three?" Hano asked, a little impatiently. "How?"

"Some say it was the bidding of dark magic procured by Po'omanu," Kaleo said ominously, then snapped his mouth shut as two high-level chiefs approached.

Hano immediately recognized them as Kaihikapu and Ohikimakaloa, brothers of Po'omanu and principal chiefs on O'ahu. Both were dressed in red-and-black feather ensembles. Kaihikapu had the more common, short-haired appearance, while Ohikimakaloa was distinguished by a mane-like crest over the center of his crown, with long grayish locks reaching down to his shoulders. Unnerved by their approach, the two Maui chiefs turned hastily and shuffled away.

"Old friend," said Ohikimakaloa, his strong, intense face offset by kind brown eyes. "A welcome reunion!"

"It's been nearly two turns of the season," Hano realized as he said the words. "Apologies for not arriving sooner. It seems Ro'o had other plans for our journey."

"Knowing you, I'm sure the unexpected obstacle was a welcome adventure," said Kaihikapu, grabbing Hano's shoulder and touching noses with him. "Far too long, old friend."

"And many gray hairs, it seems!" Hano joked.

Ohikimakaloa nodded dourly. "Yes, well, this has been a rather trying year."

Kaihikapu shot an alarmed glance at his brother. "But certainly no more challenging than managing any other island," he interrupted, producing a feigned smile for Hano's benefit. "As the son of a ruling chief, I'm sure you understand the complexities of leadership?"

"All too well," Hano admitted, gesturing to his own chiefs, who had formed a human chain to unload cargo from the canoes. "Upon hearing your needs, my father didn't hesitate to share the abundance of Taua'i."

Kaihikapu nodded gratefully. "Ruling Chief Vahanui's generosity is beyond appreciation."

"Yes," Ohikimakaloa agreed. "How can we ever repay you?"

"Nothing more than an opportunity to meet with your esteemed brother," Hano answered.

The sibling chiefs shared a glance riddled with embarrassment.

"Well, he's very busy these days," came Kaihikapu's flimsy excuse.

"I understand," Hano said, "but in addition to these plentiful offerings, my father has also sent a most special gift for Po'omanu."

Matani stepped forward, holding the neatly folded red feather cloak.

Kaihikapu's eyes lit up as he reached for the cloak. "Oh, we would be happy to give this to him oursel—"

Hano pulled Matani backward, keeping the cloak just out of reach. "Yes, well, my father specifically asked that I hand it directly to him."

Seeing no room for negotiation, both brothers finally blinked, followed by an uncomfortable silence until Ohikimakaloa spoke. "Of course. We'll take you to see him now."

Hano gave Matani a subtle but pleased smirk as they all followed the O'ahu chiefs through the crowd along the beach, past smoldering remnants of bonfires, evidently from their own water splashing ceremony the night before. Reminded of Heiana and the real Vatua, and what may or may not have transpired between them last night, Matani maneuvered his thoughts to the strange inflections he was hearing in the O'ahu language. First, the odd pronunciation of Ka'ena Point. And then how the chief's names also sounded strange. On Taua'i, they would be called *Taihitapu* and *Ohitimataroa*.

"They talk funny here," Matani whispered to Pui.

Pui chuckled. "Only the people of Taua'i and Ni'ihau use the old language. Everyone else uses the *K* sound instead of *T*, and the *L* sound instead of *R*."

"Why is that?" Matani asked, "if we all came from Tahiti?"

"Who knows?" Pui shrugged. "Maybe because Taua'i and Ni'ihau are farther away. Listen, I've been to all the islands and many of the traditional Tahitian customs have developed differently on each one."

Making their way up a landscaped path into the foothills of Waimea, Matani couldn't help but notice how each of the Shark Warriors walked with an unhurried, graceful, and dignified gait—very much in contrast to the nervous temperaments of those who lived on the island. It wasn't long before they came across a crowd of off-island chiefs—both men and women—wanting to catch a glimpse of their procession, but the onlookers quickly retreated as they neared the heavily guarded walls of the royal compound. This was when Matani first realized that tattooing appeared to be a solely Tauaian trait. He saw no one here with any such bodily decorations as the Shark Warriors or others back home.

Ohikimakaloa waved them all past four unsmiling guards at the entrance, leading the way past shaded walks lined with flowering trees of every kind. It was difficult to ignore that not one of them bore a single fruit. Even the animals appeared emaciated, lying listlessly in the shadows. Even the sultry morning air itself carried a defiling, sour scent.

"Ro'o is very upset with this island," Tari'i whispered to the others, as they arrived before an impressive mansion of wood and thatch.

The O'ahu chiefs led them past another guarded entryway into a cool, high-ceilinged room with a perimeter of woven grass walls and finely hewn pillars of wood. The centerpiece of this impressive interior was Ruling Chief Po'omanu himself. He was stretched out on a couch of mats, gazing with dreamy pleasure at four female attendants, who were giving him an exceedingly thorough and vigorous full-body massage. Normally, the physique of someone at such a height of nobility would be large and muscular, but this ruling chief was a shockingly cadaverous-looking figure.

As the masseuses rubbed, kneaded, pressed, thumped, and pulled the frail chief's body, a number of personal attendants of lesser nobility stood at the ready to accommodate his every pampering need. Beside the ruling chief were his head steward and the royal staff bearer, who was slowly waving a tuft of painted plumes—more to stave off the clouds of flies than anything else. There was even a spittoon bearer seated at a respectful distance behind them, among three women Matani assumed were the ruling chief's wives.

It was an upper-class picture of absolute power and opulence, to say the least.

Despite Ohikimakaloa's ginger approach, Po'omanu startled with a grunt, knocking over a bowl of scented oils. "Where am I?"

Ohikimakaloa seemed embarrassed by the outburst as he knelt beside his brother and spoke, making the ruling chief raise both his arms expectantly. The massage specialists quickly backed away as two attendants rushed forward to help their leader into a seated position. A bright, if crooked, smile formed under unhealthily yellow eyes that were bloodshot and barely able to focus.

"Is he sick?" Matani asked Pui in a low voice.

Pui shook his head in disgust. "Drunk."

Hano stepped forward, bowing respectfully. "Ruling Chief Po'omanu, we thank you for your chiefdom's hospitality during this holiday of peace and prosperity."

"Prosperity?" Po'omanu spat, fresh perspiration forming on his brow. "I'm sure you've seen the drivel my lazy commoners have produced this year. What I wouldn't *kill* to have as bountiful an island as yours—"

Ohikimakaloa quickly jumped in. "Great One, Ruling Chief Vahanui has delivered us an entire fleet of canoes generously filled with provisions."

"Along with a most special gift from my father," Hano added, motioning to Matani, who came forward to display the handmade cloak. "Made by his own personal cape maker, just for you."

Moving closer to Po'omanu, Matani forced himself to keep his emotions neutral upon noticing that the entire surface of the chief's body was covered with a white, leprous scurf—clearly the effects of an overindulgence in 'ava.

Po'omanu's mouth formed a perfect O, as his boney fingers twiddled in the air, reaching up for the beautiful red cloak. "My, my, my! Even your birds have brighter feathers than ours. Dress me in it this instant!"

Several attendants graciously took the cloak from Matani and moved into position around the feeble chief, fastening the collar around his scrawny neck.

"What do you think?" Ruling Chief Po'omanu asked, rather innocently. "Would I make a good Kauaian high chief?"

Hano's gaze hardened. "Since you ask such a curious question, I have one of my own. Are you planning to invade our island after the peaceful season is over?"

Kaihikapu stepped between Hano and the ruling chief, his eyes dark with anger. "Sheathe your words, Hano! Others have been slain for less."

While Hano remained calm, the chests of the other Shark Warriors inflated defensively behind him. Ruling Chief Po'omanu's eyes were blank as one of his wives whispered something to him from the shadows behind, her face and body hidden under a hooded robe.

"Yes, yes," he muttered, clumsily adjusting his position so he could clap his hands. "Enough talking. Let's celebrate!"

With an imperious gesture, the ruling chief summoned four young male attendants, each directing the guests to be seated on piles of fine mats covering the open space at the center of the room. Not a moment later, a parade of servants brought out countless platters of steaming food wrapped in leaves.

"Don't throw up now," Hano warned Matani, giving him a playful nudge.

Off to the side, an elder woman Matani recognized as a hula teacher clapped her hands, summoning a troupe of musicians, their nervous faces glistening with sweat. After a nod from their teacher, the musicians began rhythmically slapping gourds with their hands and tapping them on the ground, calling forth sixty female *hula* dancers adorned with matching grass skirts, tutuʻi nut accessories, and floral headpieces.

The dancers took center stage, and their soft, beautiful voices instantly took command of the room. Each one stood poised and practiced, gliding and swaying to the beat of the drums, counterbalancing each step on the balls of their feet.

Native shell leis and anklets of the hula maidens shook in perfect rhythm to the music as their bodies magically transformed into flying birds, swimming fish, falling rain, thunderous clouds—and even Roʻo himself.

Matani's attention was immediately captivated by one particular dancer with long black hair, and he found himself smitten. Her exposed stomach, athletically firm and flat, combined with the circular rotation of her hips and the graceful, hypnotic motion of her delicate hands, stirred feelings of attraction that he hadn't felt since—

Imo elbowed Matani in the ribs. "Your eyes gonna pop out your skull if you keep staring at her like that," he whispered.

Matani looked away, further embarrassed by huge grins from Pui and Tariʻi, startled when he looked back to find the gorgeous hula girl looking right at him. Still, he couldn't find it in him to move his eyes, utterly enraptured by her graceful movements as she crouched and spun with practiced precision, her sleek, muscular legs not missing a single step. With every spectator captivated, a light wind entered the house, flickering the torch flames that surrounded the interior's perimeter, adding a layer of magic to the performance.

With the grace and precision of a heavenly breeze, the hula dancers enacted the ancient tale of a frugal and malevolent chief who brought destruction and strife to his land. With each movement, the highly skilled artists conveyed deep symbolic meaning, their gestures and steps a vivid depiction of the story unfolding before the audience's eyes. The soft features of their faces mirrored the suffering and sorrow that gripped the land as the chief gathered all the food on the island in a carrying net and flung it into the sky.

As the performance continued, the enchanting movements of each performer grew more frenzied and intense, their shapely hips swaying in time with the pounding of the drums. They artfully embodied the arrival of a brave rat, whose delicate movements were depicted with skill and precision as he climbed up the tallest mountain and leaped onto a rainbow.

Reaching the stars tangled in the carrying net, the dancers conveyed the rat's determination with each bite that loosened the ropes until the food finally rained down all over the land. The graceful motions of the dancers conveyed a sense of joy and celebration, their every move a vivid depiction of the brave rat's triumphant victory over putting an end to the suffering.

Then came a conclusive pound of the drums, freezing the dancers in place like beautifully carven idols. The astonished silence that followed was deafening as everyone in the room held their breath, reluctant to break the spell that had been cast. As one, the spectators lifted to their feet, cheering and applauding the beauty and power of the performance, a powerful reminder of the strength of determination and hope in the face of adversity. Even Ruling Chief Po'omanu attempted to sit upright, a feat that required the assistance of three attendants. He clapped and smiled approvingly at the hula master. "Well done!"

Realizing that an end had come to the feasting and entertainment, Hano stood quickly, "Supreme Ruler, your hospitality has refreshed our spirits."

Po'omanu nodded and smiled. "Kaihikapu, arrange quarters for our fine visitors in my court. They've had a long journey and need good rest!"

Kaihikapu smiled bitterly. "It shall be done."

Hano nodded respectfully. "Before I leave, may we share a moment of words—"

Once again, the mysterious third wife interrupted, whispering something to her husband from the shadows.

"Ah, yes!" Po'omanu blurted. "You're all invited to a special celebration at Waimea Falls this evening. Warriors and chiefs from every island will be there!"

"We look forward to it," Hano said, unsettled by the rude interruption. "In the meantime, may we speak more about—"

Before Hano could finish, the third wife whispered again.

"Yes, everyone out!" Po'omanu seemed to repeat mechanically. "It's been a long day, and I must rest."

Taken aback, Hano could only nod as guards quickly ushered him out, along with all the other visitors. Servants rushed over to pick up stray hairs that had fallen around the ruling chief so they could be buried in secrecy, preventing them from being used in sorcery. By the time Matani and the Shark Warriors reached the doorway, attendants had already doused the torches and covered the windows in preparation for the ruling chief's nap.

Once outside the mansion, Pui spoke first. "Well, that was interesting."

"Yeah, Po'omanu's definitely up to something," Hano said. He turned to Imo, Pui, and Tari'i. "You three see if you hear of any unusually large amounts of supplies being gathered or weapons being built anywhere on the island. Timoa, I want you to keep an eye on Kaihikapu."

"Already on him," Timoa answered, quickly departing the group.

"Can I help?" Matani asked.

"Maybe you can find out something from the younger chiefs," Hano said. Noticing the hula girls passing by, he called them over with a debonair smile. "A most impressive performance, ladies!"

Giggling shyly, the hula dancers were clearly excited to be acknowledged by the venerable leader of the Shark Warriors.

"We're so glad you liked it," said the pretty girl with the wide nose.

In the daylight, Matani could see her eyes for the first time. Brown with gold flecks, his first thought was that they weren't as pretty as Heiana's. But they certainly conveyed a sexy playfulness.

"What's your name?" Hano asked.

"I'm Malela," she said, smiling shyly.

"Malela, meet Vatua! This is his first time on O'ahu."

Malela fluttered her brown eyes at Matani. "Oh, would you like me to show you around?"

Rendered speechless, Matani felt Hano grab him by the neck. "In case you've forgotten how conversations work: she speaks, you say something back, and so on."

"Oh, okay. Y-yes, I'd like me to sh-show you around," Matani stuttered awkwardly. "I mean you, me—"

"Just go," Hano laughed, giving him a gentle shove.

"This way, Vatua!" she giggled, grabbing Matani by the hand. "There's lots of fun things going on here today!"

Matani followed Malela, his heart a whirlwind of anticipation and unease, as they ventured hand in hand into the uncharted realms of this new and unexplored island, where every alluring step into the unknown felt like a leap into the extraordinary.

✦ CHAPTER 9 ✦

Still holding hands, Malela led Matani to the sprawling sports field down by the beach, where countless visiting chiefs were gathered. Merging with the crowd, Matani tightened his grip on her soft fingers, fearing that if they were separated, he might never see her again. Or worse, that the daunting horde of bodies might swallow him whole.

They passed under a tall, wooden pole with a crosspiece hung with white strips of bark cloth. Feather leis hanging from its crossframe fluttered in the breeze to attract game participants as well as spectators. Though of a slightly different design than he'd grown up with, Matani recognized *Akua Pa'ani*, the female god of sports, who presided over all Matari'i-hiti games. Or, as it was called on this strange new island, *Makahiki*.

All around the perimeter of the field, elders sat beneath the shade of palm trees on opposite sides of stone tables, engaged in games of strategy that used pieces of white coral on one side and black lava stones on the other. A large group of older chiefs rolled stone disks between two wooden stakes, while others threw banana stalks at targets. Some younger chiefs nearby were fiercely engaged in a competitive game of tug-of-war.

At the center of the field, the largest crowd by far had gathered around a bare-fist boxing match between two high-ranking chiefs, cheering with every punch thrown and every hit taken. Along the shoreline, highborn children ran up and down the golden sand, flying kites in the shapes of birds and fish. Older kids entertained each other with string figures or spun tutu'i nut tops. Beyond them, out past the breakers, more adventurous nobles rode wooden boards in the winter surf in friendly competition, racing to a buoy of coconuts anchored in the shallows.

Taking in the sights and sounds of this scary new world, Matani found himself comparing Malela to Heiana, the only girl he'd ever really known. Malela seemed to have a refreshing lightness about her that was easy to be around, and unlike with Heiana (in recent years, anyway), their conversation flowed easily. Holding her hand, the slight feeling of intimacy gave him a pang of guilt, but while he missed Heiana, he couldn't deny how exciting it felt to meet someone new.

"Up there is our temple of refuge, where we used to practice hula," Malela said, pointing to the eastern bluff above Waimea Bay, at the sprawling grounds of an impressive temple. The ruling chief's flags rippled in the wind just outside the oracle tower, its wrapping of white bark cloth reflecting the afternoon sun. "It's called *Pu'u o Mahuka Heiau*," she said, *Hill of Escape.* "Do you have places of refuge on Kaua'i?"

Matani couldn't help but laugh.

"What?" she asked, a confused wrinkle on her nose.

"Your accent," he said. "It's pronounced *Taua'i.*"

Malela looked surprised, then laughed. "Here on O'ahu, *you're* the one with the accent!"

Choosing not to argue the point, Matani asked, "Why don't you practice hula there anymore?"

Malela's eyes turned anxious. "Well, after High Priest Nanamaulu took up residence in the temple at the beginning of the summer, he placed a tabu on it and hasn't left since."

This surprised Matani. "Not even to perform rites for the new year?"

Malela shook her head. "Some say Nanamaulu tried to warn Po'omanu of his marauding ways, advising him to lead the people more peacefully or risk provoking the wrath of gods. But Po'omanu ignored him." Then she dropped her voice. "Almost everyone thinks Nanamaulu stays in the temple to separate himself from the ruling chief."

"That makes your hula dance about a rat saving the island from a tyrant really bold," Matani pointed out.

"It was," Malela whispered, impressed by his keen observation. "But our hula master knew Po'omanu would be much too arrogant and drunk to compare himself to that old story."

"When we first landed, someone told us Po'omanu has been sacrificing commoners every day," Matani mentioned with a more serious tone.

"Is that true?"

She bit her lip, as if trying to decide something. "Mostly healthy young men," she said, nodding dourly.

"How many are left?"

"I don't know," she replied. "Large groups went into hiding or fled to other islands."

Matani found it difficult to comprehend any possible reason for such appalling genocide, but he kept on the task at hand, thinking he might be on to information that could be useful to Hano. "Were these sacrifices the priest's idea?"

"Never," she answered in a much louder voice. "Nanamaulu has always been on the side of the people."

"Then who?" he asked.

"Many say Po'omanu's newest wife caused the rift between them."

"The one in the hooded robe?"

"Yes," Malela replied, looking around to see if anyone was listening. Then she whispered, "My hula master says she wears it to hide her skin."

"Is there something wrong with it?"

"Well, I haven't actually seen for myself," she said. "But they say it's darker than anyone's on the island."

"What island was she born on?"

"Oh, she wasn't born here," Malela said, leaning forward confidingly. "My hula master says some fisherman found her on the other side of the island one or two dry seasons ago, barely alive." Her face became strained, grim. "They say her right arm was missing. Chewed off—"

The words were no sooner spoken before Malela covered her mouth, as if realizing she'd said too much. Then she saw something that made her eyes widen with delight. "Ooh! You'll love this! Come on!"

Malela grabbed Matani's hand and pulled him to the beach, past a raucous crowd cheering on two roosters fighting inside a fenced corral. Before he could ask where she was taking him, Matani saw they were headed for the giant lava-whale he'd seen on his arrival into the bay.

The one all those deranged people were jumping off of, risking life and limb.

Considering how he would find Hano and tell him what he'd learned, the two of them were already stepping off the beach and onto the rock.

They climbed higher.

And higher.

And higher, still.

Until finally arriving at the end of a long line of more foolish people waiting to make the death-defying leap. Anxiety surged through Matani as he watched jumpers showing off with impressive skills. Some dove straight down while others turned one or two somersaults before hitting the water.

These people are crazy!

Matani glanced over at several younger children diving off a lower cleft in the rock. "Can we maybe try that one first?"

"Oh, don't be silly," she answered. "It's almost our turn!"

The line shrank quicker than Matani's courage could grow. He watched in horror as three more people leaped off the cliff, one after the other.

"We're next!" Malela giggled, pushing Matani ahead of her.

Nearly losing his balance, he clumsily grabbed her around the waist. "Hey, careful!"

Liking the feeling of his arms around her, Malela purred, "What fun would that be?"

As they inched forward, the sunbaked surface of the jagged lava underfoot made Matani's bones tingle. Arriving at the unnerving edge of the cliff, he looked down just as two people hit the water far, far below.

Feeling his heart pounding in his teeth, those soft fingers of hers found his again, followed by a single word. "Ready?"

Matani looked over into Malela's lovely brown eyes, mesmerized by their shimmering flecks of amber. "To die?"

She laughed out loud, then leaned forward and kissed his ear. "Don't overthink it. Just jump."

It was in that moment Matani knew he'd follow this girl anywhere. He nodded, and she flashed him a wink of encouragement. Together, they inched forward until all twenty of their toes were curled over the rocky edge.

With their fingers interlocked, both took a long, deep breath—then jumped.

Malela screamed with delight.

Matani screamed with terror.

Both plunged into the water.

It seemed an eternity before Matani could determine the outcome of his fate. Blinded by a rush of tiny bubbles fizzing up and down his body, Malela's hand found his again, but with a gentle tug this time, allowing him to reorient to the bright, liquid sky above. Feeling the air in his lungs nearly spent, he kicked his feet until he broke the surface, smiling.

The two bobbed up and down in the water, holding each other's gaze for a moment before Matani finally exploded with adrenaline.

"Woo! That was amazing!"

"Told you!"

"Let's go again!" Matani said with flaring eyes. This time, he was the one to take Malela's hand, pulling her from the water and back up onto that gloriously terrifying cliff.

There are plenty of cliffs on Taua'i. How come I've never jumped off one before?

Because you're too afraid to try anything new.

How many things have I missed out on because of fear?

A lot, probably. But at least you're still alive.

Maybe physically, but not spiritually!

After an exhausting rotation of climbing and jumping, Malela brought Matani to the west end of the beach, where fresh water filtered down through the sand on its way to the ocean. Realizing how thirsty he was, Matani drank voraciously from the stream until an absent glance into the crowd caused him to spit out a mouthful of water.

It was Timoa.

He was just a short distance away, talking intently with a group of high-ranking chiefs. It wasn't just his presence that set Matani off; there was a certain energy to Timoa's wild gesticulations that conveyed something similar to when the aloof warrior had first set his suspicious eyes on him.

"What?" Malela asked, seeing Matani's concerned expression. "What is it?"

Right then, Timoa glanced over at Matani and pointed, directing the gaze of the other chiefs. Matani quickly grabbed Malela by the wrist and dragged her over to a nearby grassy lawn, where several families were in the middle of playing long darts.

"Ooh, I love this game!" Malela squealed, claiming an empty lane of grass defined by a rectangular wooden frame.

"Ladies first," Matani murmured, nervously scanning the crowd.

She picked up a handful of darts made of the large, silvery flower tassels of mature sugarcane. "Okay, but what are we going to wager?"

"Oh, I don't really have anything—"

She just looked at him with that smile of hers. "You have lips, don't you?"

He blinked. "Well, yeah."

"Okay, then if I win, you have to kiss me!"

Instantly losing any and all concerns for Timoa, Matani turned. "What?"

"And I mean a good one!" she said, shaking a playful finger at him. "Not just a lame peck on the lips."

"Okay, fine," he laughed. "Deal."

Matani looked over the pile of darts and picked one that looked right, testing the weight of its earthen tip. With a sly smile, he stepped onto the thrower's mound and, with little effort, tossed the dart. It barely slid a few feet across the flattened grass, falling far short of its mark.

"Aw, too bad," Matani groaned with fake disappointment. "I lost!"

"Hey!" Malela shouted, pretending to be upset. "You did that on purpose!"

Both stood for a moment, staring into each other's eyes. And then that feeling came to Matani—that awful, terrible feeling that this was the moment that could very well ruin the entire day ... or make it the best one ever.

Uh oh. What was I thinking?

You remember what happened the last time you tried this, don't you?

Matani's mind took him back in time to the first kiss he'd ever attempted with Heiana, making him pause, wondering how Malela seemed so comfortable in the moment.

Conquer your mind; don't let it conquer you.

Sensing his hesitation, Malela interlocked her fingers with his. "It's okay," she whispered. "I'm nervous, too."

He exhaled uneasily. "Just jump, right?"

Malela nodded and smiled.

The two closed their eyes, letting their lips find each other—

"Who's this poi brain?" someone interrupted from behind, popping their fragile bubble of intimacy.

"Go away, Kahiko!" Malela shouted at a handsome and strapping chief coming toward them.

Although young, it was obvious from his short yellow-and-red feather cloak that he was a high-ranking chief. With a dull, familiar rage that reminded Matani of Uanini, he also sensed quite strongly that this arrogant highborn was more than just Malela's friend.

If he isn't her boyfriend already, he definitely wants to be.

Or used to be.

Five of Kahiko's friends came running up behind him, each one an equally healthy royal specimen, ready to offer assistance with whatever situation might arise.

"Why should I?" Kahiko laughed, his disdainful grin framing a wide gap between his two front teeth. He looked down at Matani and jabbed him with his finger. "You like playing baby games?"

"Sure," Matani said. "How about we all take turns kicking coconuts between that gap in your teeth?"

Everyone in earshot burst out with surprised laughter. Everyone except Kahiko. His grin was wiped clean by embarrassment.

"Don't do anything stupid," Malela warned. "Vatua is a Shark Warrior!"

"Shark Warrior?" Kahiko could all but hold in his laughter as he circled Matani, sizing him up. "This scrawny runt?"

Reminded of the warrior trainees, Matani felt dark emotions welling up inside, filling his tightening fists with years of bottled-up oppression once more. In the distance, dark clouds curled over the mountains.

Careful.

An unreasonable number of human sacrifices.

As if there's a reasonable number.

"If he's a Shark Warrior, why isn't he wearing sharkskin clothes?" Kahiko sneered. "Did he have an accident in them or something?"

"I'm still waiting for them to be made," was all Matani could think to say.

"Waiting for what?" Kahiko asked. "For you to get some muscles?"

Which, of course, sent his friends into hysterics.

Remember, they don't know you're a commoner.

"Leave us alone!" Malela protested.

"Us?" Kahiko jeered, poking Matani in the chest as his friends urged him on with laughter. "You think you're both a couple alrea—" Kahiko began, but his words were sheared off by Matani's knuckles smashing into his mouth.

The young chief fell backward onto the sand, his eyes registering a combination of surprise and disbelief. After a stunned moment, Kahiko slowly rose to his feet, spitting a gob of blood from his bleeding lip. "Well, maybe Shark Runt's got some teeth in him after all!" He grinned snidely, then lunged at Matani.

They hit the ground in a clatter of grunts, flying sand, and swinging fists. Kahiko rolled on top of Matani, punching him hard in the face. Matani was momentarily blinded by the pain but managed to grab Kahiko's head and slam it into the sand before both were up on their feet again, circling one another like rabid beasts. Matani touched a throbbing sensation on his cheek, seeing blood on his fingertips.

"Stop it!" Malela screamed in a trembling voice.

Startled by the intensity of her words, Matani blinked the ferocity from his eyes. As his blinding emotion faded, he found an awful look on Malela's face. He'd seen it before, and it made him nauseous. A few years back, he'd gotten into a scuffle with another farmer back home for one thing or another. While he couldn't even remember now what that thing was, he did remember that Heiana was there, and he'd never forgotten her awful expression. The same look of sheer disappointment that Malela wore now.

Here he stood again, feeling ugly inside.

Don't screw a good thing up with this one the way you did with Heiana!

While Matani had no idea what was developing between himself and Malela—whether it was something meaningful or just a fling, having never really experienced either—he found himself, once again, lost in the puzzlements of his own feelings when it came to women.

"How about some friendly competition?" Matani asked with forced civility, fumbling for a fresh handful of darts.

The narrow bone of a smile appeared on Kahiko's face. "Yeah, okay," he said bitterly, knocking the darts from Matani's hand. "But how about something more like that?" he countered, jerking his thumb at the sports field where a large crowd was gathering from all directions.

"What's going on there?" Matani asked.

"Kukini race," Kahiko said.

Matani knew the word as *tutini*, which typically meant *messenger* and referred to the ruling chief's couriers who underwent intense periods of training to build up levels of running speed and endurance unmatched by any other class. But in this case, the word was used to describe a seminal foot race that revolved heavily around excessive wagering. Considered the most revered sport of the season across all the islands, only highborns were allowed to compete. On Taua'i, this would have been a problem.

But not here.

Matani (aka Vatua, the highborn) touched his tongue to his upper lip and smiled at the opportunity to prove that this gap-toothed, obnoxious, overindulged brat—and anyone like him—wasn't any better than he was.

"Sure, I'm in," he said. "Let's prove who has better blood."

Kahiko flashed him a hostile smirk. "After you."

Somewhere behind him, Matani heard Malela's upset voice telling him he was crazy, but before he could reconsider, he realized he'd already arrived at the sports field. Only then did the harsh reality of his situation catch up to him. Any runner who entered the race would have likely been priming themselves for the competition for months, if not longer, undergoing a very strict diet and exercise routine. And here he had just stuffed himself with decadent foods fit for a ruling chief.

Malela shook Matani's arm. "You have no idea what you're doing! Kahiko is one of Po'omanu's fastest couriers! He's won this race three *Makahiki* in a row!"

"Maybe he's tired, then," Matani quipped, trying to hold on to whatever shred of confidence he had left.

By the time they reached center field, it seemed every living soul on O'ahu had assembled for the racing event of the season.

Malela gave Matani one last, desperate look. "It's not too late."

Her words seemed to convey more than just backing out of the race. She was giving him an ultimatum.

"I can't," was all he could say. "I gave my word."

Visibly hurt, Malela crossed her arms. "And what good is the word of a fool?"

Ouch.

"Clear the way! Clear the way!" All eyes followed the voice to see Kaihikapu, the ruling chief's brother, running devotedly at the front of an incoming procession. Excited cheers erupted as twenty royal guards and attendants arrived, widening a path through the crowd. Ruling Chief Po'omanu came into view, seated comfortably upon a wooden palanquin carried on the shoulders of four royal bearers drenched in sweat.

Kaihikapu waved his hands to get the attention of three royal servants carrying rolled-up mats. "Hurry up! Prepare the ground! Quickly now!" The attendants sprinted ahead and prepared the sand beneath the shade of a coconut tree with layer upon layer of woven mats, calabashes of fresh water, and, of course, several wooden jars of 'ava.

Matani couldn't hide his surprise. "What's he doing here?"

"That's what I've been trying to tell you!" Malela groaned, raising her hands in exasperation. "This race is a very big deal!"

The royal bearers arrived under the tree and carefully lowered the esteemed litter onto perfectly arranged mats. As Ruling Chief Po'omanu struggled to stand, glancing about with red-rimmed eyes, his reaching fingers were already being met by the awaiting hands of his attendants, who helped him disembark. As the court of attendants got the ruling chief settled, a stubby man—broad of shoulder and deep in the gut— appeared from the multitudes and stood beneath the god of sports. Matani recognized him as the officiator of the race by the bamboo trumpet he held in one hand and a wooden stick topped with a feather tuft in the other.

The officiator blew a solid note from his instrument, ostensibly quieting the pandemonium, but he still had to shout to be heard above the pervasive bellow of the crowd. "Welcome, honored visitors, to a Makahiki tradition on O'ahu! The rules are simple. Each runner will race to the fishpond in Haleiwa. There, each must catch a fish by any means possible. The first contestant to return with a fish for Ruling Chief Po'omanu wins!" Pausing for dramatic effect, he finished with, "Oh, I almost forgot. The fish must be alive!"

Fish?

Overwhelmed by all the people and noise, Matani looked around at the other competitors, noticing for the first time how each of them possessed various fishing paraphernalia—mostly fishhooks strung around their necks, but one had a small net stuffed in his loincloth, and another had a small basket trap slung over his shoulder.

"Looking for this?"

Matani looked toward the voice and found a sight for sore eyes. It was Pui, holding up the fishhook made of his father's bones.

"Oh, Pui, no," Matani said in disbelief. "I know how special this is to you."

"Don't worry, my father had many bones," Pui laughed, placing the hook around Matani's neck. "So, how'd you get involved in this race, anyway?"

"I did what Hano asked and made some new . . . friends," Matani said dryly, then his glance shifted.

Pui followed Matani's gaze to Malela, who was regarding them with narrowed eyes.

"Going well, I see?" Pui laughed.

"Not exactly," Matani answered thinly. "There's this other guy—"

"Say no more," Pui replied, waving it off. "I've gotten tangled in a few love triangles myself."

"Blessings, Pui, really," Matani said, appreciatively patting the hook below his neck. "You have no idea how much this means to me."

"No troubles!" Pui beamed.

The optimistic phrase brought a much-needed smile to Matani's face.

"Last call for contestants!" rang the officiator's cry. "Runners, line up!"

Matani shared a parting glance with Pui before taking a position third from the left of eight runners. On his right, a contestant focused on intense preparations, walking in circles on the balls of his feet. To his left was a skinny but incredibly muscular opponent.

"'Ano'ai," Matani said, smiling meekly. "I came from Taua'i with the Shark Warriors."

The runner regarded his attempt at name-dropping with an unimpressed smirk. "Maui," was all he offered, then turned away.

Completely surrounded by the eager audience, Matani heard fragments of people placing bets. Some used animals as collateral, others put up their homes or entire crops. He even heard one man trying to use his own wife.

But the most concerning thing was that almost everyone seemed to be betting on Kahiko. Waves of anxiety crashed over Matani, and he felt like he was drowning in a terrible predicament for which he could only blame himself.

"And what are we gonna bet, Shark Runt?" asked Kahiko as he shoved aside the runner from Maui to make room for himself.

Matani shrugged, confused. "Winning should be enough."

"Oh, I don't think so," Kahiko whispered darkly.

The officiator raised his wooden stick, its feather tip magically quieting the crowd to a dull rumble.

"It's settled, then!" Kahiko yelled, making sure everyone around them heard his words. "This runner from Kauaʻi and I have agreed to bet our bones on the outcome of this race!"

Matani opened his mouth to object, but it was too late.

The officiator dropped his wooden staff.

"Go!"

More bets changed hands even as the line of runners bolted across the beach. Right at the start, Kahiko rammed Matani hard enough to numb his right arm down to the wrist, adding a hateful glare that promised more where that came from.

And he wasn't the only one playing dirty. Matani saw how ferocious the other runners were, shoving, pushing, and elbowing each other to keep or claim that winning edge.

Racing into a lush green jungle through dusty shafts of sunlight, the roar of the crowd faded into softer sounds of birds and insects. The rising elevation quickly put a strain on the runners, evidenced by the amount of huffing and puffing. To conjure up his own fortitude, Matani imagined Uanini chasing him with his skull-smashing stone club. He adjusted quickly to the terrain, passing one runner with a noticeably bulbous butt but whose short, thick legs moved with impressive tirelessness.

Passing trees with vines and moss sagging from their branches, an earthen trail fed the runners onto the rough contours of a black lava cliff. Barely wide enough for one foot, Matani tried to ignore the deadly drop to his right. Scouting the way ahead, he witnessed Kahiko shove a runner out of his way, sending him flailing off the cliff to the beach below. He looked away, but couldn't unhear the distant, horror-stricken roar of the crowd.

The thin trail etched into the cliff widened before merging with a stretch of ground overgrown with ferns. Matani jumped over rotted logs, dodging and ducking low-hanging branches until the ground cover dropped into a muddy ravine, where he spotted a thin stream. A few runners used the slippery slope to their advantage by sliding on their feet or rumps to the bottom, then used branches and plants to pull their way up the other side to an area of even ground.

The runners eventually spread out, each carefully balancing energy with speed to work their way into the lead position, which was currently held by the runner from Maui.

But Kahiko was right behind him and closing fast.

While it was obvious that his competitors had undergone disciplined training for this race, Matani hoped that the amount of running he'd done from random people he'd upset back home was enough. Glancing back, he saw four runners not far from his own heels. When he looked forward again, someone was crossing right in front of him. Without enough reaction time to pivot, the two collided in a blur, sending them both tumbling across the ground. Matani sat up, thinking he would see a fellow runner, but realized he'd plowed straight into a commoner.

Matani sprang up and yelled, "You fool!" A few runners snickered at the mishap, while others, intent on the race, darted past him. In the blink of an eye, Matani was in last place. "Do you know who I am? I could have you killed for that!"

"Begging your forgiveness! I'm blind in one eye!" the commoner pleaded fearfully, prostrating himself face down in the mud. "P-please don't have me sacrificed, chief!"

Both the commoner's muffled words and terrified reaction sent a shock wave of guilt through Matani's very soul. Especially when he noticed the wooden plowing adze the commoner had dropped.

He's a farmer.

"'Ano'ai," Matani lamented, the greeting a humble reminder that he was no better than anyone. Then he reached down and helped the man to his feet. "You did nothing wrong. The fault is mine."

The farmer looked up warily as he stood, clearly not used to such compassion from a highborn. Then he looked down at Matani's hands and smiled with camaraderie. "Only a farmer has calluses like that."

Unable to deny his keen observation, Matani couldn't help but smile, too. "Not so blind after all?"

"I won't tell anyone," the farmer whispered with trust in his eyes.

"Is the rumor of so many commoners being sacrificed true?" Matani asked.

"Unfortunately," the farmer replied grimly. "But many have gone into hiding among the trees of Pūpūkea."

"How are you still alive?"

"The highborns think my blindness will offend the gods, so I'm left alone."

"That's good," Matani said.

"You're going to the fishpond, right?"

"Trying."

"I know a shortcut," the farmer said, pointing out a slightly different direction than the other runners had gone in. "The rest of them will be taking the coastal route, but my inland path will get you there much quicker."

"Blessings," Matani said with a grateful smile, then turned and followed it.

It's no wonder people born into the idea of superiority, like Kahiko, Uanini, and so many others, act the way they do. Barely playing the part a few days, here I am already talking and acting like one of them.

Maybe it's not the highborns' fault, after all. It's what society has taught them.

And that means what?

Society is a human construct, an illusion.

Then what's real?

Barely aware that his legs were moving, he reflected on the countless number of times he'd run away from one thing or another over the course of his life.

Here I am, as far from home as I've ever been, still running from all the same things. Clearly pointless because only now do I realize that everything I ran from wasn't actually on Taua'i, here on O'ahu, or even in people like Kahiko or Uanini. It's all inside me.

Much to his surprise, the farmer's trail brought him to the fishpond before anyone else. He jumped over the wall of fitted rocks and coral into shallow water. By the time he removed Pui's fishhook from around his neck, the remaining six runners arrived, each jumping into the pond to claim their own spot.

"How'd you get here before us?" Kahiko shouted with an accusatory tone.

Matani just looked over at him and winked. "My feet!"

Kahiko stared at him suspiciously, then shook his head.

Turning his attention to the water, Matani waited for the disturbed surface to clear, quickly spotting several small, dark shadows darting around his ankles. He lowered the fishhook into the water and waited.

"Oh, great roving fish, swim this way," he whispered, borrowing the opening line of Pui's fishing chant.

At the far end of the pond, somebody shouted in triumph.

Everyone looked up to find that the runner with the fishing basket had caught something, but when he removed his catch, everyone laughed to see how tiny it was. He impatiently snapped off the fish's head to use as bait and tossed it in the basket for another attempt.

Next to Matani, Big Butt howled with glee, holding up his bamboo spear with a good-sized milkfish squirming on the tip. He quickly made his way across the pond, purposefully stomping his feet through the water to scare all the fish away from the other competitors.

Matani remained focused, finally spotting a large, dark shape slithering through the water straight toward his hook.

He felt a tug, but waited. Another shout of excitement came from behind, but he was careful not to look. Spotting something in his periphery, he glanced over and found Kahiko talking to someone hiding behind the far corner of the fishpond, closest to the ocean. It was one of Kahiko's friends handing him a large silver fish with black stripes through the wooden slats of the seaward sluice gate. And not just any fish: It was a six-finger threadfin, reserved for only the most esteemed members of royalty.

Matani was about to point this out to the others when—

Tug!

He yanked hard on his line, pulling up a striped mullet of good size. Although he couldn't tell if his fish was bigger than Kahiko's or Big Butt's, he knew he didn't have the luxury of being picky. Gently gripping the fish with both hands, he leaped over the fishpond wall and took off running.

Just give up. There's no way you can win.

Maybe not, but I have to try.

The last leg of the race was a straight shot up the beach to Waimea Bay. Kahiko was currently in the lead, but Big Butt was catching up to him fast. Aware of feet pounding the ground behind him, the runner from Maui suddenly appeared on Matani's left, carrying a striped mullet about the same size as his.

Or does it look bigger?

Matani glanced down and saw his own fish's gills pumping furiously, trying to extract oxygen from the air, choking and gasping.

Oh gods! Please don't let it die!

Pushing himself to speeds he didn't know his body was capable of, Matani surveyed the way ahead for the most direct route, realizing he was coming up fast on a beach he'd seen earlier while sailing in on *Mano'nahu.*

Something about it gave him a bad feeling, but he couldn't remember exactly why.

Out of nowhere, a massive albatross swooped out of the sky and snatched Big Butt's fish right off the tip of his spear.

"Hey! Give that back!" he shouted, chasing after the bird.

More birds swarmed the runners, filling the air with harsh flapping, chattering, and screaming, until there were so many, nobody could see where they were going. Racing through the gauntlet of wings and beaks, Matani thrashed one hand blindly above his head to protect the gasping mullet he pressed against his chest with the other.

When the cloud of birds finally cleared, Matani found himself right behind Kahiko and the runner from Maui. Beyond them was a huge crowd of jumping, shouting, and cheering bodies gathered around two chiefs holding opposite ends of a vine that served as a finish line.

Pushing himself to the brink of physical capacity, squeaking past the runner from Maui, Matani felt a sudden wrench in his stomach that was so painful he nearly dropped his fish. His indulgence of Poʻomanu's feast had returned to haunt him. Wheezing from the excruciating cramp, he clenched his jaw and focused on the last and only person ahead of him now.

Kahiko.

You can't beat him. He's faster than you.

Matani tried to move left and sneak around, but Kahiko stepped with him.

He dashed to the right, but Kahiko did the same.

Just as Matani began to seriously question if highborns were actually better than commoners, Kahiko made a fatal error. He let insecurity steal his focus, glancing over his shoulder to see where Matani was.

Now!

Matani faked left and dodged right, confusing Kahiko enough to get shoulder to shoulder with him. By now, finer details of the faces in the crowd were visible—some cheering them on, others shouting words of condemnation in a mix of hot-blooded fervor. Matani tore across the beach, hair plastered to his skull in sweaty strings, arms pumping. He breathed in huge snatches and exhaled in harsh bursts as Kahiko pushed his own legs into a final dash.

Expecting this, Matani charged ahead even harder, only to be hit with another blinding cramp. Kahiko spotted the weakness and punched it hard. Teeth gritted, chest exploding, Matani managed to keep his momentum, now gasping at the same rapid pace as his dying fish. The screaming assembly ahead fell silent, until, with some irony, all Matani could hear was the blood pumping through his body.

Kahiko and Matani approached the finish line, neck and neck, mere steps away from a universe where one of them would be a winner, the other a loser.

The next thing Matani knew, he was collapsed on his knees just past the finish line as sounds of the world returned in a hurricane of screaming voices.

"Who won?" he gasped.

"I did," Kahiko wheezed snidely.

Cheering voices agreed, others hissed, and even more broke out in vehement arguments that quickly turned into physical altercations.

"Both crossed at the same time!" came the officiator's final verdict as he approached Matani and Kahiko. "Their fish will now determine the winner!"

Kahiko handed over his catch, then Matani. The officiator laid them both on the sand, one beside the other. Cradling his chin in the web between his thumb and forefinger, the officiator poked and prodded each fish.

Time hung still until he raised his head.

"Kahiko's fish is bigger!" the officiator shouted, pausing to allow for some cheers from the crowd. Then, he raised his hand to indicate that he wasn't finished. "But . . . it's dead. Vatua from Kaua'i wins!"

Seeing Kahiko staring a hole through him, Matani wanted to tell the smug, gap-toothed spoiled brat who he really was. But thinking of the humble farmer, he settled for a more gracious response.

"You can keep your bones," Matani said, but then couldn't help adding a slight smirk to his words before turning and walking away.

The reality was that both had cheated, and neither had actually outrun the other. It was only the matter of one fish breathing instead of the other that had determined the outcome of the race. Still, Matani couldn't help but feel that he'd proved something he'd long suspected: blood did not make one person better than another. And perhaps the most valuable lesson he had learned was that there was a skill and art to competitive running. Because the type of running he'd done back on Taua'i had been an endless, mindless, psychological circle, fueled by fear, doubt, anger, and unhappiness.

But competitive running like this was more controlled.

It had a goal.

A finish line, with winners and losers.

A purpose.

Out of nowhere, Hano's large, blistered fingers grabbed Matani's face hard enough to squeeze the insides of his cheeks together.

"Well, what have we here?" Hano exclaimed, his eyes searching Matani's. "Looks like there's a champion in there, after all!"

Pui and Imo playfully shoved Matani back and forth before lifting him onto their shoulders—which was a good thing, because if he'd had to take another step, he'd have probably passed out.

"Where's your girl?" Pui asked. "This should impress her!"

Matani searched the crowd, but Malela was nowhere to be found.

And so ends another tale of lost love. Way to screw that one up.

I know, I know.

Off Matani's crestfallen expression, Pui shrugged. "Ah, don't worry. If it's meant to be, it'll be. You still have that girl back home, yeah?"

Wrong!

"What are you waiting for?" the officiator shouted up at Matani, his tone more scolding than friendly. "Best not offend the ruling chief by presenting him with a dead fish!"

Imo and Pui promptly carried Matani over to the ruling chief, who was lounging sumptuously under the shade of palm trees.

Matani jumped down onto the sand and bowed low, holding out his still-breathing fish with both hands. "Great Ruling Chief, for your hunger, for mine."

Ruling Chief Po'omanu's bloodshot eyes remained unfocused until Kaihikapu whispered into his ear, "Congratulate him."

The ruling chief took the fish as he coughed out, "Congratulations!"

More cheers erupted, levitating Matani's spirits along with the proud, smiling faces of Pui, Imo, Tari'i, and Hano.

Kaihikapu stepped before the ruling chief, cupping both hands around his mouth. "Friends of O'ahu, we hope you've enjoyed the first day of Makahiki on our island! Ruling Chief Poʻomanu now invites you all to a grand and special feast at Waimea Falls. Just follow the torches!"

Following the announcement, an attendant carrying a torch appeared, swinging it from one sconce to another in a ritual motion, lighting the way up a dirt path that stretched into the heart of Waimea Valley.

Matani felt a hand drop onto his shoulder. "Malela—" He turned with a smile, surprised to see that the hand belonged to Timoa.

"Congratulations," the warrior said with bizarre geniality. "I'm sure your family will be proud to hear of this most prestigious accomplishment, don't you think?"

"I guess," Matani answered uneasily.

"Then why wait?" Timoa replied, his fake grin turning humorless. "I have your uncle right here."

Moving aside, Timoa revealed a man who lost the expectant pleasure on his face the moment he saw Matani.

"He's not my nephew!" the enraged man shouted.

And off Matani went.

So much for never running again!

✦ CHAPTER 10 ✦

The forest fell under an eerie spell of silence as Matani raced through it, tears of shame and guilt streaming from his eyes. Now there was only the sound of Timoa ripping breath from the air somewhere behind him, slowly closing in. Above, lightning engaged in a brilliant swordplay of white and violet, bringing forth dark, lumbering clouds overhead, completely erasing all that was left of the twilit sky. Thunder followed with a powerful crack, so loud it caused Matani's ears to ring. Plunging into some trees, the cramp in his side reawakened, stealing his breath, but he knew he could never, ever stop running.

Not after what I've done.

For a chief, any interaction with a commoner risked diluting their god-given life force, bringing bad luck upon themselves, their family, their friends, and the island they served. In order to restore lost or tainted mana, the only way to appease the gods was to kill the offender.

"I'll wring your bones and feed them to the fire when I catch you!" Timoa's voice echoed from somewhere in the dimming atmosphere.

"I'm sorry!" Matani pleaded. "I didn't know what else to do!"

Once again, his only hope for penance was to reach the temple of refuge that Malela had shown him earlier. Unfortunately, based on his own waning sense of direction, that was in the exact opposite direction. And while he had wished for his own death many, many times over the years—despite never actually visualizing how it might happen—only in recent days had he come to understand just how much he actually wanted to live. Not a waking-up-every-morning-and-making-it-through-the-day type of living, but to be truly awake and vibrantly alive—with meaning, purpose, and intent.

It's too late for that now, and you know it.

Don't you ever have anything helpful to say?

Just being honest.

What's wrong with me? I won the race! If proving I'm as good as a highborn doesn't fill this void inside me, what can? What am I doing wrong?

You keep making bad choices.

Is that all life is? A sum of my choices?

Yes. And for you, really bad ones.

Entangled in unhelpful, contradictory thoughts once more, Matani had no idea how long he'd been running. Despite the humid weather pressing against his flesh, for someone who thought he'd never run again—and with a debilitating cramp, to boot—he was making pretty good speed. But in the fading light, he had no good sense of where he was going.

As usual.

His pounding feet slowed as the ground ended abruptly at a steep drop. Standing at the edge of a deep gorge, Matani searched the jungle behind him for any sign of his pursuer but there was nothing but trees and more eerie silence.

Timoa is a stealthy warrior. You won't hear him until his knife is already at your throat.

So where do I go from here? Is there another temple of refuge somewhere on this island?

How would I know?

Glancing up at the dark and roiling sky pressing down on the sunken gorge, the faint glow of a waxing crescent moon through the clouds sparked a jolt of fear deep inside Matani, for it reminded him that this second night of the monthly lunar cycle was the *Tabu Night of the Phantom Moon.* Knowing that spirits could cross over from unseen realms on this particular night, it was customary to stay indoors after sunset. Not that Matani believed in such things, but this was also a night when practitioners of dark arts called forth malevolent spirits to carry out their evil bidding.

"There's no such thing as ghosts," Matani whispered to himself. Only half-convinced, another part of his mind prayed he wouldn't encounter any shadowy apparitions in the forbidden moonlight as he hastily attempted to climb down into the gorge.

Surrounded by a heavy mist that reduced visibility in every direction, the jungle awakened with the sounds of dusk. Unseen things skittered through the underbrush between thick stands of trees. He passed several hot springs that soaked the earth, creating a thick fog that hung motionless in the air. Forcing his way through heavy tangles of foliage, Matani's eyes shifted from side to side, nervous that Timoa might jump out at any moment.

Then, through the heavy mist, he saw something.

A temple.

As he launched into a sprint, a flash of lightning revealed a secret edifice built on raised ground. Though sections were still under construction, its imposing walls of compacted stone surrounded most of the grounds. The nearby screech of an owl made him jump. Turning in its direction, he saw some branches shaking. Unsure if his eyes were just playing tricks, Matani made his way around the base of the hill in search of a way up to the temple, slamming head-on into a figure lurking in the mist.

"P-please don't k-kill me!" Matani pleaded, shielding himself with his hands. When nothing happened, he looked up and realized he was talking to a stone idol.

Lightning raced through the clouds above, strobing across the image's monstrous face and outstretched arms, holding human skulls in each hand. Clearly this was some malign guard meant to ward off unwanted visitors. His conditioned impulse was to turn and run, but something behind the idol caught Matani's eye. An opening into the side of the hill, partially hidden by a man-made lattice of ferns. With a wary approach, he pushed them aside to reveal a hidden passage. Considering whether to enter or not, the sound of crunching leaves behind him forced Matani's decision, despite every bone in his body warning him otherwise.

"Choices," he said with a derisive chuckle, entering the earthen tunnel.

The narrow passage grew darker as it bored deeper into the hill, until he saw a dim glow ahead, highlighting a bamboo ladder at the end of the underground corridor. Climbing up its cold, wooden rungs, Matani emerged into a hollow tower of wickerwork enclosed with white bark cloth that was thick with the scent of burning tutu'i torches.

Surrounded by various stick and free-standing idols made of wood, stone, and feathers, Matani gathered he was inside the newly built temple's oracle tower. This was an extremely sacred space where only the reigning priest could enter to communicate with the gods. While someone more religious might be utterly terrified in such a place, Matani's skepticism couldn't help but focus on the ingenuity of the underground passage from a worshipper's perspective. Having the priest suddenly "appear" from the tower would certainly inspire wonder and fear.

First, the Shark Warrior costumes. Now this. Is everything the highborns do just a performance?

Through a low opening in the tower, past a fence of wooden stakes surrounding its perimeter, Matani saw a large crowd gathered before the temple's principal idol. At a poor angle to see the object of worship in question, he adjusted his vantage point just as a priest stepped into view. Not knowing whether he'd been seen or not, Matani scrambled up three levels of the tower to a platform at the very top.

Lying flat on his stomach, he peered down through a crowning fence of sharpened sticks, giving him a much better view of the entire temple. Its foundation had three descending terraces paved with waterworn pebbles and stones. There were also several thatch structures of various sizes positioned throughout the torchlit grounds. Directly below him, several priests in black robes were gathered, chanting to thousands of kneeling worshippers on the second and third levels, each one covered from head to foot in what looked to Matani like dried gray mud. The men wore necklaces made of human teeth and the women wore hairdressing pins made of human bones. Between the priests and their supplicants were ten steaming earth ovens, the reddish glow of their contents hidden by coverings of ti and banana leaves.

While certain aspects of this temple were familiar to Matani, others were not. Holy structures of this size were almost always built at the behest of a ruling chief under the guidance of his high priest. Some were dedicated to one particular god, such as Ro'o, to ensure fertility of crops and fishing grounds. Others might be dedicated to the god Tū, for success in war.

But Matani had never seen this temple's god before.

Its obscene rendering depicted a vile creature with a fanged mouth biting down on the head of a victim in its clawed grasp. But instead of looking terrified, the victim was sculpted with an awed smile, as if at peace with giving its life willingly. The sight of it chilled Matani to the very hollows of his bones.

A fear that was further compounded when a forest of silhouetted hands grew in the air as mud-covered worshippers began to chant in unison:

"We gather in the *Well of Shadows*, calling forth Mafuteo.
Mafuteo with the maggot-dripping mouth.
Mafuteo with the sharp teeth.
Mafuteo with the bloodthirst.
Mafuteo with the power.
Mafuteo with a hunger for human flesh.
Cross over! Cross over!"

A heavy pounding of drums rang throughout the temple as worshippers voiced their foul cravings. Matani was horrified to see that every single one of them had an array of fanged teeth, emulating the appearance of the malicious god before them. The death drums grew louder, somehow triggering blasts of thunder in the distance, as if the true gods of these islands were voicing their outrage at this blasphemous gathering. The chanting ended abruptly as the nefarious underpriests pulled back the leaf coverings of the long earth ovens, revealing a sight so grim, so unspeakable, Matani could barely make sense of it. Though he forced himself to believe that what he saw were just pigs or dogs, the putrid smell, combined with the unmistakable imagery of pale, sinewy arms and legs, refused him this mercy.

All ten long ovens were filled with headless human carcasses, only distinguishable as belonging to highborns by the remains of feather cloaks smoldering beside them.

The underpriests raised their arms, prompting the worshipping mob to rush forward and bite their fangs into the corpses' steaming organs and bubbling flesh with a diabolically frenzied hunger, annihilating their victims both spiritually and physically. The smell of burned meat and coagulated blood wafted past Matani, sickening him. But it was the ichor dribbling from the corners of their mouths that made him turn away in disgust.

"Cannibals," an unexpected voice whispered, followed by a head popping up from the platform.

Matani's eyes grew wide and shiny with horror, but a rough hand clamped his mouth before he could scream. It was as if he'd screamed anyway—as if he'd leaped down the oracle tower, ran past the wooden gods, back through and out of the hidden passage, across the sea, and returned to the boring but safe taro fields of Tauaʻi.

"Keep quiet!" the voice commanded in a hateful whisper.

It was Timoa.

Giving him a hard look that clearly said —*be quiet or else*— the warrior released Matani's mouth and climbed up next to him, staring down at the morbid scene below. "Now we know where all the missing commoners went."

Still dazed with fright, Matani looked over at Timoa. Seeing only the undamaged side of his face, he thought briefly how handsome the warrior must have been before his accident. "Do you think Ruling Chief Poʻomanu is behind this?"

"Indirectly, maybe," Timoa grunted softly. "He might be the reason these commoners gather in secret, but he's way too drunk to manage something this big."

"Then who?" Matani heard the fear in his own voice and knew the warrior must have, too, but he was helpless to hide it.

"Some chiefs told me that Poʻomanu's high priest disappeared a few months ago."

Matani felt a nervous need to reply. "Nanamaulu?"

The warrior looked directly at him, surprised. "How do you know that name?"

"Malela, that dancer from this morning. She told me he'd been arguing a lot with Ruling Chief Poʻomanu over poor treatment of the commoners."

"Interesting," Tariʻi considered. "And now he's taking matters into his own hands."

"Arm yourselves and be on your way!" a voice shouted with a harsh, militant tone. "The ceremony at Waimea is about to begin!"

Matani followed the voice to a strapping figure covered from head to foot in red mud. He had curly black hair and eyes full of fiendish anger. Behind him stood a group of equally hulking men painted with red mud, each carrying a long spear.

"The ones in gray mud must be the less experienced infantry," Timoa determined. "Those guys covered in red are definitely more skilled. The one who spoke is probably second-in-command."

"Second to whom?" Matani asked.

"That's what we're gonna find out."

"Tonight, we reclaim our home from tyranny!" Angry Eyes shouted. "O'ahu will soon flourish with abundance again!"

All the worshippers began to chant, "Praise Mafuteo! Praise Mafuteo! Praise Mafuteo!"

The ranks of gray cannibals lined up outside one of the temple's thatch houses, where awaiting underpriests handed out spears they dipped in large calabashes filled with a dark-purple liquid.

"What's that stuff?" Matani asked.

"Poison," Timoa said, annoyed at having to state the obvious.

Each cannibal received their weapon along with a black gourd battle helmet decorated with gray feather plumes before proceeding to the exit. Once the temple cleared, Timoa elbowed Matani in the ribs—and not in a friendly way. "Move it. We have to get to Waimea before they do and find the others."

"But—" Matani began apprehensively. "Aren't you going to kill me?"

"Later," Timoa said, barely looking back.

Uncertain if he was kidding or not, and not wanting to be left alone to decide, Matani nervously followed Timoa down the ladder. The two crawled from the oracle tower out onto the upper terrace of the eerily lit temple. Matani glanced up and saw amorphous clouds sliding across the sky, fueling a cold, strange wind that moaned like a dirge for the masticated corpses around him. A dark, suffocating energy suddenly enveloped him.

"Where are you going?" he whispered loudly at Timoa—maybe too loud, but he didn't care. "The underground passage is right here!"

"Need weapons," Timoa grunted, disappearing into one of the nearer thatch houses.

Matani gulped nervously, then held his breath as he ran after him, trying not to inhale or even glance at the half-eaten corpses in the ovens. They passed several trees with bones placed in their forked branches.

"What are those for?" Matani asked.

"Trophies," Timoa replied as he entered a torch-lit side chamber.

Matani followed him into a walled enclosure that contained an enormous natural pit filled with a matting of peaty material. Timoa jumped in and started digging underneath the dark-brown moss, using whatever was under it to slather his body from head to toe.

When Matani finally saw the warrior stand with outstretched arms, proudly displaying his entire body covered in gray mud, he understood. This was the same material that the cannibal infantry had used to uniform themselves with. And now Timoa looked just like one of them.

Matani leaped in and was hastily smearing the slippery clay over his own body and limbs when two temple guards rushed through the chamber entrance with spears in hand.

"Why haven't you left with the others?" shouted the taller of the two guards. "The ceremony at Waimea starts soon!"

Matani's heart stopped dead in his chest.

Timoa gave a subtle nod that told Matani to relax, then calmly climbed from the pit to stand before the guards. "Our night of glory has finally come, yeah?"

Tall Guard cocked his head suspiciously. "Let me see your teeth."

Timoa merely shrugged, maintaining a close-lipped grin.

Short Guard held the poisoned tip of his spear to Timoa's neck. "Your teeth!" he demanded once more.

Timoa nodded thoughtfully at the guards standing between them and the chamber exit, flashing a smile of perfectly normal teeth.

Before they could react, Timoa grabbed Short Guard's wrist and flung him into the pit of clay.

"Go!" Timoa barked at Matani as Tall Guard lunged.

Matani dove through the guard's legs, barely escaping into the hallway. He turned right, raced for the exit, and didn't stop until he was outside the temple walls—only to discover that Timoa wasn't anywhere behind him.

You can't just leave him there!

Why? He wants to kill me!

Because you put his mana at risk!

Exactly! I'm a farmer, not a warrior!

If you don't help him, you'll be a coward!

After a short pause, and against the pounding disagreements of his heart, Matani took a deep breath, then reentered the temple with more misgivings than he could count.

Peering around the entrance of the side chamber, he saw both the tall and short temple guards circling Timoa, repeatedly jabbing the poisoned tips of their spears at him. Timoa miraculously dodged every attempt, finally disarming both guards in the blink of an eye. Infuriated, the two guards cornered Timoa and tackled him. Short Guard swung his elbow against Timoa's right arm so hard, Matani heard his bones crack.

"Broke his arm!" Short Guard laughed, gratified.

Timoa barely gritted his teeth, upsetting the guards even more. Tall Guard fished a garrote from the waist of his loincloth and hooked it around Timoa's throat. Gasping for air, Timoa sank to his knees as Short Guard reached for his poison-tipped spear.

Matani took a deep breath and began pulling energy into his body from the space around him, remembering the words of Tari'i:

Find that place between courage and fear.

With a surge of adrenaline, Matani barreled into the chamber, legs pumping, heart hammering. In one explosive burst, he sprang into the air, hurtling his full weight into Short Guard's torso. The collision sent the unsuspecting guard's spear skidding uselessly across the stone floor. Momentum carried them both forward like some nightmarish dance, and together they tumbled into the mud pit.

Timoa, surprised to be free, stood up, his right arm dangling uselessly at his side. He spun toward the other spear on the ground and kicked it up into his working hand, ramming its poisonous tip into Tall Guard's side. Tall Guard stumbled slightly before his eyes lost their focus. Timoa, Matani, and even Short Guard stopped, watching as the effects of the poison quickly set in. The impaled guard collapsed to the ground, his entire body jerking uncontrollably from severe muscle spasms. Unable to breathe, his eyes bulged with mortal terror.

A moment later, he was dead.

The remaining three stood frozen in fascination until Timoa flung his spear at Short Guard, killing him before he could even make a sound. Seeing Timoa walking toward him in the mud pit with a spear in hand, Matani lifted his arms in surrender.

This is it. My turn to die.

A muscle twitched in the warrior's jaw. "Who are you?"

Matani blinked. "What?"

"Your real name!" Timoa shouted impatiently. "What is it?!"

"Matani."

"You're a commoner, yeah?"

Matani nodded.

After a silent understanding passed between them, the slightest smile of satisfaction touched Timoa's lips, giving Matani the distinct impression that he'd just been let off the hook.

"So, what happens now?" Matani asked hesitantly.

"No idea," Timoa said, then leaned the spear against the stone wall and began to squeeze and massage his right arm. He barely made a sound but grimaced with every bit of manipulation.

Matani watched in disbelief as Timoa's right arm slowly came back to life, reminding him of an incident many years ago when his cousin had fallen and dislocated her shoulder. With one final yank and turn of his forearm, the warrior issued a quick grunt of pain, then wiggled his fingers, smiling.

"That looked painful," Matani said, staring up at him in disbelief.

Picking up the guard's gourd helmets, Timoa tossed one to Matani. "Let's go!" he yelled hotly.

Leaving the temple behind, Timoa used his seasoned tracking skills to stalk the cannibal horde through the eerie darkness. In their disguises of helmets and gray mud, he and Matani soon found themselves merged seamlessly with the deadly army.

"How much farther?" Matani asked.

Timoa pressed a finger to his lips, silently reminding Matani not to expose his teeth. Matani clamped his mouth shut, glancing around at the corrupt horde of men, women, and younger adults. To him, they looked like some phantom infantry moving through the woods, evoking chilling tales of ancient night marchers—ghostly apparitions of deceased warriors said to traverse the island on sacred nights. Sensing their quiet rage—sadly, because he could recognize it within himself—Matani ultimately found genuine sympathy for them. After all, these were commoners, just like him, taught to live in fear of death since birth.

But they'd had enough.

Every one of these cannibals—people—have seen their kind treated as disposable simply because someone, somewhere, decided a long time ago that the blood of some had more mana than others. What could be so broken in a society that it pushes people into the arms of such evil? To convince themselves that killing and eating their own kind is the only way to save themselves?

Hearing rushing water ahead, the energy of the army shifted from rage to anxious excitement. Matani saw Angry Eyes at the front of the army gesticulating with his hand as they all emerged from the trees above a waterfall that plunged down into an immense pool. Across the water, amid a glowing atmosphere of orange torchlight, every chief on the island was gathered in celebration before a raised altar that showcased four tall, wooden statues representing Tane, Tū, Ro'o, and Ta'aroa.

The first three idols were blindfolded, as was customary at the onset of the winter solstice, leaving Ro'o—the evening's sole guest of honor—with the privilege of sight. His sculpted eyes gazed down upon fifty or more O'ahu warriors performing a hula ceremony for the visitors. Ten of them played on long gourd drums, wearing matching loincloths, fern headbands, and flower leis, belting out a forceful chant that vibrated up and down the entire valley. The other forty-odd male dancers were dressed in matching ensembles of grass skirts and bracelets accented with dogtooth anklets, exhibiting precisely choreographed movements that showed off their muscular physiques.

Unlike the female hula dancers from earlier that day, *kahiko* dancers were known for a more vigorous and athletic dance style that expressed raw power and strength. Every move of the male warriors made their formative muscles bulge and ripple. Their hands were like weapons, every swing of their arms like a blow, and their feet pounded the ground, creating a percussive rhythm that vibrated out into the very earth beneath the spectators, matching the intense, almost violent pounding of the drums. Their faces were fierce, their eyes fixed on some unseen enemy as they snarled and bared their teeth, ready to do battle at any moment. It was a dance of aggression and power, a reminder of the warrior spirit that had been passed down through generations.

While the entire audience remained utterly mesmerized by the performing warriors, Angry Eyes moved methodically through the cannibals, issuing silent commands that dispersed the army of grays to spread out across the valley and encircle the unsuspecting warriors below.

"This valley is the perfect location for a trap," Timoa whispered, nodding toward the opposite end, which led down to the ocean. "Only one way out."

Matani crept along behind him until both were looking straight down onto a large crowd of chiefs and warriors enjoying themselves, completely oblivious to the danger about to befall them.

"There they are," Matani whispered, pointing out Imo, Pui, Tari'i, and

Hano.

The Shark Warriors were standing together near the front of the altar when a loud crash of drums abruptly ended the hula ceremony, leaving the performers frozen in silence, chests heaving.

Timoa seized the opportunity and cupped his hands together, blowing between his thumbs two distinct times, perfectly mimicking the sound of an owl. Matani watched as all four Shark Warriors turned their heads at once, looking exactly where they stood.

The brief silence was broken by applauding guests rising to their feet, while Timoa communicated silently with his fellow warriors. Placing the edge of his hand between his eyes, he chopped the air in a semicircle, indicating the threat that surrounded them. Matani saw Hano acknowledge this with subtle glances at the upper areas of the valley before gathering the others in a huddle.

"Do you think he saw the cannibals?" Matani whispered.

"Oh, yeah."

"So, what happens now?"

Timoa cracked the long spear in two over his knee, keeping the half with the poisoned tip. "I need to start thinning out this army."

"You want me to go with you?"

"No," Timoa said, allowing Matani to exhale with relief. "I want you to get down there and tell Hano everything we saw."

"Okay," Matani said, peering over the steep descent on either side of the falls. "Get down how?"

Without missing a beat, Timoa shoved Matani off the cliff.

When Matani's head broke the surface of the freezing water, his mind wanted to scream, but his body was too numbed by the shock. Grateful for the clamoring crowd that had covered the splash of his impromptu high dive, he looked up and saw Timoa throw him a short wave before disappearing behind the cliff. Yanking off his gourd helmet, Matani swam to the edge of the pool and climbed out, discovering that most of the gray mud had been washed off his body. By the time he circled around the perimeter of the plunge pool to the gathering of chiefs, the reality of seeing the other Shark Warriors suddenly hit him, and he lost his nerve.

I can't do it. They're going to be furious with me.

Oh yeah. They'll probably kill you.

I don't blame them. I'm a liar.

Agreed. Just run away and don't look back.

Turning to leave for somewhere, *anywhere* else, Matani heard Pui whisper loudly, "Hey, Vatua! Or whatever your name is, get over here!"

Matani stopped to go back, but as it turned out, he didn't need to go anywhere at all. The four warriors had already circled him.

"M-my real n-name is Matani," he immediately confessed. "I'm sorry I lied. I'm just a farmer."

Fully expecting a lecture of some kind, or worse, the Shark Warriors shared a nonplussed glance among themselves.

"As long as you and Timoa worked things out, we're good," Hano finally said.

Matani looked at the others, who simply nodded in agreement.

And just like that, what Matani had thought was going to happen beyond a shadow of a doubt turned out exactly the opposite. What a powerful, life-changing epiphany it was for him to understand just how unhelpful his thoughts had been all those years. And it made him wonder how many more times they might have misled his choices, impacting his life in ways he only now began to comprehend.

How they made him fearful and made him second-guess himself.

How mercilessly they betrayed, tortured, and lied to him.

How often they were just flat-out wrong.

Where do these stupid thoughts come from? Are they coming from me? Or is there someone else in there? Hello?! Say something, you coward!

"Where's Timoa?" Hano asked.

"Up there," Matani said, nodding to the top of the waterfall. "Taking out as many cannibals as he can."

"Cannibals?!" Pui blurted, quickly shushed by Hano.

Matani nodded gravely. "This entire celebration is a trap."

"Who organized it?" Imo asked pointedly.

"Well, Timoa doesn't believe Po'omanu could so something like this," Matani said. "He thinks the supreme high priest is behind it."

"Impossible!" Tari'i protested. "Nanamaulu is a direct descendant of Tane! He would never worship a flesh-eating god!"

"We just came from a hidden temple that says otherwise," Matani argued. "There were thousands covered in mud and with fangs for teeth."

"The missing commoners," Imo speculated.

"Was Nanamaulu there?" Tari'i asked. "Did you actually see him?"

"No," Matani said, thinking back. "Six or seven underpriests held a ceremony that ended with everyone eating people cooked in earth ovens."

"They've been cursed with a hunger for human flesh," Tari'i said, shaking his head. "None of this makes any sense."

Hano's face darkened. "Gathering all these chiefs under the guise of a celebration is a coward's strategy."

"But a good one for someone planning an invasion," Imo said. "Slaughtering everyone here would weaken the defenses of every other island in a single night."

"This is the evil Hunumaniani spoke of," Hano reminded them.

Drums crashed, startling Matani, followed by the high-pitched whistle of nose flutes. Criers shouted above the boisterous murmur of the crowd.

"His Greatness approaches like the sunrise, the stars, and the heavenly clouds!" called the royal herald, running alongside Ruling Chief Po'omanu as he was borne all the way to the altar in a palanquin on the sturdy shoulders of six human mounts. On this particular occasion, there were nearly three hundred in his entourage—including twenty chiefs as a guard of honor, wearing feather capes and helmets, and armed with javelins festooned with leis of flowers and tinted feathers.

"Be ready for anything," Hano warned, prompting each of them to remove the ropes tied around the waists of their loincloths. To the undiscerning eye, these were harmless accessories, but in the hands of a highly trained Shark Warrior . . .

All eyes watched as the ruler of O'ahu was lowered onto the center of the raised altar. He was garbed in full ceremonial dress with a high, arched wicker helmet decorated with red and black feathers, complementing the red feather cloak gifted to him by Ruling Chief Vahanui. He offered a dull smile of praise to the kahiko performers as they quickly retreated to the outer edge of the platform.

Stumbling from his carrier, Po'omanu walked across the dais to the young priest at the rear of the procession, who was holding a portable idol of the Long God, the embodiment of Ro'o. Or *Lono*, as he was called on this island. Similar to the image of Ro'o back on Taua'i, this staff was much larger, featuring an image of the god at the top, just above a long crosspiece draped with white tapa, *pala'ā* fern, a colorful feather lei, and several black-footed albatross pelts. Every single person present fell to their knees in reverence as the emaciated ruler gazed up lovingly at the idol, calling upon the spirit of Lono to enter:

"Your bodies, O Lono, are in the heavens.
A long cloud, a short cloud,
A watchful cloud in the heavens;
Behold Lono's place in the stars,
That sail through time.
This image of Lono links us with our ancestors from Tahiti!
Rise up! Prepare yourselves for play!"

"Prepare yourselves!" the audience of chiefs replied.

"Welcome, image of Lono!" sang Ruling Chief Po'omanu.

"Hail to Lono!" came the unanimous reply.

Ruling Chief Po'omanu turned to the assistant priest. "How was my prayer?"

The young priest cleared his throat, waiting for complete silence. "There was no rain, no noises. It was excellent!"

Po'omanu nodded and smiled, mostly pleased with himself, then returned to face the image of his beloved Lono. Overcome with genuine emotion, his crusty eyes filled with tears of affection as the Long God was lowered before him. "With the land now freed, I hereby surrender my power to Lono, presiding ruler of O'ahu during the Makahiki season."

With some difficulty, the ruling chief stood on his toes and splashed coconut oil onto the idol's head, then removed the prestigious whale-tooth pendant that hung from the sacred necklace of his ancestors' hair. Placing it around the idol as a symbol of his stepping down for the season, he reached into a calabash held by one of his attendants and fed cooked meat to the young priest. Upon completion of this most important yearly ritual, Po'omanu moved to the edge of the platform and stretched his arms to the sky.

"Waimea is set free from kapu! Let Makahiki season officially begin!"

The audience of chiefs jumped to their feet, roaring with adoration. Ruling Chief Po'omanu basked in their sentiments even as a shadowy figure carrying a wooden staff emerged from the dark spaces of the altar. Po'omanu seemed confused as the mysterious person walked right up to him, yanked the royal cloak from his shoulders, and shoved him off the altar.

The entire crowd gasped into a dead silence, watching Po'omanu topple to the ground. His attendants and both brothers rushed forward to help him to his feet. Even in the glow of torches, everyone could see that Po'omanu's face was red with embarrassment when he realized that his royal helmet had been crushed beyond repair.

Infuriated, the flustered ruling chief called out to the hooded figure. "Rabulakai? What is the meaning of this?!"

The slight figure pulled back their hood, revealing an intense-looking woman with unusually dark skin, just as Malela had described. Her matted hair formed an arch over the top of her head from one ear to the other, with long, thin dreadlocks dangling down past her shoulders, and stars tattooed onto each of her cheeks.

"The wife who hid in the shadows," Hano whispered.

"She's not hiding anymore," Imo replied. "She obviously hooded her actions just as she hooded her face."

Po'omanu stood in complete and utter shock. "But why? You promised to help me save my island!"

"I *am* saving this island," Rabulakai said, her broad lips spreading in a cheerfully dismissive grin. "By taking it from you!"

Kaihikapu, the ruling chief's brother, shouted at the kahiko performers standing on the platform beside Rabulakai. "Warriors, do something! That woman has disrespected and defiled your ruler!"

The male warriors moved, but instead of seizing Rabulakai, they formed a protective stance around her, shocking everyone when they all bared mouthfuls of sharpened teeth.

"And now the real ceremony begins!" she sang, prompting eleven underpriests in black robes to appear at the back of the altar with torches, setting the Havaiian gods on fire. Several chiefs in the audience roared at the horrid desecration but were immediately struck down by spears with deadly accuracy. Convulsing violently upon the ground, they were all dead within moments.

"Their spears are poisoned," Matani warned the Shark Warriors.

"Now he tells us," Pui said dryly, smirking at the small piece of rope in his hand.

Several chiefs behind them attempted to run from the valley, only to be stopped by a wall of spear-wielding gray cannibals.

"My army of commoners has had enough of your oppression!" Rabulakai shouted. "But you needn't worry," she said with obvious sarcasm. "Since you royals hold your genealogies in such high regard, by your own rules we shall inherit your power after consuming your prized flesh and blood!"

Every chief gathered into groups of those from their own island, watching helplessly as an endless stream of ghostly looking cannibals emerged from behind trees and boulders on the sloped hills all around them.

"There's no escape!" Rabulakai screamed. "Only allies will be imbued with the power of Mafuteo! Enemies will be consumed!"

"Who do you think you are?" Tari'i demanded, stepping up to the platform. "And why have you brought this evil thing to our islands?"

Rabulakai cast a chilling gaze upon the warrior.

"Tari'i, don't!" Hano hissed.

"I was once the priestess of a village far beyond your horizon, but many of us were forced to leave because of overpopulation and waning resources," said Rabulakai. "Searching for new land, our vessel was destroyed in a catastrophic storm, and I drifted at sea for weeks in a broken hull, slowly wasting away. Then one night—one glorious, fateful night—an ancient god appeared before me, offering great strength and power. And all this god asked of me was an offering of meat from my arm!"

Pounding her staff on the altar platform, Rabulakai summoned six awaiting underpriests, who rushed out and raised a massive wooden idol. Similar to the hideous object of worship Matani had seen back at the temple, this one was nearly twice in size, carved from an entire tree. After securing the repulsive deity, the priests turned to the crowd and uttered terrific yells to encourage their own warriors and unnerve the enemy.

"After witnessing the poor care of this island and its people by that fool," Rabulakai said, pointing a scornful finger at Po'omanu, "I understood why Mafuteo brought me here."

"I knew you couldn't be trusted!" Kaihikapu shouted angrily. "You've kept our brother drunk all this time, controlling him with your whispers!"

"It's true," added Ohikimakaloa, turning to address the other chiefs in the audience. "Before she came, Ruling Chief Po'omanu would never have harmed anyone. She's the one who told him to sacrifice the common—"

With a subtle nod from Rabulakai, the guard beside her flung his spear at Ohikimakaloa, killing him where he stood. Another nod, and Kaihikapu suffered the same fate.

"Tell your tales in the underworld," Rabulakai said with a hateful scowl.

Po'omanu sank to his knees between his dead brothers, looking the most sober anyone had seen him in a long time. "What have I done?" He looked up woefully at his traitorous third wife. "Why do you not kill me, too?"

Rabulakai sneered at Po'omanu with utter disgust. "Your feeble life is not worth the spear it would take to end it." Then she turned to the vicious object of worship behind her. "Now, there's but one final act to bring Mafuteo into this world!"

At her words, four more black-robed underpriests dragged an elderly man to the center of the altar, his arms bound tightly against his body.

"High Priest Nanamaulu," Hano whispered.

"I told you he had nothing to do with this!" Tari'i reminded them.

"Priests have the true power," Rabulakai proclaimed. "Even warriors, chiefs, and their rulers must answer to the gods, but priests are the ones who communicate with them."

High Priest Nanamaulu tried to keep his eyes on Rabulakai as she walked behind him, but his restrictive bindings prevented him from turning his head.

"The gods will bring calamity upon you—" he said evenly, only to have his words cut short by the twin blades of a dagger shoved through his neck.

"Not this night," Rabulakai said coldly, relishing the sight of Nanamaulu collapsing at her feet. "Tonight, my god will bring emancipation!"

A palpable shudder ricocheted through the crowd. Rabulakai's show of disrespect for the ruling chief was one thing, but to commit such an unspeakable act of violence against a priest—the direct mediator between mortals and gods—was simply beyond comprehension.

At first, Matani thought the weapon she'd used to murder Nanamaulu was attached to her right arm, but then he remembered her saying how she'd sacrificed its flesh to Mafuteo.

That was when he noticed it wasn't an arm at all.

In a flash of lightning, the entire audience discovered with mounting horror that the bones of Rabulakai's forearm were not only exposed, they had been gruesomely sharpened into twin, spear-like prongs that protruded from a lump of flesh seared by fire at her elbow.

She jabbed the disgusting prongs of her exposed bones into the old priest's chest, yanking out a hunk of jiggling flesh. Matani looked away, but not before seeing the murderess lick away the priest's blood from her vile appendage.

One of the underpriests came forward, carefully plucking the glistening meat from her bones using an ornate, three-pronged wooden fork. He then climbed up the towering idol and placed her offering of flesh into Mafuteo's mouth.

The moment the high priest's blood touched the wooden effigy of death, the sound of crickets was silenced, followed by a hot, baying wind from the south that shuddered the leaves of every plant and tree around them.

Through a fortuitous break in the clouds above, every warrior in the audience that night shared the same horrific spectacle of the white crescent moon slowly turning blood red, casting a fiery glow onto the world around them.

Rabulakai's gore-coated fangs glistened in the unnatural crimson light. "He has arrived."

✦ *CHAPTER 11* ✦

T he island trembled with such a force that even the strongest warriors fell to their knees. The earth split open directly beneath the altar, swallowing the ashen remains of the discarded Havaiian gods in a belch of sulfuric flames. From the bowels of the chasm came a deafening roar and, in a matter of moments, the island was consumed by chaos and terror. It seemed as though there was no hope for survival.

Rabulakai leaped off the altar before the platform collapsed. She stood in eerie red radiance, sweating with excitement at the unholy events unfolding around her.

The night hummed and moaned, followed by a blinding bolt of scarlet lightning that tore through the dark underbellies of the clouds above, unleashing a heavy, blinding rain.

The drops felt awful and sticky on Matani's body. He looked down at his hands and arms, seeing them covered in a dark, viscous fluid. "Something's wrong with the rain!"

"Not rain," Tari'i said, unfazed. "Blood."

Every cannibal tilted their mouths to the sky to drink the unearthly substance, chanting in unison, "Mafuteo feeds us! Mafuteo gives us strength!"

Pushed to the limits of reason and sanity, Matani could barely make sense of what he was experiencing.

It wasn't a dream or a hallucination.

A massive, supernatural event was occurring all around him.

And it was undeniably real.

Tari'i lunged forward, but Hano grabbed his arm, pulling him back. "We'll lose if our emotions lead us into this fight," he said sharply. "We have to be smart."

Unfortunately, Tari'i wouldn't have it. He yanked free from Hano's grasp and sprinted toward Rabulakai, easily dispatching every guard who tried to stop him. As more guards tightened their ranks, Rabulakai ordered them to stand down, allowing Tari'i to get right in front of her.

"Death comes for us all, eventually," she said. "No need to run and meet it."

"Woe to the land that drinks Nanamaulu's blood," Tari'i warned, his words haunted by a prophetic tone.

Slowly, they began to circle one another, tightening their distance. One with her twisted weapon of bone, the other with his length of rope. Rabulakai was the first to break loose with an awful shriek as she lunged with her skeletal weapon. Tari'i blocked her advance using the taut cord to force back the prongs of her forearm. Rabulakai spun, freeing herself in a blur of movement. Suddenly standing apart, facing each other, Tari'i was clearly surprised by her agility and strength.

"Your maggot-eating god isn't welcome here," Tari'i said, his eyes filled with focused anger.

"What a waste of such handsomeness," Rabulakai purred, then thrust herself forward so suddenly that Matani, and everyone else, could hardly register what happened.

Tari'i appeared confused, until he noticed the tips of Rabulakai's prongs stained with fresh blood. A fine red mist sprayed from his carotid artery. Pressing his hand to the wound, Tari'i sank to his knees, well aware of the life draining from his body.

"You won't win," he said in a liquidy voice.

Rabulakai flashed the fallen warrior a fanged grin. "We already have." Then, she kicked Tari'i in the chest, knocking him backward into the chasm of fire beneath the altar.

As Hano, Pui, and Imo stood in silent shock at the incomprehensible death of their friend and fellow warrior, Matani couldn't contain his hateful rage and screamed loud enough for them all.

The cry was torn violently from him, calling down a blinding jag of purple-white lightning from the sky, striking the idol of Mafuteo that skulked behind Rabulakai.

Barely reacting, the priestess scanned the chaos around her, easily finding Matani. Her emotionless gaze paralyzed him, and when he tried to scream again, he found he could neither speak nor move. What he saw in her cold, intelligent face was nothing—nothing at all. Rabulakai's eyes were flat and lifeless.

"Where did that lightning come from?" Pui yelled.

Hano didn't immediately answer, paralyzed by his own emotions. "Where do you think?" he asked, at last, thrusting his chin at Matani, whose eyes were rolled up to the whites.

"What's wrong with him?" Imo asked.

"He's not ready to face this kind of evil," Hano said, following Matani's gaze to Rabulakai in time to see her order several guards in their direction. "Not until he completes the journey his 'aumakua have sent him on."

Pui gave him a sober look. "And if he doesn't?"

"My gut tells me the future of our islands—of us all—will be lost forever."

"Consider it done," Imo said, turning to all the other warriors around them. "Warriors! Looks like we're outnumbered ten to one. Anyone see a problem with that?"

"No!" the warriors answered defiantly.

"Didn't think so!" Imo yelled back, grinning.

Moving into shoulder-to-shoulder fighting positions, Imo, Pui, and Hano led the warriors in an ancient war chant.

"HA! HE! HU! HA! HE! HU!"

One by one, the other warriors began feeding off their mounting energy. Confidence and bravery slowly returned as each of them flexed their muscles and pounded their chests, adding their voices in thunderous solidarity.

"HA! HE! HU!"

"We gather Tū in our spirit!" Pui called out.

"Tū is with us!" the booming voices of the warriors returned (some using the more modern pronunciation of Kū).

"Warriors, ready!" Hano commanded.

"Ready!" answered the warriors, as they made hideous expressions to intimidate their opponents.

"Contemptuous fools!" Rabulakai jeered, then raised her staff, screaming at the top of her lungs, "Attack!"

On her command, the cannibal army—now covered in streaks of blood and gray clay—swarmed down both sides of the valley like wraiths, rushing, roaring, screeching.

Hano looked at Pui. "I'll consider this night a success if even one of us survives."

Pui's face stretched in a grim smile. "If only we had time to wager."

There was a growl from somewhere past the bloody curtains of rain just before an enraged cannibal launched himself at Hano, barely a flickering dark shape against the red lightning. Hano turned and grabbed his enemy by the neck and slammed him to the ground, neutralizing him with one punch to the jaw.

Another cannibal wielding a dagger raced up to Pui. He whirled on one heel and grabbed the attacker's hand, pulling apart his thumb and forefinger, forcing him to drop his weapon. The cannibal screamed until Pui silenced him with a hard knee to the face.

Feeling wet leaves brush his legs, Matani was vaguely aware of Hano pulling him along as they attempted to escape from the valley. Confused by all that was happening, he forced words from his lips.

"Why aren't they protecting us?"

"Who?" Hano asked, his eyes scanning the darkness for any sign of the cannibals hunting them.

"The gods."

"I don't know why they come sometimes and not others," Hano replied, pushing a branch out of the way.

"But Tari'i prayed to them constantly. Why wouldn't they save him?" Matani's voice broke as he stumbled over a root, "Is evil more powerful than good?"

"Mortals don't have these answers," Hano said, catching Matani's arm and pulling him faster through the bloody rain.

A third cannibal advanced on Imo with fists held high, relishing his enormousness with flesh-eating hunger. "You'll make quite the feast!"

"You can start with my knuckles!" Imo said, driving both his fists into the cannibal's mouth, knocking out most of his fanged teeth. The cannibal dropped to the ground, his bloody mouth screaming, before Imo gave him one final kick to the head, putting the assassin out of his misery.

Matani's vision swirled into a blur, somehow detaching itself from his body until he was suddenly, somehow, looking down on the carnage from above. It was disorienting, to say the least. Unable to control where he was looking, he was simply pulled along for the ride as his vision jumped from one violent interaction to another.

For a moment, his heart was nothing but blood thundering in his ears, when a chilling thought entered his mind, like cold, invisible hands reaching deep inside him.

After a season of preparation, and all that I sacrificed to convert one believer at a time to build my army, I can't believe this day has finally arrived.

Matani knew the thought hadn't come from anywhere inside him. It carried a feeling of sick pleasure at the murderous rampage carrying on below, as it scanned the chaotic landscape, focused on a single figure standing motionless in the middle of it all.

That was when Matani realized the figure he was staring at—was himself.

He was somehow seeing through Rabulakai's eyes, hearing her thoughts.

Then, rather unsettlingly, he became aware of an energy that was so filthily evil, he barely had the faculties to comprehend its horrid existence. Matani felt it touch him, making his tongue grow thick and curdling the spittle in his mouth.

It was as if death itself had entered him.

That one is dangerous. We must consume his power before he learns how to wield it.

Matani knew instinctively that these thoughts were coming from the flesh-eating god speaking inside of Rabulakai's mind. It was a predatory, vile feeling, like the claw of an unholy beast piercing his very soul.

Wait, he hears me. Matani, is it?

Leave me alone.

There's nothing to fear, young man. I'm here for people just like you. People who have had enough of highborns and their selfish sense of superiority. People who want to be treated with respect.

Stop talking to me! I don't want anything from you!

You don't want the power to control your own life?

Of course I do.

I can give it to you.

Matani sensed the immensity of Mafuteo's power seeping into him. And while he knew on some level it was wrong, his conscience—that which held his moral sense of right and wrong—couldn't deny that he liked how it felt.

All my life, I've been powerless under the rules of a society created by someone else.

Oh, I know.

So, who decided one life is more valuable than another?

Some human with a selfish, unhealthy ego.

And who decided that one group of humans would control another?

Someone with blood no different than yours.

In agreement with the dark forces invading him, Matani sensed something else in Mafuteo's energy.

If you're a god, why does it feel like you're afraid of me?

You already know, Matani. You've always known.

I have?

All you have to do is say it.

I don't want to.

Yes, you do.

I can . . . control weather. Summon storms.

No, it's much more than that, and you know it.

Matani did know. Deep down in his secret heart, he'd always known.

Go on. Tell me. What are you?

I AM the storm.

Yesssssssssss.

Uncoupled from Rabulakai's mind, Matani felt years of pent-up rage and oppression detonate somewhere in the depths of his existence.

The ground shivered under his feet.

Then, somewhere in the blinding, bloody rain, came a deeper rumbling from the waterfall, which he now encouraged to surge and grow.

Break free.

Its cascading white waters obeyed without delay, mixing with the red mud of the land as it swelled to three times its original size. All around him, dozens of smaller streams began to spout from the surrounding hills and cliffs.

By this time, courage was wavering among the exhausted warriors, as they found themselves clashing fists with yet another horde of helmeted gray cannibals standing between them and the beach.

Hano was the first to notice the reddish water—a mixture of bloody rain and mud—filling the valley floor. He looked back up the valley at the waterfall just as its headwaters ruptured over the cliff. "Here it comes!"

A mighty rumbling followed his words, so loud and so ominous that fighters on either side stopped and stared in awe at the colossal wall of black water roaring down the valley toward them, trampling everything in its path.

The mounting tidal wave snapped full-sized trees like twigs as it surged down the valley toward them. In an unlikely conspiracy of survival, warriors and cannibals together turned and ran.

Hano wrapped both arms tightly around Matani, sharing a final sentimental glance with Imo and Pui before they were all consumed by the tidal wave.

Submerged in rushing water, Matani snapped from his catatonic state. He surfaced, confused and disoriented, finding himself held tightly by Hano as both were dragged at a terrifying speed by the current, narrowly avoiding the top of a passing palm tree.

"Welcome back," Hano shouted, struggling to guide them past deadly obstacles coming at them in the water, one after the other.

Matani looked at him, bewildered. "What happened?"

"A lot," was all Hano had time to share as more submerged projectiles flew past, banging and scratching their bodies.

A flailing cannibal appeared in the rushing water beside them, too busy fighting off the massive burning idol of Mafuteo barreling down on him to be any threat. He struggled to pull free of its momentum, but his loincloth was caught on one of the statue's wooden fangs. Though he tried to keep his head above water, the base of the figure slammed into a tree, spinning it sideways. Now being pushed ahead of it, the cannibal's fate was sealed when the idol rammed into a boulder, crushing the life from his body.

"Nice god," Hano muttered, racing past the deadly scene.

Little else could be heard above the deafening roar of water except endless screams of death and terror. Ahead, Matani saw foaming waves plowing into canoes on the beach just as they would in a few short moments.

This is it. You're going to die.

Awash in regret, Matani found the need to apologize once more to Hano. "I'm sorry I lied to you about who I am."

Hano looked at him with a steady gaze. "You can't lie about something you don't know the answer to."

Matani dropped his head in shame. "But I endangered your mana?"

"I have seen commoners rise to greatness and nobles fall," Hano said. "It's an unpopular belief, but the only thing that endangers mana are people of bad character."

Hano's words, never spoken with anger or disdain, but with understanding and compassion, made Matani lift his head. "It's been an honor to know you these past days."

"Wish I could say the same," Hano replied with a sly grin.

The unbridled flow of floodwater and mud abruptly dropped the height of a tree, crashing onto the beach like an unleashed demi-god, tossing beached canoes like twigs and sending them careening into one another. The sound was deafening, a roar of rushing water mixed with the screams of cannibals and warriors. Matani screamed, too, as he fought desperately to keep his head above the surface. The onslaught of water seemed unending as it crashed through overturned canoes, sending them into torches lining the shores. A soaking-wet dog climbed up onto an outrigger as its sail lit up in flames just before several more canoes caught fire, illuminating all of Waimea Bay with a baleful glow.

Escaping the confines of the flooded valley, the tidal wave lost its momentum and quickly deflated as it reached the bay. Dark forms of glistening bodies seemed to eerily rise up as the water sank away into the sand and surf. Hundreds of cannibals and warriors lay still and silent. Trampled and battered by the flood, it was impossible to know how many were alive.

Matani looked over, relieved to see Hano still with him. "I don't see the others!" he shouted, looking up and down the beach for signs of Imo or Pui—even Timoa.

All across the beach, small groups of cannibals and warriors regained consciousness.

"Over there!" a voice shouted.

Both Matani and Hano found Angry Eyes at the far end of the beach. He was pointing right at them.

Several more figures rose from torchlit shadows across the shoreline of unmoving bodies, like corpses reanimated by ancient magic. Though they were only covered in faint streaks of red mud, Matani recognized them as the elite fighters of the cannibal army.

"Go!" Hano shouted.

"What about you?"

"They don't want me. That priestess, Rabulakai—she knows what you can do!"

"Am I evil?" Matani asked, his voice trembling.

"There's good and evil in everyone," Hano said, his words calm and steady. "The question is, where do you stand between them?"

Closer now, Matani counted six cannibals racing toward them, led by Angry Eyes, who was carrying a broken spear. The others picked up whatever weapons they could scavenge along the way—broken oars, branches, stones. Washed clean of muddy costumes meant to project a unified identity of intimidation, Matani thought they looked more human than ever, their god-given teeth shaved into fangs out of devotion to something they believed could change their lives for the better. And in that moment, Matani felt incredibly sorry for them all.

"I have a good friend that lives on the north shore," Hano said. "His name is Kanahua. Tell him you need help getting back to Taua'i so you can warn them."

"Me?" Matani said, not liking this idea at all. "No, you're coming, too!"

"I have to find the others," he said with urgency. "I can't stop Rabulakai and her army without them!"

"You really think she'll attack the other islands?"

"Yes, and I think Taua'i will be first because of how remote it is," Hano said. "Once they get a foothold there, they'll have as long as they need to prepare in secret."

Matani felt confused and dizzy. "Even if I had any idea how to get home, why would anyone believe me? I'm just a commoner!"

Hano shook his head. "Trust me, you're anything but common." Aware of the rapidly approaching cannibals, there was no mistaking the sudden gravity in his voice. "Something beyond this world has sent you on a spiritual quest, and you must see it through to the end!"

Matani just looked at him. "But why me?"

"Let me ask you something," said Hano. "Have you figured out what star you're supposed to follow yet?"

"Not yet."

Hano smiled. "Don't worry. You will." Then he pushed his forehead against Matani's, sharing the customary breath of life. "Everything I have,

I give to you."

The warrior's action and words startled Matani, for this was a ritual highborns only carried out on their deathbeds, gifting their final breath to a worthy individual before it escaped them.

"When you get home," Hano said, "and you *will* get home, say these words to Hunumaniani exactly as I tell you: *Clear skies bring evil to our shores.* Got it?"

Matani nodded, but followed it with a nervous swallow. "What if I fail?"

"There's no cliff so tall it can't be climbed," Hano said, then turned and launched himself at the first approaching cannibal. A blindingly fast punch to his attacker's heart dropped the man to the sand. Glancing back, he was clearly upset to see Matani still standing there, gawking at him.

"Don't think! Run!"

Matani's body obeyed, though he could have sworn he'd forgotten how to move. But after barely a few paces, his mind caught up, and he stopped to look back. He could see Hano standing before five remaining cannibals, slowly walking toward him. Very slowly, Hano withdrew backward, both eyes on his enemies, trying not to stumble as he gingerly wound his way past debris on the beach.

"Run," Matani begged, wishing he could trade his powers of controlling the weather for the power to control Hano. "Please."

Wait. There's a cannibal missing.

A shadow grew from beneath an overturned canoe. Hano spun to meet it, only to be struck by a broken spear. Standing without a sound, the deadly shadow had two fiery eyes reflecting the burning flames rampant across the bay.

It was Angry Eyes.

Hano stumbled back, unable to comprehend the bloody wound he saw in his side. Before he could react, Angry Eyes ran the weapon through him again.

And again.

And again.

Matani screamed until he thought it might drive him insane. Or maybe it already had.

But for some reason, there was no thunder or lightning this time.

Your body is exhausted. But I can teach you how to make it stronger.

It was the voice of Mafuteo again. So close this time, Matani swore he could feel the wicked god's very lips tickle his ear.

"No!" Matani shouted defiantly.

Even before the last echoes of his voice disappeared, the other cannibals had already gathered around Hano, clubbing him over and over again.

Softening him for consumption.

The bravest warrior and best navigator Matani had ever known fended them off for as long as he could, dodging the first few blows, but it was painfully clear that Hano's strength was dwindling and he wasn't going to be able to escape.

Hano looked back at Matani, dazed, and with colossal effort, forced a smile that slowly turned to a look of bewilderment, and then more rapidly to a cold, vacant expression, which Matani recognized as the awful moment of his death.

Gods, where are you? Are you so afraid of evil things that you hide? Can't you hear the dying screams of the innocent? Why won't you show up the way Mafuteo has? Can you only do things that can be explained away as coincidence, chance, or luck?

As always, so many questions.

And, as always, no answers.

Not one.

"This one's finished," Angry Eyes said coldly, then looked up at Matani. "Get *that* one."

Unable to think clearly, Matani saw the other five cannibals fix their hateful eyes on him. He turned and ran, dodging rocks and spears that sliced through the air, whizzing past him on either side with the melodies of death. He wished desperately that one of the other warriors was there to bring Hano back to life with the power of their mana, hating himself for not knowing how. Just as he turned back to see where his pursuers were, Angry Eyes was already tackling him.

"I'm not going to kill you," the cannibal growled, subduing Matani with the forced weight of his body. "Rabulakai wants you alive."

Speechless but in survival mode, Matani kneed Angry Eyes in the testicles, freeing himself from the howling cannibal's grasp. He scrambled into the surf and dove under several untethered canoes, where dark waters shimmered with burning auras of firelight.

Breaking the surface to breathe air into his lungs, Matani barely missed having his head crushed between several unrestrained hulls, before he finally climbed up onto a capsized outrigger. He stood, staring in shock at the chaotic wreckage of the bay. Dozens of canoes raged with blazing fires, filling the air with a smoky, infernal glow. The heat was so intense it evaporated the bloody rain before it could even touch the water.

Angry Eyes spotted Matani and dove into the surf, swimming straight for him. Matani jumped from one canoe to the next, nearly slipping each time, as he made his way across the bay—before running out of canoes. Just beyond the grainy firelight, he made out foaming breakers pounding against the reef that separated him from his last and only escape route: a terrifying sea enraged by a supernatural storm.

Forced to make an impossible choice between capture and suicide, Matani felt himself succumbing to an all-consuming fear.

Then, one end of the outrigger he was standing on dipped sharply.

Seeing Angry Eyes pulling himself over the front hull, Matani grabbed the folds of the bundled sail and flung himself behind it. Angry Eyes grabbed at him from one side, then the other, but Matani ducked and swerved each attempt. Circling the mast, the cannibal made a desperate lunge forward. Matani leaned back a little too far off his center of gravity and teetered backward, landing flat on the bottom of the hull. Angry Eyes immediately jumped on top, clamping both hands around Matani's neck. Feeling a familiar object resting on his collarbone, Matani instinctively reached up, locked both hands behind the cannibal's head, and pulled down as hard as he could.

Infuriated, Angry Eyes yanked his head up, screaming. The familiar object was Pui's fishhook, and it had caught the cannibal's upper lip. The bloodied cord necklace it was attached to broke, and Matani's head snapped back hard against the bottom of the hull. Angry Eyes attempted to remove the hook, but the barb made it painfully difficult to return through the hole in his lip. He howled with rage, blood and spittle dripping from his injured mouth.

"You're dead!" the cannibal screamed, then clamped both of his hands back around Matani's throat, squeezing as hard as he could.

Matani looked up at the sky, eyes wide. The dark, flickering clouds became blurry, insubstantial. Thunder boomed, vibrating the canoe. And the unholy red rain fell harder, dripping down the soulless cannibal's face.

"Please," Matani croaked through lips that felt numb. "I'm not . . . a chief. . . I'm a commoner . . . like y—"

"Shh," Angry Eyes soothed, gently choking him into submission.

Looking up just as a flash of lightning exploded through the guts of compacted storm clouds roiling overhead, Matani could feel consciousness slowly escaping his body. Searching for a weapon, his fingertips found a wooden cleat wound tightly with the sail's rigging. With some difficulty, he managed to loosen it just a little.

But it was enough.

The sail hoisted up the mast and wrangled the stormy wind with such force that the front of the canoe bucked straight up off the water. Angry Eyes lost his balance and toppled overboard. The muscles of Matani's throat relaxed, and by the time he was able to lift his head above the hull's edge, he could see Angry Eyes being carried away by the waves.

Now it was just Matani and the wild sea.

If he had learned nothing else from his experience on *Mano'nahu*, Matani knew he needed to drop the sail. But gathering the cordage, he found his shaking hands too numb from the cold winter wind. Noticing an object stuffed under the front hull of the canoe, he crawled over and pulled out a short fisherman's cape made of leaves. It wasn't much, but enough to protect his body from the needling rain, allowing him to free his mind. Making another attempt to lower the sail, a sudden gust whipped across the bow and tore it completely from the mast.

"*Now* you help?" Matani shouted, then started laughing maniacally.

Under a bare pole, the canoe was left to the will of the storm, throwing Matani's entire body from side to side, numbing both shoulders with pain. The only thing that kept the waves from capsizing him entirely was the outrigger's pontoon, but even that was bending in ways that it clearly wasn't meant to. Hearing something rolling at the bottom of the hull, Matani looked down and found a paddle sliding around at his feet. He picked it up and jammed it into the water, keeping the hull pointed into the waves as if his life depended on it. Because it did.

Off to his left, the eerie outline of Ka'ena Point appeared through the sheets of bloody rain like some great, looming demigod. But its physical significance informed him that he'd just gone past the farthest western point of O'ahu.

The Leaping Place of Souls.

For some reason, the image of Malela dancing in Ruling Chief Po'omanu's house came to mind. Matani even thought he could hear music somewhere behind the storm. Then, his thoughts jumped to Hano and everything he'd learned from him. Then Tari'i, Pui, Imo, even Timoa, and, finally, his parents.

What happens to all that knowledge, talent, and skill someone acquires throughout their life when they die? Or the love they felt for and received from others? Parents, children, brothers, sisters, family, friends. Does it all disappear? Lost forever?

The violent skies were black with wrath, pounding relentless waves and wind against the godforsaken craft as it heaved and rolled. Matani screamed, the sound ripped cleanly from his mouth by the roar of the open sea. Great patches of foam blew through the air in thick white streaks as colossal waves came at the small outrigger from every direction, slamming against it again and again. Feeling the canoe beginning to split at its seams, Matani crouched low in the hull, working desperately to keep the bow before the wind to prevent it from taking on too much water.

"No troubles, no troubles," he repeated to himself over and over again.

Out of the darkness, two enormous waves collided, snapping the outrigger clean from its lashings. The entire canoe lurched to one side, and Matani flew onto his back, cracking his head on the bottom of the hull. Touching the base of his skull, he looked at his fingers. They were covered in blood.

Neither royal nor common—just—plain old blood.

The idea that one person could be any better than another because of a fluid in their body seemed more ridiculous than ever to Matani. He forced a weak chuckle of irony before collapsing under the blasting sounds of the storm that melded together into an almost comforting monotony. The anger and fear at war within him faded into a buzzing sensation that danced across his cold, shivering body.

"No troubles," he said again, but this time in a disoriented whisper.

Head spinning, Matani thought it might be his imagination, but he could've sworn he saw the flicker of something with a blue tail scurry under the front hull just before the canoe beneath him started turning into something else.

Grass, maybe?

Suddenly he could smell, very clearly, the respirating earth of a rainforest.

No, must be my imagination.

The last image to flash through Matani's mortal mind was of Heiana, and only then did he genuinely understand just how catastrophically sad he felt, knowing he'd never, ever see her again.

This is it. I'm really going to die.

And with this final and terrible thought, all the mysteries of existence—as far as Matani knew them—unraveled in the stormy darkness.

. . . a web of pulsing, undulating light shifted

Matani's consciousness into a weatherless place,

followed by an eerie, unnerving sensation

of becoming untethered from the world . . .

ISLAND WORLDS

WORLDS

THE SECOND JOURNEY

✦ CHAPTER 12 ✦

A warm, tranquil breeze fluttered Matani's hair and filled his nostrils with an array of exotic, earthy perfumes. Neither night nor day, the sky was a striking emerald green full of yellow stars. Confused to find himself standing amidst the gentle sway of long, whispering grasses, his gaze came across several unusually shaped snowcapped mountains. Other strange land formations towered above the forested hills surrounding him, painted with iridescent streaks of amber waterfalls and rivers. Above the far horizon, a shimmering orange sun—three times larger than any he'd ever seen—cast long, dark shadows across an unfamiliar tropical landscape.

Wherever this place was, the soft evening air and warm sunlight was a welcome replacement to the stormy winds and biting, cold rain Matani had been experiencing just moments before.

"Land of the dead," he murmured. It was the only explanation he could think of that made any sense.

Opposite the abnormally huge sun, in the dark-green heights of the stratosphere, were immense ribbons of sand, like floating shorelines among the vast sea of yellow constellations, appearing to weave between moons of many different sizes, shapes, and colors.

Even stranger were several behemoth trees floating through the air, tangled clumps of roots dangling beneath them, each casting shadows over a wide expanse of furrowed cliffs and gorges. As Matani considered how they could survive without being planted in soil like normal, gravity-abiding trees, a blinding meteor stole his attention, etching a brief, but spectacular, rainbow across the green sky. Beyond confused, Matani wandered into a grove of sweet-smelling woods where he could hear skittering wildlife and peculiar birdsong. The massive trees, covered in spiral sashes of moss and vine, reached through the air with impossibly long branches that merged with one another in a thick, tangled canopy overhead. Upon closer inspection, what he'd at first thought were oddly shaped birds were actually majestic fish somehow swimming through the air.

It was dreamlike, surreal, yet—familiar, somehow.

A flash of white-hot lightning followed by an ear-shattering crack of thunder made Matani cry out in surprise, but when he looked up through the languid sway of the soaring treetops, all he could see was the cloudless, green night sky.

For the first time, Matani realized he was wearing only a loin cloth—no rain cape made of soaking wet leaves. But at the same time, in another place, a version of his body being pummeled by freezing rain was.

Am I really dead?

And slowly began to comprehend—

Or dying?

—that he was in two places at once.

But that's impossible, isn't it?

If you say it is so, then so it is.

The unexpected response startled Matani because he knew it didn't belong to the doubting voices he often heard inside his head.

His throat tightened with fear. "Who said that?!"

As if in response, the rainforest slowly began to disappear, and he felt himself returning to the other place—where his physical body was. Not exactly unconscious, he was having an out-of-body experience, somehow separated from his mortal vessel that was, even now, lying at the bottom of an outrigger canoe lost at sea in a tumultuous storm.

Not wanting to leave this strange place—or for it to leave him?—Matani instinctively focused on the strange, buzzing vibrations of energy he felt flowing through him. All at once, the faded colors of the curious world around him became clear and vivid once again.

Am I dreaming?

Always.

Who are you?

I am an ascended spirit immersed in divine, uncorrupted consciousness.

In his periphery, Matani caught a blurred figure walking—no, floating—toward him along an overgrown path that meandered through the dreamlike landscape. Frightened beyond reason, he turned and ran, stumbling past a pyramid of moss-covered boulders where several small creatures hid in the shadows, tracking him with large, glowing eyes.

You can't run from yourself here, young man.

Silhouettes of furry, long-armed creatures swung on creaking branches overhead, flashing through orange shafts of sunlight. Matani leaped over one exposed root after another until he arrived at a thicket of shoulder-high grass. He was about to go around it when some invisible force parted the long green blades, forming a deliberate path.

For a moment, Matani forgot to breathe.

You have nothing to fear, young man. Love is the host in these strange lands.

While these words weren't as comforting as perhaps intended, Matani followed the mysterious path anyway. Walking in a daze, he emerged from a ragged tree line into a picturesque hanging valley that gently unfurled downward, towards the sparkling sand beach of a glowing blue ocean.

While the panoramic vistas all around him were vast and beyond explanation, something was missing. Something so obvious, yet he couldn't quite put his finger on.

Wait, I don't see any flowers.

Add some when you're ready.

I don't like flowers.

We shall see.

Not far ahead, Matani spotted the ruins of an old farm from some distant time. Upon approaching, he discovered crumbled stone walls encircling a man-made pond of amber-colored water. It was built on a grassy slope that fell in a series of eroded agricultural terraces, like the stairway of some ancient giant. A dry streambed etched a path of cracked red earth down through clumps of withered taro that appeared to have, at one bygone time, diverted water using above-ground aqueducts and ground-level ditches to irrigate the site, much like his own family's farming method. But judging by the overgrowth of lichen and other invasive weeds, whoever built this place clearly hadn't tended to it for a very, very long time.

Looking back to see if the blurry apparition was still following him, Matani found it standing right beside him. He yelped and dropped to the ground in a prostrated position, every ounce of his being shuddering with fear. But after a few quiet moments, an unambiguous energy of love and compassion descended upon him like a warm blanket. Gathering his inmost courage, Matani opened his eyes and looked up.

The nebulous figure shape-shifted into a tall, thin, elderly woman with a rich brown complexion, flowing white hair and a wide nose. The next thing Matani noticed was her piercing blue eyes, eerily reminiscent of his mother's. Draped in a vibrant yellow robe imprinted with red lizard patterns, she held a tall, ornate wooden staff crowned with a carved lizard head. Upon closer inspection, he observed that each of the lizards etched on her robe had light blue tails, with two arcs hovering above their heads, reminiscent of rainbows. From the sleeves of her robe, Matani caught glimpses of partial tattoos on both of her arms. But it was the mysterious tattoo on her forehead that captivated him the most: two circles, one larger than the other, containing two columns of three dots. A symbol he had never encountered before.

Before Matani could ask about it, the old woman let go of her staff, which—much to his surprise—somehow remained upright. She smiled and placed her right hand over her heart and her left hand over her sacrum.

Eye to eye, breath to breath, heart to heart, we are.

Unfamiliar with this greeting, Matani stood and imitated her stance, right hand over his heart, left hand over his sacrum. "Where I come from, we touch foreheads, offer our breath, and say—"

—'*Ano'ai,* the old woman finished in his mind, taking hold of her gravity-defying staff. "Not one greater than another."

Matani returned a confused nod. "That's right."

Our greeting evolved long ago, with the feminine left hand over the sacrum as an affirmation of intuition and safety. And the masculine right hand over the heart as an affirmation of courage and presence. Identical in this moment, there is no hierarchy, allowing us to share each other's mana.

Curious how the elder woman's lips weren't moving, Matani had to ask, "How am I hearing you?"

Telepathy. A much more efficient mode of communication between minds.

How so?

No translation is necessary, even among different languages and dialects, removing any risk of misunderstanding.

His face took on wonder. "Who are you?"

"I *really* don't like repeating myself," the mysterious old woman spoke with her voice this time, and quite sternly.

"Oh! Uh, w-well," Matani stammered nervously. "I mean, what's your name?"

"A much better question," she said, raising a peeved eyebrow. "I am your tūtū, Ona Waikalua of the Moʻo Clan of Halawa Valley, a teacher and mystic through the lines of Nalukaʻlaniʻmanumanu, Ona, Lae, Kea and Mahi, with a lineage that extends to the ancient era of Papahānaumokuākea."

Matani tilted his head, confused by the combination of ancient and modern vernaculars. "Where I come from, *tūtū* means *grandmother*."

"Yes," she replied. "As it does where I come from."

It took a moment for her words to register. "You mean you're my . . .?"

Tūtū Ona smiled. "I am."

"But I've never seen you before in my life!"

"Of course you haven't," Tūtū Ona giggled in a way that made her seem younger than her gray-haired appearance. "I joined my ancestors five generations before this version of you arrived."

Making a rough calculation in his head, Matani blinked with disbelief. "That's over one hundred and seventy lunar years ago!"

"To be precise, one hundred and seventy-four," she corrected. "But our entire lineage goes back much further."

Sensations of thumping earth drew their attention to a group of four-legged creatures with brown fur running past them, each with odd, branch-like appendages growing from their heads. The strangely beautiful animals raced down the dried taro fields in graceful leaps and bounds before disappearing into the trees.

Matani turned back with an almost comical expression. "Okay, what *is* this place?"

Tūtū Ona stared at him with a bright but stern intensity. "You've made your way to the other side of the rainbow, young man. Welcome to the Island Worlds. This is Middle Island, the spiritual realm of the physical world."

"What's it in the middle of?" Matani asked, just as three small orbs of white light darted past his feet through the grass.

Tūtū Ona adjusted the position of her walking staff. "Lower Island, the spiritual realm of nature, and Upper Island, an ethereal dimension of ascended spirits."

"Do you mean like gods and goddesses?" he wondered. "So, are Tane, Tū, Ta'aroa, and Ro'o real?"

"Like anything, they are as real as you believe them to be," Tūtū Ona said. "Every culture develops different names and religions, but they all stem from the same source of incomprehensible power one senses out in the universe: *The One Who Creates All Things.*"

Matani nodded slowly, not entirely disagreeing with her words, but not fully convinced, either. "How did I get here?"

The old mystic gave her grandson a rueful look. "Though there are much easier methods, you reached a level of fear so traumatic, your unconscious mind inadvertently opened your psychic threshold."

He tilted his head. "Psychic what?"

"An inner doorway that connects the world of flesh with the world of spirit."

Glancing around, Matani seemed confused. "Middle Island is a farm?"

"It can be anything you want," she said. "Everything you see now is derived from your most beloved experiences, memories, and dreams."

"Spirit Farm," Matani dubbed this place, his attention caught by several giant orange and yellow butterflies flying overhead, each leaving a trail of colorful fire that lingered in the air behind them. "It's beautiful."

Tūtū Ona's face hardened, her voice grim. "But for the wicked, it can become a desolate and lifeless prison of eternal darkness. A place of true death."

"So, you're saying I'm—" Matani's voice went weak with fear. "I mean . . . did I die?"

Tūtū Ona hummed lightly, staring past him with an opaque expression. "Not yet. But this is where you'll come when you do."

Matani's heart fluttered with hope. He might still have a chance at seeing Heiana again. However slim.

"And what do you feel you need to tell this girl that's so important?" Tūtū Ona asked.

Despite being surprised again by the elder's ability to read his mind, Matani found his answer easily. "Everything."

Tūtū Ona returned a light smirk. "Yes, well, she won't hear a word of it until you apologize."

"Me, apologize? The reason I'm even here is because of her!"

"So, you mean to offer her your gratitude, then?" she asked.

"Not at the moment, no," Matani mumbled under his breath.

"Focus, boy!" she replied, but then her face became more serious. "A family meeting has been called to sort out the absolute mess your life has become."

"A family meeting?" Matani's eyes bulged with disbelief. "While I'm in the middle of a storm?"

"When a meeting is called, you come!" Tūtū Ona shouted. "No matter if you're dead or dying. This is the way it's always been."

He shrank like a toddler under his ancient grandmother's stare and made no further attempts to argue the point.

"Everyone must take part in family gatherings, regardless of health or location," she said. "Especially those held for the purpose of solving serious problems between so many family members."

"Sounds like we'll be here all day, then," Matani retorted with a wry grin.

"Undisciplined emotions and a very, very bad attitude have put you sorely out of balance with nature, the gods, and humanity at large," she told him. "It's why we set you on your journey in the first place."

"Wait . . . you?" Matani's face fell with disappointment. "But . . . I thought the gods—"

"Pssh!" Tūtū Ona interrupted, waving an irritated hand. "Ascended beings don't have time to solve every little self-absorbed problem the flesh and bone have! They'd never get anything done. No, this is a family matter!"

"What family are you talking about? The only person I see here is you."

"I can assure you that all three hundred and fifty-six generations are present in spirit but, as the backbone of our lineage is so severely fractured, only I am able to communicate directly with you at the moment."

"Why only you?"

"I come from an ancient line of mystics skilled in penetrating dimensional barriers. No matter how tangled. For this reason, I've been chosen to mediate these proceedings—which means my word is law."

Matani raised an objecting finger. "But what if I don't agree with someth—?"

"Ah-ah-ah!" Tūtū Ona barked with absolute definitiveness. "Once you are a contributing member of this family, you can disagree all you want. But until then, no back talk! Are we clear?"

Withdrawing his finger, Matani nodded.

"Good!" she said, then pounded her staff on the ground three times, igniting a thrum across the ground so powerful, the branches of every tree in the vicinity shook. "Now, let us open our hearts wide and pray:

O Moʻo Kiko,
Great Lizard Goddess,
our ʻaumakua and sacred spine of ancestry,
who stands at our back and front,
we ask for your guidance to help our descendant Matani,
to be brought into connection with his inner source
of wisdom and power,
to enlighten us with our own faults,
and heal the sacred blood and bond of our lineage.
We have called this family together in search of entanglements
of culprits, offenses, and victims.
Of emotions, actions, and reactions.
Our ancestral line is fractured.
We now seek to peel away all layers,
to release the physical, spiritual, and emotional ills that bind us,
so that we may restore the flow of our mana.
The prayer is lifted; it is free."

After finishing her opening prayer, Matani watched in amazement as angelic wisps of clean white light flew from Tūtū Ona's body and swirled up into the sky.

"Moʻo Kiko," Matani said, repeating the name using his grandmother's unusual dialect. "Your ʻaumakua is a lizard, too?"

"A giant and powerful lizard," Tūtū Ona corrected him. "She still lives today on Molokai near the temple at Kapualei."

Overcome with dizziness, Matani held his head to steady himself. "I don't feel so good."

"All illnesses have a spiritual root," she said. "They are messengers that help us understand the deeper lessons of life we may be refusing to learn. Now, let's begin with hearing your side of things."

"How truthful can I be?" he asked hesitantly.

Tūtū Ona's expression showed that she was pleased with the question. "In order to bring about a meaningful righting of wrongs, we must all speak with the highest quality of truth, honesty, and sincerity."

Matani nodded, then took a deep, shivering breath. "Okay, well . . . my mother died right in front of me, because I gave her a stupid flower. I wasn't ready for her to go, but she left anyway. My father, who blamed me for her death, lost his own life in a meaningless battle that society pressured him to take part in. After that, I was abandoned by every single one of my relatives for reasons I still don't understand. At least, everyone on my father's side. I've never even met anyone from my mother's family because they all live on Maui."

"Well, you've met one now," Tūtū Ona said with a glint in her eyes. "And I can tell you this. Your mother's family is *not* from Maui."

Matani stopped cold, looking into his grandmother's blue eyes, seeing something very familiar. "You have her eyes," he said in disbelief.

"Their blue coloring is all that remains of our honored ancestors," she told him. "Now, go on. What else do you have to say?"

"Well, after my mother died, I prayed over and over to the gods and my ancestors for help. But no one answered. Then, when my father died, I stopped believing in such things. Any praying I did after that was just out of habit."

"Not everyone is attuned to hearing past the veil that hangs between spirits and mortals," Tūtū Ona said with a compassionate nod, her eyes reflecting his pain. "Is that everything?"

"No," Matani grunted, fighting back stinging tears of guilt. "I'm angry at my parents, too."

"Well, go on then," she urged. "Get it all out."

Swallowing back an impulsive reply, Matani paced back and forth, looking down at the abandoned taro terraces. For some reason, this further stoked flames of anger and frustration inside him.

"I'm angry at my mother and father for bringing me into this god-for-saken world as a commoner, then leaving me all alone in it to fend for myself. And I didn't even get a chance to say goodbye!"

Tūtū Ona's eyes focused elsewhere for a long moment, listening to muted, whispering voices in the breeze. She nodded earnestly, then focused her attention back on him.

"We appreciate you being so open and articulate with your truth, young man, and agree that we all take equal part in this fragmented lineage of ours.

It's also clear that you've inherited some karmic burdens that don't belong to you, and we'll work on clearing these together."

Matani wiped the wetness from his eyes. "How?"

Tūtū Ona cast a loving smile on him. "Reparations through the ancient practice of hoʻoponopono will be where our work begins. It's time to set things right and put this family back in balance."

Hoʻoponopono is an age-old cultural tradition of getting the family together to solve personal issues through a process of discussion, repentance, restitution, forgiveness, and prayer.

"Then, I'd like to start by knowing why the rest of the family on my father's side abandoned me. What did I ever do to any of them?"

Tūtū Ona gave a look Matani absolutely could not read before speaking. "There have been many secrets in your family's house," she finally said.

"Secrets?" Matani repeated, awaiting further explanation.

"Before the next wave of settlers came to what you call Havaiʻi, there were people already living there," she replied in a slow and deliberate tone.

"Who?" Matani asked, intrigued.

"During the time of Elsewhere, Hawaiki-kua-uli-kai-oʻo, the ancient and spiritual land of origin for all Sea-Traveling People, was born from the primordial union between Earth Mother Papahānaumoku and Sky Father Wākea. This was a divine, unbroken land of natural beauty that stretched across the sea toward every horizon and served as the beginning for many beloved traditions and customs. But after several passings of sun and moon, massive volcanic eruptions broke apart this great continent into many segments that fell into the ocean depths, leaving only their highest mountaintops above water. In open canoes, ancient tribes who managed to survive these cataclysmic times made new settlements on island remnants that were scattered throughout The Great Ocean Of Kiwa, nearly ten thousand in number.

As the present became the past, and the past became memories, two siblings, a brother named Kūhiva, the root of masculine power, and a sister named Hina, a powerful and wise female entity, fell in love and sailed from the sky in a canoe made of starlight in search of a place to settle down. After many prayers, they came upon several isolated volcanic landforms separated by long stretches of open sea; each rife with undisturbed reefs and lagoons, sandy beaches, dense inland forests, precipitous cliffs, soaring peaks, and lush green valleys. Geographically hidden from the rest of the mortal world, it was here that Father Kūhiva and Mother Hina made their home and populated the entire archipelago that they called *Mū*, meaning *to hide* or *conceal*."

"Wait, I thought you were talking about Havai'i?" Matani asked, his dark eyebrows pushing skeptically toward the deepening vertical furrow between them. "But that's not how the Creation Chant tells us the first humans came into being."

"Historical chants often vary from person to person," Tūtū Ona replied. "As does reality," she added with a smile playing at the corners of her mouth. "Besides, those I'm referring to weren't exactly human . . . yet."

Matani lightly chewed his bottom lip, trying to keep an open mind. "Then what were they?"

"After becoming pregnant, Kūhiva and Hina returned to the stars for an unknown period of time where they spawned two tribes of supernatural beings we now call the *Originals*," she explained. "They were *Mea'uli*, the *Blue Beings*, who had blue skin and possessed great magical powers—"

"Why was their skin blue?" Matani interrupted with a doubtful look.

"The material aspect of their bodies wasn't controlled by gravity like mortals, allowing them access to higher dimensions." She paused then looked at Matani in a way that warned him not to interrupt again. "The second tribe was called *A'ā'ena*, the *Shining Ones*. These beings had a distinctive shimmer to their skin that resembled the stars, and who had the ability to take the form of animals at will. They could also heal the sick and control the elements."

Standing with both arms skeptically crossed, that last part caught Matani's attention. "But if these Originals were born among the stars, how did they end up living in Havai'i?"

Instead of reprimanding him, Tūtū Ona seemed impressed by his question. "After a time, the Originals found life among the void of space to be monotonous and without much excitement, so Kūhiva and Hina suggested they spend time on Mū.

The first days among the islands were filled with wonder and discovery, though the two tribes did experience sensory overload. After living in the sterile, featureless environment of space for so long, they were overwhelmed by the vibrant colors, the varied and exotic plant life, and the abundance of different smells and sounds. While they still enjoyed being weightless, they found interactions with the ocean, with its vast and teeming marine life, and the sandy beaches and palm trees to be something out of a dream.

Through the ebbs and flows of time, the Blue Beings and Shining Ones encountered a variety of exotic human cultures that stumbled upon the islands—some by accident, others on purpose. And with those who didn't flee in terror from their outlandish appearances, the Originals swiftly adapted their style of voiceless communication to the spoken word, imbibing the linguistic diversity of the different voyagers. Through these actions, they made a revelatory discovery. Regardless of skin or speech, they found humans to be a fervently emotional species who, above all else, desired peace, harmony, and spiritual enlightenment.

And so began the *Time of Meaning,* when the Originals founded a mission referred to as *The Grand Purpose."*

"Grand Purpose," Matani repeated in a whisper. "What was it?"

"Unfortunately, like voices of the ancestors, all that information was lost through time," she replied. "Though many descendants of the Originals have spent their lives trying to reawaken these memories through dreams and prayers."

Matani threw his hands up with discontent. "How could something so important get lost?"

"As the Originals were lifetimes into developing methods of sharing their Grand Purpose with the rest of the world, an adventurous chief named Havaiʻiloa had set sail from *The Land of The Yellow Sea of Kāne.* He brought many canoes filled with family members in search of land to establish a new dynasty."

"Now this part I've heard," Matani injected, and added, "Known for his long fishing excursions, Havaiʻiloa followed migrations of the plover and curlew for several months before coming upon a chain of islands that were fertile and pleasant. He named four of the islands after himself and his children: Havaiʻi, Maui, Oʻahu, and Tauaʻi."

"One of many stories describing early settlement of the islands," Tūtū Ona pointed out. "However, few explain how Havaiʻiloa recklessly introduced concepts of genealogical rank and material possessions to the Originals."

"Why would those things matter?" Matani asked, though his heart already knew the answer.

"As the younger generation chose to embrace the Sea-Traveling People way, imaginary hierarchies formed within their communities that created resentment," she explained. "Cravings and attachments to material things corrupted their minds so severely, they lost all memory of the Grand Purpose."

"They abandoned their own culture over titles and . . . things?" Matani blurted judgmentally, despite secretly recalling his own greedy desires for the same.

"Don't think there weren't consequences," she said. "These choices caused a major shift in the spiritual practices and beliefs of the Originals, drastically altering their entire society."

"Do the Blue Beings and Shining Ones still exist?"

"Not as they once were," his grandmother replied with mournful yearning. "Becoming identified by superficial things, meaning itself became so confusing that the Originals, both blue and shining, became capricious and unpredictable, using their supernatural abilities to play tricks on their human neighbors instead of helping them."

"So what happened to them?"

"Over time, the Blue Beings succumbed to gravity and the Shining Ones dimmed, mutating their vibrations into fixed matter," she said. "This caused their children to be born with a more earth-locked, carbon-based hue."

"The Mū," Matani deduced.

Tūtū Ona confirmed his assumption with a nod as she looked up— looked straight at Matani. "Today, descendants of the Blue Beings can be recognized by the genetic trait of blue eyes, and tribes who identify with the legacy of the Shining Ones honor their celestial ancestors through the philosophies and practices of inner illumination."

Matani's gaze shifted from his grandmother's shining skin to her blue eyes with growing confusion. "You have both."

"As do all in our family fortunate enough to carry mixed blood of the Originals," she replied.

He looked utterly flabbergasted, utterly shocked. "So I have *four* different lines of blood in my veins?"

"A most potent combination," Tūtū Ona said, and her words seemed to hang in the air.

Standing with both arms crossed, everything Matani had just been told filled him up in ways he couldn't explain. "Why don't the highborns ever mention the Originals in their stories or chants?"

Rather than answer, Tūtū Ona replied with a patient but empty smile that told him all the truth he needed to know. "After the sky turned enough times for memory to become legend, and legend to become myth, a high and powerful priest from Tahiti followed the ancient path of Havai'iloa. Upon arrival, he was outraged to discover that the pristine lineage of Havai'iloa's descendants from all those generations before had become shamefully degraded by intermarriages with Mū inhabitants, quick to judge us as godless primitives."

"You're talking about Pa'ao," Matani concluded, realizing he was leaning forward with great interest now because this person was a well-respected historical figure revered in many chants for modernizing the entire social and religious structure of Havai'i.

"He who would take away free will and introduce violence," Tūtū Ona added bitterly. "Because of this and his white robes, we called him *The Priest Who Wore Death*."

"What's wrong with white robes?"

"White is a colorless shade that symbolizes lifelessness," she bluntly replied. "We use it only to bury the dead."

"I still don't understand," Matani began, his eyes now completely fixed on hers. "Why did Pa'ao despise the Mū so much?"

"Why indeed?" Tūtū Ona asked, though her version of the question was cold and ironic. "The invaders called themselves chiefs and they called us *Manahune*, meaning *small power*, because they thought we knew nothing of murder, weapons, or war."

"But you did?"

"Of course, but having learned from the stumbles of our cosmic ancestors, Mū embraced a life that was simple and pleasant, focusing on people, their feelings, family, and personal growth. Even the descendants of Havai'iloa sometimes resorted to violence to solve problems, but we patiently taught them new ways."

Matani looked at her, astounded by the concept. "So, you're saying none of you ever fought?"

"There were occasional squabbles here and there, but Mū were an innately gentle and peaceful people without chiefs or system of law."

"No chiefs?" Matani asked, envious of the concept. "So who bossed everyone around then?"

"Guided by the wisdom of our past, we removed temptations of hierarchy, including the separation between men and women," she said. "Our ancient Mū elders had developed powerful methods of keeping relationships in balance."

Matani's eyes widened further. "That actually worked?"

"For many generations," Tūtū Ona said, flashing a radiant smile that quickly dimmed. "But this concept upset Pa'ao to no end because he'd been raised under a much more rigid society."

Then her wizened face moved with a thought, though she said nothing.

The next thing Matani knew, he was seeing into the past through the eyes of his grandmother as her voice continued narrating telepathically:

Deciding the descendants of Havai'iloa had been brainwashed through Mū sorcery, Pa'ao and his army sailed throughout the archipelago, building new temples for the tiki gods he'd brought from Tahiti, forever changing religion across the islands with a new tabu system of forbidden objects and actions.

Mū don't worship tikis?

We worship only the pursuit of purpose, though natural objects are used to communicate with our ancestral parents. An upright stone represents Father of All, Kūhiva, and a prostrate stone represents Mother of All, Hina. Using heartfelt prayers to call upon their assistance, we managed to keep those who would destroy us from the shores of Molokai O Hina for many years.

How would prayers be any help against weapons?

All who kept the rules of family had great power. Ona, Lae, Kea and Mahi were the last five lines of full-blooded Mū that had lived on Molokai for a thousand generations before the invaders arrived. A tribe of omen readers, mystics, and prophets, we called ourselves The Ones Who Keep the Sacred Light. Unfortunately, the forces of darkness proved so great we could no longer protect our home.

What happened?

Fueled by impure beliefs that genealogy established social status, Pa'ao organized an army of warriors to seize our island and end our mythic lineages. But shortly after they arrived, Pa'ao quickly ordered his warriors to return to their canoes.

Why? What did they see?

They had stumbled upon our Mana Temple at the tip of Halawa where several Mū children were gathered in a circle, their eyes closed.

Praying?

No, they were in a deep trance; engaged in an ancient breathing technique that produces deep, vibrating sounds. Pa'ao and his warriors watched in disbelief as a large boulder began rolling around the open space between them by unseen hands. Terrified by what they had witnessed, the priest and his army retreated from Molokai, calling it the Island of Sorcery.

So they just left?

Only for a while. As we would discover nearly three lunar months later, The Priest Who Wore Death returned to Tahiti and brought back an even larger army of warriors to conquer the islands. He also brought a chief of the highest lineage to repopulate the islands. Outnumbered by an army of darkness, the beaches of Molokai turned red with the invader's feather cloaks, then with the blood of slaughtered Mū.

How many Mū were killed?

Thousands of men, women, and children. Pa'ao savagely used their bodies as human sacrifices for his newly constructed temples, and their bones to decorate the wooden statues of his foreign gods. Only Tahitian-Mū mixes were spared, though forced to live as slaves.

What happened to you and your family, Tūtū?

We were among a small group that barely escaped with our lives, scattering throughout remote mountains and caves across the eight primary islands and beyond, to the northwestern ends of Papahānaumokuākea, living as outcasts waiting for peace to return to the land.

Are there Mū still hiding in the islands?

Yes, though in the beginning we risked exposure every now and again to help enslaved Tahitian-Mū build ditches, fishponds, and temples demanded by the chiefs.

That sounds dangerous.

It was, but we only came at night, completed the project before dawn, then returned to our caves and mountain hideaways without a trace.

Why would you risk being captured?

Because if the slaves didn't complete these projects in the few days given, the invaders would murder them and their families as punishment.

How many generations has it been since all that happened?

Enough for all the different languages and dialects brought with each wave *of inhabitants to blend through interaction and intermarriage, evolving into an entirely unique culture all its own.*

Matani blinked, as if startled from a dream. "Havaiians."

Tūtū Ona replied with a slow, single nod.

"So, what does any of this have to do with me?" he asked.

"Over time, the younger Mū who escaped into hiding eventually had offspring of their own. But the new generation that didn't experience the massacre firsthand grew impatient with hiding. They wanted to see and learn more of the world that their people had originally inhabited before the colonizers took it by force. One day Namahanaʻiloa, one of my grandnephews, had a daughter who grew very curious about the invaders, and against the family elder's wishes, she often snuck off to spy on them. Her name was Mahina, and during one of her outings, she met a young Tauaian taro farmer named Tumatua."

Matani tilted his head inquisitively. "My parents?"

Tūtū Ona confirmed it with a nod. "They fell deeply in love, and your mother eventually left her family and the caves they hid in to live among the Tahitians."

"So . . . I'm Manahune?"

"Oh, I really despise that name," she said, furrowing her brow. "It has nothing to do with race or lineage!"

"What am I, then?" Matani asked.

"Just as you've been told, you are second-generation Havaiian, because, like your father, you were born on Tauaʻi. But your mother's blood makes you Havaiian–Mū."

Beyond puzzled, Matani could only shake his head. "Why didn't my parents ever tell me about my Mū heritage?"

"Because it would have put you all in danger," Tūtū Ona said grimly. "Paʻao placed a lifelong bounty on all those who did not conform, as well as to prevent the mixing of bloodlines. To keep her lineage a secret, your father told everyone that she came from Maui."

"That's why I've never met any of her relatives," Matani said in realization. "They were in hiding."

"Partly, yes," said Tūtū Ona. "Unfortunately, after making the difficult decision to leave her family, Mahina caused so much hurt, they demanded she never return."

"But I still don't understand," Matani said, shaking his head in disgust. "Why was Paʻao so determined to wipe out the Mū if he thought they were so inferior?"

"Because he came to learn the truth that we already knew," she said with a look so serious, Matani felt a deep chill go up his back. "That ours is a sacred lineage steeped in the knowledge of *Mind Power*, here from the beginning of time."

"Mind Power," he repeated, tasting the words in his mouth as much as asking a question.

"Mū are taught from birth that humans are capable of remarkable things," she said, knowing her words were spectacular. "Like reading the weather, making the sky rain or clear up, sharing consciousness with nature, traveling anywhere without moving, or even visiting spirit family on the other side of the rainbow."

"So it's my mind that controls the wind?" Matani asked uneasily. "And summons storms?"

"Pssh! Weather manipulation is child's play. Your undisciplined tampering with the elements has been nothing short of negligent and dangerous!"

"Well, I wasn't even sure I was actually doing it!" Matani responded defensively. "I don't know how this stuff works!"

"A sober reminder of just how dangerous ignorance is!" she reprimanded him. "You lack concentration and proper training!"

"Well, who's fault is that?"

"Your father's," she snapped. "He wouldn't allow it."

"Because it has nothing to do with farming," Matani muttered. A reflection in the glowing amber water of the fishpond drew his attention to a dilapidated thatch structure sitting on the hill behind them. "Has that house been up there this whole time?"

"It's there now, isn't it?" Tūtū Ona answered with little explanation.

As Matani slowly approached the grass house, he could see that its gable roof had a number of sagging holes in its thatch. And the raised platform of fitted lava stones in its foundation had crumbled in several places, putting the entire structure on a slight tilt. Still, the house seemed oddly familiar. Everything from its shape and size to the precise placement of the tall, protective ti plants growing at each corner. Even the dusty gourd containers hanging in nets outside the entrance looked familiar.

Arriving at the house, he crouched through the low opening, careful not to let the braided stem on the left of the entryway scratch his back.

That can't be the same stem. Can it?

Once inside, Matani immediately recognized his childhood home. He had abandoned it after his father's death, because the memories it held were much too painful. Over the years, each time he'd passed his old home on the way to the taro fields, he would see it slowly disappearing as people scavenged materials from it, until nothing was left but a few stones. But now, standing inside it again, dilapidated though it was, he felt as if he'd been reunited with a long-lost family member. Matani smiled at the stone lamps glowing in each corner of the windowless house, remembering how his father kept them lit to ward off mischievous spirits that roamed the night. His smile widened when he found three rolled lauhala mats stored in the few remaining rafters, right where they were the last time he'd seen them.

I've never felt safer than inside this house.

Matani tried to force one of the fallen support poles back into position, only to have a clump of thatch drop on his head. Embarrassed, he quickly brushed himself off. "How did my house get here?"

"This is more of a spiritual re-creation of that place," she explained. "The first thing you must understand is that everything in the world of spirit is symbolic of something in the world of form."

"Am I able to fix it?"

"You can do anything you want," she said with a sly grin. "This is your Spirit Farm, remember?"

Matani was suddenly drawn to an energy at the center of the single-room house, where he found a pile of frayed thatch and broken rafters. He cleared them away, revealing a ring of lava rocks that contained a burning fire. How the debris hadn't caught fire was beyond him, but then he saw an object hovering just above the fire that was even more mysterious.

It was a small, simple, wooden bowl.

Although he couldn't recall his family owning such a bowl—and certainly not a floating one—he couldn't help feeling that he'd seen it before.

"What's this bowl?"

"The very first gift we receive at the moment of earthly conception," said Tūtū Ona, pulling back the left sleeve of her robe, revealing the top part of a crescent-shaped tattoo on her forearm. "A *Bowl of Light.*"

Leaning closer, Matani examined the inexplicably levitating bowl. It was crudely made, without markings or decoration of any kind on its smooth exterior. He felt a twinge of concern when he saw stones and pebbles of various sizes filling his bowl, smothering a golden light struggling to shine through.

"Looks more like a bowl of stones."

"Indeed, it does," Tūtū Ona said. "It's a symbolic expression of spirit. Throughout life, our bowl reflects all the choices we make. Good ones add to the purity of its birthlight. Bad ones take the form of stones, slowly pushing us out of balance."

"What happens when—" Matani stopped himself. "What happens if stones completely fill the bowl?"

"Once the light is extinguished, its owner becomes stone," Tūtū Ona said, lifting her eyebrows significantly. "Incapable of movement or growth."

"Well, let's dump out the stones, then!" Matani suggested, grabbing the bowl to turn it over.

But no matter how hard he tried, neither the stones or the bowl would budge.

Tūtū Ona shook her head. "These stones are far too complex to be emptied by impatient shortcuts."

"Then how do I get rid of them?"

"The same way you put them there," Tūtū Ona said, squeezing Matani's shoulder. "Free will."

Matani's shoulder slumped under her gentle hand. "Great."

"Every choice you make, every attitude you form, is reflected in your bowl. When a change is made in the physical world, it's reflected here in spirit."

"You're saying every bad choice I make puts a stone in there?"

"And every good choice removes them," she added. "Only you, and you alone, are responsible for what goes in or comes out of your bowl. No one else."

"Seems kind of important to know about a bowl like this at some point," Matani said with a hint of scorn. "Why didn't anyone tell me about it before?"

Tūtū Ona's gaze sharpened. "Long ago, all Mū had a natural relationship with their bowl. But over time, the attachments and cravings of the physical world distanced their connection with it."

"Of course they did," Matani said sarcastically, noticing a group of small creatures that looked like they were made of water. The flutter of their wings created a beautiful tinkling melody.

"Do not take this lightly, young man," she said firmly. "Only you can decide when you've grown tired of all these stones weighing down your light. The time has come for you to look deep within yourself. To separate from the illusion of who you *think* you are and become who you *really* are."

Matani just looked at her, genuinely lost. "Sounds like a great idea, but then what?"

"One who consciously tends to their light will grow in strength and be able to do all things—swim with sharks, fly with birds, and understand all things."

Before Matani could respond, his Spirit Home began to swim away, taking the comforting warmth and mixture of delightful smells with it.

"Hey, what's happening? I'm not ready to leave yet! I still have a lot of questions!"

Tūtū Ona placed her right hand over her heart, left hand over her sacrum, nodding conclusively.

Fear not. The night rainbow will guide you.

Then she, too, disappeared, along with all of Middle Island, replaced by a bright, fluid web of lights that carried Matani back across the incomprehensibly endless continuum of everything everywhere.

✦ CHAPTER 13 ✦

Total darkness finally gave way to a dull gray glow that brightened like the rising dawn, followed by the perpetual hiss and boom of the surf. His lips felt dry and stung with salt. With a gradual awareness that he was floating, the young man began to consider that he was quite possibly alive. But barely. A sharp, burning sensation along one finger submerged in water made him flinch.

He opened one eye and saw the gelatinous blue tendril of a jellyfish slide off his right index finger. The sting triggered his bladder to release a shot of warmth into the water, sending shivers through his bones. Slipping from consciousness again, he fell further and further away from the dreamlike sounds of rain tapping on skin, wood, and water.

The passing of time was vague, but at some point, prismatic flashes were followed by a deep, rumbling thunder that brought him back from the darkness a second time. Feeling a bit stronger in mind and body, he was able to raise his head and open his eyes. Somehow, he'd gotten himself stuck amid floating storm debris gathered at one end of a small, unfamiliar-looking cove along an even more unfamiliar-looking coastline. Breakers crashed against a rockbound shore, exacerbating the severe throbbing at the back of his head. He touched the area with his fingers and saw blood.

Glancing up at dark, rain-swollen clouds sliding overhead, the young man discovered that his left eye was swollen shut. Squinting the shoreline into focus with his good eye, he could make out a slightly blurred image of a very slender beach. Many steep cliffs rose thousands of feet above sea level to misty green valleys from which countless waterfalls tumbled down in bright streaks of white. An incoming wave rippled through the debris that encircled him, followed by a number of sharp, jagged sticks jabbing into him from all sides. His instincts urged him to get out of the water before something severely impaled him.

With painful effort, he swam toward the rocky shoreline of the cove, surprised to find both of his arms interlocked around a splintered hunk of wood. He was afraid to let go of it entirely for some reason and used it to push debris out of the way as he swam. Making his way ashore, clumps of leaves tugged at his body, which he discovered were attached to a rain cape he was wearing, though he couldn't recall ever owning one.

The young man ducked his head under the waves to wash the grit from his face, spotting several sea turtles hovering over enormous coral heads. Loud snapping sounds echoed through the water, broadcasting every bite of algae they harvested from the reef with their powerful beaks. A little farther along, the vibrant flash of something orange, white, and black caught his eye. It was a small clown fish nestled in the bright pink tentacles of a sea anemone. The image seemed important somehow, but then a bolt of lightning flashed above the water, making him surface right as a thunderclap exploded overhead, the sound so powerful it rattled his chest.

Making his way into the shallows of the cove, the young man found the beach to be even more narrow than he'd originally estimated—barely twenty steps to the vertical cliffs beyond, strewn with a muddle of sticks, branches, and other storm detritus. A massive waterfall slid down the towering wall of lava, muddy and swollen with storm-fueled floodwaters. The sea heaved against arm-like rock formations on opposite ends of the bay, exploding plumes of spray straight up the cliffs. He looked back and saw the reef diligently taming massive waves into gentle swells, which rolled in, sending harmless ripples of white water against the delicate shoreline.

Trying to discern what side of this strange island he was on, thick cloud cover hid the sun, making it impossible to orient himself. Even the flat gray lighting of the sky made it difficult to know if it was morning, afternoon, or evening.

The young man's good eye was still full of blur, but he was relieved when he saw a large number of people gathered at one end of the beach.

"'Ano'ai!" he shouted in a dry, tired wheeze.

But as he got closer, he realized they were a group of monk seals gathered on the beach to wait out the storm. As he approached, several of the creatures raised their smooth, blubbery heads, staring lumpishly at him behind the nervous twitchings of their whiskers.

"Can you at least tell me what island this is?" he mumbled, dispirited.

The largest seal flared its nostrils and made a soft, bubbly growl.

"*Grrrbbl* is the name of the island?" the young man asked sarcastically.

"Gah!" the seal replied, sleepily blinking its black eyes.

Frustrated, the young man inhaled deeply and trumpeted back as loudly as he could, "Gah! Gah! Gah!"

Every one of the chubby creatures raised its head in a chorus of aggressive, watery bellows before lumbering toward him with unexpected agility and speed.

"Okay, okay!" the young man shouted, trotting backward.

Quickly losing interest, the group of seals stopped where they were and resumed napping. Happy to leave them behind, he ran toward the waterfall. Snatching handfuls of fresh water from the cascade to wash the gunk from his good eye, his vision cleared a little more, offering a few more details of his surroundings.

A variety of seabirds populated the monumental black lava cliffs looming over the cove, swooping and diving from one small hole to another. The largest had white bands around long beaks, with wingspans as wide as the birds were tall. There was another smaller bird with white feathers and a red tail that entertained the young man by diving into the water over and over again until eventually resurfacing with a wriggling fish, which it carried back to its nest, hidden somewhere in the coastal undergrowth. By far, the largest population of birds in the cove had sharp, pointed beaks and came in various colors of white, blue, brown, and black.

Seeing them tilting their heads to swallow bites of freshly caught fish made the young man's stomach grumble. Searching along the opposite curve of the beach for something to eat, he spotted a pile of lava boulders at the water's edge covered in greenish-brown seaweed. Tearing off a tuft of the ocean plant, he chewed on it with a salty crunch. After pulling off a few more bites, he moved farther up the beach, where he found an ancient lava flow indented with several tide pools. Upon closer inspection of these little pockets of isolated seawater, he saw a number of limpets clinging to each of their rocky interiors. Pinching one between his thumb and forefinger, he carefully peeled away the limpet's smaller shell first and used it to shuck the tasty marine mollusk from its larger shell. The sweet, crunchy, creamy flavor definitely hit the spot, but seaweed and snails weren't nearly enough to appease his increasing hunger.

At the corner of his eye, the young man saw a dark object crawling along the bottom of the largest tide pool. Squinting past the bright reflection of clouds, he spotted a black rock crab and reflexively stepped on it. Hands shaking with hunger, he pulled away the creature's top and bottom shells, along with its gills, guts, and mouth. After a quick rinse, his tongue watered at the sight of a grayish-white lump of meat attached to its four legs. He popped it between his teeth and neatly devoured it. A bird settled near the discarded shells, picked one up in its beak, then dropped it and flew away. Lodged between the rocks where the bird had stood, the young man noticed something distinctly out of place. Carefully removing the object, he held up what appeared to be a torn fishing net.

"People," he whispered, hopeful.

Knowing he wasn't alone should have made him feel better, but his own logic prevented him. Seeing an old fishing net was very different than seeing a real person.

Staring apprehensively at the boiling sea beyond the cove, he couldn't see the coastline in either direction from where he stood. At some point, he knew he'd have to swim around one side or the other to search for whoever might have made the net he'd found, but the thought of going back into the stormy sea ignited a panic so visceral it made him dizzy.

"No rush," he told himself. "I can just stay here a few days and heal."

Looking as if it might start raining harder at any moment, the young man searched the cove for suitable shelter, but there wasn't much to be had between the steep cliffs, storm debris, and piles of lava boulders. But when he noticed a bird fly out from behind the waterfall he went to investigate, finding the opening of a small cave on the other side of the crashing flume.

The interior was cold, cramped, and dripping, but slightly warmer than outside. He crawled into the shallow, waterworn throat of lava and used his hands to rake out a small nest in the mushy, wet sand. The effort was enough to drain him of what little energy he'd gained from his meager meal of seaweed, limpets, and crab. Briefly thinking he should remove his soaking rain cape, the young man was already fast asleep.

Some time later, he awoke underwater, screaming for air.

Clawing, pushing, pulling his way through suffocating darkness for what seemed like an eternity, the young man's face finally broke through to night air and rain.

Amid the darkness, he could see that the entire cove was now completely submerged under crashing waves, swallowed whole by the incoming tide while he'd slept.

Choked by something, he realized his neck and arms had somehow gotten tangled in his rain cape. Freeing himself, a wave rolled in, broke, and slammed down, spinning his body until he could no longer discern up from down. Deafened by gurgling sounds of swirling fizz, a fierce undertow yanked his body backward and dragged him out past the coral heads until he could no longer feel sand beneath his feet.

Desperate for air, the young man spun helplessly, catching glimpses of turtle silhouettes hovering serenely in the dark water, until the current allowed him to lift his head above the surface just enough to grab a shallow gulp of air—only to have another crashing wave force him back under.

Time slowed, and a brief memory came to him from when he was about four or five. During his early years, while learning to swim in deeper waters, he'd been on a beach with someone. It took a moment, but the energy of his Auntie Mahanea finally came to mind. She'd taken the time one afternoon to teach him about rip currents.

If the water gets ahold of you, don't fight it. You'll just tire yourself out until you can't swim anymore and drown. Just stay calm. The best way to escape a rip current is to swim across it until you're free. Then make your way back to shore.

Running out of air, the young man's lungs eventually convulsed, forcing him to inhale seawater. On the verge of drowning, he followed the advice of his auntie and stopped struggling. Feeling the motion of the current, he stayed on the surface and swam across it using every last bit of strength, until a merciful wave finally drove him inland. The second his toes touched the sand, he stood up and locked his stance against the retreating water as it roared past his wobbly legs.

"Blessings, Auntie Mahanea," he wheezed, coughing up seawater.

Making his way back to shore, the young man wondered why he could remember certain things and not others. In particular, his own name. Unable to come up with a suitable answer, he hoped the slight memories he did have might lead him to remember more.

Barely able to see anything through the pitch darkness, the young man sprang through the surf until he reached the waterfall again at the back of the submerged cove. Standing in waist-high water, he was terrified the dark waves would pull him back out into the storm-riddled sea. He looked up the sheer cliff wall just as lightning exploded through the bulging rain clouds overhead, illuminating a heavy curtain of mist that swirled in the air. Pressing his body against the cliff, a deep, resounding boom of thunder vibrated the rock.

What do I do now? I'm trapped!

Expecting some kind of response from his inner thoughts, nothing came. Not a single word, positive or negative.

And it was an unnerving feeling.

Hello?! Anyone there to tell me not to give up? Or that I'm going to die? Anything?

Just then, a chilling sound came from behind. The young man glanced back and, with his slowly adjusting vision, saw a fresh bulge of surf hitting the reef, slowly curling into a wave. With little choice, he raced to the cliff and started climbing. Barely making it up a few more feet, the incoming wave crashed against his legs, fulfilling his worst fears by knocking him back into the water with ease.

Scrambling to his feet, he made his way back to the cliff, where an eerie silence caused him to hyperventilate. Looking behind him, what he saw confirmed what his body had already sensed—the bulging swell of another large, incoming wave.

So large, in fact, it sucked up every ounce of water from the beach, gathering itself into something monstrous.

The young man grabbed a fist-sized bump of lava sticking out of the cliff, took a deep breath, and pulled himself up. Despite the lava being covered with a thin coat of rain, its porous surface proved gritty enough for his hands and feet to grip. His heart pounded through his chest as he alternated between a handhold here and a foothold there, slowly but surely rising upward.

At a certain moment, without even looking, he could feel it about to happen.

Slamming his working eye shut in doomful anticipation, the young man's muscles locked as the terrible wave crashed against him with such ferocity, the force of its impact reverberated throughout the entire cliff. Expecting to be yanked back into the water, it took a few moments for him to realize that he'd somehow been spared.

Peeking from his unswollen eye, the young man couldn't believe that he'd made it just above the wave's crashing reach. Barely. But as he clung to the wall, feeling the strength weakening in his hands and feet, he was faced with the dilemma of what to do next.

I can't stay like this all night. My muscles will give out.

The waterfall to his left disappeared into the rainy mist above, making it difficult to assess just how far the climb would be to the top.

"Impossible," he said to himself, finding it hard to believe that he'd even entertained such a ludicrous idea. Then, he regarded the churning, deadly sea below, finding it very easy to believe he would drown in it. With a deep and fateful breath, the young man decided it was better to risk falling over drowning.

If I fall, I'll just end up back in the water anyway, right? So, what have I got to lose?

Again, no response.

Never mind.

Focusing on the wall of lava before him, the young man concentrated on making very careful hand and foot placements. Still having no idea how far the climb would be, he was careful to conserve his energy as much as possible. Feeling his pain-numbed fingers slipping, a bold rage took command of the young man's body, forcing him to continue with a steady, methodical cadence of right hand, left foot.

Then left hand, right foot.

Repeat.

Rarely finding full-on purchase with either hand or foot, he felt painful abrasions forming on his toes and fingers.

Rain slithered down the lava, bringing to life different shapes on its craggy surface. The young man began to hallucinate, seeing strange creatures crawling toward him, snarling and biting at his face. Horrified by the cruelty of his own imagination, he tried to blink them away and concentrate on climbing, but the burning pain in his fingertips and toes made it unrelentingly difficult.

Finally, his left hand stumbled upon a large hole that brought him some welcome relief, allowing him to firmly grab onto something. He pulled himself up, lessening the burden on his throbbing toes, and startled when several birds exploded past his face. Shouting in surprise, the young man leaned back, causing both legs to swing outward. Left dangling by one hand, he turned his body back around until it was flat against the cliff, banging the toes of his right foot into the sharp rock. His howls of pain were cut short when the three fingers supporting the entirety of his weight began to slip.

Not a second too soon, the young man's left big toe found a small ledge just wide and sturdy enough to transfer his weight onto. Another massive wave hammered the cove below, sending loose pebbles and stones rattling past him down the cliff face. Looking up, he couldn't believe his eyes. Through the mist, he could finally see the top of the waterfall roaring over the precipice.

Pressing his cheek against the cold, wet rock, he chuckled deliriously. "Almost there."

He glanced up just as lightning flashed, highlighting a lip of stone not too far above his head. He reached up with his right hand and stretched his joints and fingertips as far as they could go to grab hold of it. As he started to pull himself up, the stone unexpectedly shifted under his weight.

Slowly—very, very slowly—he transferred his weight from right hand to left, searching for a sturdier handhold.

To the left, nothing but smooth, flat rock.

To the right, not a bulge or indentation to be found.

Unable to believe he'd made it so close to the top only to run out of options, the young man searched the dark wall of lava above him for something—anything—he could use to pull him up a little more. Waiting patiently, another flash of lightning revealed a slight indentation above him and to the left. But in order to reach it, he'd have to jump. Just the thought of doing this made his joints tingle. Closing his eyes, hoping to find some lost inner courage, the young man found himself suddenly springing up as high as he could. Both hands flailed about in slow-motion—reaching, grabbing blindly and frantically for that precious indentation.

The moment he felt himself drop, he knew he'd made a terrible mistake, but at the very last moment of last moments, the index and middle fingers of his right hand managed to catch hold of something. It was thin and shallow, but enough to crimp.

Slowly reaching his left hand up and over the top of the cliff, his fingers felt a small plant or tuft of grass.

"Please have strong roots," he prayed.

Rising up on his toes, the young man sprang hard, transferring all of his weight to the unseen plant somewhere in the dark above him. Half-expecting the roots to give out at any moment, he swung his left leg up high enough to be able to pull his entire body over the ledge.

He rolled onto his back, gasping for air. "I don't believe it."

As the young man lay breathing heavily under the falling rain, an intoxicating blend of woodsy sweetness wafted over him. He lifted his head and saw the sharp black outline of a ridge in the distance cut from the stormy, glowing night sky. It had the distinct shape of a giant lizard. As he stared at it, the ridge suddenly became transparent, allowing him to see straight through physical matter somehow. Although not perfectly clear—like looking through scattered light underwater—beyond the lizard-shaped cliff, he could make out what looked to be the tallest mountain on the island.

Thinking sheer exhaustion was causing him to hallucinate again, the young man perched himself up a little higher on his elbows. Blinking in awe, he watched as a hole opened in the thick ceiling of clouds above him, framing a bright crescent moon in a patch of starry sky. It was tilted in such a way that it appeared to be smiling down at him. A mixture of moonlight and rain created the rare spectacle of a ghostly white arch across the sky, which landed directly atop the mysterious mountain peak.

"The night rainbow will guide you," the young man whispered with vague recollection, then passed out.

✦ CHAPTER 14 ✦

His father was outside their home, ranting about one thing or another, sparking that all-too-familiar fear deep in his gut, like a hidden predator was nearby and waiting to strike. But something about this particular outburst sounded different. Anguished.

Peeking around the frayed edge of the doorway, the boy was appalled to see his father ripping up his mother's beloved white hibiscus bushes. She'd spent weeks planting them around the property when he was born, and the sound of their roots being torn from the earth made the boy cringe with heartache. He couldn't comprehend why his father would destroy something his mother had cherished so dearly.

"Father, what are you doing?!"

"If your mother's ghost sees these flowers, she'll bring sickness upon us!" his father replied, angrily pulling out the last of the bushes. Then, he dropped to the ground on his knees with his fingers laced behind his head, wailing to the heavens.

The boy was more surprised than concerned by his father's mournful recital. It was the first expression of grief he'd shown since his mother had died. His gut-wrenching cries filled the air, triggering an even deeper pain no child should ever have to endure. Clamping both hands tightly over his ears, the boy tried to hide from the awful sounds, but his father's high-pitched bawling penetrated his fingers no matter how hard he pressed them against his head.

Then, a thick, heavy energy fell on the boy that fueled demons in his heart to bang with anxious savagery. He turned slowly, seeing the dead body of his mother laid out on a bier of logs covered with strips of trunk from a banana tree.

The boy slammed both eyes shut, gasping with horror.

His father barged in through the entrance of the house, tears streaming down his face. "Oh, no you don't!" he screamed. Then he grabbed his son's head and forced him to face his mother's ashen corpse. "Look what you did to my wife!"

"No!" the boy screamed back, struggling to free himself from his father's grip. "I don't want to remember her like this!"

"Then why did you give her that stupid flower?"

"I thought it would make her feel better!" cried the boy.

Clunking sounds on the floor drew the boy's attention. He looked up at the decomposing remains of his mother as she struggled to sit up, strips of bark sliding off her pale body. Both the boy and his father watched in horror as she turned her head with painful cracking sounds, staring at them with two lifeless, milky-white eyes. She opened her lopsided mouth to speak, but instead of words, a fat, pulsing taro bulb pushed out between her broken teeth. The boy tried to scream, but his father's unrelenting choke hold made it impossible for him to utter a sound or look away.

Then, a drop of water splattered on his forehead, waking him.

Soaking wet and shivering, the young man had no recollection of falling asleep. On his back, the only change in weather was that the brooding night sky had lightened, and the rain had become an intermittent sprinkle. Wiping an oily crust from his left eye, he was relieved to discover he could open it slightly. He sat up, adjusting the tattered rain cape around his shoulders, stretching cold, stiff muscles as he peered over the edge of the sheer drop.

"I can't believe I climbed that," he whispered.

The feat looked even more impossible in the dim morning light, but the bloody lacerations on his feet and fingertips proved otherwise. And the tide that had compelled him to risk his life had since retreated from the tiny beach, resetting its cruel trap for the next unwitting victim.

The cold morning sea reflected a grayish-silver panorama of clouds moving slowly through the sky. Farther out, a distant squall dragged a veil of rain across steely waters, erasing a segment of the horizon. Closer to shore, heavy winds generated dangerously large swells that battered the outer reef of the island, which the young man could feel thrumming up through the cliff he sat upon. Looking inland, overcast skies cast an even, shadowless gloom upon the forested landscape of . . . whatever this place was called.

O'ahu?

Uncertain why that particular island came to mind, the young man knew he'd never been anywhere else but Taua'i his entire life. At least, anywhere he could remember.

Still unable to locate the sun among the thick storm clouds, the young man realized he couldn't plot a trustworthy course without a way to orient himself. And being uncertain of only three of the seven directions—up, down, and within—which weren't much help, not knowing north, south, east, or west made him feel unsettlingly adrift. Yet, something was quietly pulling on him.

Something more than a sense of direction.

This seemed more like an urgent sense . . . of purpose.

Kneeling beside the muddy stream that fed the waterfall, he soaked his injured fingers and toes in the freezing water, receiving much-needed relief from the searing pain. Splashing a few handfuls into his mouth, the liquid tasted mostly of silt and earth, but it moistened his parched throat just the same.

Looking inland, he saw more of the rain-swollen stream cascading down a descending path of lava boulder clusters that paved the bottom of a steep and narrow green canyon. Farther up, past great tufts of mist drifting slowly between soaring mountains like enormous white whales, stood the verdant wall of a distinctly shaped landmark.

"Lizard Cliff," the young man breathed intuitively, remembering its peculiar shape from his vision.

And somewhere behind it, a mountain that's important somehow.

But the thought of hiking up the rugged canyon on two injured feet made him groan miserably.

Do I really have to go that way?

Considering that the fishing net he'd found was reasonable evidence that people would more likely be found somewhere along the coast, he took a closer look at his surroundings for any other possible options. Even if he waited for his hands and feet to heal, the thought of climbing back down the way he'd come was not welcome in the least. Nor was the idea of returning to a sea that he'd so narrowly escaped from with his life.

But there was something else nagging him.

Something to do with running out of time.

Unfortunately, this was a riddle he didn't have enough information to solve. Facing inland again, he guessed he could reach the ridge, or *tail*, of Lizard Cliff in about a day on undamaged feet, so it was reasonable to assume that it would take him at least two or three to get there. But before committing fully, the young man stood up and took a trial step, igniting a pain up his foot and leg so severe, his teeth clenched.

"Impossible," he grumbled to his throbbing feet. "I can't walk anywhere on these until they heal."

Spotting a clump of leaves and sticks floating down the swollen river, the young man dropped to his knees and reached out as far as he could, snatching several of them before they could be sucked over the falls.

The first few sticks were way too short. A third was broken. But the fourth one stood a little higher than his head and seemed sturdy enough. Adjusting his rain cape, he planted the stick on the ground and used it to lift himself up into a standing position. Again, he took a few trial steps, putting as much weight on the stick as he possibly could. Although painful, the walking stick alleviated the pain enough for him to think he might actually be able to endure at least a certain amount of hiking.

"I doubt I'll make it very far," he said as he began limping his way up the canyon.

Toward a mountain he couldn't see.

Leaving the ocean behind, the young man found himself swallowed by acres of plants, lava rock, and trees. Using landmarks to keep himself moving in a straight line up the canyon, he picked out a cluster of hardy shrubs as his first goal. Next came a dead tree—its brown branches reaching up like a skeleton's hand drowning in the leafy landscape—followed by a black wedge of lava that looked like a bald spot on a massive head of green hair.

The subtle differences between beach and forest became vividly apparent in the layered depths that shifted with every excruciating step he took. The cry of lofty seabirds and sounds of the perpetual surf were replaced by a chorus of insects, chirping forest birds, croaking frogs, wind-fluttered leaves, and the burbling of a cascading stream. Under different circumstances, he might have found more appreciation for the dramatic beauty of his surroundings.

But not today.

For every sound on the beach, there were two in the canyon. This was the result of an echo effect that was most evident when thunder rumbled overhead. Or when the young man screamed in pain after stepping on a shrewdly hidden stick or rock. In fact, these types of injuries happened so many times that he developed a rather morbid game: rating his screams of agony from one to ten fingers. So far, the winner had happened just moments earlier when he stepped on the upended point of a stick and pulled six splinters from the open sores.

An eight-finger scream, easily.

Forced to duck under branches and climb over logs, the once simple, practically unconscious act of walking now proved to be the most painful experience he could have ever possibly imagined. Hot streams of sweat slid down through smears of dirt on his face, continuously stinging his eyes. He felt like a decrepit old man the way he was hunched over, sidestepping his way very slowly up the canyon.

Even when he thought he'd reached the absolute peak of suffering, an overlooked stone underfoot sent the young man yowling past a new threshold of torment.

"What am I doing?" he shouted at the sky. "This is insane! I'm literally insane for doing this!"

Yet, a substantial worry that he might be punished by whatever forces had given him the vision of a mountain kept him moving forward, however reluctantly. At regular intervals, the blisters on his feet filled with sweat, forming tiny bubbles on his skin that became unbearably itchy—though, he found the warm liquid that spilled out when they popped to be oddly satisfying. He also came to grow wary of a certain low bush with long, serrated leaves that cut and slashed relentlessly at his legs. And although there was no visible sun, humid air trapped beneath low clouds was enough to keep his entire body covered in a perpetual layer of perspiration.

Lost in thought, a very clear memory emerged in the young man's mind, the clearest he'd had since coming to on the beach. It was the face of a young girl with unusual eyes. They were bronze near the edge of the iris, with tiny streaks of brown, green, and gold around the pupil. At barely twelve months old, she had somehow unriddled the puzzle of walking.

Which wouldn't have been that annoying except for the fact that—even though neither could speak yet—this precocious little girl seemed to lord her new ability over him. It would be another eight months, but with her help, he eventually learned how proper balance and alternating steps could make one more efficiently mobile.

Unable to recall her name, the young man stepped into a small trickle of water that snapped him from his thoughts. It wasn't enough to drink from, but over a considerable amount of time the tiny stream had diligently worn away the grass and turned into a slippery obstacle of red mud. Despite taking slow and careful steps, both his feet and ankles became caked in the stuff. Making it across without too much trouble, he climbed over a decayed log covered with moss, shocked to discover how bruised and battered his toes had already gotten in just a short distance.

Coming around a black lava cliff with several ti trees growing from it at odd angles, the young man was met with a glorious blast of wind that washed away the heat from his body. Leaning against the cliff to rest, he glanced down into the steep ridge and saw a forest of topless trees sticking up from the valley floor like dying fingers. Victims of some ancient hurricane.

I'm gonna pass out if I don't find something to eat soon.

Slowly making his way farther and farther inland, the pitter-patter of rain came and went, but the sound of squishing mud under his steps remained irritatingly constant. With each step, the young man also became aware of one particularly annoying knot in the mesh of his rain cape rubbing on his shoulder. But no matter how many times he adjusted and readjusted it, the knot kept returning to the exact same spot. To distract himself from the monotony of it all, he closed his right eye to see if he could catch a glimpse of his nose.

Yep. I can see the tip of the left side.

Then he closed his recovering left eye and found he could see the right tip of his nose.

I can't see my lips if I push them out though. Wait. If I pucker them like a fish, I can. What am I doing? I can barely think straight. All I hear now is the sound of my own breath. Hiking is hard. My face is hot, and I can feel the sweat on my forehead. The sound of birds everywhere. I feel small. Unimportant. This forest could swallow me whole. Maybe it already has.

As his tired thoughts rambled on, the world oscillated between light and dark under an endless parade of clouds. Growing hungrier and weaker with every step, the young man used every available plant or branch along his path as momentary crutches to keep himself moving. And to make things worse, it seemed like every five steps or so, some bedeviled branch would snag his loincloth and yank him backward, no matter how carefully he tried to avoid them.

The young man resented every bug and dragonfly he saw zipping past, wishing he could fly as they did. At the very least, he discovered that the red mud on his feet, when dry, gave his wounds a buffer of protection. But as soon as he walked across anything damp or wet, the stiff shell of clay would soften, exposing them again. It wasn't long before feelings of misery and suffering quickly compounded themselves, and the young man considered the possibility that he'd made a huge mistake.

Why am I following a hallucination? I should've looked harder for another way down to the coastline! What was I thinking?!

Trapped under heavy clouds, he could only guess it was around midday by now, but it didn't really matter, because he felt like he'd already been hiking for generations. Catching glimpses of Lizard Cliff here and there through breaks in the thick canopy of leaves, he was able to, at the very least, know he was going in the right direction. Seeing someone walking among the trees, he experienced a brief moment of hope, only to discover it was just the light and shadow of the wilderness playing tricks on him. Still, he couldn't quite shake the feeling he was being watched.

Suddenly uneasy, the young man recited a quick prayer with a thin hope that it might protect him from whatever evil spirits dwelled on this strange island.

As the day slowly wore on, heat trapped beneath the trees became increasingly unbearable. The young man stopped to rest by the stream, splashing the sweat from his eyes. Two frogs launched from clumps of grass along the bank, landing in the water—*plip-plop!*

When he looked down, two small shadows darted across the bottom of the stream.

Prawns!

Repositioning himself on his stomach beside a small cascade of water plunging over some rocks, the young man reached down and moved a few slimy stones. A small shadow shot out. Using his left hand, he guided the tiny creature over the miniature falls to his awaiting right hand and snatched it up. Lifting his fist from the water with an expectant gaze, he uncurled his fingers only to find an empty palm. After a few more failed attempts, the young man ended up with nothing more than a limp leaf and two waterlogged twigs.

Grunting loudly, he punched the water. "Prawns taste like poop anyway!"

Sitting up, the young man glanced down at the moss-edged stream, startled by his own reflection. He realized that among his lost memories, he'd also forgotten what he looked like. His face was streaked with mud, and his puffy, swollen left eye looked much more painful than it felt. But that wasn't what concerned him. What concerned him were the angry, furrowed brow and clenched jaw of the face staring back at him.

It was the face of his father, which he suddenly remembered all too well.

"Stone Boy," he whispered. But these haunting words came from a memory only his voice seemed to recall.

Giving up on the idea of catching any prawns at this particular stream, the young man got to his feet and continued onward through woods, woods, and more woods. The canopy of trees eventually opened up, revealing dark thunderclouds moving along steep rows of cliffs just ahead.

Better move faster before that storm gets on top of me.

Vaguely aware of his surroundings, the young man fell into a nearly blissful, pain-free daze for a while—until something skittered out from under some leaves on the ground. In a heartbeat, he calculated that his foot was about to squash whatever it was, so he leaned his weight back, forcing himself into a painful stagger that ended with him stepping on something pointy. Yowling in agony, he shifted his weight onto his walking stick, which promptly cracked in two.

Falling hard on his side, the young man experienced an entirely new level of pain that scorched through the aching joints of his lower back. Curled in a fetal position on a bed of damp leaves, he looked up and saw the reason for his dramatic fall.

A shiny brown lizard with light-colored stripes and a sky-blue tail.

Perched on the hollow edge of a rotted log, the tiny creature's head twitched in quick, jerky motions, studying the young man for a long, solid moment.

"Look what you made me do!" the young man shouted, throwing the remaining half of his walking stick at the nuisance.

But the lizard was already gone.

Struggling to right himself, the young man crawled around in a wide semicircle, searching through plants and underbrush for another suitable crutch. The first few pieces of wood he came upon were barely as long as his forearm, but then he finally pulled up a stick that he estimated was at least as high as his waist.

"You'll have to do," he said, looking up through tiny holes in the canopy of trees.

Finding Lizard Cliff again to reorient himself, the young man forged on with a slightly bent posture to accommodate his new, shorter walking stick. He shouted angrily at every tree that forced him to adjust his path. Even their passing branches were combative, grabbing at him like lifeless corpse arms. And with every glimpse ahead, the landscape promised to be brutal.

Around the time the sky darkened into the final glow of evening, the young man heard an unusual sound. At least, unusual for out here in the middle of nowhere. At first, he thought it was forest winds playing tricks on him, but as he stood still and listened, he could hear the unmistakable sound of a barking dog.

"Someone there?" he called out, hoping with all hopes the animal had an owner.

The young man followed the barking into a muddy ravine, where he found a deep sinkhole formed by a cave that had collapsed long ago. At the bottom, he spotted a small brown dog clawing helplessly at the ringed layers of sedimentary rock that encircled the hole.

Since meat was too valuable, most domesticated dogs were fed poi. As they got older, the heads of these *poi dogs* became flattened as the result of a soft diet that didn't require strong jaw muscles for chewing. Typically sluggish, fat, and dim-witted, this little dog was different. It showed none of these traits, having clearly been fending for itself in the wild since birth.

"Looks like someone's day is off to a great start," he said, the words feeling sentimental somehow.

The dog stopped and looked up with two frightened but uniquely colored eyes. The left was brown, like most dog eyes, but its right pupil had a striking ring of green around it.

"Nice eyes," said the young man.

The dog tilted its head, then barked impatiently.

"Not in the mood to talk. Got it. Let's see if we can get you out of there."

Searching the immediate area, the young man found a small, thin tree that had been torn from the ground by its roots. Not thinking twice about it, he got down and pushed one end of it into the sinkhole.

The dog cowered against the rock.

"Oh, don't be scared. Just grab it with your teeth, and I'll pull you up!"

But the little dog continued barking, refusing to budge, so all the young man could do was shake the tree, hoping to annoy the dog enough to bite down.

After a while, it finally did.

Yanking the branch up with force, the young man sent the dog cart-wheeling across the ground. Quickly righting itself onto all fours, it snarled, then turned and trotted off.

"You're welcome!"

Right then, a light breeze came through the forest, carrying an awful, rancid stench. Before the young man could speculate about it, an enormous dark blur raced from the ground cover, knocking his legs out from under him. Splayed on the dirt in a daze, he looked up and saw a hulking black boar standing in front of him. It had matted, bristly hair and long, sharp tusks stained with filth and blood. The young man could see that its beady black eyes were focused on the departing dog, having obviously been lurking nearby, waiting patiently for it to escape the sinkhole.

Pigs weren't native to the islands. And while most of the ones that had been brought by early Sea-Traveling People were domesticated and harmless, a few had escaped, wandered off, or gotten lost over the years, mutating into feral boars with long hair and tusks, forced to become more aggressive in order to survive in the wild. And this one standing before the young man inspired both awe and fear because it was immense, dwarfing even the largest pig in his village.

"Get out of here!" he shouted at the dog, rattling the dead tree to distract the boar.

It worked.

The beast's eyes shifted from the dog to him, and it roared deep, guttural sounds before charging with a piercing squeal. The young man scurried to his feet, barely dodging one of the boar's tusks as it knocked him down. Watching the boar circle around for another attack, the young man struggled to get back onto his feet, thinking he was dead for sure. When all of a sudden, the little dog shot out from some underbrush and bit the wild animal's hind leg.

As the boar squealed with rage, the dog looked at the young man as if to say, *there, we're even*, then took off running, with the boar chasing after it. The young man threw down the dead tree and grabbed his walking stick, blindly limping off in the opposite direction.

Glancing back, the young man saw a large boar launch the little dog high into the air with a savage toss of its head. His conscience getting the better of him, he winced and turned back to where the dog had landed, finding it unmoving. Keeping his eyes peeled for another surprise attack from the wild boar, he reached down to see if the dog was even alive—only for it to leap up and snap at him before racing off again.

Hearing something grunt, the young man turned to find the boar standing close enough for him to feel the heat from its chugging breath. There was no mistaking that its beady black eyes were full of revenge. This creature wanted blood.

Knowing his damaged feet couldn't outrun the boar, the young man waited for it to get close enough, then jammed the sharp end of his walking stick into the creature's right eye. Hearing a watery pop, he forced the stick deeper into its skull socket. Fetid slobber sprayed from the boar's mouth as it squealed in surprise and pain. It lunged backward, the stick sliding out of its punctured eye, then made a wide circle, centering its head on the young man before charging at him again with a shattering roar.

Launching to his feet, the young man raced up the ravine as fast as he could, fear and adrenaline barely diluting the pain. As he ran, memories of Ro'o's lore and traditions shook loose from his amnesia, reminding him how killing or injuring a pig during Matari'i-hiti was a sign of disrespect. Among the many body forms the shapeshifting deity could take during his tour of bringing fertility to the land, *Tamapua'a* was a mischievous half-man, half-pig creature who could manifest into different forms of nature.

Did I just make an enemy of a god?

Perhaps in answer to his question, the young man burst through a tree line and found himself sliding helplessly down a steep hill. He jammed the bloody tip of his walking stick into the ground to stop himself—only to have it snap in half, too.

Again? Seriously?

He hit the slope on one shoulder and somersaulted down the hill. His loincloth hitched up, and he felt sharp pieces of rock tearing into his thigh as he flung out his feet to slow his descent, launching an anguished scream from his mouth, easily the winner of the day.

Nine fingers, for sure.

Careening faster and farther down the slope, the young man saw a tree jutting out over the last steep drop like the bow of a canoe. He flung his body onto it, hugging its trunk with both arms. Below him yawned a precipitous drop that ended in a pile of rotted trees. Shallow by the standards of this wild landscape, but deep enough to kill him if he fell.

Catching his breath, the young man slowly persuaded his arms to loosen their death grip on the tree. Feeling the pain return to his feet, he slowly inched his elbows back until his butt was in the air, then walked his knees behind him. But before he could repeat this enough times to make it all the way back across the tree, it unexpectedly tilted forward. He froze, but the tree didn't. Teetering for a breathless heartbeat, it slammed onto the ground and slid down the bumpy slope.

With barely enough time to think, the young man jumped off the sliding trunk into a roll that ended with a loud *pop* under his rain cape. Not wanting to find out what that was, he jumped to his feet and tried to outrun whatever pain was coming for him. It worked for barely a moment before he realized something was terribly wrong with his left arm. The slightest movement detonated an unbearable, throbbing pain throughout his entire body that sent him to the ground, screaming as if he would never stop.

Ten fingers and three toes, easy.

He yelled at the sky. "What have you done to me? My arm is broken!"

Knowing that he could die from such an injury out here in the middle of nowhere, the young man sat up with his left arm dangling lifelessly at his side, feeling sorry for himself. Surprisingly, the sight of his deformed shoulder triggered another memory.

He'd been about three or four seasons old, out collecting ti leaves with Uncle Numuʻiʻua and his daughter, Etene. Climbing a boulder, Etene slipped and fell, dislocating her shoulder. Uncle Numu, who was familiar with bone medicine, acted calmly and quickly.

Control your heartbeat, and don't give in to panic, he said, encouraging his daughter to breathe and relax. He examined her shoulder closely. *If it were broken, you'd still be able to move it, but there would definitely be some bleeding and torn skin. I don't see that here, so I think your joint is out of place.*

She looked up at him with a worried look. *So, what are you going to do?*

Uncle Numu replied matter-of-factly, *I'm going to put it back.*

The young man nodded, then wiped away the tears of self-pity and pain. He sat up and assessed his arm. There was no torn skin, bleeding, or open fracture. And while definitely painful, he couldn't move it at all.

Okay, maybe it's not broken.

As he felt himself calming down, the young man recalled how his uncle instructed Etene to sit up straight with her back against the trunk of a tree. Then he told her to close her eyes. As soon as she did, Uncle Numu took hold of her injured arm and gave it a quick yank. She screamed so loudly, birds flew from the trees. But after a short while, she was back up, running and laughing, as if nothing had happened.

Wishing more than anything for his uncle to be here to help him now, the young man knew that he alone was going to have to pop his shoulder back into its socket. Not taking too much time to think about it, he extended his arm the way he remembered his uncle doing with his cousin. The pain was unimaginable, but he breathed in deeply, then took hold of his left wrist with his right hand—and yanked his left arm forward.

Crack!

Just like his cousin, the young man let out a brief howl and fell onto his back, staring up at the trees in a painful stupor as several startled birds launched themselves away.

"We have a winner," he said with a tired chuckle. "All ten fingers and all ten toes."

Lying still and exhausted for a while, the young man eventually sat up to test the mobility of his arm. Squeezing his fingers into a fist while bending his elbow a few times, aside from a little soreness, he was pleased to discover that his arm felt almost as good as new.

"I'm still here!" he shouted defiantly at the sky. "That all you got?!"

Not actually expecting a reply, the young man seemingly got one with a timely burst of rain.

"Okay, that's it! I'm done!" he ranted. "I hate this island! I hate this forest! I hate hiking! I hate clouds! I hate rain! I hate my feet! I hate that boar! And I hate being hungry! So, guess what? I quit!"

In the dimming atmosphere of the canyon, the young man found himself with a mostly unfettered view of the moon's fourth phase, the irony of its timely appearance not lost on him. Its crescent form, now slightly wider than the night before, was considered to be a celestial omen for a life in balance. It portended an important day for strengthening bonds with family and friends, restoring relations with guardian spirits, and reconciling differences between seen and unseen worlds. However, this was only possible for those who refrained from bad behavior, as that proved to create unnecessary obstacles.

"Oh, mind your own business," the young man muttered at the moon, even as it quietly assisted in his search for a place to sleep for the night.

Stumbling upon a large tree with a hollowed-out trunk, he probed the interior of its cavity for any unwanted surprises. Clearing out a few dead bees and a spiderweb before crawling inside, he leaned back against the trunk's interior, finally allowing his tense body to relax. Barely a moment later, every single muscle, scratch, cut, and bruise began pulsing and buzzing, topped off by a severely pounding headache.

Of course, the suffering didn't stop there.

The hollow shelter of the tree proved to have tremendous acoustics, amplifying the pounding rain in such a way that it felt as if his already throbbing head was inside a wooden drum being banged on by a thousand tiny fingers. And it might have just been his imagination, but gods be cursed if the rain didn't start coming down just a little bit harder. The time between now and waking up stretched like a grim, blighted expanse in the young man's memory—an endless nightmare without peace, rest, or respite from excruciating pain.

I wish this day would go away and never come back.

Startled by vague stirrings in his flesh, the young man's body went rigid with paralysis, followed by a loud buzzing that filled his ears. Focused on the pitter-pattering of rain and movement of leaves through the jagged opening in the tree trunk before him, his vision blurred into an oddly familiar web of lights, followed by an extraordinary sensation of his expanding awareness . . .

· CHAPTER 15 ·

The young man found himself standing once more inside his childhood home. While he still couldn't remember much of his life, he did remember most, if not all, of his last encounter with Tūtū Ona.

With grateful relief, he quickly noticed that his body, form—or whatever he was in this place called Middle Island—was perfectly intact. No bruises or abrasions of any kind. Not even on his fingers or feet. His muscles weren't sore, and he wasn't the least bit cold, hungry, or thirsty.

Through large holes in the sagging thatched roof of his Spirit Home, the young man saw an enormous tree floating across the beautifully odd green sky with triangular winged creatures perched on its branches. Three large sea turtles hovered just below the tree, using powerful beaks to scrape food off its exposed roots. And in the sky itself, a lighter shade of emerald this time, a striking moon glowed with hues of blue, like the ocean, and green, like an island, with a delicate shell of white swirls.

That is the holy artifact, warm and nurturing among the vast, dark sea of space. The island world upon which all human life is connected.

Pondering the beautiful but mysterious thoughts of his grandmother, the young man glanced around his house, noticing that its framework had collapsed further at one end since his last visit, offering a wider view of the surrounding landscape. Remembering his bowl, as well as its significance, he turned to find it suspended above the rock fireplace.

It was lower than last time.

And had a little less light.

At first, the young man denied that he'd done anything wrong to deserve whatever might now be weighing down his bowl further. But as he looked over the accumulation of stones, the young man was shown projections of the day's lowlights in his mind: his consistent bitterness and negativity, how he blamed everything around him without taking any responsibility, threatening to quit, and perhaps worst of all, his overall disrespect for nature.

"What about saving that dog?" he asked whomever might be listening. "That was good, wasn't it?"

A proper show of character, Tūtū Ona's voice answered in his head before she appeared beside him, lizard-headed staff in hand. "But one good deed doesn't outshine a handful of bad."

Exasperated, the young man's gaze sharpened. "How can I stop putting stones in my bowl if I don't even know I'm doing it?"

"By developing a more conscious relationship with yourself."

"That's going to be difficult, since I can't even remember who I am."

"Ridding you of past distortions was a gift of fate," his grandmother said.

The young man's brow wrinkled. "How is not knowing who I am a gift?"

"Our future projections are shaped by past experiences," she explained. "You've been freed of corruption, false identities, and unhelpful beliefs so that you might now finally have a chance to reclaim your sovereignty."

The young man shot her an annoyed look. "My what?"

"Personal sovereignty," she clarified. "It means that even when caged and bound, you still have the choice to be free."

"Okay." He shrugged. "Can you at least tell me my name?"

"Of course," she said, grinning with an expression of quiet insight. "When you're ready."

"Great," he said, throwing his hands in the air. "More riddles."

"Not riddles," she said patiently. "Lessons."

The young man snorted. "Whose side are you on?"

"Our ancestral collective's, of course," Tūtū Ona said, eyeing him narrowly. "I won't be making it a habit to repeat myself, but as I've already said, only you choose what goes into and comes out of your bowl."

Her words struck him deep. "You keep talking about choices like they exist. Exactly when, throughout my entire day, did I have a choice?"

"At each and every deciding moment," she said, then made fists with both of her hands. "My left hand is happiness. My right is suffering. Which do you choose?"

Thinking she might be playing some kind of trick, the young man thought himself rather clever when he came up with a third choice. "Neither?"

"So, you choose to become stone, then?"

"What? No!"

"Well, the only result of doing nothing is becoming nothing."

"Okay, you got me," he said disdainfully. "I should've picked happiness."

"Pssh! No one's trying to *get* you," she replied in a satirical tone, then lightly slapped him across the cheek—with her *suffering* hand, of course.

"Hey, what was that for?"

"If happiness is the correct answer, why, in all the stars above, do you keep choosing to suffer?"

"I don't know," was the best answer he could come up with.

"The answer is because you keep letting your past govern your present," Tūtū Ona said. Then her face softened. "Ultimately, you are the creator of your life, and any given situation or predicament you find yourself in is brought about by the choices you make."

"How can it be my fault?" he shouted, tightening his fists. "I never have any power over anything that happens to me! Ever!"

Tūtū Ona's eyes widened. "Ah, there they are."

His gaze was on fire. "There *what* are?!"

"Your emotions," she said. "You don't even realize when they take over, do you?"

The young man glanced down at his balled-up fists, quickly shaking the anger from them.

"You really mustn't keep blaming others for your problems," she continued. "Stop being so negative and take responsibility for your own actions!"

"You're telling me I need to find a way to be positive about my memory loss? About being lost and hungry? That I should be optimistic about hiking on injured feet? Or being attacked by a god taking the form of a wild boar? Or falling off a cliff and dislocating my shoulder?"

Tūtū Ona looked up, raising both arms dramatically to the sky. "Hail the firmament! He's finally getting it!"

The young man shook his head, unimpressed by his grandmother's theatrics. "What does any of this have to do with why I keep choosing suffering over happiness?"

"Somewhere under all that stubbornness of yours," she said, tapping his chest, "you already know what you're doing is wrong, yet you keep punishing yourself because you think you deserve it."

These words hit the young man like a stiff punch to the gut. "How do I stop doing that?"

"Our actions speak truth more than our words. Maybe if you start acting like life is a blessing, it might actually start feeling like one," she said, staring at him a thoughtful moment. "Let me ask you something. Do you like yourself?"

His mouth was grim. "From what I know of myself so far? No, not really."

"Then why would anyone else?"

The young man surrendered to this blunt statement with a partial nod, suddenly overcome with a familiar, almost comforting, depression.

"Here's another clue to living," she continued. "If you can accept the world as it is, there's no pain. No suffering."

The young man just stared past her at a tree with branches that seemed to move with a will of their own. "Accept what exactly?"

"Where to begin?" she said, inhaling a deep breath. "Certainty, change, human nature, imperfection, unforeseen events—"

"Okay, okay, I get it," he interrupted. "Pretty much everything."

"Everything *outside* yourself," she corrected him. "Otherwise known as reality."

"Yeah, I know it well," the young man replied bitterly. "So, what's inside me that I *can* control?"

"That which you say you don't have," she said, clearly delighted by the question. "Your mana."

"Mana?" he snorted impatiently. "That's just something royals came up with to control commoners."

"Not at all," Tūtū Ona said earnestly. "But sadly, the concept has been manipulated over the years by selfish charlatans."

"What is mana supposed to be, then?"

She met the young man's interested gaze. "True mana is a limitless source of power generated by The One Who Creates All Things, manifesting in everything, everywhere. We all feel its presence at some point in our lives, but how we choose to respond, or not, decides just how much mana we're able to acquire."

"Do I need to be religious to get mana? Or spiritual?"

"Young man, you need not be bound by religion or spirituality to receive mana," she said. "*Mana* means force-energy, and *ho'o* means to make. Together, *ho'omana* signifies empowerment, informing our identity, both individually and as human beings."

"Is it possible for all three work together?" he asked. "Religion, Spirituality and Empowerment?"

"Not only possible, but imperative, for each is a sacred expression of our connection to the divine and the land. Religion is the path of ceremony and tradition, honoring the gods. Spirituality is the inner journey, communing with the divine within. Ho'omana is the sacred practice of nurturing and awakening the mana that lies dormant within, awaiting only conscious acknowledgment and embrace. Together, like a river's flow, all three can be used to guide us on the journey of spirit, embracing the sacredness of life."

"So, your saying it's not about blood or what family I'm born into?" the young man interrupted, his eyes flickering with hope. "That I already have mana in me? And can have as much as a chief?"

"There are no limitations except those you place on yourself," she explained. "Every single living thing is born with permission to access mana, but it's important to remember that this power can never, ever be owned."

"Why not?"

"Because mana is a gift from the universe. If you live honorably, your mana strengthens."

Considering this, the young man asked, "How long can I keep my mana if I live honorably?"

"For all time, in body and spirit," she replied. "It is this flow of mana that keeps genealogies connected across time and space, life and death, in constant support of ascension, generation after generation."

"So, I have no mana right now because of our family's problems?"

"In part, yes. Our entire ancestral line is tangled, blocking its flow through us all," she said, clasping her hands together. "These knots cause spiritual illness and depression, greatly slowing our family's evolution."

"How do we untangle the knots?" the young man asked uneasily.

"Forgiveness and resolution," she said. "Two things many in our family refused to do in life when they had the chance."

"I forgave my father's relatives for abandoning me, but I can't say it hasn't been hard facing so many of life's challenges by myself."

"To say that one forgives but doesn't forget is not to forgive at all," she explained. "This is one of the largest stones in your Bowl of Light."

"So if I practice forgiveness, I can remove it?"

"Blessedly, every sunrise brings a new opportunity to change ourselves for the better," she replied. "Healing this family will strengthen your own mana and help you reclaim the light in your bowl."

"I'll try, of course," he said. "But will you help me?"

Her eyes heavy on him a moment, Tūtū Ona let out her breath. "No," she said, planting her staff on the ground. "But I will help you help yourself."

For the first time since he'd arrived, the young man smiled. "I had a feeling you were going to say that."

"Then maybe you *are* paying attention." Tūtū Ona smiled back. "Do you remember what I told you about how making changes here, in the spirit islands, will have a direct impact on aspects of your physical life?"

The young man nodded. "I remember."

"See anything around here in need of change?"

"Well, this house could definitely use some work," he said.

She nodded. "There must be good reason for it to be shown to you in this way."

"Could it be a symbol for family?" he suggested, going with his first impulse. "And that mine is in ruins?"

She lifted both eyebrows, impressed. "Very insightful."

He blinked, expecting her to say more. "Okay, so now what? Is it up to me to fix everything?"

"Perhaps."

"But how? I was raised a farmer and know nothing of building houses!"

"Here, in your Spirit Farm, when you need help with something, just ask."

This time, the young man raised his eyebrows. "Ask who? You?"

"Goodness, no," his grandmother laughed. "I don't know the first thing about building houses, either. But there are many spirit helpers around here who do."

Not exactly sure what she meant, the young man looked over his family home, saddened by its dilapidated appearance. Looking in no particular direction, he asked, "Is there anyone here willing to help me fix up this place?"

Tūtū Ona clicked her tongue impatiently. "Young man, you really must learn to create more meaning with your words. Even before learning to speak, Mū children are taught the importance of being a poet."

"What does being a poet have to do with speaking?"

"Seeing life through carefully chosen thoughts and words can add meaning and manifest powerful healing," she said. "Not only for ourselves, but also those around us."

The young man nodded and thought a good long while before trying again. Following his intuition, he closed his eyes and opened his heart.

It hurts deeply to see a place that has always meant so much to me in such a shambles. A place of safety and special memories. Watching it slowly dismantled piece by piece over the years, like some dead and forgotten carcass, I couldn't do anything about it by myself. But now, with a little help . . . maybe I can.

When the young man opened his eyes, his family home was gone.

The only thing he saw was an empty plot of land, untouched by human hands.

"Where'd it go?" he asked, alarmed. "Did I do something wrong?"

"Be patient," she said, calmly raising her hand. "In this place, teachers take many forms when a lesson needs to be learned."

As soon as he released control of what was happening, the young man began hearing voices. A large group of people came up over a hill—men, women, and children—each holding the largest stone they could carry. They were led by a young man in a simple loincloth with black hair and a short black beard.

"This way, everyone!" he shouted, grinning excitedly. "Our esteemed priest has chosen this very spot to build our new home for its favorable protection from winds, rains, and other elements!"

At first, the young man thought he was seeing things, but as each person came closer to where he stood, he realized they were all transparent. "Why do they look like that?"

"You are seeing a memory of your family's history that's been recorded in your blood."

Studying their faces, the young man didn't recognize any of them. "My family?"

The bearded man ran from one person to the next, guiding the position of each stone that they had brought to the site.

"Well done!" the man applauded. "Many hands make for easy work!"

After every stone had been placed on the ground, forming the start of a large, rectangular outline, he turned to a toddler standing beside him. "Tumatua, do you know the importance of these rocks?"

The young man looked over at Tūtū Ona, surprised. "Tumatua?"

"Your father," she confirmed with a slow nod. "And that bearded man is your grandfather, Namotahaʻi."

While young Tumatua considered the question, a slightly older boy standing beside him answered, "It holds up the house!"

"Hey! He asked *me*, Numu!" young Tumatua shouted.

Only then did the young man see the face of his Uncle Numuʻiʻua in the older sibling.

"Very good, Numu," Namotahaʻi laughed. "But I wanted to hear your brother's answer!"

"It holds up the house," young Tumatua repeated glumly.

"Right again," Namotahaʻi laughed. "And all these stones that our family and friends have carried up here are infused with endless amounts of love, giving our new home the strongest foundation possible."

"But how long will it last?" asked young Tumatua with a worried look on his face.

Namotahaʻi stared intently at his son. "For as long as we don't chip away at it with lies or half-truths," he said, then quickly burst into another smile. "Now, what are we waiting for? Let's get to work!"

Cheers and laughter erupted as images of the young man's family faded away into the landscape of his Spirit Farm.

"I wish I could go with them," he said yearningly, watching the ruins of his old house reappear before him.

While the vision was still clear in his mind, he walked over to the sunken parts of the foundation and began repositioning the rocks. Amazingly, each time he touched one, it felt like some kind of magnetic energy was pulling at it. After moving a few more, he realized that the rocks were actually trying to tell him where they wanted to be placed.

Such a strange island this is!

The young man continued to attempt reconstructing the house's foundation, only to discover when he was nearly done that one of the largest stones was missing. He looked around the immediate area without any luck. Searching farther and farther out and away from the house, he ended up following a glowing amber river.

"Don't wander too far," he quietly warned himself.

Strange voices howled in the distance, jump-starting his imagination. Off to his left, a trail of leaves slithered along the ground, which he realized was being carried by large white bugs with long red antennae. The river meandered past a small pond, where several boneless, fleshy creatures with six eyes bobbed up and down in the water, eventually leading to a foaming waterfall tumbling into a larger pool of glowing amber. Down below, at the outer edge of the water, he finally spotted the perfect stone to complete the foundation of his home. He climbed down the embankment, finding it to be much bigger than he realized.

After he spent a good amount of time digging, Tūtū Ona appeared at the top of the falls. "Struggling quite a bit with that stone, aren't you, young man?"

He looked up at her, annoyed. "The size is perfect, but I can't figure out how to get it out of here."

"Did you know that every single rock, piece of wood, plant, and thatch was asked to be part of your family home before the project began?"

He rolled his eyes. "Well, I looked everywhere for the original missing rock back there, but I couldn't find it."

"Perhaps finding the final stone for the foundation of your Spirit Home is important, wouldn't you say?"

"Okay, then, what do you suggest?"

"You're asking this rock to let you walk, sit, and sleep on it, aren't you? Think about that. Would you like it if someone you didn't know forced you to carry their burden without your permission?"

The young man bobbed his head in thought, realizing his mistake. "Well, no."

"Of course not. No living thing wants to be taken for granted. Being respectful to any and all things is an important part of creating a meaningful life experience." She raised a finger to her lips, lightly tapping them. "Are you familiar with ʻohana?"

"It's a word from the taro plant that means *many oha*, a symbol for family," he dictated more from repetition of his father's lectures than memory. "As a taro plant matures, offshoots called ʻoh grow from the parent plant and, over time, they mature and produce new generations of taro."

"Very good. And it also refers to more than just blood relatives," she articulated. "In Mū culture, there are no strangers, and all are treated with respect, be they a person, place, or thing. 'Ohana is the animate and inanimate working together—caring, teaching, inspiring, encouraging, supporting, and even disciplining those we love. But constant cultivation and nurturing are needed to deepen these bonds, which, in turn, help to strengthen mana for all."

He looked up, tired. "Okay, I get it. This rock is my brother or sister in nature. So, what do you want me to do?"

Tūtū Ona raised one eyebrow that conveyed the answer was obvious. "Ask permission before moving it!"

The young man looked down at the rock, then back up at his grandmother. "Ask? A rock?"

She didn't bother to answer him, of course. And he rolled his eyes in disbelief at what he was about to do.

"Okay, rock. Would you like to be part of my home?"

"Not very poetic," she critiqued. "Try again."

Reining in his frustrations, the young man bent down and gently placed his hand on the rock. "I understand you've probably gotten used to living in this spot, but if you come with me, you'll be a part of a home. If you want, we can be family. Wouldn't that be better than sitting way out here all by yourself?"

A sudden burst of positive energy shot from the rock, straight up through the young man's arm. He looked up with a huge grin. "I think it just answered me!"

"Of course it did. All nature asks of humans is to remember our connection with it," Tūtū Ona said in a steady voice. "*Now* try moving the rock."

The young man laid both his hands on the rock, thinking he might now at least be able to unwedge it from the earth. Much to his surprise, the rock lifted up entirely off the ground, floating before him in midair.

His eyes went wide. "Are you seeing this?"

Tūtū Ona smiled. "I am."

The young man effortlessly guided the rock back up along the river, needing only the slightest nudge here and there to maneuver it through the forest. The moment he lowered it onto the foundation of his house, it fit as perfectly as if it had been chiseled to exact specifications. As soon as the rock clicked into position, the ghostly images of his family reappeared around the property, this time with all sorts of building materials scattered everywhere.

Men shared jokes and laughed as they raised fitted studs and timbers, building the framework of the house. Ignoring complaints, elders showed their grandchildren how to fill in spaces between the foundation with small, river-worn pebbles, then cover it over with soft *pili* grass. Women sang beautiful songs of inspiration as they attached freshly cut thatch to the walls and rafters.

It wasn't long before every rock, corner post, wall plate, rafter, and ridgepole was in place. Every inch of the new home was just as the young man remembered it, down to every last purlin and lashing. As several women finished braiding the grass at the front opening, Priest Nereite, who had chosen the location of the house for the family, arrived to conduct its sacred birthing ceremony.

"Harmonious is the prayer to the multitude of gods," the priest's voice rang out. "With these words, we sever the umbilical cord attached to the House of Tumuhana!" Using a wooden dagger, he cut a tuft of grass that had been purposefully left hanging in the doorway. "We stand! We cut! The naval string is cut!"

"It is cut! Lo, it is cut!" recited all friends and family standing together.

The priest raised his hands to the sky. "The ceremony is complete! A new home is born unto this family!"

Before anyone could enter, Namotaha'i came forth with the final blessing.

"If a man in trouble enters this house, may he be well.
If a dying man enters this house, may he be well.
Grant life to me, grant life to my wife and children, grant life
to my parents and relatives, to my family, and to all on earth.
May this house become our home."

Inside, lauhala mats were spread across the floor, and the thatch walls and ceiling were decorated with scented *maile*, *'ie'ie*, fern, and flower leis. With the house birthing ceremony complete, Namotaha'i announced a customary feast for all those who had helped him build it.

"Great gods above, here is vegetable food and everything else provided for the new house," he recited, offering the meal's essence. "This house is given to you. Take care of your children inside it. As the house shelters against rain, wind, cold, and heat of the sun, so may the gods protect us from misfortune."

As everyone gathered to partake in the celebratory feast, the young man beamed with misty-eyed nostalgia, watching everyone eat, laugh, and share stories of the old days until, one by one, each of them slowly faded away.

"I always loved it when we'd all get together like that," he said wistfully.

Tūtū Ona smiled. "Gatherings are important for keeping family connected. And like any good working relationship, how well everyone gets along is vital to living a happy and healthy life," she said. "Not unlike the three energy centers of self."

"Three what?" asked the young man.

"Come," she said. "Walk with me."

Outside in the cool afternoon air of his Spirit Farm, the young man followed just behind Tūtū Ona through verdant fields of high grass that rippled like ocean waves. He looked up just as a large bloom of jellyfish floated through the air before a perfectly circular orange sun, their tentacles glowing with an ethereal light. Dashes of shadow and light flickered through the silky spaces of atmosphere between their flowery silhouettes and onto his face. Glancing behind him, in the opposite direction, the now familiar three crescent moons—each slightly larger than the next—were just lifting above the distant mountains, burning yellow and delicate.

"I'm sure you've noticed this tattoo on my forehead," she said, stopping to face him beside a large, shaggy tree, green with what looked more like feathers than leaves.

"I have," he nodded, squinting at the markings. Two circles, one larger than the other, containing two columns of three dots. "What is it?"

"It is called Waihona Manaʻo, an ancient Mū symbol for memory depicting *The Anatomy of Being*. The two columns of dots symbolize three non-physical aspects of *Self* that mirror the three corresponding levels of consciousness: ʻUnihipili mirrors the physical body and operates at an unconscious level," she said, gently placing her left hand over her sacrum. "She is our sister, the feminine, our source of emotions, memories, and instincts." Then she rested her right hand over her heart. "*Uhane* mirrors the conscious mind. He is our brother, the masculine, our source of will and intentionality."

The young man paused with uncertainty. "The part that makes choices?"

"Yes, but based on beliefs one holds to be true," she elaborated. "You see, at birth, we're each given a clean slate. No preconceptions."

The young man winced. "I'm guessing preconceptions are a bad thing?"

"To put it mildly," Tūtū Ona replied flatly. "Throughout childhood, your 'Uhane receives input from past experiences and cultural conditioning. Without healthy guidance, this part of you learns to accept things to be true, even if they aren't. Or untrue, even if they are. Over time, these unchallenged beliefs can become the foundation for the remainder of your life."

The young man's eyes flashed. "Like how I always think the world is against me?"

"Exactly like that," she said with a tight snap of her fingers. "Your 'Uhane has internalized this belief as an absolute truth, causing you to see yourself as a victim who is unable to make positive changes in his life."

"So, I've been a prisoner of my own mind all this time without even knowing it?"

"Yes, but fortunately your 'Uhane has the ability to evolve and change as you gain more knowledge and experience," she said. "By training it to think more critically, and challenge perceptions, you can live a much more empowered life."

"Okay, so how do I teach my 'Uhane to do that?"

"By developing emotional intelligence through your *'Aumākua*, the third aspect of Self that's connected directly to the vast web of existence. Not to be confused with *'aumakua*, which refers to the physical form ancestral spirits take to visit the living," she clarified, then gently placed a hand on her head. "'Aumākua is the androgynous seed that mirrors the superconscious mind. It enters the physical body with your first sacred breath, and stays with you until your final exhale at life's end."

The young man glanced upward with an unsettled expression. "If my 'Aumākua is always there, why won't it help me make better choices?"

"While this higher aspect offers assistance through dreams, visions, and intuition, it will never tell you what to do."

"Why not?" he replied with a bitter tone. "Wouldn't that make life a lot easier?"

"To put it simply, free will and mistakes are where the lessons are," she said. "Consider these as opportunities that help you learn and grow."

The young man groaned, his face flushed with embarrassment. "After all the dumb things I've done, I can't imagine what my ʻAumākua must think of me!"

"Oh, nonsense," Tūtū Ona scoffed. "This part of you isn't judgmental, though it does share in your defeats and cheer you on with every success."

"Where does the higher Self even come from?" he asked. "I mean, who created it?"

"The ʻAumākua is not created, it simply exists among the mystical tapestry of the universe," she replied. "With each lifetime, this sacred aspect infuses its consciousness into your physical body and combines with energies from your biological mother and father."

The young man considered her words. "What makes me, me."

With a nod, Tūtū Ona validated his assumption. "This is how you share similar characteristics and physical traits with your parents, like having a similar walk to your father or the same eyes as your mother."

He looked at her abruptly. "Can I inherit anger from a parent?"

"Without question," she replied. "Blood carries memories of both the strengths and wounds of our ancestors. Their wisdom enriches our lives, while unresolved issues can manifest as emotional and mental challenges and prevent the entire lineage from evolving."

"Stone," the young man whispered eerily, finally beginning to understand how all these different concepts of consciousness related to him and his overall life experience.

"Your personal stagnation is the result of an imbalanced Anatomy of Being," she explained. "The weight of your own past traumas and negative beliefs have rippled outward, impacting all aspects of your life."

"Of course it has," he mumbled, but then caught his grandmother's disapproving gaze and quickly backtracked. "I mean—how do I fix it?"

Tūtū Ona cocked an eyebrow. "As always, by starting with good and clear intentions," she said, then turned to the sky with her staff held high. "Let us open our hearts wide and pray:

O Moʻo Kiko,
Great Lizard Goddess,
Mother of our ancestors,
With the light, with the weather, with the elements,
Support our process of healing.
Show us your care, and bless this young man's efforts,
Act with empathy, act with righteousness.
Replace his unhelpful beliefs with positivity and light.
Fill his darkest corners with righteousness, with love,
And help his physical and spiritual parts find balance."

Tūtū Ona lowered her staff and turned to face the young man with a determined look in her eyes. "Now," she began, her voice unbidden and powerful as she pounded her staff on the ground. "Let's rid you of all this negative energy!"

With a grand flourish, she swept her staff between them and the young man suddenly found himself lying face down on a luxurious bed of lauhala mats in the corner of his Spirit Home. Tūtū Ona was kneeling beside him, her eyes glinting with steely resolve as she prepared to lead him on a challenging journey of healing.

"The final components of your Anatomy of Being are symbolized by these two outer circles of my tattoo that surround the three mirroring levels of Self," she said, gesturing to her forehead. "The smaller circle represents the Physical Body, and the outer circle represents the *Kino Aka*, meaning *Light Body*, an invisible field of luminous energy that connects your physical and non-physical parts. Through this field, insight and guidance arise, unlocking potential and illuminating the way," she explained as a bright, colorful aura appeared around her. "When healthy and strong, it shields against external negative energies and allows for communication with the surrounding environment, both seen and unseen."

Something like confusion grew on the young man's face. "How does something that I never even knew was a part of me become unhealthy?"

"Imbalance and illnesses of the physical body are direct results of disruption to the Kino Aka," said Tūtū Ona, frowning at several things attached to the young man that only she could see. "To fix this, we must identify any emotional traumas, toxic thought patterns, unhealthy habits, and resolve them."

"Oh, is that all?" the young man quipped.

Ignoring his sarcastic remark, she rested her hands on her lap, closed her eyes and took a deep breath before opening them again. "Get ready to experience the *true* magic of spirit medicine," she said. "Through the ancient family tradition of *lomilomi*, we will restore balance to your Anatomy of Being and get you back on a path of wholeness."

"Will it hurt?" he asked uneasily, looking up at her.

Without reply, she spun his head back around and pushed her ten radiant fingertips deep into the young man's shoulder blades, immediately sending a rush of energy flowing throughout every level of his being.

He gasped in surprise, feeling an intense warmth emanating from his grandmother's hands that felt like rays of sunlight. "What are you doing to me?"

"I'm working with your *Aka cords*," she explained, "ethereal conduits formed through relationships and interactions between all things that carry positive and negative energy. You have far too many negative ones, young man, and we need to remove them."

With masterful abilities passed down through countless generations, Tūtū Ona could easily locate every one of these energetic cords that connected her grandson with all the people and experiences in his life, some glowing with vibrant light while others twisted and snarled with dark energy. She applied rhythmic pressure, kneading and pulling at any negativity that sapped the young man's vitality and hindered his growth, ensuring that only his positive and nourishing cords remained intact.

As she did this, the young man experienced sensations of pulling and tugging on multiple levels of his being; physically, emotionally, and spiritually, like weeds being pulled from a suffocating garden.

"Now, this next step in our healing process won't be easy," she warned, "but I need you to be strong and summon your darkest, most destructive beliefs."

The young man closed his eyes and listened for those all-too familiar voices in his mind. Surprisingly, none came. "I think they're gone," he said, his face flickering with hope. "You did it! You got rid of them!"

"Trust me," she replied, tempering his enthusiasm. "Those little cowards are hiding in there somewhere."

As Tūtū Ona continued pulling away all the unhealthy Aka cords tangled up in his spiritual essence, it felt to the young man as if she was peeling back layer after layer of despair, revealing a lightness that he hadn't known existed inside him. But just as he was about to surrender himself to these new and lighter sensations, a dubious belief slithered from the shadows of his mind, risking exposure out of spite in order to sabotage his first glimpses of inner peace.

You're powerless.

With this belief, a surge of heavy energy erupted from the young man's body, twisting and contorting into a roiling cloud of darkness above them.

You have nothing to offer.

You deserve to suffer.

You are not important.

"Good!" his grandmother shouted, honing in on pathways to other stifling beliefs that had taken root within him. "Flush them out!"

Feeding off the young man's pain and anguish, the dark cloud of negativity quickly swelled into a seething vortex of malevolence, sprouting crooked tendrils that lashed out with fiery hatred, fighting desperately to impede Tūtū Ona's healing work. The young man slammed his eyes shut, terrified by the roiling manifestation of his own hate and cynicism that threatened to consume him once more.

"You're a failure," sinister voices whispered from the cloud.

Sensing the young man's heightened anxiety, Tūtū Ona worked with fierce determination to massage the oppressive energy away from his body.

"You're unlovable!" the malignant cloud taunted, pulsing with renewed vigor. "You're going to die miserable and alone!"

"Acknowledge whatever it says, then let it go," Tūtū Ona calmly instructed. "Believe that you are strong, you are decent, you deserve happiness, and you are loved!"

"I'm trying," the young man replied, but he wasn't being entirely honest. Years of unhealthy thoughts had convinced him that pessimism was a more comfortable position than the unfamiliar freedom of optimism waiting patiently just outside their captivity.

Undeterred, Tūtū Ona reached up and wrangled the cloud, enveloping it in a swirling tornado of colorful light that she conjured from her own protective aura.

The destructive entity fought back with all its might, unleashing intimidating screeches and horrible banging sounds as Tūtū Ona grappled with its unholy power. With a primal grunt and mighty heave, she finally managed to contain the monstrous force in a cocoon of potent energy and hurl it toward the center of the room. Twisting and screaming through the air, it crashed into the flames beneath the young man's Bowl of Light with a violent explosion that shook the very foundation of his Spirit Home.

Both watched in suspense as all that corrosive energy crumbled into a thousand shimmering fragments, twinkling like stars in the night sky. A flurry of smoldering embers scattered across the far corners of the house as a fleeting burst of divine light illuminated the entire room, evaporating every last splinter of negative energy in its wake.

Tūtū Ona looked down and smiled at the young man, the sparkling glow from her hands dimming as she lowered them. "The past is gone," she declared, brushing a white lock of disheveled hair from her face. "You are now free to move forward into a future of your own conscious creation."

Tears welled in the young man's eyes as he sat up, feeling an overwhelming sense of liberation and peace. "Th-that was amazing, Tūtū."

"You did the hard work," she modestly replied, brushing dust and debris from her sleeves. "I just helped you see it through."

Enjoying sensations of a lighter energy filling his Spirit Home, the young man's eyes were drawn to a flickering movement among the glowing embers of his fireplace. To his astonishment, several of its flames began to transform into tiny creatures that appeared to whirl and dance with one another.

He smiled, though he wasn't sure whether or not to trust his eyes. "Do you see that?"

"Those fire sprites are all that remain of your negative beliefs," Tūtū Ona said, visibly delighted by the gleeful chittering sounds of the adorable little elementals.

"I don't understand," he said. "How can they be so happy having been born from something so awful?"

"All sentient beings of nature find great purpose in helping humans," she told him. "Through their own unique powers of alchemy, these precious things are celebrating the successful transmutation of all that heavy energy you carried into something light and positive, confident that it will give you a fighting chance at a more meaningful and productive life."

Feeling as though a heavy shroud had been lifted from his body, a joyful giggle burst from the young man that surprised him. "I don't know why I just did that."

"Everything matures and your soul is no different," she said in a voice that made him unembarrassed. "That giddy feeling is the very essence of who you are expanding. In the days to come, as your newly rebalanced Anatomy of Being settles into place, your mana will surge with renewed strength and vitality."

Hope dawned in the young man's eyes. "Tūtū, am I completely healed now?"

"Young man, spirit medicine is a journey," she imparted as the ethereal veil between worlds began shifting between them. "Not a destination."

As the young man's Spirit Home faded into the ether, he caught a final glimpse of the tiny fire sprites, spinning and whirling triumphantly upon the smoldering remains of all the dysfunctional beliefs that would no longer hold him back.

✦ CHAPTER 16 ✦

They were walking through the mists of a rainforest, mother and son, on an overcast day that was unusually cold for midsummer. The shivering kind of cold that chilled you to the bone.

"Hurry!" called a voice he hadn't heard in a long time. It was his mother, now just ahead, appearing just as she had before she'd gotten sick.

"Mother, wait!" he cried out, much younger now.

She looked back with those beautiful, blue-galaxy eyes of hers, but something was different. They were fraught with confusion as she turned and continued up a worn path that cut through the shadowless green landscape. The hairs on the back of the boy's neck prickled with an unshakeable feeling that they were being watched. His mother didn't seem to notice, but he was certain something was out there.

Something bad.

"I see them!" she shouted, waving absently for him to catch up.

Something was off, but he couldn't quite put his finger on it. It was her, but at the same time, it wasn't. Despite moving his legs faster, he couldn't seem to close the distance between them. Eventually, the footpath curved to the right, revealing a massive grove of hibiscus shrubs speckled with white flowers.

"Oh, poor things," she said. "I keep telling your father they need water to be beautiful!"

Although these were her most favorite flowers of all, the boy didn't want her to go near them. In fact, something inside said these particular flowers were different.

Dangerous.

"Mother, stop!" he pleaded. Then, he remembered something he'd been told either recently or long ago.

White represents death.

"Mother!" he shouted again, trying to stop her. But she wouldn't listen.

When he finally caught up, his blood turned cold when he saw her delicate hand reaching for one of the flowers. The branch came to life and wound itself around her wrist. She screamed as more branches wrapped tightly around her waist and legs, pulling her into a giant maw of fanglike sticks.

Leaping forward, he grabbed his mother's reaching hand with both of his smaller ones, screaming in pain as the sharp stick-teeth punctured his forearms. Leaning back with every ounce of strength he had, his bare feet slid across the dirt as he was pulled closer and closer to the flower monster's chomping jaws.

"Leave her alone!" he cried. "I hate you! I hate you!"

Long red filaments growing from the flower's center flapped like tongues, mewling and laughing as they spat embers of pollen into the air.

"My love, why won't you save me?" she accused him behind terrified eyes, then finally screamed as the squirming branches gave one final yank, swallowing her whole.

An icy fist of terror squeezed the young man's heart. He tried desperately to pull her out, blindly tugging at branches that whipped his face, cheeks, and legs, leaving burning scratches of blood on his skin. One hissing branch curled itself around his neck and began to tighten. He opened his mouth to scream, only to be stifled by several knuckled branches ramming themselves down his throat.

The young man's body jerked awake from a fetal position, his face stark and horrified, his hands crammed against his mouth to muffle a scream erupting inside him. He sat up, fighting off invisible branches, hitting his head on the low ceiling of the hollow tree. Grunting hoarsely, he rubbed the discomfort from his scalp and looked out into a forest dulled by thick, rainless morning mist, wondering how long he'd been asleep.

A light breeze whooshed through the trees, sending down sporadic bursts of dewy rain from the leaves. Stretching tight muscles, the young man noticed a trail of impressions in the damp earth around the outside of the tree and shuddered, wondering if Tamapua'a had found him. Then he spotted the more clearly defined paw print of a small dog.

"If you're looking for food," he said out loud, "that makes two of us!"

Grim renderings of the flower-monster nightmare lingered, but the young man quickly diverted his mind to more positive thoughts.

"Forget that dream," he told himself. "Today is going to be a good day." Then, for some reason, he added, "Even if it isn't."

Okay, maybe that's not the best way to frame things, but considering that having only one near-death experience would put me ahead of yesterday, the odds are still in my favor.

Scooching out from the hollow enclosure of the tree, he braced himself for a painful reunion with the injuries on his feet.

Surprisingly, there was hardly any sting at all when he stood up.

He carefully lifted one foot, then the other, flummoxed to discover that, at first glance, the wounds on both soles appeared to have healed quite a bit during the night.

Impossible.

This was the first thought that came to mind, but conscious of this, he quickly formed a more positive one.

But . . . I can see the healing with my own eyes. And I feel it . . . with my own feet.

The young man plopped onto the ground, cross-legged. Brushing away the dried mud and dirt from the underside of his arches and heels, sure enough, the open and bloody abrasions that had been there just last night were replaced by delicate, puffy, pink scarring.

Changes in the spirit realm make changes in the physical world.

Elated by the potential of a dramatic new reality, the young man sprang up and whirled around in a full circle to test his rapidly healing lower extremities. In doing so, he also realized he could open his swollen eye almost entirely now. And taking a deep breath, he could feel his lungs expand with fresh, clean air, and the world around him seemed more vibrant and alive. Moving his limbs, the young man marveled at the improved flexibility in his muscles.

After just two visits, this new understanding of the vast complexities of the Island Worlds had shifted his perspective into a whole new dimension, filling him with an insatiable need to open more doors that had been closed before, or that had been previously unknown to him.

"Tūtū was right," he whispered. "Spirit Medicine *is* magic."

Possible.

Looking back, the young man noticed for the first time that the type of tree he'd spent the night in was a koa tree, highly regarded among royalty in the making of everything from bowls and tools to instruments and canoes. Walking around the hollowed-out trunk, he found a number of branches scattered in a wide radius throughout the ground cover, snapped off by animals, heavy winds, and time.

The first branch he picked up was a little thin, but it seemed to be a good length and sturdy enough. Remembering his experiences in the Island Worlds and not wanting to repeat the ill-timed mishaps of yesterday's hike, the young man held the branch firmly and with full awareness.

"Are you willing to help me on my journey?"

Despite being in the middle of nowhere, and not having seen a single human being in two moons, the young man couldn't help but glance around just in case anyone might be watching him converse with a piece of wood. Confident that no one was, he waited for a sign.

Nothing happened.

The young man made a thoughtful sound to himself, accepting the lack of response, then tossed the stick away. "Auwe!" Realizing what he'd done, he raced over and placed the stick back exactly where he'd found it. "Sorry!"

Looking over several more branches of various sizes and shapes, none seemed to be or feel what he was looking for. That was when he spotted the striped lizard with the blue tail again, this time perched on the tip of a branch farther out from the tree.

"Found something for me?"

As the young man approached, the tiny creature dropped to the ground and was gone in a blink. He reached down and picked up the branch it had been sitting on, testing its sturdiness. Admiring its fine grain and deep, rich color, he turned the stick vertically and was pleased to discover that it stood about shoulder height.

"Up for a little adventure?" he asked the potential hiking partner. "I have an important journey ahead of me and could use your help."

The young man waited patiently for an omen of acceptance like he had with the foundation stone in his Spirit Home, wondering how it might work here in the physical world.

A light wind rattled through the leaves.

Was that a sign?

Shadows and sunlight danced across the top of the stick.

Maybe that's it?

Then a jolt of energy shot from the branch, straight up into his right arm. "Oh! That feels like a big yes!"

He walked several paces, trying out the new stick, noticing a clump of ferns growing from the base of a large boulder. Closer inspection revealed several young, savory fiddleheads.

"Well, look at that," he said to his official new walking staff. "You've brought good fortune already!"

Acknowledging the collection of fiddleheads with gratitude, he popped one of the crisp curls of green into his mouth. Then another, followed by several more. Feeling a renewed energy coursing through him, the young man hiked up a steep incline with ease until he could look through an opening in the foliage at the rough but gorgeous country ahead.

With considerably less haze than yesterday, he easily located Lizard Cliff.

With my feet not hurting as much, and a strong walking staff at my side, I believe I can make the tip of its tail by the end of the day.

An ambitious goal now set, something gave the young man pause before he started off again. Gazing out at the grass spilling down the mountains into a sea of green, the raw power of the earth brought on another long-forgotten memory. This one was of his grandfather, Namotaha'i, who had passed away when the young man was barely four seasons old. Having only known him for a short time, the young man had always carried an impression that his grandfather's relationship with the elements of nature had been very strong, always greeting every plant and tree he passed as an old friend.

Grandfather, are you trying to tell me something?

Almost immediately, the abstract memory developed into something Namotaha'i had told him once, very long ago. They'd been at the center of Taua'i, looking out across a canyon formed by a collapse of the very volcano that had shaped the island eons before, carved out over time by wind and water into a gorgeous display of red ravines and green-treed gorges.

Boy, there's a calm feeling when we stand in the heart of wilderness. It's the living world claiming us as kindred. So, remember, when you're out among nature and feel sacred mana like this, always ask permission before entering its hallowed realms.

Knowing he needed to do better and be more respectful of nature, the young man smiled at the well-timed reminder. "Blessings, Grandfather."

He bent down, took some red earth into his hands, and rubbed it onto his neck, collarbone, and both wrists. And then, as was customary, he placed a leaf on a nearby boulder and put a small stone on top of it.

"Land before me, accept my presence and open the way," he requested of the mortal garden before him. "I trust you will guide me well through this day."

Feeling good all morning, the young man attributed this to his grandfather's sage advice. And rather than continuing to complain about it, he took time to fix the dratted knot of cord that had been incessantly rubbing against his shoulder by winding a few leaves around it.

But as the heat of the rising sun intensified and his muscles began to ache, he could feel his patience growing thin. It seemed liked forever that he'd been hiking through a veritable cave of trees, catching only brief glimpses of sky here and there, making him feel more and more claustrophobic. But all he could do was follow the stream as it slithered through the trees, widening here, becoming thinner there, before diving under a thicket of bushes.

"Okay, who put these bushes here?" he complained.

Going around them, the young man slipped on a rock, landing hard on his hip. After a brief but blinding pain, he rolled over onto his back and closed his eyes with simmering frustration.

"Didn't mean to yell," he surrendered. "I'm just tired and my muscles hurt."

As he lay there, the young man smelled something in the woods that sparked another memory from when he was about five or six. Out exploring the woods with his older cousin Tana'tanui, he'd slipped and fallen, badly scraping his leg. Disappearing for a bit, his cousin returned with some greenish-yellow fruits.

Ugh! What's that awful smell? he asked, wrinkling his nose.

She laughed. *They're noni, but my mother calls them vomit fruits. They stink, but guess what happens when I rub them on your scrape . . .*

Following his nose downstream, the young man immediately recognized noni hanging from a tree. As he got closer, he found several ripened fruits had already fallen to the ground and picked one up. Pulling it apart the way he remembered his cousin doing, he applied the stinky pulp to his hip. Almost immediately, the burning sensation faded under its mysterious healing properties.

"Blessings, Tana'tanui," the young man whispered gratefully, then took a bite of the remaining half, pleased that it didn't taste nearly as bad as it smelled. In fact, it had very little taste at all, and the cool juice softened his dry, cracked lips.

There's magic in this world, too.

After a short rest, the young man walked back to the bushes that he'd accused of purposefully blocking him, realizing that if he hadn't slipped as a result of going around, he wouldn't have found the noni or, more importantly, received the gift of a forgotten memory about his cousin.

"Blessings, bushes," he said with a friendly wave. "You're perfect exactly where you are!"

After all, does it make more sense that the gods would place bushes in front of me to make my life more difficult, or that the bushes were here long before I was born?

And in that brief but important moment, the young man was fully conscious of how he had just prevented a negative belief that nature would actually plant things in his way from ruining the rest of his day.

For a little while, at least.

Walking for what seemed forever through shards of light splintered by overhead leaves, the young man began wondering if he was even going in the right direction anymore. And it wasn't long before all that wondering took a toll on the positive attitude he'd worked so hard to maintain. Looking up frequently for openings in the trees, all he could see were bright points of sunlight through miniscule spaces between the branches and leaves, glimmering like stars in the otherwise thick, dark tapestry overhead.

"Come on," he pleaded. "Can't these trees open up already, so I can at least see where I am?"

As concerns of being lost gradually approached their breaking point, the young man came upon an unexpected rise in the landscape that finally lifted him from the shadowy depths to a bright, panoramic view of the entire canyon floor.

He turned slowly in a circle beneath a great patch of blue sky, hearing the distant tapping of a honeycreeper foraging in the trees. The breathtaking expanse before him looked entirely different than anything he'd seen the past few overcast days, bursting with a tableau of vivid colors glowing in a pool of sunlight. An earthly ocean of red earth and green forest decorated with yellow, pink, and lavender flowering trees amid black lava boulders—as far as the eye could see. And, of course, the great, wrinkled emerald face of Lizard Cliff stood directly ahead, crowned with a mantle of fluffy white clouds.

"Not as far as I'd hoped we were," he told his walking staff. "But close enough."

Having recalibrated his bearings, the young man's next moment of relief came when he noticed something that hadn't been visible since he arrived. *Shadows!*

Judging by the short length and angle of the shadow cast by his stick, the young man was able to quickly calculate some vital information using the sunlight. First of all, it was late morning. Next, that he'd come from the northwestern side of the island and was now heading in a south-easterly direction toward the mountain from his vision. And although he still wasn't sure if he was on O'ahu or not, at least knowing his position on whatever island this was made him feel a little less lost.

As the sun's rays cast long shadows over the land, the young man found himself at the precipice of another serious choice—as in life and death. High upon the hill, where the winds whispered their archaic chants, he studied the options before him. Below, the stream slithered like a shimmering snail's trail, leading to thunderous falls that poured down the rightward head of Lizard Cliff.

But the more accessible route to the top lay far to the left, where the tip of the great lizard's tail hung just below the canopy of trees, which was also the path of no visible water. Hunger was an old companion that he could host from the passing of new moon to full, a test of endurance passed down by the ancestors. But thirst—thirst was the unyielding fire that could consume a body to death in mere days.

In silent reverence, the young man knelt by the water's edge, offering his gratitude to the guardian spirits of the stream for helping him get this far. He drank deeply, hoping to carry the essence of its life-giving mana for as long as necessary. With courage set, he turned his gaze to the leftward waterless path, picking a new landmark in the distance—a clump of lauhala trees standing sentinel amid the untamed wilds.

Taking a deep breath and giving his walking stick a hearty squeeze for reassurance and strength, the young man set forth, bravely parting ways with the stream, each step an act of unwavering resolve, toward an unknown destiny forged by the mysterious will of his ancestral spirits.

✦ CHAPTER 17 ✦

W alking in silence for a long while, his mind quiet, the face of the mysterious girl emerged in the young man's thoughts again. She was about seven or eight this time and seemed to constantly force herself on him, even though he recalled preferring to be alone.

"What are you doing?" was one of her favorite questions, usually followed by, "And why are you doing it?" And her laugh—a cross between a bird and a dog—really scraped his nerves.

Once, as she stomped through the taro fields without a care in the world, his father yelled at her, "Why aren't you with your grandparents?" To which she replied with that bird-dog laugh, "Because they just want me to pound bark cloth all day like the other girls!"

While men were mostly responsible for fishing, farming, and cooking, women were expected to care for the children, collect shellfish, and make clothing and bedding. Knowing this, his father wrinkled his brow, as always. "What are you going to do then?" To which she smiled and said, "Whatever I want!"

At a time when others accepted their roles in society without question, this girl decided she didn't want to be told where her place was. And it was this natural desire of hers to question everything that greatly influenced the young man's own attitude, planting seeds that made him wonder why people had to be divided into commoners and highborns. While others told him it was dangerous to consider such things, this precocious girl challenged his thinking by asking, "Why do we have to be one thing or the other?"

Yes, that was the thing about . . . whatever her name was. She accepted everyone she met for who they were. Including him. And while he couldn't place who this girl was just yet, he definitely remembered her being annoyingly ambitious, a born protector.

And very special to him.

Huffing and puffing with exertion, the concept of time eventually became so meaningless the young man felt like he was moving in slow motion. The afternoon sun began drawing moisture from the rain-soaked plants all around him like hot rocks in an earth oven. At one point, he passed through a pocket of humidity so stifling, he could barely breathe. The only sound of water he'd come across so far was the sloshing of his stomach, but even that came to an end after peeing a few times.

"I've decided I like rainy, overcast skies best," he wheezed. "But I'm thankful for two things right now. Eyebrows, for catching the sweat pouring down my face. And toenails, for the countless times I've rammed my feet into one thing or another."

Despite hiking for so long under a thick cover of trees, the young man swore he could hear the humming of heat radiating from the sun overhead. A few sporadic showers passed through the lush canyon and drizzled down through the leaves, giving him barely a swallow of water. With every step, it became harder and harder to ignore the dry, swollen lump of flesh in his mouth, the grumbling pangs of his hungry stomach, or the combination of rough terrain and hot weather. Though he did his best to stay positive, it was difficult to bury the thought that if he didn't find water soon, he could di—

Shh! No! Don't even think it!

Aware that another limiting belief had begun to form, the young man noticed this time that it had been generated by an emotion that seemed to raise its ugly head far more often than the rest.

Fear.

After all, how could he be afraid of something that he had no knowledge or experience of?

It must be one of those preconceptions Tūtū Ona talked about. My imagination is creating all kinds of scary scenarios right now. But the truth is, I have no idea what will happen to me between here and the mountain. What I do know—or better yet, believe—right now, at this very moment, is that I can make it to the boulder up ahead that looks like a fist.

Choosing another landmark, a bend in a dried-up creek, and then another and another, the young man gradually made his way farther and farther up the canyon without getting lost once.

Or dying of thirst.

And while the canyon certainly appeared impossibly large, it wasn't deadly. Sure, there were plenty of opportunities to get hurt by slippery rocks and low-hanging branches, but as long as he was careful and made good steps, there was no point giving in to his fears.

"Fear can't be trusted," he said, hoping that speaking the words out loud might help program this new directive in him. "From now on, I'll always recognize fear, question where it's coming from, and listen to what it's really trying to tell me."

With each new landmark achieved, the young man gained more and more confidence in himself and his abilities to overcome whatever challenges might present themselves next. Before he knew it, his fears had soon been replaced by feelings of gratitude. And the more he chose empowerment over victimhood, something incredible happened.

The young man was actually enjoying the experience of being in such a gorgeous place.

Around this time, the sun had climbed to its zenith and moved on already. Black boulders and rocks peeked out from the rising land of green canyons like curious heads of giants buried in the earth. Farther off, Lizard Cliff gleamed in the waves of heat. Lost in thought, the young man had no idea how much time had passed before he noticed his shadow was now dragging behind him.

I should be at the tip of Lizard's Tail by now. Did I make a wrong turn somewhere?

Too tired to find an answer to his question, the young man sought to spend his energy on singing a song to accompany the rhythmic cadence of his footsteps.

"Five little butterflies, flying in the air.
Four little lady bugs, jumping on the leaves.
Three little ants, marching on the ground.
Two little flies, buzzing in my ear.
And one dumb human . . . suffering from thirst!"

The young man stopped to let out a dry chuckle. "Well, it was my choice to leave the stream, so I have no one to blame but myself."

The terrain grew ever steeper, going up now more often than down. Entering a muddy ravine full of trees and dead leaves, the young man trudged through filthy muck that reached his knees until his walking staff found sturdy ground. Liberating both feet of the mud with two loud, sucking plops, something occurred to him.

What could be making the ground wet?

Standing quietly, both legs covered in rich, dark sludge, he listened intently. Sure enough, mixed with birdsong and insects, a certain sound made hope flutter in his chest.

A watery, liquidy, wonderfully thirst-quenching sound!

Using branches and bushes, the young man pulled himself up the slope of the ravine, crawling on hands and knees through a low hanging archway of decayed tree trunks. Once able to stand upright again, he saw something massive and white through a lattice of swaying branches and leaves.

Is that wind? Am I coming to the edge of a canyon? How long will it take to go around?

The sound grew louder with every step until the interlacing trees spread apart, revealing a shimmering waterfall spilling over a concave lava cliff.

The young man stood in silent awe, bathing in the cool wind generated by the impressive force of falling water and spray that drifted into the surrounded forest, swirling in rainbows of color. The mist swept across the plants that carpeted the outer edges of the plunge pool, bringing them to life in a perpetual dance. A golden-headed dragonfly skipped across the water, passing two small white butterflies that danced in a twirling routine.

"A thousand blessings," he whispered repeatedly, beyond grateful.

Wasting no time, he carefully laid down his trusty walking staff and jumped in. The water was so cold, it took his breath away. Screaming with delight, his voice echoed over the bellow of falling water. He scooped up handfuls of the cool liquid to douse his hot hair and sweaty face. After gulping down enough to quench his thirst, the young man lay still and weightless in the pool for a long while, feeling life slowly being restored to his body.

Now, if I could only find something to eat.

Through the surface of the water, he stared in a blissful daze as the mud covering his legs dissolved away, revealing several dark bruises on his thighs, calves, and every single one of his toes.

Then, something shot out from a rock by his foot.

"Prawns. Again," he whispered. "I don't suppose any of you would let me catch you this time?"

Getting permission from a fiddlehead or a stick is one thing, but asking another sentient creature to let me eat it seems wrong.

Once more trusting his intuition, the young man focused on the mesmerizing sounds of the waterfall, quickly falling into a gentle trance.

Unlike the complete separation from his physical body as before, this experience was slightly different. His surroundings were still visible, but a swirling field of energy appeared before him.

Breathing in, he felt himself move through it and down into the water.

Here we go.

Descending through a whirlpool of light, the young man sensed he was going much deeper than was physically possible into the plunge pool he'd just been sitting in. Going farther and farther down, he found himself suspended in still waters, just beneath the reach of sunlight. His first thought was to worry about running out of air, but trusting in the experience, his body relaxed, and he quickly discovered breathing wasn't necessary in this place.

And then he was aware that something was in the water with him.

He couldn't see what it was, but it was definitely there.

Where am I?

You've found your way to Lower Island, a place inhabited by spirits of all animals, trees, plants, and rocks.

Is it always underwater like this?

Lower Island can be experienced as many different environments.

Which spirit are you?

I am the Immortal Soul of Prawns.

Prawns have souls?

Not individually, the way humans do. I am the transcendent source for all prawns in the physical world.

So, you're like the chief prawn?

If that reference helps you understand, then yes.

Through midnight-colored water, the young man could swear he saw the hint of a figure in the dreamy, muted light. As his vision adjusted—or at least, his ability to comprehend what he was seeing and experiencing—he could make out what looked like a prawn floating just a few yards in front of him.

But it was the size of an upended canoe, with long, twitching antennae and two huge pincer claws.

The rest of its eight spindly legs clicked quickly and quietly, collecting animal material that floated around it. Below the transparent shells of its upper body and abdominal segments, the unusually large prawn hovered in place by subtle and hypnotic movements of its fan-shaped tail.

Then he saw its eyes—large black spheres, gleaming in the darkness.

They were looking right at him.

I—I suddenly feel uncomfortable with my request.

No need. Humans have always been dependent on the souls of nature for their survival. This is the eternal flow of life. In, through, and beyond the physical world.

In exchange for what, though?

This is not a trade. We want nothing in return.

I see . . . well, all I know is that if I don't eat something substantial soon, my body may not be able to finish this journey. I wouldn't need very many prawns. Would two be reasonable?

Search the pond for a single white stone. Then wait. Four prawns will present themselves to you. After being eaten, their souls will be released back to me.

Four? But I only requested two.

You will know what to do with the others.

Is there anything else I need to know?

All we ask is that you take a moment to celebrate the noble gesture of the prawns you consume with music and prayers of gratitude.

Music?

Oh yes. All things of nature adore music. The insects enjoyed your song about them very much.

At first, not understanding what the Immortal Soul of Prawns meant, the young man remembered the silly song he'd made up earlier to pass the time. Before he could explain how delirious he'd been in that moment, his consciousness lifted back up through the dark tunnel of water.

Back inside his body, the young man gradually regained awareness of his surroundings, finding himself seated in the plunge pool.

Exactly where he'd been when he left.

"Incredible," he whispered, then stood slowly and looked around.

Near the outer edge of the pool, where the surface was less disturbed by the falls, he found a white stone that stood out clearly among the other brownish, algae-covered rocks. Seeing tiny feelers poke out from beneath it, his breath caught. Forcing himself to remain still, even as chills raced up and down his spine, it was only a matter of moments before a large, healthy-looking prawn crawled out from under the white rock, followed by a second one about the same size.

Then a third.

And a fourth.

The exact number given by the Immortal Soul of Prawns.

The young man lowered his hands into the water, positioning them before the four healthy prawns. Instead of darting off backward like before, they crawled straight to him. His face was stuck in a mask of bewilderment as he lifted the willing crustaceans from the water, guessing each to be about as long as his forefinger—the most impressive specimens of prawn he'd ever seen.

"For your hunger, for mine," the young man recited, then popped two of the prawns into his mouth.

The taste was mostly gills and guts, but he wasn't about to complain. For the first time all day, his mind cleared and his stomach stopped grumbling. Still trying to figure out why the Immortal Soul of Prawns had arranged for four shrimp to be under the white rock instead of two, he turned and noticed two scruffy ears sticking out from behind a boulder near the water.

"Ah!" the young man declared. "I think these are for you!"

He approached the dog, but not too close, and held out both prawns. The dog peeked around the boulder, cautiously sniffing the air. It's different-colored eyes looked at the young man anxiously before finally answering him with a defiant bark.

The young man lifted a brow, giving the dog an annoyed look. "How about we meet halfway?"

Moving closer to the edge of the pool, the young man held out the two glistening prawns.

The dog flinched, then turned in a circle with a childlike whine.

Certain it would run, the young man was surprised when it stopped and looked back over its shoulder.

"Come on," he said, keeping his tone calm and unchanged. "Aren't you hungry?"

The dog finally stepped out from behind the boulder, twitching its hindquarters. The young man noticed for the first time that it was male, with two thin white slashes across the matted fur of its left side.

"I don't have all day. If you don't take these, I'll eat them myself!"

The dog cocked his head but still didn't move.

"Boy, you're a defiant one, aren't you?" he said with a chuckle. "How about I call you Nahoa?"

The dog winked one eye in a way that made the young man laugh out loud.

"Well, at least one of us has a name now. Come and eat, Nahoa."

The newly monikered dog stepped out from behind the boulder, his slender nose twitching at the smell of food. He came forward until his whiskers tickled the young man's fingers, then sniffed the prawns before wolfing them both down in a single bite. When the young man stood and clapped the dirt from his hands, Nahoa spun with a start and skittered off.

"Hey, where are you going?" the young man shouted, kicking up a rain of water.

Spinning back around, Nahoa landed with his front paws stretched out, butt in the air, and his tail waving back and forth.

"Oh, he wants to play now, does he?"

Nahoa yipped with excitement.

The young man ran forward, slipping on a slick film of algae lining the bottom of the pond. Landing face-first in the water, Nahoa came up fast and used the young man's own back as a springboard to launch himself through the air into deeper water. As the dog swam past, the young man could have sworn he was laughing. Only after a while of chasing the dog in and out of the water did the young man realize his fur was actually white.

"Okay, that's enough," he said, on the verge of collapse. "That's about all the energy I have right now."

Spotting a welcoming slab of lava perfectly positioned in a wide swath of sunlight beside the falls, the young man swam over and climbed up onto it.

The hot, smooth surface instantly soothed his sore, achy muscles. He lay back and gazed up at a patch of blue sky framed by treetops, feeling instantly relaxed and at peace.

This place feels like a lot like heaven.

Remembering the promise he'd made to the Immortal Soul of Prawns, the young man closed his eyes in silent prayer.

The food we received today lives for the body,
Sacrificing its own life for the survival of Nahoa and myself.
We celebrate this gift with respect and gratitude.
The prayer has flown; it is free.

"And now I guess I owe you a song," he said reluctantly, gazing out across nature's panorama.

For want of music but lack of instruments, the young man lifted himself up into a seated position and started patting a spontaneous rhythm on his legs. After a short while of doing this, a warm feeling of appreciation enveloped him, giving him an absolute sense of knowing that the spirits of the freshwater shrimp he and Nahoa had consumed were happy, at peace, and that all four of them had returned to their source of spirit in Lower Island.

We rely on nature so much. Not just for survival, but for meaning.

As the young man continued drumming, nature itself seemed to join in: the high-pitched tweets of birds, the deep, thunderous roar of the waterfall, and the gentle rustle of leaves. Each adding their own beautifully harmonic texture to his performance.

And while he'd never considered himself to have any particular talent for singing, the young man suddenly felt inspired to try—though not with words. He began voicing primal sounds that conveyed a universal expression of happiness. In return for letting the music pour from his soul, the young man sensed a powerful connection taking place between himself and the unconditional love of nature.

After finishing his song, the young man lay back on the warm lava with an overwhelming sense of peace and calm. The rise and fall of insect sounds combined with the waterfall led to a heightening of awareness.

Feeling himself about to leave his body, the young man's intuition led him to convey his intentions for visiting the Island Worlds.

*To The One Who Creates All Things and to all my ancestral spirits,
I humbly ask for guidance in experiencing a powerful journey and protection
over my physical body until I return.*

Blood pulsed, a rhythmic hiss that echoed through the chambers
of his mind, and for a fleeting moment, he teetered on the edge of the
known and unknown. The air thickened, gravid with invisible forces,
and he felt it—the thrumming of primordial energy, a resonance that
coursed through the very fabric of his being.

Exhaling into the vastness, he surrendered to the cosmic tide, and
in that moment, his inner doorway opened. A web of effulgent lights,
a celestial tapestry, ensnared him, drawing him through the threshold
and beyond the bounds of mortal perception.

There, amidst the eons and the æthers, he journeyed to the Island
Worlds once more.

✦ CHAPTER 18 ✦

The young man arrived in the backyard of his Spirit Farm amid dreamy scents of forest perfumes and crisp evening dew. A galaxy of stars shone brightly overhead, reflecting off bioluminescent waterfalls in the distance. When he looked up, he saw the three yellow crescent moons hanging in a dark, emerald-green sky. Their combined light cast blond highlights onto the rugged mountain silhouettes and floating trees all around him. Down valley, the ocean shimmered with its own soft blue glow, which held the young man's gaze until he noticed his newly repaired home in the darkness, its single, square entrance flickering with a warm golden light.

A ripple of unease moved through him.

So . . . did I put any more stones in my bowl?

Only one way to find out. Get in here.

Slowly walking toward his Spirit Home, several round, furry creatures burst from the tree line, skittering through the patches of dried-up taro. After making a few steps, the young man became aware of a gentle rise and fall of the earth breathing beneath his feet. By now, he'd come to accept such things in this strange, beautiful place.

Crouching through the doorway, sure enough, Tūtū Ona was already inside, waiting beside his levitating Bowl of Light. This time, stone lamps were in each corner of the home, glowing with oily tutu'i nuts, casting their own slowly burning lights onto the thatch walls. The young man nodded a silent greeting to his ancestral grandmother, then peered inside his bowl.

"Maybe a little brighter, yeah?" he said in a high voice, casually pushing the bowl with one finger. It didn't budge, of course. Feeling his grandmother's gaze upon him, he looked up at her and shrugged. "Had to try."

The old mystic smiled patiently. "Boldness forges paths where none exist."

"Well, you were right about working with nature instead of against it. I think that's why I was able to access Lower Island."

"Yes, you've begun to reconnect with many powerful resources."

He looked up, surprised. "You saw that?"

"We don't see so much as sense what you experience." Then she looked at him and winked. "Cute song, by the way."

The young man rolled his eyes in embarrassment. "I'm glad so many of you heard that, but did you *sense* how I kept myself from thinking unhelpful beliefs, too? Before they could ruin my attitude?"

"Indeed, we did," she said, clearly pleased.

"And it's hard to believe," he said, "but I think I actually felt happy more times than I felt sad or angry today."

"An accomplishment to be proud of," said Tūtū Ona, watching him carefully. "But you've only touched upon difficult emotional layers that must be explored in order to heal."

"What do you mean?"

"You've buried many unresolved emotions in order to survive, but burying something doesn't make it go away."

"I know. I can feel them twisting inside me every day."

"These painful emotions express themselves through your subconscious as depression, victimization, and disappointment, making you unconsciously repeat the same impulsive, self-sabotaging decisions over and over again."

The young man stirred uncomfortably. "Ever since my mother and father died, it's like a part of me died with them."

"Yes, this is called *Soul Loss*," she told him. "It has weakened your personal mana and left you in a state of spiritual depression."

Gazing at the stones suffocating the light in his bowl, the young man had to ask, "Is there a way to make my soul whole again?"

Tūtū Ona nodded, but her eyes carried a hint of foreboding. "I suspect that some symbolic aspect of the pain you carry is lurking somewhere around here."

"Oh," the young man said, peering nervously over at the doorway-shaped wedge of night. "And I'm guessing you want me to confront it?"

His grandmother leaned forward on her staff. "I suggest choosing a battleground away from here, somewhere you feel strong. Then call it out."

Considering several possibilities, a single place came to mind where commoners and royalty gathered to watch the strongest and fiercest chiefs engage in competitive games of wrestling, boxing, and spear throwing.

The sports arena.

No sooner had the idea presented itself than the young man suddenly found himself standing in a large amphitheater carved from the hillside behind his farm. A ring of burning torches rose from the ground as stones dropped from the dark-green sky, forming an oval-shaped perimeter, followed by eighteen larger stone idols spaced out evenly, completing the outdoor arena.

Tūtū Ona appeared on a raised stone platform at the outer ring of the field, staff in hand. The other hand she placed beside her mouth. "Remember, nothing is experienced in your Spirit Farm that you haven't created. But be warned, this part of your inner work requires the deepest dive into yourself yet. If you're not ready, it's best to stop now."

Straightening his spine, the young man replaced his fearful expression with the bravest one he could muster, but felt the lie on his lips even before speaking it.

"I'm ready."

A muffled, unearthly roar bellowed somewhere underground. The sounds of insects and birds went abruptly quiet, followed by an earthquake so violent, flocks of long-legged birds burst from the surrounding trees.

Tūtū Ona moved to the edge of the stone pedestal, staff raised high. "It's here!"

Feeling the earth shiver under his feet, the young man's face went pale as death. At the center of the arena, mounds of earth churned and buckled as something clawed its way to the surface.

Then out it climbed.

The awful flower monster from his nightmare.

The young man stumbled back with a small, whining cry. The hideous creature looked much larger than he recalled. Its searching eyes found him, although they weren't really eyes at all but crazily spinning white flowers.

"I changed my mind!" the young man shouted. "I'm not ready!"

"Too late!" Tūtū Ona said, pounding her staff on the stone platform with a resounding thrum. "Only with bold wishing and brave action can one accomplish anything!"

The young man looked to the ground and scrambled to pick up a good-sized rock in each hand. He readied himself and faced the creature, asking the first question that came to mind.

"What are you?"

The flower monster cocked its head and hissed, wriggling its long, fleshy tongue through circular rows of tiny, sharp sticks. Stalking toward him, the creature's long, blossoming branches flicked and lashed like the tails of irritated animals. Waiting until the monstrosity was barely ten paces away, the young man flung his puny rocks at it. The creature easily caught them in its armlike branches and, much to his surprise, began juggling them. Higher and higher the stones went, making tall, tight circles in a weirdly comical performance. Then came the big finale as both rocks dropped, landing on the creature's head with two hollow *bonk-bonks*.

It stumbled dramatically from side to side before falling flat on its back.

Disarmed by the flower monster's unexpected whimsy, the young man laughed to cover his confusion.

"Don't trust it!" Tūtū Ona warned.

The flower monster sat up, casting a bitter sneer at Tūtū Ona.

"Try me," she said in a voice that was quiet, but powerful as thunder.

Cowering under the mystic's forceful gaze, the flower monster turned its attention back to the weaker energy of the young man.

Run, the beast warned telepathically, rising up on its branchlike legs. *Isn't that what you always do?*

Terrified by the hollow, lifeless eyes that stared at him straight out of his nightmares, a moan slipped from the young man's throat as he realized the frightful creature was charging toward him.

Unsure what to do, he glanced over at Tūtū Ona. "Are you just gonna stand there?"

Her face was wooden but wise. "This is not my battle."

With the beast nearly upon him, the young man had never wanted to run more in his life. But this time, he knew he had to stay put and face his fears. Though uncertain of the outcome, he defiantly held up his hand and yelled at the beast.

"Enough!"

Instead of mauling or attacking, the flower monster simply stood there, its gaping mouth contorting in a series of gurgles, as if trying to speak.

Suddenly unimpressed, the young man finally understood the power he actually held over the symbolic representation of his deepest, darkest pain. Leaning in closer, he realized that it wasn't the creature speaking but a muffled voice coming from somewhere deep inside its throat.

"Mom?! Is that you?"

The heavy scent of rotted flowers sickened him, but the young man didn't think twice about reaching into the black eternity of the monster's filthy maw. Cold branches immediately began winding around his arms and legs, their flowered tips mewling and screeching as they crept toward his mouth and eyes. The inside of the thing reeked of painful sadness and unending darkness. Grunting with disgust, the young man felt his fingertips graze something. He pushed his shoulder harder against the horrid beast's mouth, stretching his arm as far down as it would go until his fingers wrapped around a clump of hair. Closing his eyes in a quick prayer, he pulled with all his strength, toppling backward.

Lying on the ground, the young man found himself staring into the frightened eyes of a young boy on top of him.

"Who are—" The words stopped dumb in his throat.

He already knew the answer, though the boy belonged to the past.

When my bowl had more light than stones.

"That boy is the childlike aspect of your subconscious mind," Tūtū Ona said, giving voice to his unspoken thoughts.

The young man faced his younger self but remained seated on the ground so as not to frighten him. The boy rolled over onto his feet, his small face drawn, his jaw trembling anxiously.

The flower thing circled them both, severely agitated. It clearly wanted to take the boy back, but every time it tried, the twisted branches of its arms cracked against an invisible barrier.

The young man glanced over at Tūtū Ona.

She nodded confidently, her outstretched hand conjuring whatever magic she was using to protect them. "Don't worry about that terrible thing. Finish what you need to do."

The young man nodded, confident in her words, then looked over at the boy, who was now crouched in a shivering ball of emotion.

"It's okay," the young man said, scooching forward to comfort him. "It can't hurt us."

The boy jerked away, his upper lip curled in contempt. "*You're* what scares me!"

"Me? What did I do?"

The boy raised a fist, ready to strike. "You forgot about me!"

These words stung the young man deeply. "But I *am* you!"

"No, you aren't!" the boy snapped. "Not for a long time!"

The young man turned to Tūtū Ona, flustered. "What is he talking about?"

"He needs to be able to love himself again, but you won't let him," she said with a sympathetic smile. "The deep-seated anger you carry is getting in the way."

"And self-loathing," he added, realizing.

"These destructive behaviors of yours are the temper tantrums of your inner child crying out for help."

"Temper tantrums?" the young man said, offended. "I'm not a child anymore!"

"Simply getting older doesn't make you an adult. True adulthood is accepting and carrying on the responsibility for loving and parenting your younger self. Since you haven't emotionally matured enough to do this, your inner child is left feeling ignored and abandoned."

The young man's face went gray with remorse. "I had no idea that this part of me still existed."

Tūtū Ona's gaze softened with understanding. "Yet, somehow this remarkable boy manages to hang on, preserving the innocent capacity for wonder, sensitivity, and playfulness you once had, even as he suffers from your trauma, fear, and anger."

Seeing the vulnerable child trembling at his feet, the young man's heart ached. "So, how do I help him?"

"With empathy," she answered. "Age comes with many gifts, but pride and resentment aren't among them. When experiencing conflict, these narcissistic traits blind us from being able to listen and communicate."

The flower thing circled the invisible barrier, licking the unseen wall with two forked, slimy tongues. Feeling the hideous pressure of its hateful regard, the young man did his best to ignore it as he sat on the ground, eye level with his younger self.

"I'm so sorry for abandoning you," he whispered earnestly. "Can you please forgive me?"

"No!" the boy shouted, hugging his knees to his chest. "I don't trust you anymore!"

The young man nodded with understanding. "I know how it feels to lose faith in someone, believe me—"

Tūtū Ona interrupted, "Commiseration and pity only feed that child's victimhood. Whatever you didn't receive growing up no longer matters!"

The young man threw his hands in the air. "Well, what do you want me to do, then?!"

"Grow up!" she shot back. "You're that child's parent now, so do your job!"

Sighing, the young man turned again to his inner child. "Listen, you don't have to be afraid anymore, okay?"

"Why are you being nice?" Tūtū Ona interrupted again. "You're not his friend. You're his father. Act like one!"

"Boy!" he shouted with a much harsher tone. "It's time for hoʻoponopono between us!"

The boy looked up, startled.

Having his inner child's full attention, the young man nodded with satisfaction. "After our parents died, I didn't realize when I ran from my emotions, I ran from you, too."

The boy sighed. A weeping, tired sigh. "You made me feel so alone."

"You're right. I did."

The boy looked up at the flower thing, sensing its hunger to consume him into the darkness of its fetid gut. "The nightmare monster still wants to eat me."

The young man's gaze met that of the creature—a manifestation born of his own torment. "My guilt brought that awful thing into our world."

The boy—a reflection of his own innocence—unfurled his limbs and peered up, curiosity gleaming in his eyes. "Guilt from what?"

"Giving Mother her favorite flower," the young man's voice quivered, the wound still raw, still bleeding. "I thought it would ease her suffering. But I—" He choked on the words, his heart constricting.

"Ridiculous!" said the boy, his innocent, youthful voice piercing the veil of sorrow. "The last thing our mother experienced before she died was being given her favorite flower by the child she adored more than anything in the world."

The young man trembled. "I never thought of it that way."

"I forgive you," the boy said, extending a tiny hand filled with seeds—each one a promise, a potential for something new. "But can you forgive yourself?"

After what seemed an eternity, tears managed to escape the pain that had plagued the young man's eyes for so long. Real tears of long-suppressed emotions. Each droplet a release, a liberation, slid down his cheeks. They dangled like dewdrops at the edge of his chin, before falling onto the seeds below.

The boy exhaled a gentle breath, and the seeds took to the sky, swirling in a dance of healing and rebirth. Before the young man's eyes, the flowerless landscape of his Spirit Farm transformed, and ethereal white hibiscus bushes blossomed everywhere.

"They're beautiful," the young man murmured, inhaling the fragrance that stirred memories of a love undying. He knelt and cradled the boy's shoulders. "Don't give up on me."

"I won't if you don't," the boy replied cautiously. Then he stood up and embraced the young man, igniting a brilliant light of hope between them.

The flower monster, a grotesque embodiment of sick and salivating guilt, could only recoil in horror at the immediate loss of control. Its tendrils, once manipulative and suffocating, now writhed in impotent agony as the young man and his inner child tightly held one another, their hearts beating in unison.

"Go away!" the boy shouted, making the light expand even more, swallowing the despicable creature looming over them.

The flower monster convulsed in unbridled rage, its twisted branches thrashing in a frenzied dance of malice. Its hatred seethed, erupting in guttural screams and screeches, the tantrums of a petulant entity denied its feast. Conquered by forgiveness, a virtue both tender and unrelenting, the beast unraveled before their very eyes.

In a flash of triumph, the creature vanished into oblivion, its tempestuous echoes fading into the silent expanse.

Finally left alone in the warm light of redemption, the young man and boy held one another, suspended in an eternal instant, where past and future melded into the boundless now. And as the world dissolved around them, they remained—a testament to the indomitable spirit, to the enduring power of love, and to the unwavering faith in whatever obstacles may lie ahead.

"Alright," the boy said with a twinkle of playful wisdom in his eyes. "Let's go finish our journey, Matani."

✦ CHAPTER 19 ✦

"Matani," the young man gasped, re-entering his physical body. Adrenaline quickly followed with a joyful cry. "Matani! My name is Matani!"

The echo of his name bounced across the surrounding rocks, followed by a high-pitched yelp and skitter of nails beside him that ended with a watery *plunk!*

Peering over the edge of the lava slab, Matani laughed when he saw Nahoa paddling through the water with a surprised look on his face. "Sorry, boy!"

The little dog climbed back up next to him, his expressive, mismatched eyes full of worry.

"What's wrong?"

Ever so timidly, Nahoa stretched out his neck and licked the tears from Matani's face.

"It's okay," he said appreciatively. "They're happy tears."

The little dog cocked his head, then licked Matani's face again, this time a bit more vigorously.

"Okay, okay," he laughed, then glanced around at the sun and shadows, surprised at how little time had passed.

While it felt like he'd been in the spirit world for the better part of a day, it seemed that barely a few moments had passed in the physical one.

"We should get going," he told Nahoa. "I want to make it to Lizard's Tail before sundown."

Looking down at his feet, now polished clean by the water, Matani inspected them for travel. Remarkably, the puffy red scars were now faded and white, almost completely healed.

"Stranger and stranger," he whispered.

After retrieving his rain cape and staff from the outer edge of the plunge pool, Matani found the sun and quickly calculated his bearings. "I say we go that way," he decided, pointing confidently at the foothills of Lizard Cliff.

Saying the words out loud, Matani felt a slight edge of fear in them. Recognizing this, he acknowledged the arrival of this troublesome emotion. "Fear, I know why you're here. You think I won't come across water again. I appreciate your concern, but this waterfall I wasn't expecting to find tells me to believe otherwise. Now, go away."

And just like that, his fear of never seeing water again—and of dying of thirst—went away.

Wow! It worked!

Forging ahead, the dominant sounds of the waterfall gradually faded into the quiet hum and vibrations of the deep woods. After a long while, he stopped to wipe the sweat from his brow and looked up absently, startled by the sight of a completely green sky.

But he quickly realized that it wasn't the sky at all.

At long last, he was standing at the foot of Lizard Cliff.

"Look, Nahoa! We made it!" Matani shouted, beaming. And in that moment, he noticed a small cloud nestled in the shadowy spires, reminding him of a parallel image back at the cove; a clown fish and a sea anemone.

I never realized how connected land and sea were before.

Nahoa suddenly raised his head, sniffing the air just before Matani heard leaves crunching under footsteps. Thinking they sounded more human than animal, he scanned the woods, more curious than afraid.

"Someone there?"

No one answered, but Matani could've sworn he glimpsed a distant figure wearing bright-yellow clothes duck behind a tree. But when he and Nahoa raced over to investigate, there was no evidence anyone had been there at all.

"The heat must be getting to us."

Continuing onward, Matani found himself sifting through some new memories that hadn't been there before. There were fragments of an ocean journey and people he didn't recognize doing things with fishhooks, cooking boxes, steering oars ... and an island he didn't recognize. This island. Which he believed, however flimsily, must be Oʻahu.

"I was supposed to find someone," he told Nahoa. "I just can't remember who or why."

After walking for quite some time through the sweltering forest, they came upon a dry streambed full of lava boulders. Crossing it, Matani stepped on something hard. Lifting his foot, he found a single tutu'i nut embedded in the earth.

Now, this wasn't particularly unusual, because the ancient settlers had brought tutu'i trees to Havai'i long ago for their many uses, including potent medicinal remedies and a variety of colored dyes for clothes, tattoos, and painting canoes. But even more important than these uses, the general population relied most upon the kernel inside, which secreted a highly flammable oil that could be burned for light like the stone lamps in his Spirit Home.

Matani looked around and saw no signs of any tutu'i trees, easily recognizable by their silvery green leaves. "An animal or bird must've brought it here," he decided, then bent over and picked it up.

The nut was dark and smooth. And its shell had the distinct shape of a heart.

About to crack it open for the tasty morsel inside, Matani noticed some scratches on its outer casing. Looking closer, the markings appeared more deliberate than accidental.

There was a wavy, horizontal line with a counterclockwise spiral in the center that wound inward three times. At first, he thought his mind was creating meaning from something that wasn't actually there. Like seeing a face in forest shadows at night. But when he touched the symbol with the tip of his finger, three distinct words entered his mind all at once, in no particular order:

Before

After

Between

Too exhausted to solve this particular riddle, Matani rolled the nut into the waist of his loincloth.

"I'll try and figure you out later."

After passing through an old forest where the light slanted in aging, dusty beams, Matani and Nahoa finally emerged from a line of trees at the base of Lizard Cliff. Its green, dizzying heights loomed before them, resembling a giant hand with its fingers pushed into the earth.

Each of its verdant knuckles rose higher than the next in a gradual climb to what Matani hoped was the day's final landmark—the very top of Lizard Cliff.

Shielding his eyes from the sun, Matani evaluated the ascending landscape. "I think we just hike straight up its spine, all the way to the top. Don't you think?"

Nahoa, easily convinced, started trotting off ahead.

"See that bald spot about halfway up?" Matani called after him. "We can make that in no time!"

From a distance, the spine appeared easy enough to climb, but closer in, the reality of the landscape proved to be both unpredictable and deceptive. Nahoa passed the time snapping at dragonflies while Matani used a combination of his breath, footsteps, and the thump of his staff to keep himself focused and motivated.

Left (huff), *right* (thump), played his one-man band. *Left* (huff), *right* (thump).

When thinning air and absolute exhaustion forced things to a halt, Matani dropped to his knees and toppled over flat on the ground, moaning with ecstasy. "Oh yeah. Not walking is much better."

Staring in a daze at the blue sky above, a single, fair-weather cloud the size of a mountain floated into view. Whether it was ambition or exhaustion-fueled delirium, he had the puckish urge to initiate a little self-training.

Matani concentrated on the cloud in a casual attempt to change its shape. Focused on the outer fleecy edges of the white nebula, he watched them slowly churn and merge. At first, he thought it was his doing but quickly realized its constant changes were simply its natural state of being. Chuckling, he didn't feel too disappointed. After all, the very idea of sculpting a cloud with his mind seemed a bit far-fetched.

Suddenly, his hands involuntarily curled into fists, followed by a loud buzzing inside his head, as if he'd just been infused with some kind of invisible lightning. Fingers of energy skittered up and down his flesh, igniting a stretchy string of white light that shot from his chest all the way up to the cloud.

How can I help?

Startled, Matani assumed his negative thoughts were interfering again, but he quickly understood that the words belonged to someone that wasn't him. "Who said that?"

I'm the cloud you just connected with.

"Oh, well, I didn't realize—I mean, I was just trying to see if I could make you look like him," Matani said, pointing at Nahoa. "My dog."

Well, you can't make me do anything. But you may ask.

"Sorry," Matani replied. "Could you please consider changing your shape to look like my dog?"

Sure, why not? Sounds like fun!

The cloud drifted over until it was directly above Matani. Then it began to spin and merge, its fluid white body moving in and out of itself before finally shape-shifting into the unmistakable image of a dog. And not just any dog.

"Nahoa," Matani whispered, pointing at the cloud. "Look up there, boy! That's you!"

Nahoa's ears perked up, more excited by Matani's voice than the cloud.

"Can you maybe make him bigger?"

I sure can.

The cloud rendering of Nahoa grew until it was large enough to block the sun. Continuing to grow even bigger, its bright, luminous body darkened and started flickering with lightning and rumbling with thunder.

"Uh-oh!" Matani shouted, jumping to his feet. Grabbing at the tether of light connecting him to the cloud, his hands passed through it like smoke. "Smaller, please! Smaller!"

At his behest, the storm cloud immediately shrank, returning to its original size. Feeling himself become disconnected from the cloud, Matani saw the tether of light disappear. Relieved, he bent down and stroked Nahoa's dusty, matted fur.

"I think that's enough training for the day," he whispered.

His mind still reeling at what he'd just accomplished, Matani heard the faint call of a bird. It was an inexpressibly lonely sound that made him think of home. He tilted his head back and found the bird floating through the dimming colors of the afternoon sky on outstretched wings.

I wish I had wings like that, so I could fly us up to that mountain.

Struck by a conspicuous burst of energy, his vision swirled. Experiencing a prickling sensation, it felt like his mind was being sucked out of his body. The next thing Matani knew, he was looking down on the island from unimaginable heights.

I'm flying!

Thinking he needed to be doing something, like flapping his wings, Matani encountered a confused resistance that sent him plummeting straight down toward the ocean.

Just let go and enjoy the ride.

Quickly realizing that he was interfering with the bird's consciousness, Matani relaxed into the truly incredible, dreamlike experience.

Using his lofty view to figure out what island he was on, he quickly scanned his surroundings, but nothing about the landscape looked familiar. To the west, he saw a long shadow through the clouds—possibly another island—but the watery ocean atmosphere backlit by a late-afternoon sun obscured whatever it was.

Understanding his unique position as a passenger of the bird he'd been watching just moments prior, Matani made a telepathic request of his benevolent host. Floating through the air, the bird responded by folding its wings and dropping like a stone. His stomach tightened with tickles of breathlessness as his controlled descent brought him closer to the island's surface until he spotted Nahoa, appearing as a minuscule fly on the spine of a great green lizard's tail.

Already pushing the boundaries of what he believed and understood to be possible, Matani became unsettled when he noticed himself sitting in a trance beside the dog. It was an extraordinary moment, because in all that he'd experienced in the spirit realm thus far, he'd seen no greater example of how the human form was merely a vehicle for consciousness in the physical world.

All that I am—my Anatomy of Being—really does exist somewhere in the mystery and magic of time and space.

In a blink, Matani was back on the ground, seeing through his own physical eyes again, with Nahoa's curious and very physical nose sniffing his face.

"I can't imagine what you must be thinking," Matani said, scratching the dog's ears. Then, he got to his feet, looking to the west just in time to catch a glimpse of the bird he'd just inhabited disappear into the setting sun.

"We better keep moving, Nahoa," he whispered. "It'll be dark soon."

The higher they climbed, the narrower and narrower the spine became until Matani and Nahoa were forced to walk one in front of the other. While the dog trotted briskly ahead without a care in the world, Matani experienced a sudden fear of heights, which made him stop.

"I don't think I can do this," he said, unnerved.

Retreating back down the spine to find a safer route to the mountain, a glimmer in the sky made him stop. Far out across the sea, hanging above the eastern horizon, he found the crescent moon in its fifth phase, indicating that today was a good day for working on the balance between mind, body, and spirit.

I've never understood what this phase of the moon means.

Impeding the will of the universe on this day endangers your healing and empowerment process.

Meaning what?

Go with the flow.

Sensing a trustworthiness to his thoughts, Matani turned back. "Okay," he said, taking a deep breath. "Let's keeping going."

Rotating his walking staff horizontally so he could use it as a counterweight, he accidentally kicked a stone that tumbled down the steep slope on his left. Watching it swallowed up by dark mountain shadows below, he gulped nervously before moving forward one careful step at a time. Concentrating on each and every one of the sixty-four steps his feet made, Matani was surprised when he glanced up to discover that he was barely a stone's throw from the top of the spine.

"We made it!" he shouted with relief.

Focused on safer, much wider ground ahead, he was about to walk forward when something blocked him. Squinting in the darkness, Matani looked down and saw Nahoa standing in his way. "What are you doing, boy? What's wrong?"

The little dog peered ahead of them, drawing Matani's attention to something hidden in the darkening atmosphere.

A deep chasm about the length of a good-sized palm tree.

Matani reached down and stroked Nahoa's head. "Well, we can either go back down, or sleep here tonight and wait for the sun to show us another way across."

Considering these two options, a third one presented itself unexpectedly when the ground crumbled under his feet.

Feeling his body tipping to one side, Matani tried to rebalance himself with his walking staff, attempting to urge his center of gravity forward.

But it was too late.

With no choice but to launch himself across the chasm, Matani held his breath and jumped. Suspended above the drop for what seemed like forever, his body finally slammed into the wall of rocks on the other side so hard, his teeth cracked together. Realizing that he'd let go of his staff at some point, he clung with both hands to some ferns growing from the rock. While they stopped him from sliding down any farther, he could feel their roots slowly ripping from the dirt like hair from a scalp.

"Nahoa!" he yelled. "I could use some help here!"

Nahoa answered the call by vaulting his tiny body across the chasm, landing on a boulder just above Matani that was wedged between a V-shaped split in the rock. He leaned down and clamped his jaw on the neck of Matani's tattered rain cape, giving him just enough support to grab hold of a small tree. Locating a small foothold with his toes, he spun his entire body around so his back was against the cliff.

"That was close," Matani said in a shivering whisper.

Another strong gust of wind came rushing down, bringing more clattering pebbles and stones rolling past him. Feeling a vibration in the rocks, Matani looked up just in time to see the wedged boulder Nahoa was standing on shift forward.

"Nahoa! Off!"

With barely a moment to flatten himself against the cliff, the dislodged boulder grazed Matani's back before striking more rocks in the darkness below, igniting bright-yellow sparks as it bounced and rolled all the way down. Contemplating any number of deadly scenarios that had almost happened, Matani frantically searched the darkness.

"Nahoa? Are you still here?" Hearing two sharp barks, he was relieved to find the little dog's shadowy figure standing above him with the walking staff in his teeth. "Good boy!"

Taking hold of the stick, Matani used it to climb up the steep, shifting ground. As he carefully climbed higher and higher, the already steep incline turned even steeper, and he found himself needing to take a lot more breaks at shorter intervals to catch his breath. Seated and hunched over with barely the energy to breathe, he waited for the strength in his body to replenish itself just enough for him to get up and make it as far as he could before having to stop and do it all over again. So close to the top, his legs felt like they were ready to give out, and he wanted to quit right then and there. Dragging himself onward until he felt like one more step would be the end of him, he mustered every last bit of strength he had until, at long last, he stood safely atop Lizard Cliff..

"We made it," he wearily celebrated on behalf of himself and Nahoa.

Arriving just in time to catch the final embers of daylight fading behind the western horizon of the sea, Matani collapsed where he stood and watched as the grainy, pastel purples and blues of the sky filled with bright-red-and-orange clouds that reflected the final rays of the setting sun.

And while it was a huge relief to be free of the canyon depths . . . something was missing.

In fact, it was the entire reason he'd even risked his life to hike to the top of Lizard Cliff in the first place.

The mountain, of course.

But where it should've been, all he saw were clouds.

Lots and lots of thick, heavy clouds.

Is there even a real mountain out there?

Doubtful.

Did I nearly kill myself for nothing?!

Probably.

Matani's entire body went rigid with disbelief.

What are you doing here?

I never left.

Then why haven't you said anything?

I had to wait for more of your memories to come back so you could remember how to overthink everything.

You're really annoying, you know that?

So are you.

Frustrated that his awful, negative thoughts had returned, Matani did his best to ignore them. By the time twilight thickened toward true dark, both he and Nahoa had come upon an overlook with a sweeping view of a small, blue-shadowed valley. Full of heavy mist, it was hard to discern any real detail, but his eyes eagerly searched the terrestrial expanse for any signs of human life.

Anything at all.

But he neither heard a sound, nor saw so much as a wink from a cooking fire in the darkening expanse before him. What he did see on either side of him, though, were several lava outcroppings with ferns growing from cracks like bushy clumps of hair. He gathered up an armful, then found a sturdy tree a few steps back from the vista's edge. Barely arranging the ferns into a makeshift mattress, Nahoa spun in a circle and flopped down on top of them in a tight, furry ball.

"Hey, that was for me!" Matani yelled, but seeing how tired the little dog was, he conceded with a chuckle and went about gathering more ferns just as a gust of frigid air rushed across the valley.

It was as if the night had given birth to a new breed of wind. Shivering, Matani sat on his own bed of ferns, moving closer to Nahoa's warm little body as feelings of fear and insecurity crept up inside him. Realizing that these emotions were coming from his inner child, he closed his eyes.

What do you want me to do?

Help me stop feeling cold and afraid!

Forcing himself to access whatever parental instincts he might have, Matani recognized a familiar, woodsy fragrance in the damp air. As his eyes adjusted to the darkness, clusters of tiny, star-shaped flowers scattered across the ground immediately told him that they were surrounded by sandalwood trees.

Like so many other things, the early settlers had found several uses for this particular tree. Its wood was used to make the decks of double-hulled canoes; shavings of its heartwood were used to perfume bark cloth; and certain doctors used the unique properties of its oil to heal a variety of skin ailments. But of all its uses, the one Matani was most interested in was its ability to make fire.

Crawling around the dark on hands and knees, he scoured the ground for any sandalwood sticks he could find. Despite finding many soaked with rain, Matani's unwavering determination led him to discover several dry ones hidden under a layer of dead leaves. Gathering enough to last the night, he dropped the bundle of sticks in a clatter right beside Nahoa, who barely twitched.

Getting straight to work, Matani proceeded to build a small pyramid of wood, keeping aside two sticks that were about the length of his forearm. Gripping the first igniting stick with both hands, he rubbed the tip up and down the length of the hearth stick, which he held between his feet. This was a long and laborious process, but eventually the deepening groove began to char and trickle with smoke, followed by the appearance of a single, tiny ember. He carefully blew the delicate morsel of light into a flame, feeding it a pinch of dry grass to help it grow. Adding a few more sticks, it wasn't long before Matani had a sturdy little campfire.

Flickering flames cast a warm glow that formed a protective womb from the cold, dreadful darkness that surrounded them. Sensing his inner child's relief, Matani leaned back onto his fern bed, stretching every tight and sore muscle in his body. Inhaling curls of the aromatic smoke, he felt something hard poking into his side. Feeling around the waist of his loincloth, the tutu'i nut popped out onto the ground.

"Forgot about you," he whispered.

The nut's smooth surface reflected the firelight, with a white-hot iris at the center of its shell, like some mystical eye staring up at him. The moment he touched the markings on its exterior, those three same mysterious words came to him again.

All at once and in no particular order:

$$Before$$
$$After$$
$$Between$$

Still uncertain if the symbol was important to his journey somehow or not, Matani didn't want to lose the thing before he could figure out the answer. He dug up a sharp stone from the ground with his fingers and used it to bore a small hole through the top of the nut's outer shell. Then, he snapped off a forearm's length of cordage from his rain cape's netting and threaded it between the two holes, fashioning a crude but practical necklace, which he placed over his head.

Lying back again on his bed of fresh ferns, Matani rolled the pendant between his fingers as he watched the earthly orange cinders from the fire float up to the heavenly stars above. At the very top of the sky, three in particular caught his focus. One large star followed by two smaller ones.

Holding up his right hand, he positioned his index and middle fingers on the stars, then tilted his thumb to estimate where its path would fall on the western horizon.

"Home," he whispered longingly, and with a sense of distant familiarity.

Trying to remember who it was that had taught him this bit of celestial navigation, a dozen streaks of light raced across the sky in a series of bright contrails. He sat up, neck tilted, eyes wide, staring at several more long, stretching lights that scratched the darkness. There was another, and another, then two more streaking in different directions. Most were quick flashes of thin white lines, disappearing so fast they seemed like hallucinations. Others lit the sky with burning stripes of orange and yellow, reminding Matani of how his village celebrated special occasions by lighting both ends of *papala* sticks before throwing them off cliffs along the north shore of Taua'i, creating a beautiful trail of fireworks that rode the trade winds far across the sea.

I wonder what the gods are celebrating tonight.

A bright-white light flickered overhead, sending a menagerie of leaf and branch shadows spinning wildly around Matani. He leaped up and ran to the very edge of the valley, watching the brilliant flying star. Feeling Nahoa against his ankle, he looked down and caught the fireball's reflection in his innocent little companion's eyes. When he looked back up at the sky, the dazzling white star arced right over their heads, turning bright orange and red before bursting into several fiery pieces that winked out above the distant horizon.

Even as phosphorescent squiggles faded from his vision, Matani noticed that the mist and clouds that had filled the valley earlier had moved off. The fifth phase of the crescent moon had moved over the island, casting whitish-blue highlights upon the dark world below . . . and there it stood as real as could be.

"The mountain," he whispered in awe.

Seeing the actual monument of his vision felt like a dream.

Yet, it in this moment, seeing it still meant nothing.

Well, of course not. Why would it?

Because I think I should know why I'm going there by now.

Just because you're stupid, doesn't mean you're right.

Maybe I'm not supposed to know until I get there.

If you get there. It's still pretty far.

The unhelpful voice wasn't wrong. By Matani's own estimation, the mountain looked to be at least another three moon phases away. As plenty more conflicting thoughts raced through his head, Matani led Nahoa back to their campsite and stoked the fire by adding a few more sticks. Repositioning the sore parts of his body a few times, he settled back comfortably on the ferns and looked up at the beautiful tapestry of stars.

'Aumākua, I'd like to hear your thoughts. Do you think I'll reach the mountain?

Yes.

What will I find when I get there?

Your true self.

Pondering this answer, Matani looked down to see Nahoa—his innocent furry face at peace in the firelight—had fallen asleep nestled beside him. It wasn't long before he finally fell asleep himself, listening to the night sounds of the deep mountain woods.

Until sometime later, when something terrible screamed in the night.

✦ CHAPTER 20 ✦

Matani awoke in the dead of night, uncertain how long he'd been asleep or even where he was. Shivering uncontrollably, he sat up in the throes of darkness, glanced down at the gray ruin of fire, then up at the sky. The stars he'd fallen asleep under had since been wiped clean by ragged clouds that flickered with an eerie green lightning.

When he glanced over at Nahoa, the little dog was already awake, ears pulled back on high alert, intently fixed on something in the woods behind them.

"What is it, boy?"

There was the steady rise and fall of cricket song.

And something croaking in the woods.

Farther off, a hooting owl.

Closer, leaves rattled in a quiet breeze.

Separately, these were just the normal sounds of night, but combined, they triggered a primal fear imprinted in the biology of Matani's most ancient ancestors, passed down generations to this very moment.

Fear of the dark.

Unreliable moonlight changed the shapes of the trees all around, turning them into distorted black skeletons. Nahoa whined deep in his throat until it became a low, constant growl. A branch cracked, launching Matani to his feet, head spinning in all directions.

"W-who's there?!"

Searching the dim forest, he bent down and stroked Nahoa's head, for his comfort as much as the dog's, when the pressure of an invisible hand shoved him from behind.

When he turned around, nothing was there.

"It's n-not a ghost," he whispered, dubiously. "No such thing."

But the words were flimsy, and he knew it. Slowly resurfacing memories reminded him that every island had its own place—be it high on a mountain or at the edge of a cliff—where a person's spirit leaped into the underworld after they died. Sometimes the deceased—either too afraid or not ready to move on—chose to stay and wander aimlessly. And everyone knew that wandering ghosts were known to create great mischief.

Trembling, Matani summoned the name of The Source he learned from Tūtū Ona in a whispered prayer, "The One Who Creates All Things, if you can hear me, please protect us."

About ten paces ahead, an unsettling mist appeared in the dark, haunted air. Nahoa gave a low woof just before a single bright flame shot up from the fire's ashes. This was followed by a cold breeze that smelled moldy, like the stale air of an ancient burial cave. Moments later, the echo of a disembodied voice chanted unintelligible words, but the emotion was unmistakably mournful.

The hair on the back of Matani's neck prickled, blasting a shot of cold down his spine. Nahoa bared his teeth and barked, the whites of his eyes gleaming in the pale moonlight. An unnatural breeze moved past them, followed by something stomping across dead leaves to their left. The unrevealed chanter continued, their voice mixed with other whispers floating on the musty air. To his right, a shadow darted between two trees. Hoping to scare it off, Matani slammed his walking staff against the tree trunk beside him—*Thwack! Thwack! Thwack!*

"Go away!" he shouted.

After a beat of silence, the thing in the woods answered.

THWACK!

Matani and Nahoa exchanged worried looks that might have otherwise been comical, but the fear Matani felt coursing through his body was anything but funny. Dropping to his knees, he searched the ground with shaking hands.

"Father told me if you pee on a stone and throw it at a ghost, it'll go away," he whispered to Nahoa, hoping it was true.

Before his fingers could find anything, a stone flew from the darkness, hitting Matani squarely on the shoulder. He froze, eyes wide as wooden plates. Leaves shook to his left, twigs cracked on his right, every sound moving closer and closer. It was only in that moment Matani realized—despite all he'd heard, been told, and ultimately didn't believe—that he actually knew nothing of ghosts.

Scanning the night, another unsettling sound infiltrated the quiet. It took a long, fear-stricken moment before he realized it was coming from the tutu'i nut pendant around his neck. Bouncing lightly against his pounding chest, the nut rattled softly inside its hollow shell. Another branch snapped in the dark, right where his eyes were looking.

Matani's words came out in a cold shiver. "Leave us alone."

Something touched his arm.

A branch?

Looking down, there was a transparent hand with black dirt under the tips of its fingernails.

"Go away!" Matani screamed, launching his body as far from its grasp as he could.

More spooky green lightning flashed overhead, brighter and more intense this time, followed by deep, rolling thunder. Trees flickered with moving shadows that brought the forest to life just before a sudden drop in temperature. Matani exhaled into the unearthly cold, breathing tiny clouds of mist.

The woeful chanting stopped, followed by a raspy moan that was both nearby and far away.

"Help meeeeee."

The air swirled with an unsettling energy as Matani felt something behind them. Despite his tongue being locked in fear, unable to speak, an inexplicable need compelled him to turn and see what it was.

There, threading its way through the trees, was a small, vaporous orb of smoke. It stopped just a few feet away, then disappeared in a flash. In its place, a pale mist formed, churning slowly like liquid shadow, until a spectral image swam out of nowhere, forming the distinct shape of a torso. Matani would have thought a human being was standing right there in front of him—if it hadn't been missing its legs.

No, this wasn't a human being at all.

At least, not a living one.

Cemented in fear, the apparition that hung in the air before Matani was both light and dark at the same time, a fragile construct of otherworldly materials stitched together by otherworldly means. Its head was only partially visible, lit from below by some spectral flame. Fatal wounds covered its body, from spears or daggers, with the most damage clearly from a ragged, gaping hole in its sternum surrounded by splintered claws of bone. But it was the ghostly thing's eyes that unnerved Matani the most.

Two eyes of a deceased spirit staring at him with chilling awareness.

Nahoa stopped barking, tilting his head back and forth, more curious than afraid. Swallowing nervously, the taste of acidic fiddleheads and prawns seeped up into Matani's throat. He would have retched, too, had the ghost not started moving toward him. It didn't sway its arms or lift its legs the way a human did, gliding through the air instead. Before Matani could jump-start his mind and tell his own legs to get him out of there, the ghost slammed into his body.

Frozen in a soundless thunderclap of shock, confused emotions and feelings crashed over Matani with the weight of a thousand waterfalls, forcing him to his knees. He heard Nahoa barking, but the sound quickly faded as the forest around him began crackling and pulsating with a highly charged, paranormal force.

The next thing Matani knew, he was seeing through someone else's eyes.

Time, although connected, was suddenly very fluid. Neither present nor linear. It was as if he were outside time, looking in . . .

Baby hands reaching for his mother.

Love.

Looking down at small, unfamiliar feet. Learning to walk, stumbling after chickens, pigs, and dogs.

Giddiness, excitement, curiosity.

Hands suddenly older and stronger, stealing cooked pig from the neighbor's earth oven.

Hunger, shame, desperation, guilt.

Taller now, learning to plant taro, the delicate corm cracks, a fracture that would impede its growth.

So frustrating! I want Father to be proud of me!

On a grassy hill overlooking the ocean with his loving mother, watching the sunset.

Adoration, sensitivity, empathy. Such a kind, strong, and loving woman.

The hands and body, older still, climbing a palm tree to get a high perspective of the sea.

What's out there? Beyond the horizon?

Searching, longing, aloneness.

Hidden among trees, sneaking a peek at a passing chief wearing a red-and-yellow feather cloak.

Fear, jealousy, resentment, envy.

Older hands, blistered and cut, confidently pushing corms of taro into mud.

Staring endlessly at the constant motion of wind, waves, and clouds against the dependable stillness of towering mountains.

Appreciation, calm. But still a sense of loneliness.

What is my place in the world? Will I ever find someone to love? And will someone love me in return?

Older now, exploring the highest regions of the island. Stumbling upon a beautiful girl bathing in a remote forest pond.

Nervous excitement, passion, lust. Who is she?

His eyes meet hers. Striking blue.

She stands naked in the water, and his gaze suddenly feels inappropriate and invasive, so he covers his eyes and takes a step forward to properly introduce himself. A sharp branch jabs him in the side, hard enough to make him lose his footing. He slips off the embankment and lands headfirst in the pond.

The pretty girl drops down into the water, letting out a startled cry, annoyed.

Shame. A rushed apology.

Her stern expression melts with amusement. She points behind him, to his loincloth dangling from a branch up on the embankment. Dropping down into the water, never more embarrassed in his entire life.

Both blushing. Laughing. Talking.

"'Anoʻai," he says. "My name is Tumatua."

She smiles at him for the first time. "Mahina."

A connection neither can deny.

Chaste days spent together, never kissing or holding hands, barely looking into each other's eyes for longer than a passing smile. She doesn't talk about her family or her reasons why. He doesn't talk about his disgruntled life as a farmer. Instead, they talk about their favorite places on the island and all the things they shared in common. They talk about the world around them. And then, sometimes, they don't talk at all.

Peace, joy. Connectedness.

After many months, they become the best of friends.

More time passes. Walking together, always together, in the woods. Mahina touches his arm in a way that feels like more than friendship. Without over-thinking too much, he risks a quick kiss on her cheek. She smiles, saying nothing.

He holds out his hand and Mahina takes it. They find a soft, private place in the woods to be together, awkwardly at first, then tightly embracing.

The day they become the best of lovers.

Her honesty and strength, her quirks and imperfections—everything about Mahina makes him want to be a better person. To be worthy of her trust.

These first precious moments of their relationship are held dear in his heart but, as time goes by, more and more complications arise. Life together becomes increasingly difficult.

Mahina turns to him with a beautiful smile, pregnant. And a secret truth. Her Mū lineage.

What will the future of our child be?

Then comes the night of a terrible storm. They find shelter inside a cave.

She's in labor, giving birth.

Mahina looks up with uncomfortable eyes. She adjusts the blanket to hide a blue blotch of skin at the base of their baby's spine.

"What is that?" he asks.

"It's everything," she replies. "The mark of Mū is proof of his lineage."

"If a chief ever sees this, we'll all be sacrificed to the gods," he warns. "Will it go away?"

"If this part of him isn't developed soon? Yes," she replies. "But then he'll be left with a lingering sense of confusion."

Days, months, and years pass in the blink of an eye.

Now, husband and wife lying on their sleeping mats in the glow of tutu'i nut lamps, whispering over their four-year-old child fast asleep between them.

"Matani called the wind again today," he whispers. "In front of my brother this time."

"Did Numu see him do it?"

"Of course he did!"

"What did you say?"

"That it was a coincidence."

"Did he believe you?"

"Probably not, but you know as well as I how suspicious my family already is. Especially since we aren't letting my grandparents raise him in these early years."

"Matani's powers are beginning to emerge. We need to take him to my brother in Papahānaumokuākea. He'll teach our son how to manage his gifts."

"Those islands are not for the living. Taua'i is his birthplace. Farming is his legacy."

"And an important one, but the legacy of my ancestors also runs through his blood and should not be stifled."

"A legacy of what? Hiding and being hunted? Being sacrificed at the altar?"

"As our child was preparing to enter this world, I had visions of his sacred name and who he is to become."

"Which is what?"

Mahina stares into her husband's eyes, searching for any signs of receptiveness. "What any of us have the potential of being when we're born. One who can change the world."

"I wish I had known of your lineage before we decided to have this child."

"Tumatua, Matani was born of love. There is no greater cause for existence."

"Then what about your family here on Taua'i? Why can't he train with one of them?"

"They want nothing to do with me after I left to be with you."

"And if my family disowns us should they learn the truth, what happens then?"

The world spins, slows, then stops. Now, he's standing in the upland taro fields across from his brother.

Angry, frustrated, heartbroken.

"Why would you get involved with a Mū woman?!" Numu'i'ua asks. "You realize the danger your wife and child have put you in? Have put us all in?"

"I love them, Numu. More than anything."

"More than your own family it seems," Numu'i'ua says sharply.

The words not only sting to hear, they hurt his brother to speak.

"Our father is Tahitian-Havaiian, and my wife's father is full-blooded Mū," he says. "But she and I were born on this island—just like you—so that makes Matani second-generation Havaiian. No matter what blood runs in our veins, he's bound to these islands by birth."

"But that's not how the highborns will see it," says Numu'i'ua. "They'll say his blood is contaminated."

"They just don't like that the Mū were here first," he responds defensively.

"There is death in your words," Numuʻiʻua replies.

"The trees will say nothing," he says, looking around them. "Will you, my brother?"

"I will be silent as the trees," Numuʻiʻua reassures him. "But we must live separately from this day forth."

Numuʻiʻua hugs his little brother, tighter than he's ever hugged him before, an embrace that needs to last a lifetime, then turns and walks off.

An ocean of sadness floods his heart.

It's the final time he'll lay eyes on his brother, who soon relocates his entire family to the north shores of the island.

Entering his home, he sees his son holding a flower. His wife. Dead.

"Matani, what have you done?"

Rage and resentment fill his heart toward the world.

Including his own boy.

But even worse is the regret that fills his soul for only thinking of himself in that moment. His son had been just a child, needing his father's love more than ever.

A need that never changes . . . at any age.

He never forgives himself.

Older now, his spirit is weighed down by sadness, depression, and loneliness as he works in the field.

Chiefs come, recruiting him to fight. Months of training follow: how to throw and dodge spears, boxing, and wrestling techniques. He stands with his fellow draftees—other commoners from across the island—hearing their complaints about the unfair situation they're in.

Why must we fight for these highborns? We gain nothing from this battle!

A battle fueled by some unpaid wager between two chiefs. Before this day, he realizes he's never actually experienced real fear.

The fighting begins.

Bodies merge, weapons clash.

Suddenly, he's face to face with an enemy he knows nothing about—certainly not enough to call him either friend or foe. His opponent lunges, swinging blindly. He directs a flurry of perfectly aimed punches at the man, just as his highborn boxing instructor taught him. His final swing is answered by a flare of pain across his right cheek, then they both fall to the ground in a scuffle.

An anger grows inside him that he never knew existed. All the things that *happened over the last several years crash inside his head. His enemy is suddenly on top of him with a shark-tooth sword, but as his instructor taught him, he pulls a dagger hidden in the leaves of his right anklet and drives it straight up into his assailant's chest. Falling back, seeing his breastplate impaled by a bloody dagger, his enemy's eyes fill with stupid wonder.*

Ashamed, he kneels beside his victim in sorrow, watching the life fade from his terrified eyes.

Days, months, years later, he tries to continue living his life but is no longer a part of it. Every moment of his days—sleeping, eating, farming—the memory of those dying eyes haunt him.

Guilt colors the rest of his life, pulling him further and further away from everyone around him.

Including his only son.

Chiefs come to the taro fields again and again, recruiting him for one pointless battle or another. There is no longer fear. Not because he's become brave, but because he's grown numb.

Then comes a day held by many in their nightmares. The Battle of Beating Heart.

The day he dies.

Engaged in reckless battle, full of anger and hatred, he's lost what made him human: empathy. He swings and lunges his shark-tooth sword at enemy after enemy, fueled by blind hatred and rage.

Something slams hard into his back. A bloody spear explodes from his chest. At its tip, an unfortunate soul's dismembered heart.

Watching, in shock, the heart still beats. His heart.

He understands for the first time that the hate and rage he feels is for himself.

Unable to breathe, he drops to his knees.

Tha-thump . . . tha-thump . . . tha-thump . . .

Muffled heartbeats fill his ears, becoming slower and slower as he feels life leaving his body.

. . . tha . . . thump . . . tha . . .

Guilt, sorrow, and regret.

. . . thump.

My son will be left all alone.

. . . on the ground, Matani's own hands clutched his chest, having just experienced the journey of his father's entire life in a matter of moments, and every ounce of feeling and emotion that accompanied it.

"Father," he finally gasped. But when he looked up, the apparition was gone.

The heavy, haunted air disappeared as quickly as it had arrived, and the irregular darkness of the night brightened with a more natural glow. Even the green heat lightning had moved off, but the night sky remained overcast.

Faithfully at his side, Nahoa watched him, those different-colored eyes full of worry. Matani wrapped his arms around the dog's neck and hugged him before taking several trembling steps back to the campsite.

"My nights of sound sleep are definitely over," he said, forcing a laugh. Then he dropped to the ground with his back against the tree as Nahoa curled up right beside him.

Adding a few more chunks of sandalwood to the dormant fire, Matani was thankful that the few remaining coals were hot enough to ignite them. Staring into the flames, a thousand questions raced through his mind. And the only person, the only family member he could think to ask for answers was Tūtū Ona.

But my last three visits to the Island Worlds happened by accident.

Did they?

Do you know how I opened my inner doorway?

Primal sounds trigger your heightened awareness.

"Yes, of course," Matani whispered, surprised that the constructive question and answer came so easily and without argument. He then focused his intentions on the crackling flames.

To my ancestral spirits, please wrap me in a blanket of strength, safety, and guidance.

Returning his attention to the fire, every now and again, a downdraft made the smoke swirl around him, and he breathed in its lovely aroma. The gentle crackle of its flames accompanied phantom shapes that danced around the incandescent core of the burning wood, mesmerizing him.

It wasn't long before his skin started vibrating and his vision exploded with a rainbow of colors as the forest faded from view. Closing his eyes, he felt the air turn, taking the dense smells of the woodland with it.

Even with his eyes closed, he knew.

Opening them, Matani found himself in the otherworldly dawn of his

Spirit Farm, inhaling the lovely fragrance of hibiscus flowers, and the sweet nectar of tropical fruits. A large herd of bulky creatures, made of what looked like sticks and grass, grazed quietly in a nearby meadow. But seeing his farm illuminated by a wide band of orange sunlight, Matani noticed something new this time. A rush of amber water was flowing down through the previously dried aqueduct, turning the lifeless dirt of every taro patch into rich and fertile mud.

My farm looks so much healthier!

Because you're finally tending to its needs.

Matani looked up and found Tūtū Ona standing beside the glowing amber water of the fishpond. He immediately raced over and hugged her hard enough to make them both stumble.

"So glad to see you, Tūtū," he whispered in a trembling voice.

Both surprised and pleased by his unexpected show of affection, she hugged him back. "I'm here," she said earnestly.

After what he'd just been through, never before had two words felt so comforting to Matani. "I just met my father's ghost."

She already knew, of course. "There's nothing to be afraid of, young man. Spirits are just another aspect of nature, no different than wind or rain."

"I've never experienced anything like that," he said, his eyes full of anguish. "I lived his entire life!"

"There is a proper relationship to be had between the living and the dead. Well spirits help us, but unwell spirits can cause problems."

Matani took a moment to process his grandmother's words. "But if my father is a spirit now, why isn't he here? In the Island Worlds?"

"He left too many stones unattended in his Bowl of Light, so when your father's spirit crossed over, none of us could claim him. It seems he's been relegated to the *Realm of Lost Souls.*"

Matani looked at her, confused. "How can a spirit get lost?"

"When a physical person dies, their consciousness transitions to a detached state," she explained. "If still carrying harmful emotions and energies, they may be drawn to lower vibrational planes in alignment with their heavy energy, preventing them from transitioning completely."

"He was asking me for help, but I didn't know how," Matani said, his voice heavy with guilt.

"His own choices in life led him to a restless state of being," she told him. "What he needs now is guidance crossing over, but he can't do this without resolving the emotional struggles he carried before passing. If he doesn't, his anguish and pain will haunt this family for generations to come."

This was a dizzying revelation to Matani. "So, I do carry my father's anger and pain?"

Again, his grandmother bobbed her head in partial agreement. "Some of your suffering comes from ancestral traumas, yes, but there's plenty of your own making as well."

"Is it even possible to resolve someone else's pain after they've died?"

"Not only possible but imperative," she told him. "You must do what your father could not—learn to control your own thoughts and emotions instead of letting them control you."

"My mind was so calm and quiet the first few days of my journey when I couldn't remember anything," Matani said wryly. "But the arguing voices suddenly came back, and now everything is getting very confusing again."

"Young man, when you see two people fighting, do you immediately go over and jump in between them?"

"No, of course not."

"Then why do you do this with your thoughts?"

"I don't know," Matani replied defensively. "I mean, they're in my head. It's a little hard not to get involved."

"It can certainly be a challenge, but not impossible," said Tūtū Ona. "You must teach yourself to pause, take a step back, and listen to these thoughts without being reactive. Then, decide for yourself which ones are helpful and which ones are not."

Matani just shook his head in frustration. "I know you said thoughts and emotions are in my 'Uhane aspect of self, but where do they actually come from?"

"First of all, they're two different things. Emotions are real, thoughts are not."

"Thoughts aren't real?"

Tūtū Ona flicked her fingers as if casting a spell with each word pairing that followed: "Blue tree. Green cloud. Red canoe."

Matani pinched his brows together. "What?"

She smiled a small smile. "Did you see those objects as I said them?"

"Yeah," he replied, but his voice sounded unsure.

"Then where are they?" she asked, feigning a quick search around them.

"Ah," Matani realized. "In my mind."

"That's right. And day-to-day thoughts arrive in similar ways, born of feelings, emotions and experiences that your mind uses to craft opinions. Unfortunately, these can often be stronger than facts."

"What's the difference between facts and opinions?"

"Facts can be proven true or false," she clarified. "Opinions can't be proven at all."

Matani fidgeted uncomfortably. "But if thoughts aren't real, why do certain ones seem to have so much power over my life?"

"*Objective* reality is like the ocean, existing independently of your thoughts," she said. "However, *subjective* reality can evoke different emotions for different people. To one, that same ocean can be a source of excitement and beauty. To another, it may trigger feelings of danger and fear."

"So two people looking at the same ocean, in the exact same moment, can experience completely different realities?"

"Yes, but based on belief systems created from their past experiences—even if they didn't consciously create them," she further explained. "Another example is when thoughts tell you you're stupid, unloved, unattractive, or that you can't do or be something. If you accept these opinions as truths for too long, they begin to shape negative beliefs about yourself."

"I don't know," Matani said warily. "When I think things like that, they feel pretty accurate to me."

"Which is why it's important to consciously challenge self-sabotaging thoughts the instant they arrive," she cautioned. "Before they can develop into limiting beliefs."

He took a moment to ponder. "What's the difference between thoughts and beliefs?"

"Beliefs are a more comprehensive set of ideas that a person holds, while thoughts are more specific mental processes that reflect a person's current mental state."

Matani's face became a dreadful blank.

Recognizing his confusion, she simplified her explanation. "Think of thoughts as seeds, and belief systems as the crops they bear."

"Ah, got it."

"We successfully transmuted the negative energy of your limiting belief systems through lomilomi," she reminded him, "but now you need to develop some mindfulness techniques to manage the constant flow of thoughts that come and go each day."

"Is that even possible?" he asked.

"Yes, by learning to allow toxic thoughts to pass through your mind without giving them any power over you," she continued. "Instead, shift your focus to more positive thoughts that will support you on your journey."

"But if negative thoughts aren't real, then positive ones aren't either, right?"

"Thoughts are just thoughts," she replied indifferently. "But positive thoughts bring light and hope, while negative ones bring darkness and despair."

"I've . . . had my share of dark thoughts before," Matani reluctantly admitted, diverting his eyes in shame.

"We know," Tūtū Ona said quietly, tenderly lifting his chin with her wrinkled hand. "And you've let them fester for so long, they've manifested a debilitating depression that constantly tricks you into believing distorted opinions about yourself that simply aren't true."

Matani blinked his tears back. "Does that make me weak, Tūtū??"

"Absolutely not," she replied, instantly dispelling his doubts before they could take root. "Depression can overwhelm anyone, no matter how strong or important they may appear."

"It's like I'm drowning in this deep, dark cave and there's no way out," he explained, even now haunted by all the self-deprecating thoughts constantly chiseling away at his sense of self-worth. "How do I find my way out when that happens?"

"By reaching out to those who love you," Tūtū Ona whispered softly, then wrapped both of her arms around him.

Calmed by her loving embrace, Matani felt the spiritual presence of his other ancestors circling around them, each having faced their own struggles and hardships in life. "Just when I think I'm making progress, something else always seems to come up that I need to fix about myself."

"You are not broken," she reassured him. "You just need to practice a little more compassion for yourself and learn to appreciate the valuable person you are."

"I see what you did there," he said with a forced smiled, trying to hide his melancholy. "Hopefully I can learn to shift pessimistic thoughts like that myself someday."

Tūtū Ona's blue eyes glinted with an otherworldly wisdom. "Small things are necessary before big things can be achieved."

Feeling the silky, ethereal grass under his feet becoming a scratchy, tangible bed of ferns under his body, Matani reached for the tutuʻi nut pendant around his neck. "Wait, I meant to ask you about this symbol!"

The necklace wasn't there, of course. It was a material object from the physical world.

"Remember," Tūtū Ona said, placing her left hand over her sacrum, right hand over her heart. "What you do defines who you are, not what you think or believe."

✦ CHAPTER 21 ✦

Kneeling in freshly irrigated mud, Matani reached for another taro stem from the tattered, earth-stained basket hanging at his side. "Never forget," his father said, glaring down with severe judgment in his eyes. "The legend of Haroa reminds us that taro is the foundation of our people."

Matani had heard different versions of this legend over the years, of course. As it was told to him, Papa and Vatea, creators of the beloved island chain, had a daughter named Hoʻohoturani, who conceived a child with Vatea that was stillborn. Naming him *Haroa*, meaning *eternal breath*, his tiny corpse was wrapped in bark cloth, placed in a basket and buried. For many long and sad days after, Hoʻohoturani cried tears of grief on Haroa's grave until, from his remains, grew the very first taro plant. It produced a corm that was removed and planted again, creating more taro offspring. In time, Hoʻohoturani produced a second child who she also named Haroa. He became the very first Havaiian.

"The taro plant is the first-born child of our people," his father lectured. "If we don't respect and care for our older brother, he will stop feeding his family!"

Only half listening, as always, Matani pushed the taro stem down into the wet earth. Feeling something squirming in his hand, a single breath caught in his throat.

His father grimaced. "What are you waiting for? Pick him up!"

"No, I don't want to," Matani said nervously, watching in horror as the freakish stem swelled into a grayish-brown bulb of taro shaped like a human baby. Its tiny mouth hung lifeless and agape beneath half-closed eyelids.

Hissing with dismay, his father shoved him aside to pick up the newborn creature. "Have you forgotten everything I've taught you?!"

Matani could no longer imprison his words. "Everything you've taught me, I never wanted to learn! I hate being a farmer!"

"Farmers are the backbone of this community!" his father snapped, slapping the mutated creature's bottom. Seeing it still lifeless and limp, he whacked the hideous thing again.

This time, it coughed to life with gurgling mewls.

"Get that thing away from me!" Matani shouted. He turned to walk away, hoping his father would pretend he didn't exist, as usual.

"Oh, no you don't," his father yelled, shoving the wriggling taro-thing back into Matani's arms. "He's *your* responsibility now!"

The pressure of his father's rough hand forced his gaze down, just as the creature looked up with its inhuman black eyes, screaming through barbed teeth. Matani wanted to scream, too, but his throat was locked in terror.

Staring into the hated, feared, loved face of his father, Matani let out a choked yell, breaking him free from his nightmare.

Nahoa jumped to his feet, his eyes worried.

"I'm okay," Matani said wearily.

Liar.

Looking up at another overcast morning sky, he adjusted his rain cape and cinched his loincloth, which had become noticeably loose over the past few days. After warming both hands over smoldering coals of fire to melt off the morning chill, he stood up and stretched with a sleepy yawn, feeling a few more leaves of the rain cape flutter down his leg.

"Come on," he said, lifting up his walking staff. "The mountain awaits."

The nightmarish imagery of the taro baby gradually faded as they made their way around the valley they'd camped alongside, bringing Matani and Nahoa to a vast landscape of the day's journey ahead. More mist-laden gorges and ridges of green lay between them and the summit of their destination which was, once more, hidden under a mysterious mantle of clouds.

Seriously, though, what do you think is going to happen when you get there?

I have no idea.

You think all your problems will just disappear?

I don't know.

Well, I think you're only going to end up disappointed. As always.

Please be quiet. I don't have any patience for your nonsense today.

Seething at this most unhelpful conversation in his thoughts, Matani did his best not to engage them any further.

For a while, he was pretty successful, and the first part of the morning proved uneventful as he and Nahoa made their way through the rolling hills and humid mists of the rain forest. But by the time the silvery blur of sunlight had risen higher behind the gray sky, the terrain had turned into a muddy swampland of submerged grasses, thickly tangled vines, and moss-covered trees ornamented with birds of every imaginable color. As Matani climbed to higher elevations, the cooler temperatures began seeping into his skin, causing him to shiver uncontrollably. With each labored breath, his lungs burned with the sharp sting of freezing air, and his fingers and toes numbed with an unbearable chill as the gradual increase in altitude began taking its toll on him.

The first ti plant he came upon, Matani used several of its waxy leaves to repair his rain cape, but they did little to insulate him from the increasingly harsh elements. The hardest part was walking through the swamplands, a laborious process. Back down along the forest floor, a hiking landmark might've taken a hundred steps or so to reach, but in this wicked mudhole, it took three times as many.

"Just keep going," Matani told Nahoa, more for his own motivation than the dog's. "She wouldn't give up so easily."

She, of course, was the meaningful girl from his childhood, who had wandered into his thoughts once more. The one who was always there after his mother died, trying to help fill the void. No matter how angry or sad Matani felt, how many times he pushed everyone away, she was the one who never left. Or at least, always came back. No one else had done that for him. And after his father was killed in battle, she was the one who demanded her parents take him in when no one else would.

But having lost both his parents—left all alone in the world—just being alive eventually became too much for Matani's heart to handle. He'd often do what she called *disappear*, where he'd go walking for long stretches of time far across the island and back again. But no matter how far he went, she'd always find him and talk with him for as long as he needed until he felt even the slightest bit better. Knowing he was afraid of forgetting his parents, she would press him with a thousand questions, though she already knew the answers. *How tall were they? What did they like to do? What's something funny they did? What did they do that made you happy?*

One particular day, feeling depressed to the point of utter numbness, Matani had found his way to the edge of a cliff. Staring down past his toes at waves churning over jagged lava rocks below, he decided he couldn't take the grief any longer. In that moment of weakness, something dark inside encouraged him to take the fatal step forward, but then, someone pulled him back. It was the girl, of course, her eyes shining gold in the sunlight. And there was something in those eyes that told him everything was going to be okay.

Once again, she saved him.

Just as she always had.

"Heiana," Matani whispered longingly, finally recalling the name of the special girl engraved so deeply in his heart.

The very sound of her name gave him the jolt of purpose he needed to persevere.

"I'll find my way back to you," he spoke with unwavering determination. "By the gods, I will."

Arriving at the threshold of another expansive bog, a fast-moving brume came rolling in, erasing every potential landmark from view—including the one Matani was currently using to guide them. *Poof*, gone. Worlds of trees and vines were erased, entire groves at a time, and then Matani and Nahoa were swallowed, too, left with barely any visibility. Although he felt his aching legs moving, Matani started to wonder if they were actually getting anywhere at all.

It was, by far, the roughest-looking terrain they'd come across, full of ragged trees contorted into bizarre shapes with large, twisting plants growing from their trunks. Wading through the endless, untamed wilderness, Matani began feeling like something was lurking in the mud, waiting to drag him down into its murky depths. He was having a much more difficult time making his way through the chaotic terrain than Nahoa, who easily maneuvered his tiny, agile body through the complex system of tangled roots and vines.

"Go on, boy," Matani said each time Nahoa sat and waited patiently for him to catch up. "I'm right behind you."

Blinded by fog, the two of them plodded through the muck and mire, continuously fooled by emerging shapes and distances. What appeared as a gentle ridgeline quickly turned into a brutal combination of hiking and climbing, further complicated by nearly impenetrable fern thickets and slippery mud pits. Slogging across a large puddle of brackish mud only served to fuel Matani's thickening anger and frustration. At one point, a branch caught his necklace, yanking and choking him.

Before

After

Between

Okay, what do these words even mean?!

Nothing! It's just a nut with some scratches on it that you dumbly interpreted to be something meaningful and magical.

Shut up!

You first.

I'm so sick of you! Get out of my head!

Unfortunately, any attempts at remaining neutral with his insidious, unhelpful thoughts while angrily struggling through mud and ever-thickening fog—and now a cold rain—was a losing battle. And it didn't help that every landmark Matani chose ended up looking the same, to the point where he was sure they were going in circles. After stepping into a quagmire of ancient slime that swirled with any number of unimaginable things, he realized how lucky he'd been with just mud. With every step came new and disgusting sensations, gushing with mucus-colored bubbles that popped with smells of putrid decay.

Impossible to maintain any sort of regular pace, Matani lost track of how much distance he'd traveled or how much time had passed. At one point, he could only move forward through the mud by pulling himself with his walking staff.

"The night rainbow will guide you," he spat, cursing the vision that had begotten this fool's errand in the first place. "If I'd known I was part Mū instead of farming taro all these years, I wouldn't even be in this situation right now!"

And your Bowl of Light wouldn't be filled with so many stones.

Exactly!

You wasted so much time being miserable.

You can say that again!

You wasted so much time being miserable.

Very funny.

As funny as Uanini's unjust oppressiveness?

Matani stopped cold. "Uanini," he said, the name poison in his mouth.

His hands started shaking as the trauma of several lost memories returned. Memories of the chief who had plagued him for so much of his life, including the incident with the border idol. While he still couldn't recall much detail about what had happened after the chubby chief chased him through the village, he recalled just enough to realize one thing.

That fool is the reason I'm lost out here in the first place! Who do these chiefs think they are? We pay them taxes, work for them, fight their wars. We live under tyrannical laws where the smallest infraction is punishable by death! Slaves to their every arrogant and piggish whim. There's nothing we have that can't be taken from us!

Tūtū Ona said one must forget in order to forgive.

How can I possibly forget what the highborns did to my father?

Just like Uanini has been threatening to do to you.

So help me gods, if I ever get back home again, I'm going to take that stone club of his and smash him over the head with it!

Now you're talking!

After what seemed like an eternity, the ground hardened into a damp, squishy undergrowth of stagnant filth that transitioned into a forest of gigantic tree ferns with enormously wide trunks. Matani found their raised roots useful to walk on, allowing him to move more quickly and to cover more ground. But, as with many things that made life easier, it came with a price. The tiny thorns growing on the trunks were continuously scraping his arms and legs.

At one point the tree ferns grew so dense he had to turn and use his back to push his way through their heavy, massive leaves, bringing even more surprises. Each disturbed frond released tiny white spores that filled the air and got caught in his throat, choking him.

Is there ever going to be an end to this miserable swamp?

Doubt it. Though there is one way to make it stop.

Believe me, I've been seriously considering it.

Oh, good. Maybe you're not such a coward after all.

Guessing at what may or may not have been glimpses of the mountain, Matani led Nahoa through the fern forest as best he could, eventually coming into an area of smaller ferns. Several of them appeared to have been uprooted, but not as the result of a natural occurrence, like wind or heavy rain. It looked to Matani as if their outer bark had been deliberately torn away by someone to expose their pulpy, edible interior.

After passing several more disemboweled ferns—careful not to let too much hope sink in just yet—Matani found a narrow path beaten down to bare earth. Nahoa pressed his nose to the ground and followed it.

"My spirit grandmother told me that the people who first lived on these islands went into hiding many years ago," he whispered to Nahoa. "Maybe we've found one of their villages."

Losing the path a few times under thick leaves and brush, Matani and Nahoa came into a kind of ghost wood standing in the rainy fog, its trees looking like giant, gnarled sentinels frozen in time. Moving past gangly branch arms, he could see their trunks had been charred black by some long-ago fire. Through the maze of broken trees, the path eventually sank into a clearing of ankle-high muck swarming with bugs flickering in the foggy air. Swatting the tiny annoyances from his face, Matani heard Nahoa snapping at his own cloud of attackers. Farther ahead, he saw what looked like ferns. Their leaves were splashed with something red.

His stomach quivered with fear.

They arrived at six or seven shallow depressions in the mud, each with a creamy brown surface fizzing with scum and hopping bugs. Matani got that old sinking feeling. He'd seen something like this once before.

"Oh gods," he realized. "People didn't make that path."

No sooner had the words left his mouth than three feral boars emerged from the dissolving fog, each of their ragged, filthy hides encased in thick hazes of bugs. A fourth boar pushed its way to the front, easily the largest and strongest of them all.

It was enormous and black and missing an eye.

"Tamapua'a," Matani whispered, barely able to breathe. "Nahoa, run!"

All four boars advanced in a squealing horde of rage. Before Matani could react, a massive black blur charged from the mist and rammed into his thigh like a boulder, effortlessly flipping him through the air. Dazed, he sat up and saw Tamapua'a not far ahead of him, its tusk dripping with blood.

Where'd that blood come from?

Aware of a burning sensation in his leg, Matani looked down, horrified to find a huge gash from knee to thigh with maggots squirming at the edges. If it wasn't for Nahoa's fierce barking, Matani would have fainted. Crawling into a half walk, half run, the pain in his leg was excruciating, but hearing the brute forces pounding the earth behind him was motivation enough to push through the agony.

Struggling to keep himself upright, Matani remembered a conversation with Heiana's grandfather, Rua'au, who had been taught from an early age the ways of hunting by his own father and grandfather. Together, the three of them would bring back wild pig from the mountains to share with everyone. On one particular hunting trip, Matani had joined them, and Rua'au imparted something very important.

Boar have a keen sense of smell and can pick up on the scent of a human from great distances. You can run or hide out of sight, and you can walk without making noise, but you can't hide your smell. And the more you sweat, the stronger it becomes. So, if you ever find yourself in boar country, travel with the wind behind you, so your body odor will be blown away from the pig's nose.

Heeding Rua'au's advice, Matani quickly adjusted from running against the wind to with it, whereupon he came upon a tutu'i tree that loomed before him, surpassing even the height of a ruling chief's palace. Its boughs spread wide, a tangle of twisting branches promised an escape route from the wild boar barreling down behind him. Dropping his walking staff, he grabbed Nahoa under one arm and used the other to climb up as high as he could go. Standing on a thick branch at about the height of three men, he felt it bending under his weight and quickly dropped into a seated position to lessen the load. A spasm of shivers riddled Matani's entire body, and his skin felt both hot and cold at the same time. Hugging Nahoa closely, he could feel himself losing consciousness but fought it off the best he could, knowing he needed to stay alert.

Loud tapping on the leaves told him it was raining now, and pretty heavily, too. Then the tree shook. Matani looked down and saw that all four boars were circled around, taking turns ramming their massive shoulders into the base of the trunk.

"Stop that!" he shouted down at them.

But the boars simply stared back up with their beady little eyes, then returned to ramming the tree. With every attack, handfuls of tutuʻi nuts rained down onto the muddy ground that the rabid beasts devoured with unnatural veracity. Noticing that the three-pointed leaves all around him resembled the snout and ears of a pig, the young man remembered how the tutuʻi tree was yet another body form of Roʻo. Even as this disturbing revelation began to fester, ominous popping sounds started coming from the upper part of the trunk.

"They're weakening the tree," Matani whispered fretfully.

From his elevated vantage, he looked out across the expansive treetops and saw a distant river dividing the landscape. And, although it was difficult to discern through the rain and fog, he also thought he could see groves of banana trees not far beyond it. Banana trees in themselves were not unusual, but the uniform way in which they grew was.

"Can anyone hear me? Please help us!"

Nahoa crawled to a corner of one of the branches and balanced himself between the thickest part of its stem and the trunk, barking and snarling at the boars below. Tamapuaʻa squealed angrily up at the dog as it dashed its shoulder against the trunk, making the entire tree lurch. Nahoa's hind legs lost purchase on the branches and flailed wildly in midair. Scrabbling with his forepaws, there was nothing for him to hold onto.

Matani dove for the dog, forgetting all about the excruciating pain of his wound, falling onto a lower branch hard enough to make his teeth clack. Clinging with one hand, he reached down and grabbed Nahoa with the other, barely catching the little dog by the scruff of his neck. The boars, eerily aware of their prey's vulnerability, began ramming the tree even harder. Feeling himself slipping, Matani locked his legs around the thicker end of the branch he clung to, feeling the congealed blood in his thigh wound pulling apart. With Nahoa slowly slipping from his fingers, Matani could see the boars waiting patiently for them both to drop.

"Leave us alone!" he screamed directly at Tamapuaʻa, cords bursting from his neck. "Isn't that what you gods are good at!"

Matani's words, rife with primitive emotion, conjured something dangerous from the air. He saw every hair on Nahoa's body stand on end just before a blinding bolt of lightning exploded down from the clouds and struck the base of the tree. He heard the splintering of wood, smelling both electricity and burning amid a deafening roll of thunder.

Blinded by the white-hot flash of light, Matani felt himself falling through cracking branches before hitting the ground with a jolt of terrible pain. As his vision slowly returned, he found himself clutching Nahoa tightly to his chest. Looking up at the tree they'd just fallen from, it was split straight down the middle by a slash of burning orange embers that hissed and smoked in the rain.

Nahoa jumped to his feet, on alert. Nowhere to be seen, it seemed the boars had scattered. Using the opportunity to take a closer look at his wound, Matani's stomach turned at the sight of mud and splinters enmeshed in the raw pink flesh of his thigh. A single maggot squirmed at the outer edge of torn skin that he immediately flicked off, making him dry heave. Falling rain cleared some of the grit, but Matani knew he needed substantially more water to flush it out before infection could set in.

If it hasn't already.

"Should be a river up ahead," he said, struggling to stand but collapsed under the effort.

Every inch of skin ached, and his thigh had already stiffened to the point where he could barely bend it without causing pain. Gathering his strength to make another attempt at standing, Nahoa came running up with the walking staff clamped between his teeth.

"Good boy," Matani said, smiling weakly.

Making their way across the mud-filled swamp at a much slower pace, the darkening atmosphere swallowed them whole as a heavy, cold rain began to fall. These weren't just meek, fleeting clouds spreading across the sky, but colossal masses breaking free from the surrounding mountains, bringing strong winds that blew through the trees. Huge, fat drops of cold rain pelted their faces as the sky unleashed its fury upon them. The only good thing about the rain was that it dispersed the heavy fog in diaphanous swirls, offering some more visibility.

Hearing the unmistakable thunder of a river beyond the trees ahead, Matani limped along as fast as he could. A sudden rise in temperature turned the air from cold to humid, followed by a powerful wind that whined at a high pitch at first, quickly becoming a deep roar that signaled the arrival of something deadly.

"Hurricane," Matani gasped. "We need to find shelter. Right now!"

He forced himself into a limping run, his entire body a medley of aches and pains. From one moment to the next, Matani and Nahoa found themselves in a dangerous gauntlet of nature's most destructive forces. Out of nowhere, chunks of burning logs from other lightning-struck trees flew past them like meteors. To the right, a massive chunk of ancient lava broke off from a cliff and tumbled down a slope, knocking down several trees in its path with a series of deafening cracks. Birds flew backward, caught in gale-force winds that bent an entire forest of palm trees horizontal. Leaves, plants, and other debris filled the air as many different types of uprooted trees flew past. More rocks and boulders crashed down a steep ridge to their left, impacting the ground with such force they made the earth shake.

Did my anger cause this storm?

Isn't it beautiful?

Searching for the village he'd seen from the heights of the tutu'i tree, Matani and Nahoa came upon a racing river of rain and red mud that blocked their path. Having worked on a farm his entire life, Matani recognized a flash flood when he saw one. It wasn't that far across, but its flow was moving dangerously fast, with clumps of plants and leaves in the water racing faster than even he could possibly run.

"Why does this have to be here?" Matani groaned, dropping to his knees in despair.

His stomach tightened, and he hunched over, vomiting bile and pieces of berry. There were probably a few shreds of fiddlehead in there, too. Dropping his sweaty face into his sweaty hands, he could feel his skin burning hot with fever. Barely catching his breath, Matani gagged again, somehow expelling more contents from his cramped stomach.

Nahoa started barking crazily at something coming up from behind.

The boars had found them again.

Without thinking, Matani reached down, grabbed Nahoa, and tossed him across the river of mud. Landing in a roll, the little dog spun himself upright with a look of complete surprise.

"Go to that village and get help!" Matani shouted above the storm. "I'll be right behind you!"

Unfortunately, throwing Nahoa to safety had drained the last of Matani's strength. He tried to get up, but his legs buckled, and his bowels tightened again, forcing him to vomit some more—this time, nothing but acidic water.

Then came the deep, guttural sounds of the boars.

Seeing them closing in, Matani knew he was out of options and decided to at least make an attempt at jumping across the floodwaters. He forced his head up as he dragged himself to the edge of the raging torrent. The closer he got, the faster it seemed to move.

Don't overthink it. Just jump.

And he did.

Clutching his walking staff tightly, Matani's toes barely skimmed a few blades of grass on the opposite bank before his entire body fell back into the freezing water. He was carried off with such force, it took his breath away. Following the sounds of barking, he found Nahoa racing alongside him. Focused on dodging rocks and trees in the water, Matani's heart stopped when he looked ahead and saw a tunnel of trees that ended in open sky.

He was headed for the edge of a cliff.

Nahoa raced ahead, launching himself onto the branch of a tree growing at the cliff's edge, then began gingerly inching his way across, his claws clinging desperately to the rough surface of the bark. Unsure what the dog was doing at first, Matani noticed the branch dropping down closer to the water.

"That's it, Nahoa! A little more!"

The leaves at the tip of the branch had just touched the surface of the mud when a traitorous wind gusted, shaking the entire tree. Nahoa's claws scratched madly for purchase before he regained his balance, crouching miserably with his eyes fixed on Matani.

"It's okay!" Matani shouted. "That's enough!"

He felt the precise moment when gravity merged with momentum, doubling the mudslide's speed toward the edge of the cliff. Offering a quick prayer—more of an abstract wish, really—he visualized himself grabbing hold of the branch. Waiting until the timing felt right, he reached up, relieved to feel its knotted wood between his fingers, his mind already picturing the relief of pulling himself to safety. But the hope was short-lived, shattered like the brittle wood that snapped in his grip. The deafening roar of the raging torrent drowned out his cries as he hurtled over the edge, his body tumbling helplessly into an abyss of plummeting silence.

✦ CHAPTER 22 ✦

Drifting in and out of darkness, Matani was immobilized, pinned down by a suffocating weight that smelled of mud, soaked wood, and plants. His skin radiated a fevefish warmth, each swallow burned, and his head felt like a cracked egg. Through closed eyelids, flashes of lightning needled a pounding headache exacerbated by the roar of rushing water. Then he lost his already frail grasp on consciousness once more.

A murky length of time later, Matani didn't so much wake up as slowly drift toward the distant sounds of a flute. It felt like a dream—one in which he thought he was awake but unable to move. As his awareness grew stronger and the glow behind his eyelids grew brighter, he forced himself to open one eye.

Half expecting to be in his Spirit Farm, and for good this time, he instead found his face half buried in a soft bed of dried banana leaves. Opening his other eye revealed a little more information.

The dim interior of a small cave.

With some effort, Matani rolled over on his back and raised himself up on both elbows. The first thing he noticed was that he was wearing a new loincloth and had a fresh bark cloth bandage wrapped around his right thigh.

Looking around for whoever might have changed him, he found several torches lining the natural ledges of the cave, filling the otherwise dank space with comforting warmth. In one corner was a small sitting area, where several stone adzes and shell knives were strewn among piles of fresh tree bark and plant shavings. To his right were neatly folded squares of bark cloth stacked beside small piles of tutu'i nuts, coconuts, and the leaves of different medicinal herbs. Lining the base of the cave walls were stacks of large and small wooden gourds full of earthy liquids. Matani assumed these were medicines based on several coconut shell dippers and other stone instruments that priests and mystics typically used for crushing dried plant tissues, seeds, and minerals.

Slightly dizzy, Matani carefully rolled onto his stomach, fully expecting a painful response from his thigh, only to be pleasantly surprised when he experienced little to no discomfort at all.

Whoever wrapped my leg knew what they were doing. But where are they?

Standing up, he walked past a small fire at the mouth of the cave and out onto a grassy hill that overlooked a secluded glade featuring a large pond. Its lightly rippled surface reflected the surrounding trees and bright sky. Large stacks of storm clouds sitting heavily on green mountains provided the backdrop for a cascading waterfall that spilled into the forest pond and continued on down through the forest landscape. Morning sunlight highlighted the treetops and filtered through their leaves in dusty fingers of light, filling the idyllic setting with a peaceful glow.

Following the light sounds of music that had woken him, Matani's eyes found someone crouched at the edge of the pond. His back was turned, and he was playing a bamboo nose flute. Dropping onto his stomach, Matani watched in amazement as the pond began to bubble and swirl into a spiral of water that lifted up into the air. Large and small pearls of liquid were somehow suspended in midair, spinning slowly like spritely ornaments, refracting sunlight into shimmering rainbows that danced across the ground.

Enthralled and enchanted, Matani could barely believe his eyes as the floating menagerie of glassy waterdrops appeared to respond to the stranger's music, merging into a single, giant undulating sphere of water full of swimming fish, frogs, and shrimp. The great watery globe began to bend and stretch like a giant bubble, forming the shape of a human head with a wide-eyed, open-mouthed facial expression.

Realizing that the water was mimicking his own expression, Matani gasped.

The enormous liquid Matani-head gasped back.

Astonished, he burst out laughing.

All at once, the great, floating, watery head popped into a burst of rain that collapsed into the pond with a loud, hissing crash. The stranger lowered his flute and turned, revealing a bearded adult male, who, even from a distance, Matani could tell was missing a few teeth.

"Well, look who decided to join the living!" the stranger shouted in a surprisingly deep, rumbly voice.

Matani quickly shuffled backward on his hands and knees, hidden just behind the lip of the hill.

Uh-oh, better . . .

"Run?" finished the stranger in his baritone voice.

How did he . . .

"Know what you were thinking?"

As the distance closed between them, more details came into focus. The bizarre stranger's hair, white as clouds, was braided in locks that fell down past oversized round eyes flickering like gentle flames above his thickly bearded chin. Underneath his banana-leaf rain cape, Matani made out a barkcloth tunic cinched at the waist by a finely woven belt of cord. Both the man's wrists and ankles were adorned with bracelets of shells and pebbles that rattled when he walked. And spread across his noticeably muscular chest was a necklace of wooden stars. But easily the most unusual detail was how the odd character's skin twinkled like starlight. A detail that made Matani jump up and take two steps back.

"They call me Krum," said the shimmering figure, tucking the nose flute inside his tattered banana-leaf cape. "Come closer."

Matani squinted, still not trusting his own eyes. "Are you a god?"

"No," Krum laughed, and as he laughed, his skin sparkled even brighter. "Not yet, anyway."

Matani couldn't help but stare in awe as the light danced across the unusual person's face and eyes. "How long was I asleep?"

"Passed out is more like it!" Krum blurted, punctuating his words with an infectious cackle that sent more incandescent ripples up and down his body. "Nearly two days. If I'm being honest, I wasn't sure you were gonna pull through!"

Matani smiled, seeing a friendliness in Krum's face that told him he had nothing to fear. But at the same time, there was something unsettling about the stranger's rather peculiar eyes.

Humming to himself, Krum walked over to the fire at the cave's entrance.

Using two sticks as tongs, he pulled out a few fist-sized stones and dropped them into a nearby calabash that was filled with a mixture of water and shredded green leaves.

"Always nice to meet a fellow Mū," he said. "Our numbers are getting smaller and smaller these days."

Following after him, Matani stopped. "What makes you think I'm Mū?"

"I can feel it on you."

"Well, I'm only part Mū," Matani replied.

Stirring the hot water mixture, Krum stopped and looked up, his raised, thick eyebrows demanding further clarification. "Really? Which part? Your knee? Elbow?"

Matani just stared at him, confused.

Krum threw back his head and laughed, not unpleasantly. "You gotta lighten up, friend! Way too serious!"

"Oh, sorry," Matani mumbled, embarrassed.

"Come now, don't be like that," Krum chuckled. "All I'm saying is, if you've got Mū blood in you, then you've got Mū blood in you!"

Matani paused with a thoughtful nod. "I also carry the blood of both Originals."

Krum stopped and looked up. "How do you know about them?"

"My grandmother just told me a few days ago," Matani replied, staring at Krum's peculiar flesh, the way it shimmered like light and fire at certain angles. It reminded him of his Bowl of Light. "Are you a Shining One?"

"No, I'm just a descendant like you," Krum said with a grin as he carefully poured the tea he'd prepared into a beautifully carved wooden cup. "But I've managed to unlock some of their magic in my blood."

"I have to admit, I didn't really believe her," Matani said, sipping a harmonious blend of sweet and savory. "Until now."

"I suppose I wouldn't either," Krum said with a smirk. "Especially since history that's passed down orally is often prone to interpretations that tend to contradict themselves."

"But why?" Matani asked. "Shouldn't everyone be passing down the same story?"

Krum laughed as he stood, envious of his young visitor's ignorance. "It seems certain *adjustments* are made to suit the motives of those telling the stories."

"Highborns," Matani said, the word dripping with disdain. "Always trying to embellish their genealogies to make themselves more important than they actually are."

"Well, with blood of the Originals coursing through your veins, you've added about ten thousand years to your lineage. No Tahitian chief can claim that!"

"Is that why Pa'ao tried to wipe out the Mū?" Matani asked. "Because he was jealous?"

"People have done worse for less," Krum replied, slowly turning his left arm in a ray of sunlight that ignited a dance of fiery embers. "That's why I've spent most of my life trying to reactivate the starlight in my own blood. So I can access the power that comes with it."

"Why?" Matani asked. "What do you want to do with it?"

"If I can gather other like-minded Mū, we can finally reclaim these islands in the names of our ancestors."

Matani's face filled with concern. "But if the highborns find out, won't they try to kill you?"

"They've already found me," Krum said, coughing up a hard laugh. "Almost caught me a few times, too. Which makes me wonder how you're still alive."

"My parents hid my Mū heritage from them," Matani replied. "I didn't even learn about what I was until after they died."

"*What* you are?" Krum repeated back. "Don't you mean *who?*"

Matani's cheeks reddened; his mouth thinned into a line.

Krum chuckled, fixing his eyes on something past Matani that turned his chuckle into a gasp of terror.

"What?" Matani asked, looking behind him. "What is it?"

Krum raced over to the cave and returned with a spear. Sniffing the air, he tilted his head in an attitude of keen attention, staring apprehensively at the many potential hiding places of the forest around them.

"Is something out there?" Matani whispered nervously, his first thought being wild boar. Then he heard something snap beyond some trees a moment before five spear-wielding warriors wearing red feather loincloths raced from the jungle.

"Run!" Krum shouted. "I'll take them on!"

Matani whirled around and limped his way into some trees at the edge of the glade. As he ran, the sound of weapons clattered amid angry voices. Looking back from his hiding spot, he saw Krum bravely mounting a defense despite being clearly outnumbered.

The unfair, unwarranted ambush outraged Matani.

It's been this way since these invaders first arrived in their red feather clothes. They take whatever they want. Our food, our women, our temples—and our lives. They give us orders and call us commoners, but we are not commoners. We are the ancient ones, who have lived on these islands long before they came to our shores.

Matani recognized Krum's voice through mind-to-mind communication.

So why do you keep letting them persecute you?

Two reasons. They outnumber us, and the darkness that leads them is powerful.

But if they believe rank and power are derived from bloodlines, and theirs is barely a thousand years old, then what does that make them in comparison to us?

Matani, ours is a sacred bloodline that goes back to the very genesis of consciousness itself.

"Then *we* are the true highborns," Matani whispered, realizing he'd been living falsely under the oppression of people who were inferior to him all this time.

Krum broke free from his captors—only to run straight into the arms of a high-ranking chief lurking behind a tree. He was easily a head taller than the others and had a permanent scowl carved into his face.

Clearly recognizing the warrior, Krum flashed him a smile. "Kapawa, I wondered when you were gonna show up!"

Kapawa smoldered, kicking Krum's legs out from under him. "You best use that maggot-eating mouth of yours to tell me where the others are."

"I'll tell you where they are," Krum said with a sarcastic lilt to his gruff voice. "In a much better hiding place than mine!" Then he laughed, which only managed to further anger Kapawa and his fellow chiefs.

"Kill this aberrant thing", Kapawa growled through his clenched jaw. He then placed a necklace of teeth and bones of slain Mū around Krum's neck, rendering him powerless. "We'll find the rest eventually," he promised with a cold stare. "And kill them, too."

Matani snuck into a position where he could better see the confrontation, locking eyes with Krum. Both knew in that moment that he was about to die. Krum struggled to loosen his restrictive bindings, but the warriors quickly moved in and pinned down his hands, legs, and back.

"You may have been here first, but these islands belong to us now," Kapawa snarled, unhitching a stone club from his red feather loincloth.

As Kapawa raised his killing weapon, preparing to bring it down on Krum's head, madness ebbed and surged throughout Matani's body, half crazed, wholly powerless.

Powerless? Are you?

"All you had to do was follow our rules and do what you were told," Kapawa said, gritting his teeth into a sick and twisted grin as he dropped the club.

Time slowed as Matani watched the weapon descend through the air. His heart pounded, his lungs heaved, but his paralyzed muscles refused to respond.

"Enough!" Matani screamed.

Parting the long green stems in front of him, Matani stepped from his hiding place. His right hand rose immediately and forcefully, its palm facing Krum's smug assailant. Every one of his fingers manifested immaterial forces that reached across the distance between them, catching hold of the stone club, freezing it in midair.

Unable to complete his deadly strike, Kapawa's eyes found Matani with a flash of angry surprise, nodding a silent order for the other five warriors to seize him.

At first, Matani wanted to run.

Just as he always had after offending or upsetting one highborn or another.

But he wouldn't, not this time. This time he refused such immature inclinations.

This time, even as the warriors bore down on him with raised spears, he stood his ground.

You don't have to be afraid, Matani.

I'm not afraid. I'm angry.

Good.

Why is that good?

Because anger is your father's greatest gift to you.

But isn't anger dangerous?

No. When harnessed properly, anger is power.

Matani went still for a fateful moment, then felt something he'd never felt before.

That he was in absolute control of not only himself but the situation at hand.

After a life of being brainwashed into believing he was unworthy, weak, and common, Matani finally understood why all those deceptive highborns had inflicted their fears upon him. Highborns like Uanini, Rock Jaw, Back Scar, Big Head, Thick Neck, and Kahiko.

They were afraid of me.

Yes. As you've always known, you're far more special than they would ever allow you to believe. They are the ones who created inhuman laws that they themselves can't even follow. But you—you are a descendant of the universe, and no mortal is your equal.

Matani's face melted with hatred. "My blood is mighty."

The time has come for you to use that might in your blood to end their sinister plot on this world once and for all.

"Yes," Matani hissed, kindling a distant smolder somewhere in a secret space deep inside his heart. A dark and shadowy space full of cobwebs and decay. He closed his eyes and exhaled all that he knew to be true but had kept buried all his life. And with that exhale came the unleashing of something that had grown tired of useless words and thoughts.

Vengeance.

Worlds trembled as Matani's vision darkened. Maintaining a psychic hold on Kapawa's stone club with his right hand, he raised the left and filled it with a buzzing energy so powerful it made him grin.

"Kill him!" Kapawa ordered his subordinates, still struggling to take back control of his arm.

Foolishly, they obeyed.

The sky blasted with lightning, and that same electricity surged through every level of Matani's being, rolling through his body and out of his clawed hand, sending the five chiefs running in all directions. But as fast as they were, none of them could outrun the blinding, bluish-gold arcs of lightning—which obliterated them into meaningless piles of ash.

Released from the mysterious power that held him, Kapawa made a desperate, staggering run at Matani, his stone club poised and ready. With barely a flick of the wrist, another bolt of lightning tore from Matani's fingertips, slashing the chief across his head, followed by another strike that devoured his heart.

Overwhelmed with dizziness, Matani dropped to his knees, feeling fear reaching its cold hands into him again. But his fear didn't come from the vengeance he'd just committed.

He was afraid of how good it felt.

Matani walked over to Krum and removed the magic-hindering talisman from his neck. But just as he started loosening the bindings around Krum's wrists and ankles, Matani noticed a striped lizard with a sky-blue tail at his feet.

"Not you again!" he shouted angrily.

Or was it shame? Either way, the very sight of Matani's family guardian unlocked a rampaging bonfire that had been metastasizing inside him like a disease for many years. Overcome with a strange, almost eerie, desire, he screamed at the top of his lungs, then raised his foot and stomped on the lizard with all the rage he could muster.

The small creature's delicate skin burst, instantly extinguished of life, its guts squishing up between Matani's toes.

Staring at the crushed remains of the lizard, numb and confused, he stumbled back a few steps. "Oh, gods. What have I done?"

"You've shed false identities that have been projected upon you," Krum answered, placing a forceful hand on Matani's lower spine. "To finally become what you were meant to be."

"Evil?" Matani asked uneasily.

"No." Krum smiled darkly. "Someone wielding the might to shape the world as they desire."

"There's only one thing I desire," Matani began, then stopped himself. "No, it's impossible."

"You've had a lifetime of others telling you what you can and can't do," Krum said. "But now that you've accepted the power you've inherited, *all* things are possible. Go on," he urged. "Just say what you want, and you will have it."

Without considering the potential consequences, Matani carelessly said the words anyway, "I wish my parents were alive."

Krum bobbed his head back and forth, twiddling his fingers in the air. "Mmm, close. You need to be more specific."

Matani nodded firmly. "I want to bring my parents back from the dead."

"That's it," Krum said, both corners of his mouth curling into a smile as he took Matani's hand and guided him down the hill.

Unable to resist even if he wanted to, Matani followed Krum into the shallow pond and waded across to the waterfall on the other side.

"What is this?" Matani asked, his own eyes aglow with primitive fire.

"Water is the expression of memory," Krum explained, his eyes focused but expressionless. "Gaze into the falls and share your most treasured memories with its flowing waters."

Hypnotic patterns of water cascaded down the lava rocks, which began to glow with a soft inner light. Moving closer, a bright spark of energy burst forth from the falls, connecting itself to Matani. With a slight stinging sensation, he felt the spark probing him, pulling out the essence of his fondest, most personal memories that, much to Matani's surprise, appeared in the veil of water before him.

Sitting by white hibiscus flowers with my mother at dusk.

Marveling at the golden halo of light around furry bees collecting pollen.

Riding on my father's shoulders during many long hikes along oceanside cliffs.

The three of us together, swimming in mountain pools and sitting around the fireplace at home, laughing and talking story.

"In just moments, you'll be able to do all of those things with them again," Krum whispered. His lips were so close, they tickled Matani's ear. "Just call them forward."

Mesmerized by the relaxing sounds of flowing water, Matani's breath caught in his throat when he saw two blurry figures appear. They were either behind or somehow inside the falls, but their shapes were immediately recognizable to him just the same.

He shouted to them, his words conveying both hope and disbelief. "Mother? Father?"

"Yes," Krum said evenly. "Now, call them home."

"I'm here!" Matani cried out. "On the other side of the water! Can you see me?"

The two figures started walking toward him but appeared to stop just behind the falls. Growing impatient, Matani tried to enter the water, only to receive a painful jolt of electricity.

He turned with an angry grimace. "What's going on?"

Krum raised both hands in surrender. "Well, bringing back the dead isn't impossible, but it's a slightly complicated process."

"Then tell me the rest!" Matani yelled. "What else do I have to do?"

"You must give an offering to the falls before it will let your parents cross back over."

"What offering?" Matani growled impatiently. "I don't have anything!"

Krum glanced down and Matani followed his gaze, startled to find that the pendant around his neck was glowing with a warm inner light.

"My tutu'i nut?" Matani asked incredulously.

"Yes," Krum said with a deliberate nod. "Before your parents can return from the hereafter, a meaningful offering must be made to the lift the unseen veil between flesh and spirit."

B e f o r e

A f t e r

B e t w e e n

Finally understanding the cryptic words that had haunted him for days, Matani stared in silent amazement as a large, glimmering hand reached out from the waterfall with its liquid palm upturned. He carefully removed the glowing tutu'i nut from around his neck and lowered it onto the—

Stop!

The voice was familiar, loud and jarring.

Who—who is this?

"What's wrong?" Krum asked impatiently. "The waterfall's waiting! Give the offering, or you'll never see your parents again!"

Tell it you're saying a prayer, then close your eyes and listen carefully.

Confused by what was happening, Matani turned to Krum. *It?*

"N-nothing," he said, flashing a fake smile. "Just praying."

Krum furrowed his bushy eyebrows. "Well, make it quick!"

Then, Matani closed his eyes and listened.

Honey, you aren't where you think you are. That's not your father or me behind that waterfall. And that thing next to you is most certainly not any incarnation of Mū.

Mother?

Matani blinked his eyes open and the idyllic landscape around him flickered like flames, revealing a cold, dark world hidden underneath.

Instead of a beautiful oasis, he now stood inside his Spirit Home. But all the repairs he'd made had been ferociously vandalized, its foundation completely destroyed.

But that wasn't the worst of it.

The tutu'i nut he was about to give the waterfall wasn't a nut at all.

It was a stone.

And he was about to place it on the very last glimmer of light in his bowl.

"Do it!" Krum yelled, sensing Matani's resistance. "Give the offering!"

His voice sounded different. *Its* voice.

Deeper.

Angrier.

Turning slowly, Matani saw Krum for what it really was.

✦ CHAPTER 23 ✦

A terrifying monster, far more unholy than any nightmare he'd ever experienced, cast its grotesquely malformed shadow upon Matani. The hidden manipulator that had been pulling the strings of his thoughts and actions all these years. He could feel it thinking, but its thoughts weren't the least bit human. A lingering, sentient creature from some unfathomable, ancient dimension, its face that of a mutated boar with long, sharp tusks dripping with puss and drool. So enormous, it was almost too overwhelming to comprehend. It was a hideous thing with a cleft nose, its bulbous lips curled back to reveal scraggly yellow fangs. Moths circled its horribly defiled body, and its wrinkled skin spewed and bubbled with the smell of things it hungered for—anger, hatred, grief.

Swatting away incessant bugs feeding off oozing pustules on its face, the boar-thing glared down at him with large yellow eyes that were chillingly wise, but with a dark, ungodly knowledge.

A disquieted sound escaped Matani, something between a squeal and a moan.

The creature issued a low growl. "Ah, so you *can* see me now?"

Mother, what is it? An evil spirit?

No, a spirit is born and reborn at one time or another. This creature is a shadowy reflection of The One Who Creates All Things and preys on those vulnerable to its influence. What stands in your way is The One That Destroys All Things.

Where did it come from?

Negative mind projections hidden in the emotions of your physical body. It's a psychic cannibal that thrives on negativity, silently dimming the empowering light of its victims.

But why? What does it want?

To destroy humanity by turning it against itself.

Has it destroyed me?

No, it needs you alive—but unconscious—while it makes you forget who you really are, assuming control of your body to spread its destructive skills. This is how it leads every human it infects across the threshold of absolute evil, from which there is no return.

Is there any way to escape it?

I'm trying to find a way, honey, but you've wandered too far down the dark path.

"Your own choices brought you here," the vile beast snarled. "Now put that final stone into your bowl and be done with it!"

"No!" Matani shouted, flinging the stone into the fire.

Flames shot up from the burning coals of the fireplace, blinding The One That Destroys All Things. Seeing a brief chance to escape, Matani dove through the slanted doorway, shocked by the complete obliteration of his Spirit Farm. Everything beautiful and vibrant had been paved over with a lifeless, unforgiving landscape. Neither night nor day, the sky was tarnished by a chilling darkness that held not a single glimmer of moon or stars. Gray moths—thousands of them—flitted through thick, smoky air in tight swarms, like ghostly apparitions. The ground was covered in black volcanic ash extending in endless marching dunes toward the only source of light—a pale, spectral glow beyond the encircling horizon.

What happened to my Spirit Farm?

It reflects the life you've chosen after giving all your mana to The One That Destroys All Things.

Strangely aware of something stalking him, Matani looked back and saw the awful monstrosity both walking and sliding across the ash-covered ground, leaving a trail of smoking, acidic slime in its wake. Its gelatinous body writhed with bulging, pulsing, tumorous lumps that dripped with mucus. This was clearly not a creature of the gods. It was a soulless thing born of an archaic, forgotten evil.

Matani took off running, but the constrictive bandage around his injured leg slowed him.

"Why are you running from me?" the creature whimpered. "I was always there when you needed me. I helped protect you from the pain, heartache, and frustrations of daily life when no one else would. Don't you remember?"

"Heiana helped in more meaningful ways," Matani yelled back. "You were poisoning me with negativity!"

"I'm the only one that never abandoned you."

Don't listen to that thing, Matani!

I'm trying not to!

The One That Destroys All Things drew nearer, quickly closing the space between them. Glancing back, Matani could see it morphing into different adversaries that caused pain and suffering in his life. At first it was his father yelling at him; then it was countless chiefs telling him what to do—like Uanini with his constant death threats and Kahiko with his conceited, gap-toothed grin. Then it was Tamapua'a the one-eyed boar, then Krum, and finally . . . Heiana laughing cruelly at him.

How could I have been so stupid? The One That Destroys All Things is a nefarious shape-shifter that has tricked you into believing its manipulative thoughts are yours. It never tells you what you need to hear, only what you want. And its greatest advantage is that you've never been aware of its existence until now.

When it's too late.

The One That Destroys All Things slithered, ran, galloped behind Matani, roaring and snapping its hungry jaws. With wriggling maggots dripping from its slobbering jaws, its menacing talons clawed wantonly at the air behind him. Matani knew if it caught him, he'd be absorbed into its horror. Unable to tolerate the sight of it for another moment, he forced his eyes away, but he could still hear the noises it made, squishing, choking, and laughing. Pushing himself to outrun the nightmarish thing, the bandage around his leg loosened and began to unravel. When he reached down to fix it, he couldn't believe his eyes.

There was no wound. Not even a scratch.

Of course! I'm in my spirit form! But then, where's my body?

Still running from the monster, trying to solve the riddle of this new revelation, that familiar feeling of being in two places at once suddenly overcame Matani, like when he'd first visited the Island Worlds. It took some effort to adjust his awareness before he could see into the physical world.

But this time, it was a much different experience.

Instead of returning to his physical body, he hovered directly above where it lay motionless, buried under a pile of muddy storm debris that was bunched up alongside a racing river of mud. Nahoa was there, too, working diligently to dig him out. Making an attempt to reenter his body, some kind of invisible barrier prevented him.

What's happening? Am I dead?

No, but the biology of your physical body is suffering from a very serious infection.

Then why don't I see any spiritual manifestations of my sickness here? Everything is gone!

The One That Destroys All Things is the spiritual manifestation of your infection. In order for your physical body to survive, you must defeat it.

What happens if my body dies?

Your detached spirit will wander in the darkness you've created, alone and hungry for infinite time.

Just like Father.

Don't give up, honey. I'm trying to find a way—

The ground trembled under Matani's feet. He looked back again to see how far away the creature was, but it was nowhere to be seen. A shiver of darkness swept down his spine.

Mother? Are you still with me?

"I don't know how she got in here," it laughed from the very core of fear itself. "But you're mine now!"

Matani tripped over a rock and belly flopped onto the ground. Rolling onto his back, he looked up and saw something in the ebony sky above. It was the beastly mutation of his negative energy, but now it had grown scaly wings that spread as wide as trees on either side of its body. It swooped down and snatched Matani with its sharp black talons, lifting him off the ground. Matani's screams were muffled by the wind rushing past him as he stared across the endless, dreary landscape.

Just kill me already.

"Death is no longer a luxury you possess," said The One That Destroys All Things. "Welcome to an eternity of never-ending punishment!"

Its hideous cackle rang throughout the darkness. Carried helplessly through the dead sky, Matani felt a searing pain in his hands.

To his horror, all ten fingertips were turning to stone.

Oh gods, it's happening.

Matani grabbed one of the creature's talons and bent it back as far as he could. The winged monster screamed, loosening its grasp enough for Matani to slip free. He tumbled head over heels from an impossible height that, in the physical world, would have been certain death. But here, in the spirit realm, he slammed to the ground and skidded across the black sand, feeling every intense moment of pain. Dazed, he looked up and saw The One That Destroys All Things circling back for him.

Matani jumped to his feet and ran to the top of a towering black sand dune, where he found a deep, narrow canyon carved into the charcoal landscape. Not sure what other ugly, torturous things might be lurking in its jagged contours, something near the entrance caught his eye. A bright fleck, out-of-place in the otherwise dim world. He raced down the dune and entered the dark canyon to get a closer look.

It was a white hibiscus flower.

With ghostly petals radiating fluorescent hues in the dreary light, its lovely fragrance wrapped itself around him, bringing tears to his eyes. Even as the flesh of his arms slowly turned to stone, Matani felt the sensation of a loving hand caress him, and it lit his heart with hope.

He pulled in a shaky breath. "Mother? I can't hear you anymore, but I still feel you. What are you trying to tell me with this flower?"

A second flower appeared, followed by another, and several more, until a trail of glowing white flowers stretched across the winding darkness of the canyon. Hearing the awful screech of The One That Destroys All Things reverberate off the rocks, Matani raced along the floral path as it grew from the black sand, one glimmer of hope after another, guiding him through the darkness to the entrance of a small cave. The cramped opening, barely wide enough for his body to squeeze through, forced Matani onto his hands and knees. Crawling through the humid darkness into a wider tunnel, he found himself among several hundred burial cists lining both sides. He became slowly aware of a strong, unmistakable feeling that these remains represented all those who had come before him, bound to one another by love in both life and death.

Ancestors.
Relatives.
Family.
Loved ones.
Friends.

Then he heard Nahoa barking frantically, abruptly pulling his consciousness back to the physical world. Hovering in the air, he looked down to find the little dog crouched beside his motionless body with both ears flattened back against his head.

What is it, boy? What's wrong?

Nahoa looked straight up at him, his one green eye glinting in the crescent moonlight.

Can you see me?

Answering with a jubilant yelp, Nahoa looked away, baring his teeth and snarling at something approaching. Matani heard a familiar, meaty grunt that drew his attention to a heavy shadow emerging from the darkness.

It was Tamapua'a, the one-eyed boar.

With no other members of its sounder in sight, it appeared that the malice in this beast's heart would not rest until it had its revenge.

The massive creature charged across the muddy ground, straight for Matani's lifeless, vulnerable body. In a blur, Nahoa raced to meet it, barking savagely. The one-eyed behemoth skidded to a halt, sizing up the furry nuisance barely a third of its size.

"Great Ro'o, I beg forgiveness for disrespecting you!" Matani cried, his voice heavy with contrition and remorse. "I'm flawed, but Nahoa is protective, loyal, and true. He deserves your mercy!"

Tamapua'a let out a low grunt before slowly raising its massive head. Difficult to tell through the darkness, but its angry black eye seemed to peer into the depths of Matani's soul, considering his desperate plea—until Nahoa rammed into its shoulder. Stumbling, the boar quickly righted itself and slammed hard into the little dog, sending him rolling across the ground.

"Nahoa, stop!"

But the little dog's fierce loyalty and protective instincts overruled his obedience to Matani's command. Nahoa raced around the colossal animal in circles, barking repeatedly, before leaping onto its back and sinking his teeth into its bristles. As the boar struggled to shake off the tenaciously fearless dog, the unstable ground beneath them crumbled, dropping both down the embankment in a roaring tangle of tusks and fangs. Before Matani could react, the two animals rolled straight into raging floodwaters that swiftly carried them off into the night.

"Nooo!" Matani screamed, abruptly yanked back into the spirit world.

The painful echoes of his cry resonated through the tunnel, returned with patronizing laughter. "You can run, but you can't hide!"

Matani gnashed his teeth. "If something happens to Nahoa, I'll kill you," he spoke in a voice as dark as his surroundings.

Again, chilling laughter answered him. "That's the kind of talk I like to hear!"

Its voice sounded much closer now.

Matani heard movement behind him, and he looked to see the beast squeezing its body through the tunnel like a boneless squid. He turned and scurried along on his hands and feet until the passage widened enough for him to stand and run.

Blinded by thick, hanging vines and other steaming plant life, he could hear squishing sounds behind him, getting louder and closer. Matani followed the humid tunnel farther and farther down through shadowy twists and turns, bursting through a wall of cobwebs into a chamber of lava rock. Adding an air of magic and mystery, a black pool of water at the center of the stone cavity was surrounded by a ring of tall tutuʻi trees and several stone altars topped with unlit torches.

Mother, where have you brought me?

"Are you sure that's really your mother you've been talking to?" suggested The One That Destroys All Things as it oozed from the tunnel.

Reshaping itself, the beast grew even larger than before, its massive form towering over Matani, its eyes ablaze with unbridled hatred. With every breath it exhaled, the air around them seemed to darken and thicken, suffocating Matani in its corrosive malevolence. Its gaping maw dripped with venom, the stench of decay wafting from its cavernous throat. No shred of compassion, goodness, hope, or love remained in this creature, only an insatiable hunger for destruction.

Matani's words quavered as it drew closer to him. "Leave me alone."

The One That Destroys All Things cackled as it held out its twisted claw, materializing a Bowl of Stones in its enormous palm.

"Give that back!" Matani screamed. "It belongs to me!"

"Not anymore," said the beast with a grin both pleased and hateful. It used the crusty tips of its sharp talons to pinch a stone from the ground. "As you are incapacitated, I'll do the honors myself." Then, making sure to have Matani's full attention, it placed the stone into his bowl with sadistic glee, snuffing out its final wisp of light.

"Please," Matani begged.

Desperately wanting to take back his bowl, Matani took a step forward but found his feet rooted to the spot. His eyes widened with horror as he watched his legs turn to stone, the petrification slowly spreading from his ankles to his knees, like a creeping death inching up his body.

The One That Destroys All Things approached Matani, laughing. Smelling of rotten eggs and death, rancid moths flittered between their two faces—one full of fear, the other evil.

"Stone Boy," hissed the voice of Uanini from the beast's stinking maw before it burst into a petulant cackle.

As Matani felt his thighs petrifying, then his waist, a memory bobbed to the surface of his mind like wood on water. Something Tūtū Ona had told him.

Only you decide what goes in and comes out of your bowl.

Fully grasping the hard truth that this awful beast had been the source of all the negative thoughts and impulsive emotions that led him to make so many bad decisions over the years, Matani consciously chose to never again believe its wicked words. And so, with supreme effort and intention, he willed the return of his precious bowl, determined to reclaim what was rightfully his.

In the wink of an eye, the bowl disappeared from the creature's vicious grasp and reappeared in front of Matani, still full of stones, but hovering faithfully at his feet.

"Nice try," snarled The One That Destroys All Things, moving to take back the bowl. "But you're too late."

The creature scurried forward, its sharp talons outstretched to rob Matani once more of his bowl. Nearly petrified, unable to move, Matani felt his consciousness slipping down a dark and desolate tunnel. As the weight of defeat bled through his mind, the sound of water echoed from behind. A sound that reminded him of a place he recognized. Not by sight, but by feeling.

He'd been here once before.

Lower Island.

The dreaming of nature, inhabited by the spirits of trees, plants, rocks, and animals.

Suddenly understanding why his mother led him down here, Matani closed his eyes and gave the most important prayer of his existence.

O Mo'o Kiko,
Great Lizard Guardian, symbol of my ancestral
spirits of the immediate past,
harbinger of my ancestral spirits of the distant past,
from sunrise to sunset,
O spirit of land that dwells in flowing waters,
a major force of life,
your head peers into the future, with wisdom and foresight,
your front feet, symbols of youth, always reaching,
touching, and examining,
your hind legs, the parents, symbols of stability and grounding.
The elders, both alive and passed on, form the spine,
the collective chant of all that came before.
Together we hold all dawns of the past,
and all those that will come after.
My loving family of ancestors, I now understand
how important you are in my life.
I now humbly ask for your help.

"Nothing can help you now," gibbered The One That Destroys All Things. "In just a few last moments, you'll become nothing but a lifeless statue, doomed to remain frozen for all eternity, with no hope of salvation."

Ever so slowly, almost imperceptibly, the noiseless hand of death wrapped its cold, dispassionate fingers around Matani, pulling him into the invisible beyond.

Feeling his chin harden, his arms and shoulders, he knew with dreadful certainty that he was coming to an end.

But more than death, this was something else.

He was moments from ceasing to exist in any time or place.

A terrifyingly definitive end to one's primordial consciousness.

My love, back at the altar in the men's eating house, before you began your ocean journey, you offered yourself as sacrifice.

I remember.

Did you mean it?

Every word.

The ground shuddered. Flames burst to life from the torches built into the ancient stone altars that surrounded the pond. The entire chamber rumbled, shaking loose a light rain from the rocks above, followed by a roar that erupted from the very bowels of eternity, powerful enough to shake several stalactites loose from the ceiling and send them crashing down into the black water below.

Unable to turn his petrified head, Matani heard the sound of churning, bubbling water. Directly in front of him, the beast was tracking something with its terrified eyes, something rising higher and higher.

"You have no business here," The One That Destroys All Things growled from the cave's shadows like a spoiled child. "That little brat of yours gave himself to me by his own doing!"

No, my son already offered himself to his ancestors; therefore, I still have the right to claim him!

Matani's heart lifted as an enormous clawed foot lowered onto the ground beside him with a powerful thud. He strained to shift his gaze upward, locking eyes with a lizard the size of a house. A great and shiny lizard with stripes and a long, sky-blue tail that glowed brightly in the darkness. And though its eyes—the size of boulders—weren't those of a normal lizard, he recognized them just the same.

They were the beautiful, blue-galaxy eyes of his mother, full of pure and infinite love, just as he remembered them.

"Turned, the body has, into glory," Matani whispered in awe, acknowledging the transformation of his mother into lizard form.

While ancestral spirits could take the form of a specific vessel to interact with the living, Matani remembered how the Immortal Soul of Prawns represented all prawns in the physical world. It seemed his mother had somehow persuaded the Immortal Soul of Lizards to let her enter its body and use it to reach him here in Lower Island.

I'm here, honey. But as with any internal battle, I cannot fight it for you.

But how? I can barely move!

The One That Destroys All Things operates in darkness. Only in the light of recognition will it become powerless.

Feeling his ears and nose hardening, Matani searched the shadows of the chamber but had lost sight of The One That Destroys All Things. Desperate, he focused on the bowl of stones below him, willing it to turn over.

But just as twice before, it wouldn't budge.

As his eyes began to harden, he could feel the sacred rhythm of his beating heart slowing down.

It's over. I've failed.

Or . . .

Or what?

What you do defines who you are, not what you think or believe.

Matani felt the 'aumakua form of his mother pushing against his spine, the symbol of generations past and present, igniting a surge of energy that exploded through him like wildfire, carrying boundless love, knowledge, and support. It was as if an ancient river had been unblocked inside him, restoring his bond with all genealogical bloodlines that ran through him: Mea'uli, A'ā'ena, Mū, Tahitian, and Havaiian.

Never before had his personal mana felt so strong and so balanced.

He felt as if he could move mountains.

Or perhaps . . . a single bowl.

With focused intention, Matani felt the power of his ancestors coursing through him, strengthening him, guiding him back into a more positive polarity.

Then he formed a single word of action in his mind.

Turn.

And, with his third attempt, it did.

Every last stone fell to the ground, setting free a blinding column of golden light from his bowl that shone so brightly it immediately exposed the sinister entity's hiding place. The stone parts of Matani's body began to recede, first freeing his face and torso. As soon as he could move his hands and arms, he grabbed his Bowl of Light and aimed it at the beast, letting its powerful illumination sing through the darkness, arrowing straight into the heartless center of The One That Destroys All Things.

It shrieked in surprise, pain, and outrage.

"Every negative thought you planted in me, I believed!" Matani screamed with heartbroken betrayal. "I gave you the power to torture me over and over all these years, destroying any chance at peace or happiness!"

"So what?" the creature hissed.

"Now that I recognize you for the meddling, soul-poisoning monster you are, I choose to reclaim my personal sovereignty and banish you from my being!"

Enveloped in a pure and absolute light, The One That Destroys All Things screeched and twisted wildly, eyes bulging as it faded from existence. Gagging and shrieking and thrashing, the beast used the last of its strength to shape-shift into something else, its body spurting foul-smelling ooze as it shrank smaller and smaller, until the next thing Matani knew— he was staring at himself.

Though, not his true self. This was a hollow duplicate that had been gestating for years inside The One That Destroys All Things.

A Dark Matani, without a single spark of light in its being.

Matani stood before the shadowy imitation of himself, overwhelmed. "I'm sorry," he finally said with genuine compassion, despite all the harm it had caused. "I had no idea what kind of person I was creating."

This more sinister version of Matani—the complete manifestation of energy accumulated by all his negative thoughts and emotions—opened its mouth in a crooked rage.

"I hate you!"

It was the only truthful thing it had ever said to him.

Matani nodded compassionately, managing his own emotions in the moment. "I accept responsibility for the darkness I brought into my heart and am grateful you've shown me what that looks like."

Dark Matani's soulless eyes bulged with hatred. "Drivel to choke on!"

Matani looked up at the lizard form of his mother. "I said I'd sacrifice myself, and I intend on keeping my word," he told her, gesturing to the shadow version of himself. "And so, I offer this part of me that's wrought of hate and negativity."

The great lizard's pink tongue unfurled across the ground and wrapped its tip around Dark Matani's waist in a firm but loving embrace.

"What are you doing?" it screamed, fingernails clawing at the earth. Then its eyes met Matani's for a moment, hellishly bright and aware.

"I'm sorry," Matani said again.

"You think you're rid of me so easily?" Dark Matani laughed with amusement. "As long as there are emotions of love and happiness, I'll be there, ready to ruin them." It's voice was dripping with satisfaction. "The next time you feel hate for a chief, neighbor, family member, or complete stranger, my dark seed will breed in your mind, heart, and soul once more!"

Then it disappeared into the lizard's cavernous mouth, swallowed whole.

Feeling as though an immense weight had been lifted, Matani was left standing with an expression of shock and wonder. "What happens to that part of me now?"

The infinite powers of the One Who Creates All Things will convert his negative energy into something beautiful.

"But can it really come back?"

There is always a chance. The One That Destroys All Things exists with the sole purpose of undermining the entire human spiritual evolution. Now that you have recognized this beast for what it is, you've freed yourself to experience limitless potential, empowerment, and conscious evolution.

As the last bits of stone dissolved from his body, Matani turned to face the spirit goddess form of his mother. Two enormous, blue-galaxy eyes stared back, reflecting the light of the ancient fires surrounding them.

"What happens to *this* part of me now, Mother?"

My son, the time has come to let go of all past limitations that you've placed on yourself and become your destiny.

Matani's gaze fell to the ground. "I'm ashamed I went so far down the dark path."

Sometimes one must pass through shadows to better appreciate the light.

Without warning, a thundering roar from the ceiling accompanied a waterfall crashing down into the center of the pond, reflecting the firelight in curtains of shimmering orange and gold. Relying on his intuition once more, Matani felt compelled to express his deepest feelings and gratitude. He removed his loincloth and soaked it in the sacred waters, then began slamming it onto the rocks over and over again in an ancient ritual of calling out all generations that had come before him by name.

"On my father's side, I am Matani of the House of Tumuhana, farmers from Taua'i and Tahiti. And on my mother's side, of Vaitarua, mystics and healers of the Lizard Clan, through the lines of Naluka'lani'manu-manu, Ona the makaūla, keeper of medicine, and Lae, Kea and Mahi of the piko, with a profound lineage that extends to the ancient era of Papahānaumokuākea. I call these names into my own so that I may embody my ancestors and carry forth the song of our family's history into the next generation."

Having spiritually unlocked access to ancestral information stored in his blood, Matani continued for what felt like many earthly days, reciting the names of relatives going all the way back to Kūhiva and Hina, the very founders of his lineage exactly 19,296 lunar years ago. When he finally finished, he wrung the sacred waters from his loincloth and tied it back around his body.

"Saying these names, reconnecting with them, I feel whole again," he said with an invigorated sense of pride. "I understand now that many insecurities have led me to make bad choices throughout my life. From this day forth, I'll work harder to carry the ancestral light of my family and let it guide me for the rest of my days."

Now that the victim in you has collapsed, you can serve your ancestors in a more meaningful way by discovering your true identity. By choosing to become Spirit Greatness, you will serve as the link that carries our consciousness forward with strength and purpose throughout time.

The great lizard spirit's blue tail glowed even brighter as she opened her jaws, releasing a gorgeous white owl that circled the chamber, glowing brighter and brighter, until its blinding light of awareness filled the cave. The light swirled in the air and hit the base of Matani's spine, leaving both inner and outer aspects of his Anatomy of Being pulsing brightly, exquisitely.

Grinning widely at first, Matani's expression slowly melted with concern. "But what happens if someone makes me so angry and hateful that I lose control of my emotions? Will this nightmare start all over again?"

Smiling with her blue-galaxy eyes, the guardian lizard form

of Matani's mother gingerly touched her nose to his forehead, sharing the breath of life.

Instead of weapons or words, throw love at your enemies and watch them disappear.

SHADOW & LIGHT

FINDING BALANCE

✦ CHAPTER 24 ✦

Matani opened his mud-caked eyelids, finding himself buried under the crushing weight of broken sticks and branches. A shiver tore through him when he realized his body was in the exact same position as he'd seen it from above. With slowly gathering senses, he was aware of a thin layer of frost covering the ground.

Crawling out from under the debris, Matani's tattered rain cape barely clung to his body. Much too weak to remove it, he assumed it would fall off soon anyway. In the dim light, he could see that some puckered tissue had formed around his thigh wound, but his fever had broken, telling him that the deadly infection had run its course. Still, the injury had a long way to heal. He tried to stand, got dizzy, and dropped back to the ground. Lying with his right cheek pressed into the mud, Matani noticed something that was purposefully placed within reach.

His walking staff.

"Nahoa," Matani said in a dry, croaky voice.

Curling his fingers around the cold wood, and used it to climb up, hand over hand, into a standing position. Making his way past an oddly beautiful labyrinth of splintered branches and other tree parts gathered by the storm, Matani carefully slid down an embankment to what was now nothing more than a swollen stream of mud.

Tufts of dog fur and boar hair fluttered in chilly whorls of wind. Some blew across the ground, others clung to broken branches. Sadly, this confirmed for Matani the terrible fight he'd witnessed in spirit form between Nahoa and Tamapuaʻa. Following a trail of muck and mire that the flash flood had carved between the mountain trees, he hoped with all hope that Nahoa was somewhere out there, still alive.

His muscles and joints stiffened by the cold air, Matani limped down along the stream until coming upon a toppled tree fern torn from the ground by its roots. This particular fern stirred a dormant voice that belonged to Amura, his father's mother. In life, she'd been a practitioner of plant medicine, and although Matani never experienced her wisdom firsthand, he distinctly felt himself receiving direct access to her knowledge.

Through the vibrancy of her spirit, Tūtū Amura encouraged Matani to kneel the best he could, which he did. He then felt her hands guiding his walking staff to scrape as many of the stalks and younger, unfurled fronds from the fern as best he could, stripping them of their silky fibers. Once he had a large enough clump to cover the wound on his thigh, she had him snap off some of the exposed sennit from his tattered rain cape and use it to bind a makeshift bandage around his injured leg.

"Blessings, Tūtū Amura."

Continuing downstream through a prehistoric landscape, passing several more fallen trees spattered with red mud, Matani followed a path through a dwarf forest of ʻōhiʻa lehua trees, easily distinguishable by their dark, oval-shaped leaves and puffy red flowers. At lower elevations, these trees grew much taller. At this altitude, they barely stood above his waist.

Following the stream to the edge of a soaring precipice, Matani found himself staring down upon a landscape of colorless gray clouds—a heavenly blanket spread out across the earthbound territories of land and ocean as far as the eye could see. Standing at what felt like the edge of eternity, his heart sank when he spotted more white tufts of dog hair swirling in the abyss before him. His imagination brought images of Nahoa's final, awful moments.

Forced to accept that there wasn't much chance the brave little dog could have survived such a fall, the dreariness of dawn echoed Matani's emotions. Dropping his head in sorrow, high-altitude winds caught the waterfall beside him, sending sheets of water drifting up through the air in glistening spirals. He took comfort in believing this was Nahoa's soul. Nodding gratefully, he stood up straight and tall to honor his brave little companion by placing his right hand over his heart and left hand over his sacrum.

"My loyal friend, your watchful spirit has guarded me well," he whispered, tears streaming down his face.

Lost for a time in the hypnotic churnings of the cloudland below,

Matani slowly became aware of a powerful presence. Following the pull of energy coming from his right, he turned.

It was the mountain.

Despite being on the verge of collapse, both physically and emotionally, Matani couldn't help but feel unspeakably moved by the ultimate landmark of his journey's end. This time, only its summit could be seen, appearing as its own island floating on a sea of clouds. Green and fertile and powerful. So close now, its features were no longer blurred by the haze of distance. Great, grassy pastures stretched up its steep slopes into a fringe of thick forests, tonsured around its peak with the low shrubbery of high-altitude meadows.

Barely a half day's journey now.

Seeing the mountain summit in such detail impacted Matani much more than he would've expected, reminding him of something else Tūtū Ona had said.

Seeing life through carefully chosen thoughts and words can add meaning and manifest powerful healing.

For the first time, he understood what she meant.

The mountain does not speak, yet it says everything.
It does not want. It does not need.
It just is.
Standing tall, it exudes confidence, dependability, and support.
With many paths to its peak,
its height offers new perspectives.
And the knowledge and wisdom it holds are sacred.
Both perfect and terrifying.
The summit of this mortal realm breaks me
open and shows me everything.
What I want to see and what I don't.
But I am grateful for the truth.
For the mountain heals me.
Asking nothing in return.
Only to serve.
And be respected.
It is an earthly temple built by gods.

To bring the heavens to mortals.
A transmitter of universal consciousness.
The mountain connects us, one and all.
If my journey should end in this moment,
I am grateful for this profound gift of understanding.

A light, rattling sound made Matani look down. It was the tutuʻi nut pendant thumping against his chest, replicating the steady pattern of his own heartbeat.

B e f o r e
A f t e r
B e t w e e n

Surprised to hear the riddle of words in his mind again, Matani remembered that the previous solution had come from The One That Destroys All Things and, therefore, was more than likely a lie. Seeing the first rays of sunrise casting an orange halo of fire behind the eastern slope of the mountain, he turned and faced it head-on.

What are these words trying to teach me?

Not to be a slave of time.

Given a new riddle to ponder, a sudden blast of wind drove away the clouds, offering Matani his first glimpse of this strange island's western coastline through the misty, early morning air below. At first, his mind refused to accept what his eyes reported. Gazing down the precipice, past verdant forests of koa and sandalwood, he was suddenly overcome with dizziness. Matani stepped back and took a moment to steady himself on his walking staff. Puzzlingly, the unsteadiness was not a result of vertigo.

It was because the landscape below him looked impossibly familiar.

It shouldn't, but it does. I'm on Oʻahu, after all.

Are you?

His mind quickly unraveled as he absorbed the familiar shape of the coastline and the unmistakable patterns of farming terraces built along the twin rivers that snaked down through the village. Of course, he knew this land like the back of his hand, having spent most of his life farming it.

"That's Vairuanuihoʻāno down there," he whispered in disbelief. "That storm must've blown me clear across the channel! I'm not on O'ahu! I'm on Taua'i!"

Leaping into the air with unbridled excitement, a searing hot pain from his thigh cut the celebration short. Settling for a few pumps of his walking staff instead, Matani glanced over at the mountain again, which offered him the final piece of confirmation.

How could I have not recognized Mount Vaiareare? It's been part of my sky since I was born!

Eager to complete the last leg of his journey, Matani took his final steps toward the very heart of his island home. After barely a few, something far, far out across the eastern sea caught his eye. Through the bluish-purple hues of dawn, orange speckles of light glimmered over the dark morning marine layer that filled the channel between Taua'i and the real O'ahu, seen only now because of his extremely elevated position. Focusing on the lights, Matani's expression slowly morphed from curiosity to horror when he realized what they actually were: thousands of torches attached to thousands of canoes.

A single, breathless word escaped his lips. "Cannibals."

The invisible dam that held back many of Matani's short-term memories ruptured. Within moments, he was overwhelmed by everything he'd experienced since stowing away on *Mano'nahu*: sailing across the ocean; bonding with Shark Warriors; dolphins and whales; arriving on O'ahu; the pretty hula girl, Malela; the bully, Kahiko, and winning the foot race against him; Timoa wanting to kill him; the temple of death; being ambushed by a terrifying army of mud-covered cannibals. And, worst of all, the awful murders of Tari'i and Hano he had witnessed before barely escaping with his own life from a deadly cannibal with angry eyes.

All this was followed by a single name.

"Mafuteo," he whispered. No sooner had he spoken the name than a strange animal cried out somewhere in the darkness. "I have to get down there and warn them!"

Matani's thoughts jumped to Heiana, and his immediate concern for her safety sent him stumbling haphazardly along the edge of the cliff, looking desperately for a way down. But there were very few viable choices. Making his way a short distance north, he came upon a sharp ridgeline connected to a series of descending rugged mountains.

It's the only way down.

He held up his walking staff and squeezed it with both hands. "Ready to do this?"

Waiting for an answer, he impatiently turned sideways and started down the ridge without one. Taking tiny steps worked for a little while but, the farther down he went, the steeper the grade became. The ground was less firm, too, forcing him to drop onto his butt. The natural forces of the earth took over, and he started sliding down faster, needing to drag his hands to control his speed. This worked right up until he swerved into a rock, sending him into a head-over-heels tumble. His injured leg slammed against the ground a few times, filling his vision with bright stars of pain. He threw his arms out, flattened his back to the ground, and prayed for the best.

Mercifully, it was a short trip that came to an abrupt end against the stump of a rotting tree. While painful and jarring, another few feet would have sent him tumbling straight off the ridge to certain death.

"Think, you dumb log!" Matani scolded himself. "You won't do them any good if you kill yourself!"

He looked over at the mountain, feeling its pull, then at the constellation of torchlights moving steadily across the ocean, feeling their urgency. By his best guess, the cannibal army would make landfall by late morning. Long before he could ever possibly climb all the way down to the coast. He doubted he would be able to make it even if he could run at top speed the entire way.

Grisly visions of his village being attacked by cannibals came in rapid and horrid detail—burning homes, slaughtered animals, and the terrified, dying faces of friends and family. Just the thought of it all ignited something unholy in the depths of Matani's soul, stirring anger and fear in his shadowy depths once more.

And what of the mountain?

Recognizing a voice that didn't belong to him, a tingling sensation raced from the base of Matani's spine up to his head, followed by an abrupt heightening of senses. The sensation was similar to what he'd experienced at the onset of his inner travels. But this time, instead of his consciousness departing, something else was arriving.

A shadow moved in his periphery.

Scrambling to his feet, Matani witnessed what he could only describe as a dimensional tear occurring in thin air, from which a soft blue orb of light emerged. As the light drew closer, floating over moss-covered logs, the familiar energy confirmed his suspicions.

"Tūtū Ona? What are you doing here?"

To advise you that your decision in this moment is crucial, young man. There's a right time for every beginning and every ending, especially on this day of the sixth moon phase, when the delay in completing your responsibilities is extremely dangerous. You must finish what you've begun—or risk altering the course of events already foreseen.

"But if I keep going to the mountain, my entire village will be massacred."

A few days of introspection and the farmer thinks himself a prophet now, does he?

"Well, look for yourself!" Matani said, pointing at the clusters of firelight in the channel. "Those cannibals aren't coming to celebrate the new year!"

Don't get smart with me, young man!

"I don't mean to be disrespectful," he said, relenting. "But I feel very conscious of my choices and believe the only right one is to get home and warn them what's coming."

I would never tell you to go against your feelings, but if you don't follow the rules of hoʻoponopono I've set forth to help you get back in balance, you risk ceasing to exist in the eyes of this family.

Matani swallowed nervously. "You know, I didn't understand what you meant about ʻohana being more than just blood relatives until right now. For better or worse, every single one of those people down there is an important part of my family, too."

Very well, then.

The blue glow of Tūtū Ona's vital essence floated gracefully back through the dimensional rift from which it had materialized. Matani watched in amazement as the portal closed behind the luminous orb, leaving a misty seam in the fabric of reality, a distortion that dwindled and contracted before disappearing into nothingness.

Move forward with strength, young man.

"I'll be fine," Matani muttered, wishing he believed his own words. "I just need to be creative."

And with these words, inspiration came to him.

With time running out, Matani knew the next few moments were critical in deciding his own fate, as well the fate of his entire village. Including Heiana. Having saved him so many times before, he knew he could never live with himself if something happened to her. Drawing in a deep breath and exhaling fully, he focused on the soaring, high-altitude vista of dawn breaking before him. He thought of all he'd learned about life and death over the past several days, the magic of the universe, and all the work he'd put in to face his flaws and fears.

All for the effort and desire to strengthen his own personal mana.

But how strong is my mana now?

Concentrating on a solution that would likely require a lot, Matani noticed a white-tailed tropicbird wheeling freely through the morning mists. He centered his mind on the cords of Aka, that tenuous thing that had connected him with other conscious beings before.

Beautiful long-tailed bird, can you hear me? The people in that village below you are in danger. Will you help me warn them?

No response came.

Please. The girl I love is down there.

Love, you say?

Without warning, Matani's intentions manifested in several bright cords of Aka that wove down through the cold mountain air and touched the bird. Through feathers and flesh, he sensed the being's nervous tension as her untamed will joined his. Strengthening his soundless call, he shared all his memories with the bird so that she might understand.

Not a moment later, two words entered his mind.

Ready yourself.

Unsure if they actually came from the bird or not, a powerful jolt of energy struck Matani, not at all like his previous experience of joining with another sentient being's consciousness. This time, an ethereal wind rushed past his ears, and his vision filled with countless points of light that exploded with an instantaneous acceleration that stretched into infinity. The movement was so powerful, it felt to Matani as if he were hurtling through the universe on a metaphysical tempest. He raced across an endless, glistening web of lights, faster and faster, until all of creation and reality flew apart into blinding-white nothingness.

As Matani's walking staff fell to the ground, he vanished in an instant, reappearing next to the pig idol at the border of Vairuanuiho'āno.

The very spot his entire journey had begun.

It took a few moments for his breathing to regulate before intuition told him he'd just been transported through space and time.

Shivering with confusion, Matani's body vibrated with the residue of entirely new feelings and sensations. In the blink of an eye, he'd gone from the very heights of the island all the way down to sea level. Gazing around the forest, he noticed that from a certain angle, every tree appeared smaller. Younger. Shifting his gaze, there was suddenly no growth to be seen anywhere at all. Just black lava floating on a sea of blue, as if when the island was new. In another direction, he could see people walking around and sensed—or felt—that they were from long ago, from now, as well as from the future.

But all at once, somehow.

Feeling dizzy and nauseated and unnerved, Matani rubbed his eyes, hoping to fix what had broken. When he opened them again, his vision was mostly back to normal, except for one thing. Faded, pulsing prisms of light appeared around any object he focused on. Slowly, Matani's curious new hypersensitivity stabilized, and as he stood beside the pig idol, barely able to comprehend what he'd just experienced, a familiar sound echoed through the trees.

That awful, wonderful sound of pounding wooden mallets.

Matani launched himself into the air, shouting at the top of his lungs, "I'm home!"

"Stone Boy?!" came a surprised voice from behind.

Matani spun and met eyes with none other than Uanini on his usual patrol; his jaw hung with confusion.

Neither of them spoke.

Then, Uanini swallowed, the click in his throat sounding like a snapped twig. "Where—? I mean, how did you—?"

"Great questions with very long answers," Matani politely interrupted. "I know you probably want to bash my head in right now, but I need you to listen to me very carefully. An army of cannibals is on its way—"

"No more lies," Uanini seethed, unhitching the stone club from his feathered loincloth.

Normally, this would've been the time when Matani took off running, either to hide, or maybe even to make another attempt at reaching the temple of refuge. And if he were being honest, both thoughts crossed his mind.

But things were different now.

He was different.

And this allowed the introduction of a new choice that Matani had never considered before. To discard old patterns and remain in the present moment, allowing himself to see past his own immaturity, bad attitude, and judgmental ways.

And in so doing, he saw Uanini for who he really was.

Neither royalty, commoner, slave, nor outcast.

But a person. Just like him.

Throw love at your enemies and watch them disappear.

Before the rightfully angry chief could fall into old habits developed from his own beliefs and preconceptions, Matani raced forward and affectionately touched foreheads with Uanini, sharing the breath of life, then stepped back and waited for fate's unpredictable whims to decide what would happen next.

Uanini stared back, dumbfounded. But his stare seemed to hold something else in it as he grabbed Matani by the shoulders and moved him into the light. Thinking he was about to receive the long-threatened blow from the chief's dreaded stone club, Matani realized that Uanini's eyes were focused entirely on his own.

"What is it?" Matani asked.

"Your eyes," Uanini said with bewildered astonishment.

Noticing a puddle of mud at his feet, Matani dropped to one knee. Looking down at his reflection, he could see quite clearly that both of his eyes had turned from brown to blue.

Miniature blue galaxies, like the eyes of his mother.

He stood back up with absolute humility. "There's a lot going on here that even I don't understand, but you were right about me, Uanini. I *was* a stone boy. A selfish, thoughtless, immature child, who blamed my own insecurities and frustrations on you and everyone around me. But I realize now how wrong I was. And I've also learned that life offers second chances. I know you have more than enough reason not to grant me one, but I'm asking anyway. Can you find it anywhere in your heart to hear me out?"

The intense look on the face of his old nemesis seemed to lighten just the slightest degree. "Talk," was all he said.

Matani nodded earnestly, then pointed to the east. "Cannibals are on their way across the channel from O'ahu right now to attack us. Thousands of them."

"How do you know they're from O'ahu?"

"Because I was there," Matani said. "Another long story, but we need to tell your father so he can prepare a defense before it's too late."

Uanini held up one finger, as if what he was about to ask would determine the action that followed. "You were hiding on my brother's canoe that day, weren't you?"

Without blinking, Matani nodded. "Yes. I was."

"I knew it," Uanini replied, almost relieved. Not only because he'd been proven right, but because Matani's story about being on O'ahu suddenly didn't seem so far-fetched. "Come on."

Walking off, Uanini looked back, annoyed when he saw Matani trailing behind. Noticing Matani's bandaged leg for the first time, he hung back for a moment, as if trying to decide something. After an awkward pause, he finally walked back, took Matani's arm, and threw it around his neck.

Matani just looked at him and smiled.

"Not a word," Uanini grumbled, then pulled Matani up past some trees to a bluff overlooking the eastern shoreline.

Through the dark morning atmosphere, both of them easily found several flickering orange lights far out to sea. Uanini looked at Matani, and his face said everything. Tightening their grip on each other, the two hurried down into the valley.

Moving past a cluster of familiar houses, Matani saw Poutoru preparing a morning meal in his earth oven. When the stonecutter spotted the two longtime rivals walking side by side, he beamed. "Friendship is the true legacy of a former foe."

"Oh, shut up," Uanini mumbled as they passed the old man, who, even then, kept the smile on his face.

Seeing the village again, his *Earth Home*, it truly was a sight for Matani's sore eyes. Animals scurried about while children played quietly in well-swept yards. Exhilarated to be back among familiar faces, Matani couldn't deny the world of experience that now seemed to separate him from those crawling from the doorways of their homes to start a new day.

While he'd only been gone a few days, everything felt smaller, somehow. It wasn't the village that had changed, of course.

He had.

But what struck Matani the most was how genuinely happy, healthy, and content everyone appeared. The relative freedoms they enjoyed and the simple lives they had each built for themselves were in great contrast to what he'd witnessed on Oʻahu. Vairuanuihoʻāno was a flourishing village comprised of good people, both royal *and* commoner.

Only now, after having posed as a highborn himself for a few days, Matani realized just how uninformed he'd been about the complexities that revolved around positions of leadership. While he still didn't agree with a hierarchical system based on the arbitrary differences between highborns and commoners, he couldn't deny that Vahanui had always done his best, under the circumstances in which he'd been raised, to ensure the relative happiness, health, and nourishment of his people.

It must be a difficult task for a leader to please everyone.

Uanini helped Matani along a winding path of crushed stones that led to the enormous, oblong thatch structure of the royal palace, where they came upon a group of apprentices guarding the back gates. Among them, Matani recognized Big Head and Back Scar. And despite strict laws that allowed only highborns access to the compound—much less a commoner who was still wanted for a serious crime—Uanini ignored their befuddled expressions.

"Hua," Uanini called out. "Canoes are coming from the east; go track them with the signal fires. Manunu, bring back your best estimate of how soon they'll be here."

Hua (Big Head) and Manunu (Back Scar) didn't move until Uanini glared at them both in a way that told them he wasn't to be questioned, leaving them with nothing left to do but race off together into the forest.

"What are you all gawking at?" Uanini shouted at the remaining apprentices. "We're about to be attacked! Gather every warrior you can and be on alert for the unexpected!"

Matani felt unsettled as the apprentices dispersed. "Do you think there's enough time to prepare a defense?"

"More time than if you hadn't seen them coming," Uanini said, pushing aside the lavish, decorative cloth of the doorway to the mansion.

Unlike the smaller entrances of most common homes, this one was large enough for both of them to walk through without even having to lower their heads. Entering the dim interior, Matani noticed finely woven mats hanging from the walls to cover the thatch, an aesthetic luxury afforded only to royalty.

Their arrival was met by several formidable guards with spears, but Uanini waved them off and boldly ushered Matani right before Vahanui, who was lounging on a bark cloth couch, finishing his morning repast under the raised hands of Supreme High Priest Hunumaniani. The royal spittoon bearer and two attendants sitting quietly behind them were the first to look up, clearly surprised by the intrusion.

Their reaction prompted the ruling chief to catapult himself into a seated position that threw Matani to his knees.

"Uanini?" Vahanui barked. "What do you want?"

"Apologies for the interruption," Uanini replied, bowing his head respectfully to his father. "I bring urgent news."

Vahanui tried not to look annoyed. "What could be so urgent this early in the morning?"

Uanini motioned to the prostrated figure of Matani on the ground beside him. "This farmer has brought to my attention that many canoes are coming across the channel from Oʻahu as we speak, which I have witnessed with my own eyes. He believes they plan to attack us."

"I knew Poʻomanu was up to something," was Vahanui's first reaction, then he seemed to debate his own words. "But during Matariʻi-hiti? How do you know they mean harm?"

Uanini looked down at Matani and impatiently motioned for him to stand, which Matani did apprehensively, taking center stage before the royal court.

"Great Chief, this may be hard to believe, but I was on Oʻahu and saw the evil that now comes this way," Matani said, then gulped nervously at what he knew he had to say next. "I wouldn't be here to tell you this if it wasn't for Hano's brave sacrifice."

Everyone in the room gasped, but the loudest came from Vahanui himself, who glanced between Uanini and Matani. "Hano?" he uttered in despair, plunging forward as if some invisible support had been yanked from under him.

Uanini glared at Matani. "Why would my brother sacrifice his life for you?"

"So that I could deliver his words to our high priest," Matani answered.

Hunumaniani tilted his head attentively. "Then speak them."

Matani looked into the priest's eyes—one alive, one dead—and told the words Hano had entrusted him with. "Clear skies bring evil to our shores."

A baleful wind entered the room, whipping the flames of every candle. Vahanui looked from Matani to Hunumaniani for affirmation. He got his answer when the supreme high priest sprang to his feet with a look of utter astonishment.

"Three times last night I heard screams of the 'alae, the bird of evil omens," said Hunumaniani. "Let him continue!"

"The celebration on O'ahu was a trap," Matani said. "At first, we thought Ruling Chief Po'omanu was behind the attack, but it was his own wife who betrayed him. A priestess from some faraway land."

"What is this woman's name?" Vahanui demanded.

"They call her—" Matani hesitated and swallowed nervously, as if saying the name might cause her to appear, "—Rabulakai."

"Sounds like a dialect from the deep southern islands," said Hunumaniani.

Feeling less intimidated, Matani took a step closer to make sure his words weren't misunderstood. "Whoever she is, and wherever she came from, this woman has built an army of cannibals using people disillusioned by Po'omanu's rule. And she's convinced them to serve a flesh-eating god that vows to conquer all of Havai'i."

Vahanui sat stunned by these words. "Cannibals?"

Matani nodded grimly. "With poison-tipped spears."

"Did this priestess kill my brother?" Uanini demanded.

"No, but she murdered Tari'i," Matani said, his eyes welling with tears. "And many others. It took an unfair match of six men to defeat Hano. The final blow was given by her second-in-command, a cannibal with angry eyes who chased me into the storm."

"You speak of the unnatural storm five nights ago," Hunumaniani interjected. It was a statement, not a question.

Matani nodded somberly.

Vahanui, however, didn't seem entirely convinced. "How could you survive such a terrible winter storm at sea? Much less travel all the way from O'ahu to Taua'i in it?"

"My ancestors helped me," Matani answered, realizing only then how far-fetched it all sounded. But Hunumaniani nodded without judgment.

The numb silence that followed was finally broken by someone bursting through the entryway curtain.

"I saw them," Manunu wheezed, out of breath. "Thousands of canoes."

"How long before they arrive?" asked Ruling Chief Vahanui.

"The winter sea has separated them into groups, but the first wave will make landfall before the day comes full. Hua's already lit the first signal fire."

Vahanui jumped up and raced out to the courtyard where many privileged retainers and officers of the court were already gathered, having heard of the strange entrance of a commoner into the royal compound.

"There!" Uanini pointed.

In the distance, far up the coast, a tendril of smoke wriggled into the air against a dawning sky in which not a single cloud could be seen.

Uanini turned to his father with a comfortless look on his face. "At the ninth fire, they'll be in our bay."

Vahanui nodded uneasily. "How many warriors on hand?"

"Three hundred," Uanini answered gravely.

Vahanui's face paled as his eyes met Matani's. "And what of the rest of my warriors who went to O'ahu? Did any survive?"

Matani could only shake his head, but his troubled expression was answer enough.

Hunumaniani approached the ruling chief. "Light signal fires on the western beaches. There may still be time for your brother on Ni'ihau to gather his warriors and bring them here," he said. "And dispatch runners to all the other districts for assistance. Hurry!"

Vahanui's eyes grew sullen, knowing full well the lingering issues between himself and his brothers. "And what if they don't all come?"

The supreme high priest returned a sober look. "They must."

Vahanui's gaze fell on Matani again. After staring at him for a long and serious moment, he turned to Hunumaniani. "Could this farmer be the *Enlightened One* of your prophecy?"

Hunumaniani deeply contemplated the provocative question. "Knowing what was at stake, by giving his life so this young man could live, Hano must have believed so."

"But a commoner?" the ruling chief asked incredulously.

"If memory serves, the farmer's eyes were not always blue," Hunumaniani replied.

"Mū?" asked the ruling chief in a hushed tone, appearing more curious than concerned.

The priest nodded slowly. "I must take him to the temple and confer with the gods."

"I'll come with you and make my own offerings to earn their favor—" Vahanui suggested.

"No," Hunumaniani said firmly. "You must make preparations to defend the island. And make certain every warrior understands that what we're all soon to face is much more than a skirmish between men. It's a war of ages, between light and shadow, that has carried on since the birth of time."

Before the ruling chief could respond, an irregular thunderclap vibrated every natural and man-made structure throughout the village. All eyes followed the foreboding sound to the eastern sky, where a second plume of smoke slithered up from the trees.

Matani was the first to recognize what the sound really was, for he'd heard it in the hidden temple back on Oʻahu.

The din of approaching death drums.

♦ CHAPTER 25 ♦

A
nimals were skittish as the smoke-filled air rang with the pounding of foreboding drums to the east. By the time full sunrise lifted above the horizon, word had spread throughout the village of the imminent assault. As was customary during times of war, groups of women, children, and the elderly gathered inside temple walls seeking refuge and protection. Relying heavily on his walking staff, Matani did his best to keep up with the surprisingly brisk pace of Supreme High Priest Hunumaniani as they passed by the warriors' compound, where preparations for battle were already under way.

Chiefs of every rank fitted themselves with gourd helmets adorned with great feather plumes, while others lathered themselves in coconut oil to make their skin slippery against an enemy's grip. Large groups of commoners had also come together, improvising their own protection for their heads with cloth turbans made from barkcloth, as they were not afforded the luxury of gourd helmets reserved for the highborn. They helped each other wrap the cloth tightly around their heads, hoping to cushion expected blows.

Younger warriors ran about the outskirts of the compound with baskets slung over their shoulders, collecting stones for slings. Among them, Matani spotted Vatua, the apprentice whose identity he'd borrowed. Wishing he could ask him where Heiana was, the two barely had time to exchange a glance before destiny pulled them in different directions. When Matani and Hunumaniani arrived at the north bank of Vairua River, two underpriests were already waiting in a canoe to take them to the private landing on the opposite side. Once there, Matani could barely believe his eyes when he saw where Hunumaniani was leading him.

Hauora, the temple of refuge.

After all the obstacles he'd faced trying to reach this venerable location just days prior, here it stood before him amidst a grove of swaying palm trees.

And I'm being escorted straight to its gates by none other than the supreme high priest himself. Never, in a thousand lifetimes, would I have imagined this moment.

"Yet, here it is," came the priest's voice ahead of him.

Matani's face flushed with unease until the great priest looked back, winking his milky eye at him. At the end of a long, wooded path, they arrived at the temple where a crown of wooden idols stared down on them from high stone walls. The supreme high priest stopped at a narrow entrance flanked by two temple guards, who bowed respectfully.

"Unfurl the white flags," Hunumaniani ordered, glancing up at the eastern sky. "The enemy arrives on the ninth signal fire."

The two guards looked up at a third wisp of smoke now climbing into the air. With comprehending nods, they departed quickly to raise the customary flags of peace and protection. Matani followed Hunumaniani through a narrow entryway, arriving in the temple's interior, where he was immediately struck by the power of what was, undoubtedly, the most sacred man-made domain in all Taua'i.

The expansive grounds were paved with smooth, flat stones and, like most temples of this size, divided into three terraces. A perimeter of stone walls framed a rectangular sky above that glimmered with the morning's blue glow, highlighting the tall, wicker tabernacle wrapped in white at the opposite end.

Crossing the front terrace, Matani and the supreme high priest passed several different-sized houses, all built with sacred wood and thatched with leaves. These included the religious houses of the ruling chief, the supreme high priest, and those of his various assistants. On the other side of these houses, they were met by eight temple underpriests.

"We must prepare a ceremony," Hunumaniani expressed in a calm voice. "Decorate the temple gods with fresh flowers. And bring three black chickens from the stables at once so I may seek the auguries of battle."

The underpriests nodded obediently and rushed off as Matani followed Hunumaniani to the central court, where he passed several more important houses. These included the *Mana House, House of Living Waters, Vaiea*

House, the *Hale o Papa*—set apart for female deities—and the *Long House*, where the sacred fire of the temple burned.

Moving past the *Drum House*, the priest stopped before a scaffolding of poles topped with a wooden platform. He bowed his head in deference to the primary god of the temple, Ro'o, sole presider of Matari'i-hiti season. As Matani gave his own prayer to the resident godhead, the tattered leaf cape that had clung to him throughout his perilous journey suddenly fell from his shoulders, as if it had fulfilled its purpose. Hunumaniani waited patiently as he picked up the weathered and worn pieces.

"You did well," Matani whispered, then reverently draped the faithful cape over the altar beside them, a fitting tribute to its unfailing support.

The high priest nodded approvingly at the show of gratitude, recognizing the rain cape's significance. "May the spirit of this cape continue to enfold you in its warmth and protect you from the dangers that lie ahead," he said, his eyes fixed on Matani's.

Dogs were muzzled and chickens were placed by temple staff inside lidded calabashes to prevent any unwanted sounds from breaking the spell of the forthcoming ritual. The long drum sounded with three measured strokes, calling forth six officiating priests, who solemnly approached the altar, each carrying a wooden knife. Several more priests came behind them—some bearing torches, others wrangling the requested three fowl offerings. The supreme high priest gave quick supplications to the other three blindfolded Havaiian gods, Tane, Tū, and Ta'aroa, accompanied by intonations from the assisting priests surrounding him. Placed upon a sacrificial table, the fowl were decapitated. Hunumaniani waited patiently until the mortal functions of the headless animals ceased, then carefully cut each one open to examine their hearts, livers, and entrails.

In low tones, the underpriests began the legendary chant of the ruling chiefs of Taua'i, calling upon the bloodlines of Teave'ītetahiari'iotamotu, Ha'aheoitamarama, Pāva'a , and finally, Vahanui-o-Tahiti. As they recited these exalted names of past generations, their voices remained steady but intense. Finally, the bleeding carcasses of the three chickens were placed upon the altar.

"Ro'o, accept this offering," Hunumaniani appealed. "We request your assistance."

A young priest carefully handed the supreme high priest a wreath of sacred ti leaves, which he placed reverently around the neck of the idol. Two older assistants placed a crown of brightly colored feathers on the figure's head. After a long silence, either by chance or divinity, a beam of light peeked over the temple walls and shone a halo of light around Matani. The other priests stared upon the commoner with utter fright, but Hunumaniani read this timely answer with a knowing smile.

"Follow me," he said, leading Matani to the northwest corner of the temple. "It's almost time."

Through a square doorway built into the stone wall, they entered a domed ceremonial antechamber built by the finest of stoneworkers honest to their craft. Matani had never seen such a room and was fascinated by the irregular pattern of eight small apertures constructed into the walls and ceiling. Even more curious was a single circular opening at the top of the dome, which cast a dusty beam of sunlight down onto a large, shrouded object positioned at the center of the circular stone floor.

"Your recent inner work serves the requirements of redemption for all past offenses," said Hunumaniani, "but there is one final task that must be completed before you can leave this temple under full protection of the gods."

"I will do anything required of me," Matani said, trusting the opinion of the supreme high priest.

"Good," said Hunumaniani. "I want you to make your confessions."

Matani accepted the assignment with a nod. "For how long?"

"Until there is forgiveness."

"From the gods?"

With a subtle but dramatic flair, Hunumaniani pulled the shroud off the object at the center of the room, revealing a large fragment of black volcanic glass. "From yourself."

Matani gasped at the stunning clarity of his own reflection in the perfectly mirrored surface of obsidian. It was as if he were standing before another human being who looked exactly like him. "What is it?"

"The *Aka Stone*," said Hunumaniani, gesturing to the mysterious object. "Forged in the volcanic fires of *Pere*."

Also known as *Perehonuamea*, meaning *she who shapes the sacred land*, this particular deity was a powerful elemental force that embodied the lava and natural forces associated with volcanic eruptions. According to oral history, she was born in the distant land of Tahiti but voyaged to the Havaiian Islands in search of a new home. Both destructive and creative in nature, she could take many forms, such as glowing lava lakes, earth-shaking fountains, and fiery streams of lava flowing down active volcanoes.

"Where did you find this?" Matani asked, unable to look away from the wondrous thing.

"Many years ago, when construction began on our temple, I had a vision. A monolith of glass lying at the bottom of a dormant cauldron on Maui. I sent three priests to the island, where they found exactly what I saw, in the exact place I described."

One by one, rays of sunlight burst through the eight mysterious portholes of the chamber, interacting with the volcanic glass. A vibrant web of lights sparkled at the heart of its mineral magnificence, projecting onto the hemispherical stone walls that surrounded them.

"This light looks familiar," Matani said, recalling a similar pattern of lights he'd seen refracted through the water onto the backs of whales during his ocean journey. He'd observed the same weblike pattern in shadows cast onto the earth by sunlight shining through swaying leaves during his mountain journey. And, of course, every time he traveled back and forth between the realms of body and spirit.

"This undulating labyrinth of light represents connectivity and can be seen and felt in all things," said Hunumaniani. "For at the fathomless heart of the Aka Stone is the *Aka Field* itself. A cosmetic tapestry, woven with threads of pure energy, stretching across the fabric of time and space, binding all of existence together in a web of infinite connection."

Matani nodded with clarity. "This gives even more meaning to many things I've experienced the last several days."

Hunumaniani's lips twitched with a smile. "With practice, one can use the Aka to completely separate from all concepts of Self."

"Why would I want to do that?" Matani asked, surprised.

As the priest walked in a slow, deliberate circle around the glowing monolith, his crisp shadow moved across the shimmering lights projected onto the stone walls behind him. "To dissolve the illusion of separation and experience a sacred oneness with The One Who Creates All Things," Hunumaniani whispered, his eyes glistening with secrets of the universe.

"Is it alive?" Matani whispered, amazed, but when he looked away from the stone, Hunumaniani was no longer in the chamber with him. Having learned to accept such things without question, Matani turned his full attention back to the Aka Stone, imbibing its cosmic radiance. He sat on the chamber floor, carefully laying his walking staff on the damp stone beside him. Experiencing no pain in his leg, he wondered if it was being muted somehow by the divine energy permeating the room. Believing this to be so, Matani took several deep, sharp exhalations and stared into the black volcanic glass. Almost immediately, he felt his consciousness merging with the stone.

To The One Who Creates All Things,
These are my offenses:
Thinking that only what I need matters.
Making too many assumptions.
Worrying too much about what other people think.
Failing to set boundaries between myself and those I have issues with.
Failing to explore the world around me.
Not taking time to plan where I'm going or who I want to be.
Letting my emotions control me.
Letting my past negatively impact my future.
Never creating space between feeling and reacting.
Never asking for help when I need it most.
Not taking potential relationships more seriously.
Not socializing enough or taking time to develop friendships.
Not knowing that judgment is at the heart of hate.
Life is not meant to be endured. It should be lived with limitless joy.
Starting now, I vow to practice discrimination
and to be more compassionate with others as well as myself.
I forgive myself for not knowing any different.
But now that I do, may past mistakes become knowledge for my future.
My confession is finished; it is free to fly away.

Matani opened his eyes.

No longer in the ceremonial chamber, he was floating freely among the Aka Field, though not, he realized, in spirit form. Incredibly, Matani was very present in his physical body. All his senses—overwhelmed in ways that seemed beyond mortal comprehension—were submerged in the elusive substance that held the physical reality of the very universe itself together, connected through all aspects of time and existence.

It was both a terrifying and exhilarating experience.

Then Matani heard, felt, sensed—a forgotten voice transmitted from the very heart of the universe, which he only now recognized as the same voice that had come to him in the moments before each of his mortal consciousnesses was born. It was this higher source to whom all prayed through the many different names informed by their culture.

The One Who Creates All Things.

What truth do you seek in this moment?

Am I a good person?

With each physical experience comes the opportunity to learn and grow. Only when your body returns its breath of life to the universe will you know this answer.

Then each night before I sleep, I'll do an inventory of my Bowl of Light and remove any stones my actions and choices may have placed in it that day, giving me a fresh start to do better when I wake.

Matani blinked, suddenly back inside the stone walls of the chamber, seated as before in front of the undulating lights of the mystical Aka Stone. The sunlight had moved slightly off the portals, causing the internal glow of the talisman to slowly fade, swallowing the dancing lights that had reflected so beautifully on the chamber walls.

Staring at the pristine surface of the dormant volcanic glass, Matani found himself once again face to face with the most detailed image of himself he'd ever seen.

A profound sense of relief washed over Matani. "There you are," he breathed in sacred affirmation.

Gone was the haunting specter of the Dark Matani that had once shackled him to the shadows of negativity. Instead, he beheld the image of a soul reborn—a reflection radiant with hope imbued with the wonder of newfound possibilities.

Tears welled in his eyes in a moment of pure, unbridled catharsis—an emotional release that cleansed the remnants of sorrow from his heart.

In that moment, Matani smiled with deep gratitude at the resilience of the human spirit. A smile that illuminated the path ahead, a path of purpose and boundless potential of a life transformed.

And his reflection smiled back.

As his profound experience with the Aka Stone came to an end, Matani slowly became aware of pounding death drums again, now much louder and nearer, beating like the malignant heart of some unholy thing. Smoke from multiple signal fires filled the air inside the chamber with a sinister haze. He walked over to the doorway and looked up through the open ceiling of the temple to find an eighth pillar of smoke rising up into the late-morning sky.

"One more to go," Matani whispered, swallowing nervously.

Prayers of blessings and protection from terrified refugees echoed throughout the grounds as both its entrances were barricaded by temple staff to protect against attacking forces.

"I fear we must prepare for many burials." It was the hushed voice of an underpriest down the hall.

Matani approached two of the portholes built into the chamber facing west and pressed his eyes to one that offered an unobstructed view across the bay, seeing several low-level priests arriving on the beach carrying a wooden palanquin on their shoulders. It prominently displayed Tū, the newly feathered war god, meant to inspire confidence and courage in all those preparing to fight. Behind the idol was Ruling Chief Vahanui, this time wearing a red-and-yellow feather helmet and matching shoulder cape designed to be less cumbersome in battle than his long cape. Three hundred warriors marched faithfully behind him, chiefs and commoners, all appareled and armed for battle.

Much to everyone's surprise, a fleet of canoes came ashore at the north end of the beach, led by Opoa, the ruling chief's youngest brother from Ni'ihau, who had brought, at best count, another two hundred warriors to the cause.

But there was still no sign of Vahanui's brothers Utumehame and Manu, or anyone from their political and personal divisions.

"Not nearly enough," Matani said, comparing their numbers to what he'd seen of the incoming attackers.

A warning blow from a distant conch sounded through the village. The urgent barking of dogs cut through the cold morning air as murmurs shuddered throughout the temple. Without having to see for himself, Matani already knew what had prompted the frenzied sounds.

The ninth and final signal fire had been lit.

A foul wind carried the echo of death drums throughout all Vairu-anuiho'āno, so loud now even the sturdy stone walls of the temple seemed to shake with fear. The entire regiment of Tauaian warriors watched in stunned silence as hundreds upon hundreds of canoes rounded the southern coastline, each carrying twelve or more cannibals. Even having thwarted the element of surprise, the daunting reality of being so dramatically outnumbered was not lost on those who stood steadfast and ready to defend their home.

Watching the brave warriors spread out across the beach, Matani saw many of their mouths moving rapidly in prayer, more than likely calling upon the protection of family guardians. Matani prayed silently for them, too, recalling the crippling fear he'd experienced through his father's eyes each time he had been forced to enter battle, knowing death could come at any moment.

As the first enemy canoes scraped ashore, the maddening echo of drums ceased, causing the mundane sounds of choppy morning waves to become more menacing somehow. Ahead of the dark army, Matani spotted two cannibals carrying a statue of Mafuteo. Just as they had on O'ahu, the cannibals wore a fearsome uniform—coated in ashen-gray mud and adorned with formidable gourd battle helmets. In their hands, they wielded spears that Matani could only assume were tipped with deadly poison.

Faithful beyond fear, the Tauaian warriors held their ground before the legion of approaching cannibals, attempting to intimidate these uninvited guests by making horrendous faces. Not to be outdone, the cannibals returned contorted grins that displayed mouthfuls of savage fangs, wantonly shaking their bloodthirsty weapons.

"Ready your slings!" Ruling Chief Vahanui shouted with such bravado, Matani heard him clearly across the bay. "Let's give our guests a warrior's welcome!"

And by his command, the battle opened.

With the roar of Tauaian warriors, anxiousness ended, and no longer did anyone have to imagine the destruction that would follow—for the moment was finally upon them. The din of arms rose on high with the wrath of men and the baying of conch shells. Land forces met ocean forces, waxing furiously on the crescent-shaped shoreline of Vairuanuihoʻāno Beach. The two armies merged with wild battle shouts, unleashing spears, shark-tooth clubs, stone hammers, trip cords, and swordfish daggers. Slingers propelled sharp and heavy volcanic rocks with deadly accuracy, as armed warriors hurled themselves against the oncoming regiment of cannibals.

Great was the clash of their meeting.

The first to die was a young Tauaian warrior, felled by a cannibal's lethal club to the head. His body slumped to the ground, lifeless. The one who'd dealt the death blow cried out for all his comrades to hear, "Mafuteo, a gift of our enemy's blood for you! Grant us victory!"

Matani watched from behind the temple walls in an agony of suspense, horrified as countless warriors stumbled across the sand, convulsing and bleeding from their mouths, quickly informing others of the poisons mounted on the tips of their enemy's spears. Cannibals thrashed in the water, daggers and spears protruding from puncture wounds in their bodies. It wasn't long before the entire bay turned red with blood.

Dusty rays of sunlight flashed off clattering spears and striking clubs all across the beach as Ruling Chief Vahanui gave short but effective orders to keep as many of his warriors alive as possible, only to find himself separated from them. Easily spotting the vulnerable ruling chief of Tauaʻi in his brilliant feather garb, several cannibals took aim and flung their spears at him. But Vahanui proved strong and fleet of foot, dodging and deflecting every projectile with near effortlessness. Many of his warriors weren't so fortunate, however, falling poisoned or injured into the surf.

"Mafuteo leads us," the cannibals shouted repeatedly.

"Your false god is not welcome here!" Vahanui answered them.

A long dagger made of bone was hurled through the chaos to silence the ruling chief—only to pierce the shoulder of a selfless warrior, who threw himself in front of his royal master.

No one was more surprised than Matani to discover that brave soldier to be none other than Uanini.

Vahanui only had time to glance down at his wounded son before both were surrounded by a horde of cannibals. Taking several blows from their war clubs, the ruling chief managed to push his enemies back, but they clung to him with inhuman persistence. As capable of an opponent as he was, Vahanui began to stagger under the cannibals' repeated attacks as they tightened their advancing circle, finally knocking him to the ground alongside Uanini. The terrible sight triggered Matani's memory of Hano's last, awful moments.

Somebody do something!

Out of nowhere, a strapping cannibal taller than any human Matani had ever seen before emerged from the surrounding carnage to deliver the final death blows to the Tauaian ruler and his son. But he stopped with surprise when three cannibals deliberately stood in his way.

Matani recognized one of their weapons all too well, for he had stubbed his toe on it many times. It was Imo's *Leg from Heaven*.

"Those aren't cannibals," he gasped.

Indeed, they were Timoa (his right arm in a sling), Pui, and Imo, all disguised in gray mud. Not only had they somehow survived the catastrophic events on O'ahu, they'd also managed to infiltrate the attacking fleet of canoes.

It didn't fully register with the hulking cannibal just who he was dealing with until the three Shark Warriors sank to their haunches, grimacing and growling. Calling upon the ancient methods of hand-to-hand combat, Timoa, Pui, and Imo began to pull invisible energy from the ground, sea, and sky, consuming these exceptional forces of the earth to bolster their strength.

"Recognize us yet, you stinking maggots?" Timoa shouted. "We are sharks among fish!"

Many of the cannibals hung back, rightfully unnerved. Even the brutish cannibal stopped cautiously a moment, despite a salivating grin on his face. Imo hefted his great tree branch and leaned forward, issuing a battle cry so fierce, several cannibals simply turned and fled. A few offered lame resistance, but eventually also thought it best to run, leaving only three behind who appeared eager to fight.

The first cannibal to tempt fate came at Imo with a spear. The bulky warrior easily dodged its poisoned tip and brought his great club down in a blur—first against the attacker's left knee, then the right, shattering them both. The doomed cannibal fell to the sand, screaming.

Cannibal number two charged at Pui with a short wooden sword. After a hasty discussion with his twin-bladed dagger, the crazy-eyed warrior knocked away the armed hand of his assailant and cleanly sliced his neck in two places.

Both Pui and Imo turned to see the brutish cannibal advancing on Timoa. As far as Matani could see, they seemed to purposefully stand back and cheer Timoa on from afar rather than rush over to assist him, despite his obvious handicap.

Timoa found himself staring up at the tight expression of the brute. The two shared a competitive smirk before Timoa threw the first punch into his opponent's gut. Barely flinching, the giant's smirk only widened. Timoa threw a resigned smile at Imo and Pui as the unfazed giant threw both his arms around the warrior and lifted him clear off the ground in a merciless squeeze. Despite the pressure crushing against his injured arm, Timoa showed no physical reaction whatsoever as he wriggled out his good arm and elbowed the cannibal's face with a painful-sounding crack, freeing himself.

Hitting the ground, Timoa grabbed the broken end of a spear at his feet and, spinning with the grace of a well-seasoned kahiko dancer, rammed its pointy end into the brute's stomach and out through his back. Before the giant could react, Timoa grabbed both ends of his makeshift weapon and yanked with all his might, tearing its entire length straight through the cannibal's left side in a gory spill of blood and guts.

The three Shark Warriors stood side by side and bent on their haunches in unison, proclaiming victory over their unworthy opponents.

"You are slain by the shark warriors! By the godly strength of Tū!"

Pui, Imo, and Timoa, quickly joined up with Ruling Chief Vahanui and the few remaining squads of gourd-helmeted warriors, diving back into the fray, dispatching one cannibal after another with their bloodied weapons. As they fought, several enemy skirmishers snuck past the thinning Tauaian defenses and set fire to a large canoe shed at the north end of the beach. Its enormous thatched roof quickly became a raging inferno, spreading to some trees beyond the beach. More cannibals came at the valiant warriors from all sides, pushing them back into the flames.

The scent of decay had already begun to rise from the corpses along the shoreline, easily overpowering the pleasant ocean smells. The rapid, hot breaths of the fighting warriors mixed with the cool winter air, creating an eerie mist over the beach—a sobering manifestation of collective fear, tunnel vision, and the pounding of hearts. Body after body fell to the sand, thrashing in pain, crying out for help from their mothers and loved ones, others making no sound at all.

Around this time, the faithful wives of the warriors rushed onto the battlefield, some bringing food and water, others beckoned by moans and cries of the wounded. A remaining few found themselves disabled by their own weeping over the awful discovery that their loved ones were beyond help. As the tide of battle turned in favor of the enemy, many of the women shifted from caregivers to warriors themselves, entering bravely into battle to receive blows alongside their husbands, friends, and relatives in a terrible landscape of destruction and death.

Flames erupted on rooftops of several more structures behind the beach. This time, it was the warriors' compound. Six arsonists covered in gray mud burst from the tree line carrying palm-rib torches, even as a group of women with weapons in hand raced to meet the intruders.

Matani's gut heaved when he recognized one among them.

Heiana, no!

Up to this point, he'd been experiencing the battle from across the bay with an odd sense of detachment. Only now did Matani understand why he hadn't yet mustered the courage to join the fight. Simply put, after experiencing battle firsthand through his father's eyes, he didn't want to die. After all, having finally shed his misguided, flippant attitude toward his very existence, why would he consider throwing away something he'd only recently realized was so precious and irreplaceable?

But seeing Heiana defending herself against a cannibal raking at her with his savage dagger, Matani understood that the time had now come to risk his own precious life.

To save the girl he loved.

He raced from the chamber, past the guards, and out of the temple as fast as his injured leg could carry him. The distance wasn't that far to the battlegrounds—about the length of a hundred and fifty men laid head to toe—but the rough winter surf was chewing away at the shoreline, further hindering his ability to run. Nearly halfway there, water crashing under his feet, Matani was surrounded by the hostile sounds of carnage that had become Vairuanuiho'āno Beach.

Limping along the water's edge, he could only watch from afar as Heiana dodged and struck at her attacker, her feet moving gracefully as any well-trained hula dancer. As she sidestepped every stabbing attempt, it reminded Matani of the friendly sparring matches they used to have. But it was clear from the panic in Heiana's eyes that she was well aware of the deadly reality she faced—engaged in a real fight with a real enemy who was really trying to kill her.

Images moved through his mind in slow motion of the girl who had always been there to save him, but who was now too far away for him to do the same.

"Leave her alone," Matani said heavily, barely aware of the energy sparking from his fingertips.

✦ CHAPTER 26 ✦

Racing through the surf onto a beach scattered with orphaned weapons, Matani dodged a flurry of stones whizzing through the air all around him. At the southern end of the coastline, Tauaian skirmishers drove against the legion of cannibals still mounting in strength. Matani lost sight of Heiana for a few suspenseful moments in the sea of clashing bodies.

"Hurry," he grunted, willing his injured leg to give just a little more.

Finding Heiana through the blur of fighting masses, she dodged a wild swing before plunging her sword into her opponent's chest, sending him stumbling. As the impaled cannibal fell back onto the sand, he managed one last, desperate fling of his blade.

It struck Heiana in the side, sending her spinning to the ground.

Matani roared with outrage as he raced past the chaos of the living, dying, and wounded, feeling a sudden flare of agony across his back. A rock had struck just left of his spine and sent him reeling. He fell beside a dead cannibal—who he quickly realized was merely pretending to be dead. The two locked eyes, but what Matani saw startled him. The cannibal was trembling with fear. Instead of alerting nearby warriors, Matani grabbed the enemy's helmet and put it on his own head before scrambling off.

Finally arriving at Heiana's side, he dropped to his knees where she lay. Her eyes were closed, and she had a glistening red wound above her waist.

It was not the reunion he'd imagined.

"Heiana," he begged, gently lifting her unmoving body into his arms.

She opened her eyes, dazed but clear, then flinched away in horror, struggling to free herself. Realizing his face was obscured by an enemy helmet, Matani quickly removed it.

"Matani?" she cried, hugging him tightly.

"I'm here," he said, hugging her back even tighter.

She leaned back, studying him in utter disbelief. "What happened to you?"

"Wild boar," Matani replied, assuming she meant his leg wound.

"No, I mean you look—" she began, more overtly studying his muscular features chiseled by days of extreme diet and physical activity. "Cute!"

Matani smiled and the two found themselves sharing a still, sweet moment amid the horror until her brow wrinkled with confusion.

As Heina looked up at Matani, her expression lit with surprise. "Your eyes—" she began, her voice trailing off as she took in the startling transformation. His familiar brown eyes that she'd known since childhood were now, to her amazement, a strange and brilliant blue.

But before she could say anything more, a sharp pain shot through her body, melting her expression of surprise into fear. "Am I dying?"

Placing his hand on Heiana's wound to staunch the flow of blood, Matani's vision plunged into the biological complexities of her body, seeing past tissue, veins, and muscle, and sensing with great relief that her injury wasn't fatal.

"You'll be fine," he reassured her, not having time to fully comprehend what he'd just done. "But we need to get you off this battlefield."

Helping Heiana to her feet, Matani sensed a dangerous energy behind him and turned. A long moan of despair filled his throat when he saw Angry Eyes staring back from afar, his upper lip painfully bruised and swollen from its encounter with Pui's fishhook. The cannibal bared his fangs in twisted glee as he sprinted across the beach, approaching Matani and Heiana like a venomous cloud.

"I know it hurts, but you have to get up," Matani pleaded.

Finally managing to lift her, Matani and Heiana barely made it a few steps before toppling back down onto the sand. A heavy shadow fell over them as they looked up, seeing Angry Eyes lifting a shark-tooth sword above his head. As he brought it down, a long spear came out of nowhere and blocked it.

"Vatua!" Heiana shouted.

Angry Eyes swept his sword, forcing Vatua into a backward stumble. The cannibal's wooden blade descended for another attempt, but Vatua swung his spear in wild desperation as he fell to the sand, its tip slicing

Angry Eyes' left cheek. The cannibal reeled, stunned at first, but then burned with quiet fury.

"You're dead," came his chilling promise, bringing his sword over Vatua with an arrogant sneer.

In excruciating pain, Heiana barely had the strength to scream at Angry Eyes, throwing anything at him she could get her hands on—sticks, rocks, sand. Matani watched it all in a kind of daze, his heart pounding furiously.

You don't have to lose anyone else. You now have access to great mana.

Evil mana, you mean.

Who cares? Mana is mana.

And what would you have me do with it?

Destroy anyone that stands in your way.

The thoughts were unwelcome, but Matani found he couldn't ignore them so easily.

Why do I have to destroy them?

Because the wickedness in people knows no rest.

Vatua growled in defiance as Angry Eyes brought down his sword. Trembling with the traumatic memories of how this same cannibal had murdered Hano, Matani was so mad he couldn't breathe. Unable to control his rage any longer, he clenched his teeth and flung out his hands. Lightning crackled overhead, stabbing through the clouds. Angry Eyes reeled back with confusion and alarm.

"For what you did to Hano," Matani said coldly, feeling an alluring abyss of strength surging through his body.

The memory of his friend, murdered the way he had been, instantly hardened Matani's horrified mind and heart. Knowing that using mana for malevolent purposes was dangerous, and had serious consequences for both the user and their victim, he channeled this arcane power into his fingertips anyway. Summoning a massive bolt of energy so fiendishly cursed, its concussive force sent Angry Eyes spinning helplessly through the air. The cannibal's muscles contracted so severely, every bone in his body made several sickening cracks before he even hit the ground.

Confusion reigned supreme as conflicting thoughts invaded Matani's mind. Before, he'd taken his first lives when Kapawa and his men attacked Krum, but that turned out to be a false experience in a deceptive world created by The One That Destroys All Things.

Now, in the harsh realities of the physical plane, he'd actually taken the life of another human being using the dark art of sorcery.

Fearing that the weight of this damning, irreversible action had driven him backward into the coldhearted embrace of evil, Matani walked over and stared down upon the smoking, writhing corpse of Angry Eyes.

"I see now why people kill," he said blamefully. "The only way evil can be defeated—is by becoming evil, too."

Heiana and Vatua looked up from the gobs of seared flesh bubbling in the sand to see Matani holding out his electrified hands.

They were shaking, but not with fear.

With power.

Unafraid, Matani threw his mighty hands against the sky.

And the sky moved.

With impossible swiftness, the rising sun was extinguished under a mass of dark clouds. Thunderheads bruised the light-blue heavens with gray and purple. A heavy wind whipped across the beach and through the trees. The ocean reflected the fury of the weather—of Matani: a collision of wind and waves churning spume from the breakwaters. All of this culminated in a booming thunderclap that broke the clouds open, drenching the landscape in hellish rainfall.

Heiana looked between Matani and the storm, her terrified eyes filled with dismay. "Are you doing all this?" she shouted above the howl of gale-force winds.

Matani heard her, but he was far too lost in the grave pandemonium playing out both inside and all around him. Staring down at the unrecognizable remains of Angry Eyes, the nameless person whose life his unbridled emotions had just taken, he ran to the ocean in tears.

When Matani turned and looked back, everything around him had become a wild blur, but at its center—like looking through the eye of a hurricane—the battle before him suddenly looked different.

He was no longer standing amid one battle taking place on the beach, but several all at once.

Isolated by noise and billowing smoke, Matani trembled. The battle-consumed worlds he was somehow seeing into were vast and endless. In one direction, the clothing was the same, but the faces were different. In others, foreign marauders with oddly shaped facial features were dressed in outlandish garments and three-pointed helmets. They had strange skins on their feet and shouted in unfamiliar languages, and they carried long sticks that barked like thunder and coughed smoke, their deviant sorcery exploding gory patches of blood from fragile human bodies.

Matani realized that in this horrifying glimpse across time, it wasn't only his ancestors who were being killed but also his descendants. He understood from this potent vision that countless foreigners would come to the islands, destroying the land and the people, ending ancestral lineages with murder and disease. Each new wave of invaders would bring a surge of ego and a pathological fixation on material wealth, with no regard for the customs and beliefs of the native people. Their sense of superiority and entitlement would threaten to erase an ancient culture with destructive ideas, and their unwillingness to understand the ways of the native people would fuel the divide between them. Their actions would be driven by deep-seated biases and fears, blinding them to the beauty and richness of a culture they refused to understand, leading to a bleak future for all.

In the same way that Paʻao, driven by arrogance and fears, imposed a severe spiritual order, darkening the once peaceful existence with human sacrifices and tabu laws that instilled fear and division among the people.

Out to sea, Matani saw the wavering image of a strange canoe that was as large as a mountain. It had thick, hollow black branches sticking out of holes in its side, belching thunder as it launched small boulders across a great distance, exploding trees, thatch houses, and entire fleets of canoes to splinters.

Caught in a nightmare of multiple battles that spanned generations of the past, present, and future, Matani spiraled further and further downward into the desperate, collective ignorance of humanity before him. There was no telling how many confrontations he was witnessing, but they all ended exactly the same: with meaningless loss of life. Staring into these other, mind-bending dimensions, Matani felt overwhelmed by how many times great-grandsons, grandsons, sons, fathers, grandfathers, and great-grandfathers had fought, were fighting, and would one day fight, so many more senseless battles, only to end up injured or dead on the sands of this very beach.

Sacrificing our lives for any battle is a waste of human potential. A senseless and tragic waste of human life.

Wanting it all to stop, Matani screamed with ungoverned rage. Using the dark sorcery boiling in his clawed hands, he brought rivers of mud crashing down hills lining the beach, ripping palm trees from the sand by their roots. But when he realized his actions were somehow impacting the battles taking place in all aspects of time, he quickly curled his fingers into fists to suppress his abilities, holding them tightly against his chest.

All at once, the multiple worlds he was somehow accessing disappeared, leaving Matani standing amid the present battle taking place between the Tauaians and cannibals. Quicker weapons flashed red with blood while slower ones fell to the ground beside their dying owners. The air was serrated by the anguished cries of cannibals and warriors with daggers sticking out of them, slowly draining of life. All across the beach, scores of men and women lay motionless, their shattered, burning bodies sprawled across the sand like some morbidly careless graveyard.

Is there no end to this cycle of killing?

As you've just witnessed, humans never learn. Generation after generation, they repeatedly succumb to the shadows of ego, power, and control.

Recognizing the pessimistic voice, a warning prickle raised the hairs on the back of Matani's neck. He slowly turned to find a shadowy object on the sand beside him.

The One That Destroys All Things had returned.

This newly born version was barely a pulsing fetus of negativity squirming in the sand at his feet, attached to his lower spine by a long umbilical cord of dripping humors.

Having summoned the return of his psychic parasite once more, just as it had foretold, Matani knew he had only himself to blame. But all he wanted now was for the death and killing to stop. Cringing at the macabre sight of fallen bodies still clinging to the crude weapons that had ultimately failed them, never had Matani felt such pity for the human race. These people—every single one of them—had unwittingly become the shadows that secretly controlled their lives, preventing peace and happiness at every opportunity.

People constantly fight, murder, and die. And why? For the wants of one ruling chief's ego or another? If those who claim to have so much power can't put an end to this battle, then who will?

Matani replied with a single, deliberate nod, then pointed his index finger down and began slowly spinning it in circles. Against the horizon, three black waterspouts joined the sea and sky, moving swiftly toward the beach. Great funnels of sand filled the air and sucked up any cannibal or warrior in their paths, flinging them into the sea, slamming them against rocks, and catapulting them into burning trees.

Only then did both sides of this pointless confrontation break free from their fixation on killing each other in a desperate clambering for shelter.

Young man, be careful not to lose yourself in false realities created by untruthful thoughts.

Matani followed this new and sobering voice to a familiar creature that stood out among the bloodstained beach. There, perched on a flat hunk of lava embedded in the sand, was a striped brown lizard with a sky-blue tail.

But this time, instead of hurt or frustration, the mere sight of his guardian spirit brought sanity to Matani's mind.

The One That Destroys All Things thrives on human conflict.

For the first time, Matani realized that the large hunk of lava he stood on was in the shape of a tear. Tumatua's Tear—the infamous spot where his father had died during the Battle of Beating Heart all those years ago. And with this realization came a stark, unspoken warning.

What are you waiting for, Matani? You're in control now. The time has come to avenge your father!

Yes, you're ri—

"Son," came a muted voice.

Startled by the presence of a familiar energy, Matani looked over at the ethereal wisps of an apparition forming beside him. Two intense eyes developed first, which he immediately recognized as his father's.

"Don't listen to that wretched thing," Tumatua warned. "I don't need or want its poisonous obsession for hatred and violence. This family has lost far too much because of it already."

Ashamed of his own part in the tragedy of things lost, Matani found he couldn't bring himself to face his father's ghost. "But if I don't stop these people from hurting each other, who will?"

"Matani, I thought I could prevent the insane cycle of murder by killing those who killed. But during my retrospections in death, I've realized that love is what gives life within. Hate and anger give no life."

Matani's downturned eyes found the tear-shaped lava fragment under his feet. "Will this hunk of rock be my memorial as well, Father? Is that what you've come to tell me?"

"No," Tumatua said, shaking his head. "I'm here to apologize for abandoning you. For manipulating you to feel weak because that's how I felt. My selfish oppression is what triggered your disdain for royalty. I unconsciously passed my pain and anger to you when I should have been passing on healing and love."

Hearing these words, Matani looked up at his father. "After seeing life through your eyes, I understand why you did those things."

"And I appreciate that, but a son understanding his father's flaws doesn't absolve them. May you one day be able to forgive me, my son."

"I already have," Matani said softly, at long last making things right between father and son.

Tumatua smiled with humble appreciation. "During my time of wandering, I came to understand how, in life, I used words as an emotional weapon. You use weather. Both equal in their destructive potential when fueled by negative emotions."

"I've tried really hard not to use my abilities for bad," Matani said, surveying his own contributions to the devastation of war that surrounded them. "But the convincing arguments of my darker thoughts have made it difficult."

"Struggling against your own negativity has consumed you, my son," Tumatua said, placing a comforting hand of spirit gently upon his son's troubled chest of flesh. "But you have yet to consider the potential for using your powers for good. Just as a farmer must tend to his crops even in challenging weather, so too must you tend to your bowl when shadows overwhelm you, for it is the guiding light through the darkest of storms."

Matani shook his head in despair, realizing he was so preoccupied with his negativity that he hadn't even considered using his powers in a positive way. "But what difference can the light in my bowl make if so many others are full of stones?"

"You have no control over anyone's bowl but your own," his father replied, a glimmer of wisdom in his eyes. "So use it to cultivate a shine that serves as a beacon for all."

And with his thought-provoking words, Tumatua faded away into the ether.

Breathing deeply, Matani felt his heart center open as he experienced a powerful moment of ancestral healing. In response, the howling, destructive forces of the storm dissolved as quickly as they had appeared, and the dark, emotional weather on his face cleared away.

Matani thought back to one of his last conversations with Hano, about how it isn't having an abundance of the finest things, the clothes someone wears, bloodlines they share, or even how dumb or smart they are that make one great.

It's good deeds and moral character.

That's what the voice in the Aka Stone was trying to tell me. Despite all the mistakes I'll inevitably make throughout my unknown number of seasons, may I reach my final moments having done more good in life than bad.

"More are coming!" a voice rang out somewhere behind him. Matani turned to see Hua gesturing wildly at the southern end of the beach. "That was only the first wave! More canoes are coming!"

Bone-weary from fighting, the last two hundred or so able-bodied warriors saw the second wave of war canoes entering the bay, full of nearly twice the number of cannibals as before. Every Tauaian warrior slumped, realizing with grim despair the hard fighting and long labor that still lay ahead of them, hope dying in their hearts.

"Rabulakai!" someone shouted. It was Pui.

Following the warrior's pointed finger to the incoming mass of canoes, Matani spotted the one-armed priestess standing on the deck of Po'omanu's royal double-hulled vessel, leading her cannibal forces ashore with an evil grin.

His entire body began to tremble.

"We've been flanked!" Timoa warned, gesturing inland.

On a grassy ridge behind the beach, treetops bristled with spears carried by swarms of an unidentified enemy. They unleashed a massive boulder from the top of the hill and sent it rolling straight over a squadron of cannibals, brutally injuring many of them.

Imo was immediately suspicious. "But why attack their own?"

Where the boulder had been on the hilltop, a dusty cloud settled, revealing a figure standing in its place. It was Manu of West Tona, Ruling Chief Vahanui's older brother. And with him, a fresh army of one thousand warriors awaiting his command.

At the other end of the beach, two more boulders came crashing down the slope, leaving a dozen more crumpled enemies in its wake. It was Utumehame of East Tona, the ruling chief's younger brother, backed by another two thousand warriors.

Realizing that both estranged siblings had answered his call for help, Ruling Chief Vahanui whirled his shark-tooth sword in the air. "Welcome home, brothers! It makes my heart glad to see you!"

Both Sun and Wind Eaters poured down onto the beach, merging into a single army, quickly moving to the fore of the battle in a crescent formation, allowing the ruling chief and his exhausted soldiers an opportunity for much-needed rest. While the arrival of additional armed forces ignited hope in the Tauaian warriors, their numbers still paled in comparison to the legion of cannibals approaching the shallows like a tidal wave.

Father was right. There must be another way people can resolve conflicts without violence.

There isn't. Trust me. I've seen it all.

I don't believe you anymore.

We'll see about that.

About to further engage his negative thoughts, a buoyant energy pulled Matani's attention across the sea to a bright and stunning rainbow sparkling above the waves. The symbol of his supportive ancestors made him smile, giving him an opportunity to relax and step back from his thoughts. Waiting patiently, he was able to discern a more positive voice offering more helpful guidance.

The voice of his 'Aumākua.

There's no such thing as a different sex, race, or species of people. The definition of 'human' in any language is simply 'person.'

Are you saying that lineage, skin color, language, and physical appearances don't matter?

I'm saying that every single human being who enters the physical world is bonded by a common parental source that transcends individual beliefs.

Matani inhaled sharply, opening his eyes.

Realizing both hands were balled into tight fists, he relaxed and let them fall open, releasing their maleficent power back to the universe. Heiana and Vatua came to meet him, their arms linked in support, both sharing the same concerned expression.

Matani turned and smiled calmly, confidently. "I know how to save us."

Heiana looked warily into his blue eyes. "No storms?"

"No storms," he promised. "Instead of weapons or words, we'll throw love at our enemies and watch them disappear."

"And how do you propose we do that?" asked Vatua, unconvinced.

"Ho'oponopono," Matani replied with a nostalgic grin. "It's time to call a family meeting."

Heiana's eyes flew wide with disbelief. "Right now? In the middle of a battle?"

Fully appreciating her familiar reaction, Matani's grin widened. "When a family meeting is called, *everyone* must come!"

"But whose family?" Vatua asked.

"Whether bonded by love or blood, we're all part of the same 'ohana," Matani explained. "Including our enemies."

Then, Matani took Heiana's hand in his left, Vatua's in his right, and pulled his shoulders back, sending out a psychic call to invoke the strength and connectedness of all families in this world—and the next.

"Mighty is 'ohana; our ancestors will protect us," he said calmly. And despite his lone voice being so easily lost in the surrounding cacophony of battle, Matani anchored his spirit in faith and said the words again.

But this time, Heiana joined him.

"Mighty is 'ohana; our ancestors will protect us."

Then Vatua.

"Mighty is 'ohana; our ancestors will protect us."

Soon, others gravitated toward them, bringing more and more people forward to hold hands with their island neighbors, extending a lengthening chain of humanity across the entire beach. Glancing to his left, then his right, Matani recognized many of the faces he'd grown up with standing alongside him. Though not by blood, they were most certainly family.

They, too, began reciting the words of his prayer, which became just a little bit louder with each new voice.

"Mighty is 'ohana; our ancestors will protect us!"

A glimmer of yellow flashed in Matani's periphery, coming from some-where behind. As he turned to look, a group of men, women, and chil-dren—all dressed in matching yellow dresses and loincloths—emerged from the smoldering, charred trees behind the beach. The moment reminded him of when he and Nahoa had seen similar flashes of color in the jungle on his journey to the mountain, realizing that they had not been hallucinations after all.

Each of them came forward, adding their voices to the weaponless line of defense. Matani noticed the red-earth imprints of lizards with blue tails on their clothing, strikingly similar to the pattern he'd seen on Tūtū Ona's robe in the Island Worlds.

The Lizard Clan of Mū.

Behind them came another tribe of unfamiliar people, dressed in orange wrappings printed with repeating images of flames. They each wore matching tattoos on their right arms and legs.

The Fire Clan of Mū, bringing their voices to support the prayer.

"Mighty is 'ohana; our ancestors will protect us!"

Then came the Turtle Clan, dressed in green, with both men and women wearing long hair made into pugs with sticks through them.

And the Shark Clan, dressed in blue, with each of the men wearing short beards and the women wearing a blue flower on the right side of their heads.

Then, clothed in bright indigo, the Starfish Clan emerged from the trees, the men distinguished by long beards and the woman by fern headbands.

Finally, the Octopus Clan, dressed in purple, joined the line. All the women had short hair, and the men's faces were plucked clean.

As each uniquely distinguished tribe of Mū came forward, it wasn't lost on Matani that the decision to reveal themselves out of respect for the ancient rules of ho'oponopono after all this time could not have been an easy one, for doing so meant putting every single one of their lives at risk.

Setting aside many generations of pain, fear, and animosity between the Mū and Tahitian descendants, every single person on the beach stood together selflessly and bravely to face those who'd come to murder them, creating a vibrant, living rainbow extending from one end of the bay to the other.

Red, orange, yellow, green, blue, indigo, and purple.

It was a rainbow, not of water and light, but of flesh and blood.

Unable to deny the powerful energy created by the growing bonds between every soul on that beach, Ruling Chief Vahanui, Uanini, Timoa, Pui, Imo, and every other warrior were inspired to drop their weapons and join hands with their neighbors. Even the Wind Eaters and Sun Eaters stood side by side to offer support—including many of Matani's aunts, uncles, and cousins from his father's side who he'd not seen for many turns of the sun.

And what had begun as a single voice suddenly became the mighty roar of thousands, sounding a prayer of protection that was powerful enough to shake the sands of Vairuanuiho'āno Beach.

"MIGHTY IS'OHANA, OUR ANCESTORS WILL PROTECT US!"

The living rainbow of people, both masculine and feminine energies entwined, stood firmly in the house of power they had manifested together. So infectious were they, that several cannibals felt inspired to lay down their own weapons and join them, including the one whose life Matani had spared. As they exchanged friendly smiles, Matani felt a glimmer of hope in the possibility of peace.

The moment Rabulakai's double-hulled canoe came ashore, she hesitated a brief but telling moment at the sight of all the stupidly unarmed people, then urged her disembarking army of cannibals to attack. Fresh with battle fury, they obeyed without question, rushing forth with flailing swords, daggers, and spears.

Still, not a single person let go of the hand on either side of them.

With malevolent cackles, the advancing horde flung spears and rocks at the human targets lined up so conveniently before them. To the cannibals' astonishment, every single weapon they hurled landed harmlessly at their opponents' feet.

Spotting soldiers from her own army standing with the enemy, Rabulakai flew into a rage and sent all her remaining cannibals to attack, only to watch each one stumble and fall into the surf, grabbing at their throats, unable to breathe.

"MIGHTY IS'OHANA; OUR ANCESTORS WILL PROTECT US!"

By now, the Tauaians' voices had become a thunderous force. Thousands of cannibals squirmed in the sand and surf, struggling to cover their ears from the potent supplication of words. Like a wave, the focused intention and united prayer hammered into them, driving through the ranks of every retreating cannibal, leaving them incapacitated by forces they couldn't even begin to comprehend.

"Rainbow People! Rainbow People!" one frightened cannibal shouted, naming those who possessed the mystifying ability to defend themselves with mere words of prayer.

Above the voices, Matani heard the frigid, perverse sound of laughter. At first, he thought it was the dark voice inside him, but he quickly realized it was coming from Rabulakai. She stood beside the broken image of her sinister god, surrounded by injured cannibals writhing in agony.

Sensing the oncoming ruin of her plans, the priestess yanked a broken spear from the ribs of a slain cannibal and locked eyes with Matani. Her lips split in a twisted grin, revealing her fangs. Then, she took aim and flung her killing tool at him with every measure of hatred in her corrupt soul.

Matani took a subtle step backward, his eyes moving from the spear to The One That Destroys All Things squirming at his feet. Feeling its existence pulsing, swelling, feeding off his fear in that moment, a black shiver ripped through his entire body. Barely a day, and he'd already allowed a new shard of darkness to infiltrate his being. Gazing at the surrounding invasion of death and chaos brought on by Rabulakai and her unholy god, he couldn't help but wonder once again if things of shadow were more powerful than things of light.

In response, arrogant laughter rang in the dim corners of his mind.

Of course I'm more powerful, you fool! Since the first moment light flickered into existence, humanity has battled its own deep desire for darkness. Only one choice remains to end this immortal struggle. Surrender yourself and come live with me in the shadows!

His heart tripping faster as the spear drew closer, Matani closed his eyes and focused on making a meaningful connection with it. Instantly feeling the spear's rage, he realized this wasn't because it thirsted for blood, but because it was a wooden creature born of nature and hated being forced to extinguish so many innocent lives against its will.

Spear, grant me the ease of catching you, and I promise you will never be used in a harmful way again.

Rabulakai's lips muttered a dark spell that carried her spear past the invisible barrier manifested by the protection chant. Whatever ritual she invoked from the shadows, its sinister power began to alter her physical appearance. Smoke burst from her eyes, her nose, her mouth. Her skin grew filthy with glowing lesions as her eyes sank deeper into her skull.

"Kuatha Rah!" she incanted, then gave a violent thrust with her arms.

The spear accelerated into a blur.

All at once, the chanting stopped, blanketing the beach in suspended silence.

Matani remained exactly where he stood and waited patiently for the spear's reply even as it screamed through the air, dead set on his heart.

"Don't just stand there!" Heiana screamed. "Matani, get out of the way!"

Then came a single word from Rabulakai's spear.

Now.

With a subtle nod, Matani calmly closed both eyes and clapped his hands together.

CHAPTER 27

Opening one eye, Matani glanced down and saw the tip of Rabulakai's spear pressed between his palms. Its deadly point had nicked his chest just enough to draw a single trickle of blood.

It was common belief that when someone caught their opponent's spear, they also captured that person's soul and could forever control it. Even Rabulakai herself gaped helplessly, like a fish drawn from the water. Refusing to accept defeat, she continued driving the last of her cannibals while fumbling to reassemble the shattered remnants of her evil god, as if it might somehow restore her malevolent abilities.

"Attack, you cowards! Or face the wrath of Mafuteo!"

But her words were powerless, and her followers no longer had the stomach to meet the mighty ancestral forces their enemy had in service. As a result, every remaining cannibal proceeded to defy her orders and retreat from the island in the stolen canoes that had brought them.

Seeing Rabulakai standing alone across the ruins—of broken helmets, of discarded weapons stained with blood, and so many bodies lying unmoving in puddles of their own blood—Matani raised his right hand with the intention of striking her down. But remembering the final words of his father's ghost, he chose to leave Rabulakai's fate to Timoa, Imo, and Pui, who were already racing across the beach to apprehend her.

Rabulakai staggered sideways like some crazed animal, one eye glaring at Matani just before an abnormal wind swirled the sand into a frenzy and erased her from view, leaving only the echoes of a sinister, disembodied laugh behind. Pui was the first to arrive at the spot where she'd been, with Timoa and Imo coming up fast behind him. All three searched with haste but found only a trail of footprints in the sand that mysteriously came to an end just a few feet away.

"She's gone," Pui said in disbelief.

"Into realms unknown, maybe," Timoa said with a wary grimace. "But not dead."

And with these unsettling words came the awful battle's end, forever known from this day forward as the *Battle of Caught Spear*.

Following the defeat of Rabulakai and her army of vicious cannibals, healers went straight to work on the wounded, and the honored dead who had not already been claimed by the sea were buried to protect them from spiritual harm on their journey to the afterlife. As the names of lost loved ones were delivered throughout the village, death chants rang dolefully through the air, singing songs in honor of all those who had bravely met their end in battle that day.

Although mentally and physically drained by the tragic, strange, and difficult day, Matani felt an underlying peace. Despite the unwelcome return of The One That Destroys All Things, it seemed fate and family had prepared him well. He was proud of himself for the precious knowledge he'd acquired on both his journeys, which had allowed him—and him alone—to determine the destiny of both the battle and its story. New, hard-earned perspectives had given him the mental strength to resist the ancient influences of The One That Destroys All Things, and the opportunity to create new choices that enabled him to lead his people to defend themselves.

Not with violence but with love.

Not with darkness but with light.

By late afternoon, conch shells sounded the all clear, calling elders and children from the temple of refuge as fresh winds blew over the village, carrying new beginnings that swept away the stench of death. But despite the victory, its cost of life compelled many pain-stricken mourners to knock out their own teeth in a customary show of grief, reminding everyone of the harsh reality that battles and wars never truly have an end.

Lines of officiating priests from all seven temples gathered at the shoreline of Vairuanuiho'āno Bay and purified themselves in the waves, invoking Ro'o through prayer to remove the stains of battle from the land and restore peace. Afterwards, earth ovens were lit and pleasant aromas drifted across the village as the Matari'i-hiti celebrations of prosperity and renewal resumed.

In an effort to encourage his people to focus on healing instead of hurting, Ruling Chief Vahanui contributed much of his own seasonal offerings of fine, rich delicacies, filling many long tables with broiled whitefish, dried bananas, baked yams, coconuts, poi, freshly picked fruits, and cooked fowl for all to enjoy. After his diet of prawns and fiddleheads, Matani hungrily devoured his fill of the diverse and delicious foods. Supreme High Priest Hunumaniani even temporarily lifted several island laws so that all members of the community could celebrate the long-prayed-for reunion of Ruling Chief Vahanui and his brothers together. And in so doing, many had already begun to feel the gathering's curative effects.

Music filled the air, as hula dancers gifted the celebration with resplendent performances. Dressed in red and yellow, they honored the noble lineage of their ruling chief on this day of glory, using hypnotic movements to memorialize the Battle of Caught Spear. Along the shore, children gathered shells and splashed in the surf, blissfully unaware of the horrors that had unfolded there earlier that day.

May they remain forever oblivious to such senseless violence.

After many shared tears and much laughter, it became widely known that Matani and Uanini had been the ones responsible for informing Ruling Chief Vahanui about the cannibals, giving the island a fighting chance. Everyone wanted to hear these details firsthand, and in Matani's account, he gave Uanini all the credit—which, of course, Uanini accepted without argument. However, Uanini's version of events mostly centered around his own heroism, as well as an overtly embellished tale of how he had intercepted the long dagger meant for his father, becoming two and even three daggers in several retellings. Despite Uanini's lack of humility, his undeniably brave act in that fateful moment had finally earned him the respect he'd sought from the other warriors for so long, and no one ever called him a lobster again.

Even the four warrior apprentices who had wanted to end Matani's life just a few days ago approached him in truce. Throughout the day, they each went out of their way to treat Matani with courtesy and respect, as was customary once a tabu breaker was officially absolved of their offenses in the temple of refuge.

But the warmest welcome by far that Matani received came from his extended family of aunts, uncles, and cousins. He had never received so many long, tight hugs and affectionate nose rubs as he did that day. He was also pleasantly surprised to learn what a diverse group of individuals his family was. As it turned out, not all were farmers; there were musicians, hunters, builders, cloth makers, stone carvers, fishermen, and several canoe builders. But the best part? Well, while he'd experienced much-needed love and support from the spirit world, there was just something incomparable to the warm, physical embrace of the living.

Among them, Uncle Numu'i'ua was the first to come forward and apologize to Matani for deserting him without explanation.

"Please don't hold any bitterness against our family," he said. "I'm ashamed to admit that my own irrational fears led us all to abandon you and your parents." He paused a moment, visibly emotional. "Matani, you taught us all just how little we know of those that inhabited these islands before us. Please believe me when I say that we're ready now to open our hearts to the bloodline you share with the Mū."

Matani hadn't realized until that moment just how much he'd needed to hear those words. "Uncle, I've come to learn that where there is love, there is forgiveness."

"Then we shall have plenty of both," Uncle Numu'i'ua proclaimed, then wrapped his arms around Matani and lifted him off the ground in a crushing hug.

After that, Matani made it a point to find and thank each and every family member who had assisted him on his journey: Auntie Mahanea, who'd taught him about rip currents and kept him from drowning; Uncle Numu'i'ua and Cousin Etene, who'd taught him how to fix dislocated bones; Cousin Tana'tanui, who'd taught him about the healing properties of the noni fruit, and Rua'au, his adopted grandfather, who'd imparted his knowledge of boars.

Without any of the useful skills they had passed on to him, Matani knew he might very well have perished out in the wilderness. And now happily reunited, he looked forward to learning even more valuable wisdom from each and every one of them.

Then Matani's thoughts of gratitude turned to those who could not be present.

Grandmother Amura, who'd shared her wisdom of plant medicine and guided his hands in bandaging his leg wound, and Grandfather Namotahaʻi, who'd taught him the importance of respecting nature, rituals of house building, and the power of family.

Also, Hano and Tariʻi, the two brave Shark Warriors who'd offered meaningful words and mentorship.

I don't know how much time passes between life and death, but I hope we'll meet again one day in the Island Worlds. Until then, I vow to live a life worthy of your sacrifices.

Then, of course, Tūtū Ona, his wise and ancient grandmother, and Nahoa, his stubborn but faithful dog.

I'll carry the wisdom you gave me, Tūtū Ona, and share it with my own children one day. Nahoa, whenever I feel daunted by any obstacle, I'll summon your name and meet it with defiance.

And, finally, he took a silent moment to honor two special people who'd brought him into this terrifying, beautiful world.

His mother and father.

While things weren't perfect, I think about you both every single day and appreciate everything you've ever done for me. I love you both more than there are stars in the sky, and I realize now how much you sacrificed for me. I miss you both deeply and will carry you in my heart, forever and always.

Yes, the celebration that day was one of profound healing and new beginnings.

At one point, Ruling Chief Vahanui took Matani aside to personally commend his bravery and fortitude in the face of all he'd endured, and Matani took the opportunity to share with him a meaningful story.

"Hano asked me if I knew what my guiding star was," Matani began. "I didn't know the answer at the time, but I realize now he was talking about my heart."

Vahanui's eyes welled with many emotions. "Blessings for this gift of words from my son, young man. I vow to hold them in my own heart with every waking day to honor his memory."

Noticing several people watching them, Matani suddenly felt very exposed with everyone knowing his true lineage. "Ruling Chief, do you think there can be peace between Havaiian and Mū?"

"After today's events, I certainly hope so," Vahanui replied. "But I've learned in my position that having ideas about such things is easy. It's executing them that's hard."

Remembering something, Matani looked away and back again. "There's no cliff so tall it can't be climbed," he said. "It's one of the last things Hano said to me."

Knowing the words all too well, Ruling Chief Vahanui both smiled and cried.

Returning to the many tables of food for yet another helping, Matani came upon none other than Pui, Imo, and Timoa gathered in a tight circle, unapologetically gorging themselves. Seeing him approach, Imo thrust Timoa aside with his rump to make room. Surprisingly, Timoa moved over without so much as a sneer. Each of the Shark Warriors asked Matani a number of questions that he patiently answered, but mostly they wanted to know how he'd made it back to Taua'i before they did. Matani summarized his journey in as much detail as he possibly could before they quickly lost interest. After everyone offered heartfelt words honoring Mau, Tari'i, and Hano, they moved on to stories of their individual experiences with each of these unique and special friends. It wasn't long before the Shark Warriors were whisked away by several women, but before Imo left, he made certain that the acclaim and gratitude wasn't getting to Matani's head by making several derogatory remarks about his penis.

A beautiful laugh rang through the air, sounding like a cross between a bird and a dog. Matani turned and saw Heiana coming toward him, helped along by a wooden crutch on one side and Vatua on the other. Realizing she was laughing at Imo's lewd comment, Matani blushed with embarrassment.

This did not go unnoticed by Pui, who yelled from afar, "Hey, is that the girl you can't stop talking about?"

"Yes, Pui," Matani answered through the corner of his mouth, now further embarrassed, then he turned, first meeting eyes with the brave apprentice warrior who'd played an important role in the story of his ocean journey. "Blessings, Vatua," he said earnestly, holding out his right arm. "I owe you more than I can say."

Vatua took Matani's arm and squeezed it. "I'd say we're even."

"Vatua?" a voice asked from behind.

Both Matani and Vatua turned to find Timoa a few steps away, standing in the frisky grasp of two hula dancers. Matani swallowed nervously as the warrior slowly approached, his eyes flickering back and forth between the striking similarities shared between a farmer and a warrior apprentice. Timoa shook his finger at Matani, giving him the subtlest of smirks, then walked off with his female companions.

"Long story," Matani said to the puzzled expressions of Heiana and Vatua.

Then he took a deep breath to emotionally prepare himself.

Okay, when Heiana and Vatua tell you they're together, just smile and act like you're happy for them.

Matani recognized this voice instantly, and it definitely didn't belong to his 'Aumākua. It was one of those annoying *thought bugs* as Hano had called them, daring to emerge even after his accomplishment of putting a positive end to the battle. Accepting that these unhelpful thoughts weren't ever going to go away, he consciously chose not to create false assumptions, simply letting them pass.

If this truly is the person her heart desires, and he treats her well and makes her happy, then that's all that matters.

"So, what's the story with you two?" Matani asked, holding his breath.

"Just friends," Vatua said, forcing a smile. "Though I have to admit, I was interested in more. But Heiana's eyes never came anywhere near to looking at me the way they did whenever she talked about you."

"Ah, well," Matani began, doing his best to be humble. "I hope I can live up to that look."

Vatua glanced over at Heiana, her gaze intent on Matani. "I'd say you're off to a good start," he said, then smiled warmly and placed his hands on both their shoulders, gently pushing them closer together. "Now, I think you two have some catching up to do."

Then, Vatua graciously stepped away, leaving Matani and Heiana facing each other with different versions of the same bashful smile.

"You didn't have to, but you took the blame for knocking over that old pig idol," Heiana said.

"Just trying to return the favor for all those times you've helped me," Matani replied.

All he could think about was how beautiful she looked, and he considered making another attempt at kissing her—only to be interrupted by a young girl who ran up to him with a flower lei made of white hibiscus. Matani regarded the timely symbolism of his mother's love and support, then placed it around Heiana's neck and used it to pull her face closer to his.

"I thought you hated flowers?" she asked, pleasantly surprised by his playfulness.

"I did," Matani said, then gathered the courage once more to lean in and kiss her, only to be interrupted yet again by a smattering of nearby laughter and whistles.

Matani glanced over to find several of Heiana's younger cousins giggling and pointing at them, the youngest of the bunch making grossed-out faces.

This time Heiana was embarrassed. "Ugh," she groaned, rolling her eyes. "Family can be so annoying sometimes."

"I know," Matani laughed. "Isn't it great?"

From that moment on, everything between them seemed easy, and Matani realized the time had come to keep the other promise he'd made to himself.

Starting with Tūtū Ona's advice.

"Heiana, there's so much I need to tell you, but I have to apologize first for being so stupid and selfish," he began cautiously. "I appreciate that you never gave up on me, and how you always gave me a chance to prove I could be a better version of myself, not the worse one that came out sometimes."

"A lot of times," Heiana added teasingly.

"Okay," Matani humbly agreed. "A lot."

Heiana looked up at him, brushing strands of hair from his new blue eyes. "Well, you always accepted me for who I was, even when I was annoying."

"Also a lot," Matani countered, trying to look serious, but eventually cracking a grin.

Heiana giggled, but then her face became serious. "I'm sorry I ran off that day you tried to kiss me."

"It's okay," he said, intending to leave it there, but finally couldn't. "Why did you?"

Searching the past in her mind, Heiana nodded thoughtfully. "I think maybe I wasn't mature enough to understand my own feelings back then, much less know if you and I were a good fit for each other."

Matani's eyes widened with agreement. "That makes a lot of sense, actually."

Then, instead of trying to kiss her a third time, Matani simply sat quietly with Heiana, taking in the joyous celebration all around them.

And that was perfectly enough.

But perhaps the most astounding experience out of the many important revelations that day was the presence of the mysterious and enigmatic Mū, who many had heard stories about but had never actually seen with their own eyes.

Countless questions were asked of them, mostly by commoners who wanted to know why they had come out of hiding to help defend descendants of the very highborns who had slaughtered and murdered their ancestors. Their responses were best summed up by how one female Mū elder eloquently put it,

"There is a long-held prophecy that describes the arrival of an *Enlightened One* who would carry many bloodlines, including that of our enemy. We've been aware of Matani's position in our heritage since before he was born, but when we received his telepathic call for help today, we knew the time had come to stop hiding."

Well aware of their contributions to the day's victory, Ruling Chief Vahanui made a special announcement, praising each and every Mū for risking their lives to help defend Taua'i, fully admitting that he'd inherited a misguided attitude toward the original stewards of these islands. After a lengthy and heartfelt apology, he officially lifted the century-old bounty on their lives.

After this stunning decree, a senior Mū leader wearing a long cape of dried banana leaves approached Vahanui with grateful tears in his eyes. Introducing himself as Ruling Elder Nana'maoa, he placed his left hand on his heart, right hand on his sacrum. Nodding, Vahanui reflected the greeting with utmost respect.

"I am grateful to be identical with you in this moment," said Nana'maoa. "But my people cannot so easily forget the tyranny of oppression waged against us for so many years."

Everyone—from commoner to chief—held their breaths, eyes wide and round, until Vahanui answered. "On behalf of all my people, I can only beg your forgiveness." Then, the ruling chief touched heads with

Nana'maoa, sharing the breath of life with him.

Facing one another, a storm of emotions passed between the eyes of the two leaders, ending with an exchange of gentle smiles, which everyone present recognized as the birth of a new era.

An era of peaceful resolution and collective empowerment.

The Mū elder smiled again, but this time his expression was somber. He looked down, exhaling years of intense feelings upon his feet, then lifted his head proudly. "We have waited generations for this land to be at peace again," he began. "After my great-grandfather passed, then my grandfather, I hoped my father would still be alive when this day came. But he has also passed away, and I was beginning to wonder if I would be dead, too. It's now time for everyone living on these islands to know the truth."

"We're listening," Vahanui said, bowing his head respectfully, allowing Nana'maoa the full courtesy of time.

The Mū chief turned to the audience, focusing on the anxious, confused, and fearful faces of the many highborns looking back at him. "During the time of Pa'ao, you took many of our chants, our teachings, and our parables. You took our women, our temples. You killed our families, forced us from our homes, and took the song from this land we love so much."

Ruling Elder Nana'maoa paused to reflect on his own words and observe the attentive reactions of his audience.

"Long before your ancestors colonized these islands, violence was a foreign concept to us. All these years watching you, we have seen that your only answer to conflict and fear is to fight. And not just your enemy; you also fight each other. Brothers fight brothers, fathers fight sons. But have you considered those who attacked this island today? Underneath those costumes of anger and mud, they're just people. People with hearts and fears, just like us. They have homes with families and animals to feed, just like we do. But they also have something heavy and painful inside them that blinds them with an unhealthy compulsion to fight. I don't know where this cannibal woman came from, but does it not make you wonder what other kinds of people exist out there beyond our horizons? If so, what might their pain, their fears, and their influences bring upon these islands?"

Matani recalled his disturbing visions of strangely garbed warriors carrying sticks that spat fire at their enemies, killing them instantly.

"If more strangers should come, we must remember what conflict has taught us," Nana'maoa continued. "Those who died today had plans to-morrow, but in the blink of an eye, everything can change. When there is war, no one wins. When there is oppression, there can be no peace. We should not divide ourselves by arbitrary titles or false identities any longer because we are all part of the same 'ohana. This means we cannot hit our neighbor without hitting ourselves, our relatives, our friends, or our enemies. We are all human and our greatest gift is free will. Let's stop wasting it making bad choices."

A long and powerful moment of silence followed the elder's unsparingly honest and heartfelt words before Ruling Chief Vahanui raised his head. "We have much to learn from your wise and ancient ways," he proclaimed with deep humility. "I must admit, I've been bound by the influences of my own uninformed history, but if you are open to the idea," he said, pausing to throw a smile and a wink at Matani, "I would welcome discussions of co-rulership between our people so that we might find a more suit-able path that respects the values of each other's customs, cultures, and presence moving forward."

Ruling Elder Nana'maoa inhaled the fine words given to him. "Mū believe that life is a tapestry, interwoven with many beautifully diverse colors and designs. What we weave is what become. Ruling Chief Vahanui, let us create a new tapestry that weaves our lives together in a meaningful way from this day forward." The Mū elder then turned to the crowd and smiled. "The true power of blood—that precious fuel within us all—is the fragile and temporary life it provides for our physical bodies. But it's the immortal light in our bowls that fuels our souls for all eternity."

Exultant cheers erupted, so great they became loud as thunder. Many leapt in the air with jubilation, while others were overcome with emotion, shedding tears of unbridled joy. It was a stark and beautiful contrast to the mournful cries of death that had haunted the air just that morning.

And while it was clear that years of oppression and murder could not be erased by a warm smile, friendly greeting, or even words, no matter how profound, Matani realized that much like an individual must take responsibility for their actions and put in the work needed to be pono—balanced in and among oneself—so it was for all humankind.

✦ CHAPTER 28 ✦

After the historic meeting between Ruling Chief Vahanui and Ruling Elder Nana'maoa, Matani discovered that the fisherman's house he'd lived in was among many destroyed by fires. But the situation wasn't so bad because it made him finally visit his childhood home. The physical version needed repairs, of course, but its foundation was just as sturdy as the house in his Spirit Home, and would have no problem providing the safety and comfort it once had. Hearing of this, family and neighbors came forward, offering to gather materials and help Matani rebuild, including several elders who'd been there to lay the original foundation all those years ago.

The next day, a little before sunrise, Matani found himself drawn back to the taro ponds he'd once so despised. Although the seventh phase of the moon was considered a bad day for planting, having developed a better understanding of just how important being a farmer was for the community, Matani tended to his current crops to ensure that the staple food his people depended on would be ready when they needed it.

"Well, looks like someone's day is off to a great start," came a familiar female voice from the forest.

"Better than most," Matani replied cheerily, then stood and turned to see Heiana, step out from behind a tree. Somehow even more beautiful than when he'd last seen her.

Limping toward him on her wooden crutch, Heiana smiled. "Your father would be proud to see you out here so willingly."

Matani quickly stood to greet her using his own crutch. It was Rabulakai's broken spear that he'd caught. By now, it had become legend, as well as his new walking staff.

With its permission, of course.

"I finally understand why he was always telling me those stories about farming and taro," Matani told Heiana, as he helped her settle onto an old stump beside the taro pond.

"Well, this I'd like to hear," she said with sweet, smiling interest.

"The legend of Hoʻohoturani and her children—one plant, the other human—symbolizes the connection between people and nature as siblings. Nature watches over us and gives us everything we need. But in return, we have to watch over her and treat her with reverence and respect." Matani looked out across the rows of taro and smiled, his voice thick with emotion. "My father was trying to tell me that our relationships with each other, our ancestors, and our land, are what truly define us all."

Heiana's eyes sparkled tenderly. "May it ever be so."

Once again compelled by unseen forces, Matani looked up at Mount Vaiareare, its lofty peak once again hidden under a thick mantle of clouds.

"Does the mountain still call you?" asked a raspy voice behind them.

Both Matani and Heiana turned, watching a figure materialize from the morning mists of the forest. It was Supreme High Priest Hunumaniani, smelling of herbs and secret powders.

"Feels like it," Matani replied. "Hiking to its peak was the purpose of my land journey, but then I saw the cannibals crossing the channel from Oʻahu and had to make a choice."

Hunumaniani regarded Matani. "Do you regret your decision?"

"Not at all," Matani answered without hesitation. "I'll see what's waiting for me up there as soon as my leg heals."

"I believe you will," said the old priest, nodding thoughtfully. "As I understand it, your house was destroyed in the fires?"

"Yes, but it's okay," Matani said. "Friends and family are going to help me rebuild the home I grew up in. The one my grandfather built."

"It is important to make these repairs," acknowledged Hunumaniani, then gestured to the faded crescent moon in the dim morning sky. "However, the first of the ʻole moons reminds us to set aside daily routines for the next four nights so that we may seek personal enlightenment. After speaking with Ruling Chief Vahanui at great length, we agreed that you should take up residence with me in the temple for a while."

Matani threw a confused stare between Heiana and the priest.

"As your gardener?"

Rather uncharacteristically, Hunumaniani erupted with laughter, surprising all three of them. "My herb garden may benefit from your farming skills, but no," he said, quickly regaining his usual demeanor. "I would like to mentor you in the ancient ways of healing and dream medicine."

"I accept," Matani replied immediately—fully aware that an entirely unexpected path into a new future had just opened up for him.

"Good," Hunumaniani said, only just noticing Matani's necklace. "What's that pendant you have there?"

"Oh, just some tutu'i nut I found on my mountain journey," Matani said, touching it with his muddy fingertips. "I thought these markings meant something, but now I'm not so sure."

"There is meaning in everything, always. Even in the most *common* of things," the old priest imparted with a sly wink. "Not only is the tutu'i nut a body form of Ro'o, it's also a powerful symbol of illumination."

Matani stared at him. "What is illumination exactly?"

"It's the moment a wave discovers it is an ocean," said Hunumaniani, pausing to let his sage words sink in before turning to walk way.

"High Priest?" Matani called after him.

The old priest stopped, looking back. "Something else, young man?"

"Did you see me on the beach that day?"

Hunumaniani looked long into Matani's eyes, his face remaining unreadable right up until the corner of his mouth slowly turned upward.

Matani could only smile at the mysterious reply. "With everything that's happened these last days, do you think Ruling Chief Vahanui might be open to a few ideas I have about revising some of our old traditions?'

"As a wise old woman once said: small things are necessary before big things can be achieved."

Matani's jaw dropped, realizing that the priest had echoed the exact words of Tūtū Ona. "How did you—?"

Again, Hunumaniani just smiled his knowing smile. "I'll see you tomorrow morning, young man."

Matani looked at Heiana, dumbstruck, then both watched quietly as Hunumaniani disappeared into the morning shadows of the woods.

"What's that?" Heiana asked, startled by a faint rustling sound coming from the trees beside them.

Tamapua'a.

Matani's heart began pounding wildly. Studying every low bush, he instinctively moved in front of Heiana just as something with filthy, matted hair burst from the undergrowth.

It had two eyes.

One brown, the other green.

Nahoa.

Matani fell to his knees as the dog flew into his arms, his muscular little body wriggling and whimpering with excitement as he licked every inch of his human's face.

"Oh, good boy!" Matani rejoiced. "My good, defiant boy!"

"Is this who I think it is?" Heiana asked, enjoying the happy reunion between the two.

"Yes!" Matani shouted, beaming.

Hugging Nahoa, tears streaming down both cheeks, Matani looked up at the sky and, in a quiet moment of clarity, he believed the god of fertility and peace had forgiven him.

"Blessings, Ro'o," he whispered with heartfelt gratitude, promising to live his life with faith, empowerment, and humility.

Eventually, all three found their way down to Vairuanuiho'āno Beach to wash the mud from their bodies, and bathing quickly turned to chasing each other in the cool morning surf. As the first rays of dawn lifted above the sea, lighting the dim landscape with soft hues of pink, orange, and gold, Matani stopped a moment to take it all in, barely able to believe his eyes. Just above the eastern horizon, the top half of the reddish-orange sunrise was completely obscured by a hard line of backlit clouds, leaving only its bottom half glowing in such a way that it perfectly resembled a heavenly Bowl of Light.

"I absorb this celestial radiance into my body with a promise to share it with everyone I meet," Matani said, knowing in his heart of hearts that this perfectly timed gift from the universe was no accident.

Then he felt something skitter onto his right foot.

Seeing a familiar, brown-striped lizard with a sky-blue tail, he bent over and placed an upright palm beside it. The lizard twitched its head before climbing onto his hand, curling its long blue tail around Matani's little finger.

He lifted it up to get a better look at the creature. "You sure do get around, don't you?"

The lizard twitched its head this way and that, then winked at Matani before jumping down onto the sand and darting off. Smiling absently at his feet, Matani did a double take, realizing for the first time that he was standing on Tumatua's Tear once more. But this time, standing at a slightly different angle than before, he realized that it also resembled something else.

"A heart," he whispered, speaking a new name for the tragic landmark into existence. "Father's Heart."

Bathing in warmth cast by the serendipitous hemisphere of light smiling at him from across the sea, Matani found himself overwhelmed by a sense of belonging in the world and peace in his soul.

"Life sure has its ups and downs," he said, "but every so often, we get to experience perfect moments like these that somehow make sense of it all."

Unconsciously placing his hand on his heart center, the tips of Matani's fingers touched the tutu'i nut pendant that hung below his chin. Again came those three mysterious words.

Before

After

Between

Examining its outer shell—just as he'd done many times before—something about the scratches on it finally made sense.

"I should have known, it *is* a symbol!" Matani shouted excitedly. "Look, it's as clear as day to me now. This inward spiral symbolizes the three aspects of Self and the three levels of the Island Worlds. And this swooping line moving through them is time, flowing in and out of the earth plane like a river. The left half of the line is the past—the before. And the right half is the future—the after. So, this spot at the center is what lies *between before and after*. The now. The present moment."

Pondering who or what wise forces of the universe had placed this tutu'i nut in his path for him to find that day, Matani offered them his profound gratitude.

"Today, right here and right now, this is exactly where and who I want to be," he said to Heiana beside him and Nahoa at his feet, to the mountain behind him, to the sea before him, and to the sky above. "Tomorrow, I'll be where and who I am tomorrow."

When Matani looked over at Heiana, her eyes sparkling with tiny fires of gold that reflected the half sun, she'd never looked prettier to him. With a new, adult perspective on how two people could come together in a mature relationship—not simply as a result of growing up together, but growing independently of one another, as well—Matani gently moved aside a few strands of hair from the gorgeous eyes of the girl he'd loved since the day they met.

And this time, rather than laugh or run, Heiana looked back deeply into Matani's blue-galaxy eyes and smiled, for she finally saw what she needed to see in them.

Someone she could trust with her heart.

And then they kissed.

Finally.

As the birth of a new day aged brighter, Matani, Heiana, and Nahoa found a comfortable spot on the beach under a lovely palm tree and settled back together on the sand, marveling at the pageant of colors blooming and simmering in the sky above them, content in the tropical splendor of it all.

With his left arm wrapped around Heiana and his right hand gently caressing Nahoa's fur, Matani drifted into a peaceful meditative state listening to the soothing sounds of the ocean in front of him and rustling leaves of the forest behind. Suddenly, a burst of energy paralyzed his body, filling him with a euphoric sense of boundless joy and a profound connection to the universe beyond constraints of space and time.

Gazing down at his skin, he saw that it shimmered with a radiant, celestial light that pulsed from within, casting an otherworldly aura around him. Silent and awestruck, he looked up at Heiana to find an expression of wonder that matched his own.

"You're skin," she gasped. "It shines like starlight."

As boundaries between self and other began to blur and dissolve, Matani's entire being felt lighter somehow, as if transcending the limits of gravity and time. Overwhelmed by emotions of love and unity, he was no longer Matani, but now one with the delicate touch of Heiana's fingers and the soft fur of Nahoa.

Offering a quick prayer of strength, everything and nothing melted together into the infinite universe as the cool, gritty sand he sat on ... disappeared.

٠ CHAPTER 29 ٠

Traveling across the immortal lights of Aka, connecting him to all space and all time, a transformed Matani found himself standing on the summit of a glorious mountain.

Before him spanned a grassy plateau with a small freshwater pond at its center, its surface rippled by continuous gusts of wind, rain, and fog that blew up from the surrounding rim. Peering over the edge, whatever secrets dwelled in the fathomless abyss below were obscured by thick, swirling clouds.

"D-did I—? Am I—?" Matani stammered nervously. "Is this . . . the summit of Mount Vaiareare?"

You should know better than to make me repeat myself. What did I say about the Island Worlds?

The familiar voice and complaint made Matani smile. "Everything in the world of spirit is symbolic of something in the world of form."

Praise the gods, he's teachable after all. Welcome to Upper Island, young man.

Even though he could barely see his own hands through the fog, Matani slowly became aware of whispering shapes gathering around him.

He realized they were spirits.

Thousands of them.

His ancestors through time.

In the silent communion of gazes, Matani encountered each ancestral spirit, individually yet concurrently, feeling himself thrust across the vast abyss of time. Each specter served as a portal, a starlit tunnel through which he could view the grand tapestry of his lineage, unfolding across countless epochs. The life saga of each ancestor unfurled before him, a cosmic odyssey from the first flutter of existence to the tranquil stillness of the end. Their emotions—ecstasy and dread, adoration and desolation—pulsed through him, echoing ancient rhythms in the chambers of his heart. Each memory, vivid and stark, unfolded before him like a visual chant, its resonant verses filled with victories savored and defeats mourned, skills honed and lessons etched deep within the spiritual spine of his genealogy. Above all, he perceived with crystalline clarity the precise place each forebear held in the intricate web of his ancestry, and the subtle ripples of their influence, shaping the destiny of generations yet unborn.

Among the spectral assembly, Matani recognized a younger iteration of Tūtū Ona. She came forward, shape-shifting into the elder form he was more familiar with, wearing a lei of white flowers and pointed silvery-green leaves that symbolized the colors of Molokai, a sentimental homage to her beautiful and beloved island of birth in the physical world.

"Well, I'd say our ho'oponopono was a success, wouldn't you?" she asked, her voice bringing a comforting familiarity that he hadn't realized he missed.

"All is pono," Matani replied, his voice soft, his smile humble.

"Having emptied your heart of so many troubles, from the stubborn crown of your head to the weary soles of your feet, to the four sacred corners of your body, we may all now move into the future unburdened and with an open mind," she said, then waved an impatient hand. "Now, quit your stalling and let's have a look at it!"

Knowing exactly what she meant, Matani held out his palms and manifested his Bowl of Light. Not entirely sure what it might look like, he was slightly disheartened to see a few new stones in it.

"Oh no," Matani said, his face creased with concern.

"Pssh! Don't be so hard on yourself," his grandmother demanded. "Our bowl isn't meant to be pristine. Its purpose is to measure the balance of our Anatomy of Being, and tending to it is a lifelong task. The stones you collect are simply reminders of the lessons that need to be learned."

Matani breathed a sigh of relief. "I won't argue with you there."

"A wise choice," his grandmother replied, arching one eyebrow.

Seeing the playfulness sparkling in her blue eyes, it made Matani think of his own. "Tūtū, why have my eyes changed color?"

She nodded, appearing unconcerned. "As a Mū descendant, with your increasing mana comes new abilities. This change of color suggests your cells are growing lighter, in both weight and luminance, bringing the potential of being less confined by earthly boundaries."

His expression turned apprehensive. "Is this why I've been able to see into different generations?"

"On a rudimentary level, yes," she elucidated. "You now have access to the fourth dimension, where time is merely a physical quantity, and past, present, and future lose distinction."

Hearing this concept, Matani remembered his conversation with Krum about the starlight in his blood. "When I first met The One That Destroys All Things, it had taken the form of a Shining One. But did the Originals actually exist?"

"Many people hold different views and theories about the past," she said with a hint of impatience. "But in the end, all that really matters is—what do *you* believe?"

Matani paused thoughtfully. "I think that maybe those stories about Blue Beings and Shining Ones are meant to remind us that connecting with nature and with each other gives meaning to our lives. Attachment to superficial things only causes us to lose focus on ourselves and weaken our mana." He looked over at the ghostly faces of his ancestors, feeling their emotions washing over him. "Like you said when we first met, it's people, their feelings, and personal growth that matter most."

"Free will comes with the burden of consequence," Tūtū Ona replied. "Sadly, The One That Destroys All Things played a significant role in using this freedom to lure many Originals into the Dark Age. But a new dawn rises, and the time has come for humanity to regain consciousness of The Grand Purpose and move forward into the Age of Light."

"What is The Grand Purpose?" he asked.

"Perhaps you will be the one to recover this ancient wisdom one day, young man," hinted Tūtū Ona, then she raised her hands as a perfectly fitted necklace of polished tutu'i nuts appeared, placing it around Matani's neck.

Matani ran his fingers across the string of smooth shells. "It's beautiful."

"A symbol of perpetual enlightenment, guidance, and peace," she said. "A most fitting gift on the day of your seventeenth season."

Reminded that this was the day of his birth, Matani felt a surge of emotion welling up inside him. "I completely forgot."

"Young man, we are all so very proud of how hard you've worked these past days to achieve mana, claiming the right to finally learn your sacred name," Tūtū Ona said, her eyes softening with affection and pride. "A name given to your mother by the very vibrations of your soul before you were even born."

Though difficult, Matani knew not to show any emotion during this most sacred ritual, quietly absorbing the importance of the name he was about to receive.

"May this mana, the gift of our ancestors, pass through me and guide you," Tūtū Ona said, then put her right hand over Matani's heart, breathed into his mouth, and onto the crown of his head. "This sacred name I am about to share with you is a reflection of your own unique path of empowerment."

Then she leaned in closer, whispering the sacred name into Matani's ear.

"*Mahiʻai Kukui,*" he repeated with reverence. *Light Farmer.*

Matani smiled, and the smile made his face beautiful as a feeling of exultation filled his entire being—a sensation one might experience being lost in a dark forest when a light suddenly shines out.

"This name holds great mana, for it honors both the farming skills of my father's family and the mystical attributes of my mother's, defining my true, authentic path of meaning and purpose."

"And what purpose is that?" Tūtū Ona asked with concentrated interest.

"To harvest and nurture the light of humanity through the collective knowledge of my ancestors," Matani answered.

Then he raised his electrified hands.

But this time, with the wisdom and intention to create rather than destroy.

Waving all ten fingers majestically in the air, Matani conjured up an expansive parcel of paddy fields on the grassy summit of the sacred mountain. Another motion of his hand, and sprouts pushed up from the earth in multiple rows, each growing into long, bioluminescent green stalks that unfurled up to three and four branches with glowing, heart-shaped leaves.

"Instead of seeds, I'll plant light," Matani said with passionate determination. "Not in gardens, but in the spiritual bowls of all who seek to cultivate their own personal empowerment, ancestral healing, and transcendence."

He knelt down and carefully pulled up one of the luminous stalks from the moist earth, its bulbous root caked in mud. Giving the exquisite plant a gentle shake, the mud fell away, revealing a beating taro bulb in a timeless shape that symbolizes the love and affection within the souls of all.

The human heart.

"It is good to share the ancient wisdom you've learned, but as you embark on this new path to becoming a kahuna of spirit medicine, know it is a narrow one," Tūtū Ona warned. "Lighting the flame of awareness is far easier than keeping it aglow, for negative forces are always lurking in the shadows with the sole purpose of extinguishing this most precious light."

Matani carefully returned the radiant plant to the earth, then stood and faced all his ancestors encircling him, absorbing their energetic bond of love and support. "I couldn't have saved our village without you all," he said with humble appreciation.

"Many hands make for easy work," answered a distantly familiar voice. Astonishingly, it was the spirit form of his long-deceased grandfather, Namotaha'i, appearing before him in the prime of his youth, strong and vibrantly alive just as he had been in life.

Matani smiled. "With my ancestors from the recent and distant past beside me, I'm confident I can do anything."

"Having come to know yourself, to know the truth, and to reengage with your ancestors, you now have unlimited access to a long line of powerful medicine holders," said Tūtū Ona. "This sacred and luminous knowledge is now your responsibility."

"I vow to never let our ancestral line become corrupted again, ensuring access for all those who come after me," Matani replied. "Something I couldn't have done without your help, Tūtū."

"I am merely an usher that met you at the threshold," she humbly replied. "It was you, young man, who had the courage to enter the realms of spirit and do the hard work." Staring proudly upon her grandson, the smile on Tūtū Ona's face grew even wider.

"What?" he asked with a puzzled look. "What is it?"

"The answer to many years of your hopes and prayers," she said, gesturing behind him.

The hairs on the back of Matani's neck tingled as he turned to see a familiar couple emerging from the swirling mist of ghosts.

His parents.

Locked in fathoms of emotion, the sight of Matani's mother and father brought dazzled tears to his eyes.

Tumatua looked entirely different than when Matani had last seen his ghost, now wonderfully unburdened of the bitter anger that had ravaged him in his later years. The harsh lines of stress on his father's weary forehead, and the deep emotional pain lodged behind his eyes, had been completely erased, giving Tumatua the youthful innocence one possesses when life is still new, bright and full of wonder.

And Mahina, no longer bent and crippled by disease, stood magnificently tall and straight as a spear. But as always, her eyes—those beautiful, blue-galaxy eyes—were strikingly vibrant and full of life. Just as Matani remembered them.

He turned back to Tūtū Ona, swallowing nervously. "What do I say?"

"Well, *goodbye* seems a bit obsolete now, doesn't it?"

"I suppose so," he replied, fully understanding the true magic of the Island Worlds as a conduit for maintaining the powerful bond between loved ones for all time. "Blessings, Tūtū. For everything."

Tūtū Ona placed her right hand over her heart and left hand over her sacrum. "Eye to eye, breath to breath, heart to heart, we are . . . and will always be," she said, then gestured toward his waiting mother and father. "Go on, now. It's been long enough."

Walking slowly, searching for just the right thing to say, a single word came to Matani that he only now understood to be the epitome of poetry. A word born of the Hawaiian culture's young evolution, imbued with many shades of deeper meaning.

"Aloha," he whispered, his voice trembling.

His parents reflected the word back with infinite tenderness, tears mounting in their eyes.

Aloha, meaning *Love for Kin*, is that first beautiful expression of unconditional affection shared between parent and child. It is a transformative power, a gentle yet potent force that shapes a child's emotional intelligence, even as they float in the quiet sanctuary of the womb.

Tumatua smiled. "As parents nurture their child with love and kindness, the tender sprout blooms with virtues of their own. But if the soil is polluted with jealousy and anger, the sapling takes on the bitter fruit of their parents' bitter deeds."

Mahina smiled at her husband's farming metaphor, then added, "So always a better choice to reflect love than hate."

With infinite tenderness mounting in their eyes, Matani threw himself into the embrace of his mother and father, where all the mysteries of love and wonder of the universe flooded his soul, melting him into nothing. And, oh! The way they smelled and the familiar feeling of their skin against his own was indescribable.

"I've missed you both so much," he said, unable to hold back his tears any longer.

Mahina caressed his hand lovingly, her matching blue eyes shining back bright and beautifully into his. She was crying, too. "My brave and noble boy, I'm so grateful for who you are. It is such an honor to be your mother."

"You instilled many beautiful things in me," Matani replied. "But I still have so much to learn about Mind Power."

A thoughtful expression crossed her face. "My brother can help."

Matani looked at her, surprised. "You have a brother?"

"His name is Hale Naʻauao Makua, a wisdom keeper and practitioner of sacred Mū magic," she said. "He returned to Papahānaumokuākea when I was a child."

Matani nodded, eyes lighting at the implication of another journey as Tumatua affectionately squeezed his neck. "Son, you've reconnected the hearts of this family, and our entire lineage rises once more because of you," he said, his voice trembling with emotion. "You have found a worthy path to become the amazing person you were always meant to be, and I couldn't be more proud."

As the debilitating sense of cosmic loneliness he'd been suffering from these last several years transmuted into something wonderful, Matani reflected the joyful expressions of his parents, reveling in the truest, most meaningful love he'd ever known.

Wiping the tears from his eyes, he stepped back to behold the magnificent joy that poured from the ghostly faces of his forebears, encircling him like a luminescent halo.

"Until we meet again," Matani said with a grateful smile. "I will draw upon your constant source of wisdom and knowledge for my strength, my inspiration, and my mana. Everything I've learned from each of you will live on through me."

"I'm curious, young man," said Tūtū Ona. "What exactly *have* you learned?"

Taking a deep breath, Matani decided telepathy would be best to answer such an important question.

So there would be no misunderstanding.

First and foremost, the Island Worlds are an amazing resource for help, healing, and knowledge. Through my travels within, I discovered that the bonds of love we share with others are the foundation of life.

Land, sea, and sky are important sacred temples and healers, but we must care for these remarkable creations just as they care for us.

For me, the sea was a very physical, masculine place, full of lessons in logic, practicality, and reason, reminding me just how immeasurably expansive life truly is.

The mountain was a spiritual, feminine experience, full of lessons in emotion and intuition, teaching me that there are many paths to the same place.

From both, I learned that our greatest guide in finding direction and purpose through the beautiful mysteries of mortal existence is the purity of light inside our bowls and in our hearts.

I've also discovered some important values to live by:

Always come from a place of love and understanding.

Accept that things won't always work out, but know that everything will still be okay.

We're here to learn. Perhaps the hardest lesson is how to handle conflict because might of the mind and force of the fist cannot exist in the same body. Energy will go to only one.

The more love you give, the more you will receive.

And despite what my thoughts, emotions, or past might inform me, I should never stop learning to trust. Not just in others, but in myself.

Lastly, I think the most important thing I've learned is that no one can heal me. While the gods, family, and friends can provide support, ultimately my life and empowerment needs are my responsibility, and mine alone.

Every single adoring face of Matani's ancestors gleamed with pride. Through the strength and totality of their collective love, he saw, sensed, felt each of them reflecting back their fullhearted appreciation for his profound revelations.

At the start of your journey, you sought answers to three important questions.

The words moved through Matani's very soul, from somewhere, everywhere, all at once, defining higher vibrations of an energy that he instantly recognized as the trustworthy voice of his ʻAumākua.

"Yes, I remember," Matani replied.

And have you found these answers?

"I have," he answered confidently.

Where do you come from?

"The One Who Creates All Things."

Who are you?

"I am . . . human."

What is your purpose?

"To be the best human I can possibly be and, hopefully, inspire others to do the same."

Covet this wisdom always, Light Farmer. And create your life extraordinary.

. . . and now, adventurous reader,
our outrigger canoe has returned to the present.

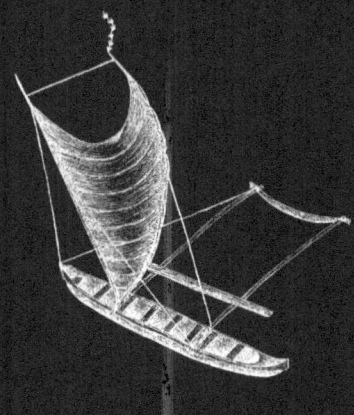

May each of you cultivate the seeds of light in your hearts
as you embark on your own wondrous journey across the
fathomless oceanic depths and lofty mountain heights of life.
Move forward with strength, knowing that your ancestors are
always there for you, waiting to help you grow and succeed.
As we part, let the rain of blessings in the form of high mana
descend into your own bowls of light, which exist to help
you fulfill the promise of who you are meant to be.

Aloha pauʻole
Love without end

Christopher Farley

. . . and Matani's journey continues . . .

✦ ACKNOWLEDGMENTS ✦

I am deeply grateful for the knowledge, guidance, and support I have received. My heartfelt appreciation goes to the beautiful island of Kaua'i, which inspired this journey, and to institutions such as the Bishop Museum Archives and Hawai'i State Archives for preserving Hawai'i's rich heritage.

I am indebted to numerous individuals for their contributions to the preservation of Hawaiian culture, including Mary Kawena Pukui, David Malo, Kaili'ohe Kame'ekua, Pali J. Lee, and John K. Willis. The Polynesian Voyaging Society and Hōkūle'a exemplify the spirit of exploration, and I am inspired by the passion of their esteemed and giving navigators Nainoa Thompson and Bruce Blankenfeld.

I am thankful for those who have shared their wisdom, including Hale Kealohalani Makua, Kalei'iliahi, Margaret Machado, Claybourne "Braddah Smitty" Smith, Adam Kolii Keawe, Abraham Kawai'i, Hank Wesselman, Sandra Ingerman, Carlos Castañeda, and Ke'oni Hanalei.

Special thanks to my triple threat editing team from Reedsy.com— Kimberley Lim, Constance Renfrow, and Becky Sweeney—and to my book designer and cover artist, André Manoel, for their invaluable help.

Finally, my gratitude extends to The Ancient Nomads of the Pacific, whose brave journeys and powerful legacy continue to inspire and guide us.

⋆ Colophon ⋆

The body text of this book was set in *Adobe Jenson* at 12 pt. The *Bebas Neue* font was used on the cover and parts. The images featured in this book were first generated with MidJourney, and served as foundations for the artistic illustrations and collages.

www.ingramcontent.com/pod-product-compliance
Lightning Source LLC
Chambersburg PA
CBHW020828030726
47496CB00001B/145